EMILY ANTOINETTE
AFTERGLOW

A SPICY SAPPHIC MONSTER ROMANCE

Copyright © 2024 by Emily Antoinette

ISBN 979-8-9883161-6-9 (paperback)

All rights reserved.

Cover art by Fires

Cover design by Emily Antoinette

No part of this book may be reproduced in any form or by any electronic or mechanical means, including information storage and retrieval systems, without written permission from the author, except for the use of brief quotations in a book review.

No generative artificial intelligence (AI) was used in the writing of this work. The author expressly prohibits any entity from using this publication for purposes of training AI technologies to generate text, including without limitation technologies that are capable of generating works in the same style or genre as this publication. The author reserves all rights to license use of this work for generative AI training and development of machine learning language models.

This book is a work of fiction. Names, characters, businesses, places, events and incidents in this book are either the product of the author's imagination or used in a fictitious manner. Any resemblance to actual persons, living or dead, or actual events is purely coincidental.

To all the babes who assumed they were straight because women are just "objectively" sexy and attractive.

Also, to my future badass domme wife.
(A girl can dream, right?)

CONTENT NOTES

Afterglow is a spicy slow burn sapphic vampire romance, with some darker themes and open door sex scenes. This means discussion and explicit depictions of sex and kink-based activities including D/s dynamics, biting, mild blood play (there's a vampire, so duh), bondage, flogging, shibari, orgasm denial, edging, praise, service, mild humiliation, and spitting.

Throughout the book, there are references to chronic pain, queer identity and experiences, grief and loss, sex work, religious trauma, and trauma and shame from past relationships.

As this is a vampire romance, there are multiple depictions of blood and the consumption of blood (both MCs).

There are brief depictions of dubious consent and sexual trauma from past partners, kink scenarios with partners other than their love interest (both MCs), mentions of past violence, mentions of infidelity (not MCs).

Characters use profanity and explicit language throughout the book.

EMILY ANTOINETTE

For a comprehensive list of content notes, tropes, and tags, please visit https://emilyantoinette.com/afterglow

If you have any questions about these notes, please don't hesitate to reach out to me at emilyantoinetteauthor@gmail.com.

1

BLAIR

Darkness surrounds me.
    A high-pitched ringing fills my ears.
    Why can't I breathe?

My hand scratches at my throat as I panic for a split-second. After what feels like an eternity, I manage to suck in a shallow, unnatural breath.

I wait for another to come. It doesn't.

The fog of dreaming slowly parts as my hands reach out to feel around me, searching in the pitch black for a way to anchor myself to reality before terror overtakes me again.

Cool, dry sheets. No blood soaking them.

I grab my left wrist to find faded bumps of scar tissue, not an open wound.

I keep my eyes shut for a minute, willing myself to calm down. When my body is completely still, no breath or pulse marking the passing seconds, I let my eyes open.

The nightvision gray-scale of my bedroom greets me, joined a few seconds later by the chime of my alarm and dim light shed from my phone screen.

Right. I'm at home. I'm okay.

Shit, that hasn't happened in a while. I stare up at the ceiling as I anchor myself in the present. The ornate mirror over the bed shows nothing but rumpled sheets outlining the form of my body.

I really need to take that thing down. It was hot when my ex asked me to put it up so she could watch herself get off, but it's pointless when I'm the only one in my bed.

It's usually simple to channel the power inside me to create a reflection, but rousing the blood in my system already feels like a monumental task tonight, so I don't need to waste what little energy I have. An ache of hunger builds inside me and my throat feels scratchy as I continue to lie in bed, working up the fortitude to move. Nothing like that awful night when I was practically feral with thirst, but not the most pleasant way to wake up.

I didn't eat enough yesterday. I had a late booking with a client at my studio in the city, and by the time I got back home, all I wanted was a shower and the cool, dark comfort of my bed.

Foolish.

I know better than to go to bed hungry. Now I'm paying the price for not taking care of myself.

When the alarm becomes too annoying to bear any longer, I summon the energy needed to reach out to my phone and dismiss it. Then I set a notification for 4am to have a snack if I don't feed at the club. No excuses now for not getting the sustenance I need.

It's irresponsible and reckless to take such poor care of myself. I can't lose control again. I won't.

I push myself up to sitting, my arms shaking with the effort. I grab my legs and swing them off the bed one at a time, then stand slowly. My muscles seize and my knees almost buckle, but I manage to shamble across the room, looking every bit the undead monster I am.

I'm exhausted by the time I make it to the mini-fridge sitting next to my bureau. I could keep it next to my bed, but I didn't think I'd ever be starving enough that walking the four feet over to it would feel like a marathon.

My legs threaten to collapse as I bend to open the refrigerator door, so I slide down onto my ass and open it from the floor. With trembling hands, I grab the bag closest to the front and tear it open with my teeth instead of using the pull tab. I throw it back, uncaring about how some of it slides down my chin.

Pathetic.

Cold B positive isn't my favorite, but it does the trick. My body temperature rises slightly as the energy from the blood invigorates my sluggish veins. When the blood bag is empty, I sigh and wipe my face with a tissue, then blot up some blood that dripped onto the floor.

Messy.

I toss the bag and the tissue into the trash and head to the bathroom. This time I have enough energy reserves to look myself in the eyes in the mirror hanging above the sink.

I look awful. Remnants of my eyeliner are smudged under my eyes, there's a bloodstain on the front of my favorite silk pajamas, and my deep brown complexion has a sickly gray tinge to it. My eyes squeeze shut, hating what I see.

Foolish. Pathetic. Messy. You can't let it happen again.

Unlike many of my clients, degrading myself does little for me. It's a shame. I'm excellent at it. It comes to me even easier than breathing did when I was alive. After all, as a queer kid raised in a born-again Christian household, I've had plenty of practice with self-loathing.

Shoving the negativity aside is a muscle I'm building. I can't wait for the day when it's strong enough to fully combat the criticisms that echo in my head.

I open my eyes and look at myself again, this time with forced compassion.

I learn from my mistakes. I'll do better next time. No one is perfect.

It helps. Somewhat.

There's a joke here somewhere that I'm doing positive affirmations after drinking B positive, but humor isn't really my strong suit.

By the time I've brushed my teeth, showered, and moisturized, the bad awakening is almost completely behind me. Slipping into the black bodysuit that clings to me like a second skin, and stepping into my favorite red-soled heels finishes the job.

It's a little after 7, which means I still have a bit before the sun sets and I can head out to the club. Enough time for a little work.

There are four clients waiting for a reply from me when I check my messages. I open up the first one with a hint of a smile.

> Nic: Good evening, Mistress Bella. Hope you slept well.

> Mistress Bella: Thank you, I did.

Nic checks in like clockwork every night. He's currently my only monster client, so he understands my sleep schedule and doesn't bother me during the day. If I had to guess, he's going to follow it up with a request for a session this weekend. He's easy to please. He'll clean and act as my footstool, secretly hoping that I'll bite him if he does a good enough job. If I weren't busy tonight, I'd consider it. My baseboards could use a good scrubbing and shifter blood always gives me an extra energy boost.

I close the chat and open up the next message.

> G: May I see you this weekend, Mistress Bella? I was so good for you. I wore the cage all week.
>
> Mistress Bella: I'm busy.
>
> Mistress Bella: If you're a good boy and keep it on, I'll fit you in on Monday.

Huh. I'm surprised G hasn't broken yet. I'm oddly proud of him. I don't think he'll last two more days, though. He'll end up getting the punishment he craves even more than my praise.

There's a flurry of increasingly panicked messages from one of my newer clients.

> X: Can you wait until Sunday?
>
> X: I don't have the money right now.
>
> X: I hate disappointing you, but $1000 is too much. I can't do it.
>
> X: Mistress, please say something!
>
> Mistress Bella: You're pathetic. You think you deserve to talk to me? I'm deleting your number unless you send me another $1000 on top of what you should've already sent.

I snort. We both know he'll send me the money, but he loves the dance leading up to it.

The final message makes me frown.

> Thumper: Do you want to carpool? I can pick you up, if you give me your address.

Ugh. You ask a sub for a favor and the next thing you know, they act like you want to be their friend. My mistake for not wording my request like a command.

> Bella: I'll see you there at 8. Wear purple. It'll match the ropes I'm using.

He replies right away.

> Thumper: Yes, ma'am.

Better.

I don't need more friends. Even if I did, I don't mix work with my personal life. Maybe if we'd met outside of a booking or even on one of the nights I was at the club for fun... but no. Even then, I wouldn't want Thumper's friendship. I'm happy with the way things are.

Life is good. Work is steady and enjoyable. The renovation of the guest bedroom is finally done. I have dinner with Mona once a week.

No, that's not a euphemism. I don't drink from my best friend, despite her curiosity about it. Her partner would try to kill me, and I don't want Mona to be sad if he ends up dead.

She eats leftovers, I bring a thermos of blood, and we talk.

It's nice. Wonderful, really. The only thing that would make our relationship more pleasurable isn't on the table. Fortunately, I'm excellent at accepting things for what they are and adapting. If I wasn't, I'd still be back on that blood-soaked hotel bed crying out for help.

With the remaining time before I have to leave, I fall back into the predictable rhythm of texting my clients.

X sends the money and adds another $500 tip as an apology. I don't reply because I know he loves to squirm. Some people might think I'm being unfair, but I'm only giving him what he wants. Getting to make a ridiculously wealthy tech bro sweat is just a perk of the job.

As I expected, Nic asks if I need any yard work done, because he's free tomorrow afternoon. He's my only client that I've allowed to come to my home, and that wasn't an intentional decision. I was unlucky enough to hire his landscaping company to help me out with my unruly yard. We both startled when he knocked on my door after sunset to let me know they were all done for the day. After that, it just made sense for him to come here so we can both skip the drive into the city to meet at my work apartment.

It's breaking one of the boundaries I set for myself when I started taking on clients after a disastrous incident when I was still working as a sugar baby. But out of all my clients, that big bear is the one I'm least worried about turning into a problem. The worst he does is unsubtly mention his monster support group meetings when we're scheduling our next session. I ignore him when he brings it up. I don't need a support group and I certainly don't need one where one of my submissives is the leader.

G sends a picture of his caged cock. It does nothing for me sexually, but there's a surge of satisfaction in seeing how shriveled and sad it looks. Cis men are obsessed with dicks. I enjoy controlling what they see as the physical embodiment of their virility. It's cathartic. It pays well, too.

I praise him, slide off my heels, and text him a picture of my feet, toes perfectly polished purple to match my ropes tonight. Nothing gets him harder than worshiping my feet. I bet he breaks and removes the cage within the next hour. I told him there's a sensor on it that's linked to an app on my phone, but in reality I have no way of knowing other than his obvious guilt when he breaks my rules.

I finish up just in time for my weather app to say that the sun has finished setting. Perfect. Time to head out and see what the rest of the evening has in store for me.

2

GRACE

Waking up every morning feels a lot like roulette, with the odds heavily stacked against me. Will my body be cooperative, or did I somehow manage to hurt myself during the time that's supposed to be restoring my body?

The stiffness in my neck, followed by sharp pain when I go to roll over and turn off my alarm, gives me my answer.

Shit.

I let out a long sigh, squeezing my eyes tight and giving myself a thirty-second pity party before I open them again. If I let myself break down every day I'm in pain, I'd never get out of bed.

I gingerly sit up, using one hand to stabilize my neck. I wince as

I look down to grab my phone and turn off my alarm, the stabbing pain in my neck unavoidable when it's this bad.

Delightful. I carefully gather my hair up into a messy bun and pad groggily to the bathroom. You know it's a bad day when it hurts to lift my arm to brush my teeth.

At least it's the weekend. It sucks to be in pain on one of my days off from work, but that means I can cozy up with my heating pad without passive aggressive messages from my boss.

It would've been better to speak to you about this in person.

No, you mean it would've been better for you to stare at my tits as you mansplain a project I created.

It's important to maintain a professional work environment, even on video calls.

Right, because my heat pad and t-shirt are worse than your mug that's shaped like breasts.

I'd report him to HR, but they were hard enough to work with to get any accommodations at all. My job begrudgingly lets me work from home when I have a pain flare-up, only allowing it because they're legally required to.

When I worked up the courage to tell my boss I needed accommodations, he laughed and said, "You're not disabled. You just want to work from home so you don't have to put on a bra." How I got through the conversation without crying or cursing him out, I'm still not sure, but I'm pretty proud of my composure.

I'm less proud of how part of me agrees with him. The guy is an asshole, and I had a goddamn doctor's note to back me up, but I still can't bring myself to say I'm disabled. If I do, then I have to acknowledge how much my fucked up spine impacts my life.

After my boss's reaction, I've kept quiet about my pain. My Dad knows I have degenerative disc disease because he was the one that took me to the doctor when the neck pain first started, but I haven't told him how bad it's gotten. I haven't even told my best friend about it at all.

What's the point? It'd just make them sad, or worse, pity me. I already do enough of that on my own. No thanks, I don't want it. Better to have everyone assume I'm okay, so I can maintain my feeble hold on the illusion that I'm perfectly fine and capable.

It wasn't too hard until recently. When you look at me, there's nothing visibly wrong. Invisible disability is what my PT calls it.

I try not to call it anything at all.

My pain is like the monster under the bed. If I shut my eyes and lie as still as possible, maybe it doesn't exist. Or at least maybe it's all in my head and I can make it disappear by changing my mindset.

Ugh, even I know that's bullshit. I have multiple scans and x-rays showing physical proof of the source of my pain. But sometimes it's simpler to pretend that my pain is a personal failing rather than an actual condition, because at least then I have some control over the situation.

Okay, enough. Wallowing won't fix anything.

I go through the mental calculations needed to determine if my plans for the day are ruined or not. If I take a hot shower, slap on the TENS unit (one of those things that uses electrical currents to try to break pain signals), and pop a muscle relaxer right away, maybe I'll be okay enough to go out tonight. I had a bunch of chores to get done and I really don't want to be a zombie from the meds, but I also don't want to be in pain, and I don't want to cancel yet another date.

That'd be five dates in a row, if I don't make it out tonight. God, that's depressing. This is supposed to be my time to rediscover myself! I'm single for the first time in almost ten years. Time to sow my wild oats or some shit like that.

Too bad my body is cockblocking me at every turn.

I stopped going on the apps so I could focus on getting my pain under control, but seeing my ex-husband's honeymoon pics with the woman he cheated on me with made me impulsively ask out the barista at Cafe Celia's that's always flirting with me.

Damn, if I cancel tonight, I won't be able to show my face there for at least a few weeks. Their honey lavender latte is the only thing that motivates me to get out of bed some days. Plus, Isaac is sweet, attractive, and the man behind those incredible lattes. If things go well, there could be a future of him making them for me every morning from the comfort of my own home.

Whoa, slow down. You've only been divorced for a year.

The whole point of dating is to have new experiences, not shack up with the first guy that's vaguely decent. I don't need a man to make me happy. I've spent most of my life living according to that false narrative, but all that got me was heartache and an abundance of emotional baggage.

No, I'm enough on my own. Though, it'd be nice to have a boyfriend right now to give me a massage. I don't get touched much these days. At least, not outside of physical therapy.

I shower and take my morning meds, then attempt a few of the exercises the PT gave me for when I'm in pain, but most of them hurt too much to do. Who knew turning your head to the side could be that unpleasant?

Deciding to go the muscle relaxer route, I take one with my coffee and some overnight oats. I'm trying to prep meals for myself on good days so I'll stop resorting to take out when I don't feel up to cooking, but it's hard to find the motivation to stay home at the stove instead of going out and doing something fun when I'm not in pain.

Once I'm medicated and fed, I microwave the heat pad and put on the TENS unit. I decide to transfer my pillow from my bed to my couch for a change of scenery. Maybe if I move around where I lie around like a lump, it'll help me not feel so pathetic.

My foot gets tangled up in a resistance band that's dangling out of the basket next to my couch and I stumble to the side, smacking my shin against the corner of my coffee table.

Stupid piece of crap.

Another bruise to add to the collection dotting my pale skin. At least I'll know where this one came from. That's the second time I've tripped on that band, and I haven't remembered to use it in a week, so I should put it away. I'm trying to get in better shape, but every time I work out lately, I hurt myself. Even when I follow the PT's advice.

I'm getting sick of all the advice. Half the time I do what I'm supposed to, and it makes things worse. My awful doctor wants me to go on a diet. And work out more. But how am I supposed to do that when I can't turn my head?

At my last visit, I told her about the increased pain and she said I'd feel better if I lost weight. That was a first for me, and though my best friend has bemoaned the treatment she gets because of her size, I was still taken aback and incredibly embarrassed.

Embarrassed and infuriated. Increased pain is the reason why I've gained weight in the first place. Turns out that if I can't go to the gym five times a week, my body doesn't stay a size six. And I can't go to the gym five times a week because my neck has decided it hates me.

It sucks. I feel trapped in a no-win scenario, and the person who's supposed to be my guide to figuring out how to manage the issue doesn't get it. Which reminds me, I still need to ask around if anyone has a doctor they like. I'm not going back to mine.

I don't give a shit about being heavier. Going up a few sizes hasn't done anything to make me feel less attractive. I've always loved the way I look, and that hasn't changed. I've got great tits that are even better now. My tummy is soft, with a pooch that looks super cute in tight skirts. I've got legs for days and long blonde hair. The only complaint I have is that none of the weight has gone to my butt, but even with my flat ass, I'm hot as fuck.

Though, I'd happily trade good looks for a body that actually works properly.

Too bad cyborg bodies don't exist yet... maybe I'm tempting the robot uprising, but I'd be the first in line to upload my consciousness out of my pretty, defective meat sack. Hmm, but if I were a cyborg, where would my allegiance lie if it came to man vs. machine?

My wandering thoughts signal that the meds are kicking in. My mind is fuzzy, and I search on my phone for information about transhumanism and the future of cybernetics until I'm too sleepy to keep my eyes open.

Fingers crossed when I wake up, I'll feel a little better. It looks like we've got a long way to go before I get my robot spine.

3

GRACE

It's after 2pm when I wake up from my muscle relaxer induced nap. Sleeping that much during the day makes me feel like I've been out for years and my sluggish mind attempts to pull me back under. I fight it, and make myself sit up as carefully as possible, bracing myself for the bright flare of pain.

Thankfully, it's only a dull throb now. Good enough to go out.

After I get up and move around a little more to test and make sure the pain doesn't come back right away, I pull up my text thread with Isaac to confirm the time we're meeting. I frown when I see an unread message from last night, as well as one from a few hours ago.

Crap, I should've checked that when I got up. I was too distracted by the pain and subsequent problem-solving mode to look at my texts.

> Isaac (11:32pm): Hey Grace! Mind if we reschedule for next weekend? A friend needs my help with something tomorrow night.
>
> Isaac (10:14am): Hope I didn't upset you. Let me know if you're still up to go out another time.

Oh. Well, okay then. Guess I didn't need to worry about backing out because he'd already done it for me. I wait for anger or disappointment to crop up, but all I feel is relief.

Isaac is cute, but I didn't imagine the date going anywhere other than maybe a few dinners and some mediocre third date sex where I pretend to orgasm, and then one of us ghosts the other person. Shit, in that scenario, I'd also have to stop going to get coffee where he works. I really didn't think things through. This is the best outcome.

I text him back, letting him know it's fine, and that I'm busy next weekend. Hopefully, he won't bring it up if I see him in person, and if he does, I'll make something up until he moves on. I'm hot, but not enough for someone as attractive as him to get caught up on.

Once that's taken care of, I chug some water, make myself more coffee, and go sit out on the back deck while I munch on some carrots and hummus. I read somewhere that being in the sun helps boost your mood, so I try to be outside for at least fifteen minutes a day, since it can't hurt anything.

The family in the condo attached to mine is out in their fenced in sliver of yard, the kids racing around with their pit bull puppy while the parents argue about something at the grill. I give them a wave and smile, cringing internally when I realize I'm still in my pajama shorts and oversized t-shirt with no bra. Thankfully, Mr. Anderson doesn't seem like he has a pervy bone in his body because his eyes don't fall from my face as the couple returns my greeting.

"Nice weather for grilling," I say, crossing my arms over my chest so I don't make anyone uncomfortable with my free-hanging tits.

"Yeah, the weather's been beautiful this week. Next week is going to be broiling though," Mrs. Anderson says amiably.

"Makes me wish I had a pool." I gesture to my equally tiny backyard and laugh. "I'll have to settle for a kiddie pool, for now."

"You're welcome to borrow ours if you'd like," Mr. Anderson says, and his wife nods in agreement.

"Thanks!" There's no way I'm going to borrow a child's inflatable pool from them and sit out in the yard, but the offer is kind.

"Any fun plans for the rest of the day?" Mrs. Anderson asks.

"Nope. I thought maybe I'd go out, but plans changed." I must sound dejected when I say it, because they both frown a little and exchange a glance that silently says "poor woman, alone again on a Saturday night".

Okay, maybe I'm a little bummed that I've wasted half a day trying to be well enough to go out, only to find myself with no plans. It's sad when the stressed out parents of three wild kids feel bad for you.

I drink my coffee to the sounds of squealing kids and happy dog barks, letting the afternoon sun bake me until it, combined with the heat pad, makes me too hot to stay outside any longer.

When I'm back inside, I survey my living room with a sigh. The couch is still set up from my morning nap. What a depressing sight. Is this what my life has come to?

There was a brief window after the divorce was finalized and I moved into this condo where I was out almost every night of the week. I was seizing the freedom of single life with both hands. Sure, that was exhausting and no doubt my way of distracting myself from my broken marriage, but it was better than this. Now I'm tired from a day of lying around.

Nope. I'm not doing this. I'm not feeling sorry for myself tonight. The day isn't ruined yet, it's only early afternoon. There's plenty of time to find something to do. If worse comes to worst, I'll head over to Nightlight and see if I can find someone to flirt with or chat with the friendly bartender, Tomas.

I pull up my text thread with my best friend, Mona. Most likely she already has plans with her fiancé, but I can check. Ever since they met, our weekend hangs have diminished. Not that I don't contribute to that by regularly backing out of plans because I'm in too much pain.

> Grace: Hey! Wanna hang out tonight?

> Mona: Hey! I thought you had a date? Did you cancel?

Ouch. I get why she assumes I was the one to cancel, but it still feels bad.

> Grace: For once, no. He said he had to help a friend. I don't care so much about the canceled date, but I was looking forward to getting out of the house for a bit.

> Mona: Damn. His loss.

> Mona: I was planning on going to see Blair perform at The Vault tonight. Come with me!

My stomach does a weird flip at the mention of our mutual

friend. Probably because a handful of months ago, I found out that she's a vampire and that monsters are real. It's an instinctual prey reaction, no doubt. Not that she's ever threatened me.

Blair comes off as aloof at first, but after spending time with her, I realized that's a well-crafted act. She spent hours helping to fix my disastrous burlesque costume for the class performance we were in, when the only connection we had at the time was our mutual friendship with Mona. She's the best kind of supportive—empathetic and helpful while not sugar coating things.

Or at least she was when we spent time together. I haven't seen Blair since New Year's Eve, which was months ago. Not intentionally. She's been busy with work, and I've been busy being pathetic. I don't feel up to going out most nights, and she's not awake during the day.

Us not seeing each other has nothing to do with that moment right before the clock struck midnight. I'm not even sure it was a moment. I was drunk and coming off a bad string of first dates, and there was a second when I had the weirdest urge to do something when I saw couples getting ready to kiss. Blair was staring directly into my eyes and I felt like I couldn't breathe. Then someone knocked into me and spilled champagne all over my dress and it was gone.

It was for the best. Blair is beautiful, but I'm not attracted to women. Kissing someone because you're lonely and intoxicated doesn't mean you want them. I'm happy about the champagne accident. It stopped me from making things really awkward between us.

Though, now that I think about it, maybe even the look we exchanged was enough to mess up our friendship. We used to spend time together at least once a week and now…

No, I'm overthinking things. We're still friends. She's just busy and I'm a forgetful mess.

The Vault is a kink club a few miles outside of town. I've been there once, for a burlesque show that Mona performed in. I wonder what kind of performance Blair is doing. She also does burlesque, but she's a professional domme. Is Mona going there tonight to see her dominate someone?

Sweat beads on my brow, and I can't blame that entirely on being overheated from the sun and my heating pad. My stomach clenches again in that strange way that makes me feel like the floor has dropped out from beneath me.

What exactly does Blair do as a domme? I've never had the guts to ask her about it.

Well, that's not completely true. I'd confessed to Mona about my unconventional fantasies after she divulged the kinky sex she and Max were having, and she said I should discuss it with Blair. We went out for drinks after my first—and only—burlesque performance, and I was riding the post-performance high, so it felt like the right time to ask.

But then Mona called… and I found out that monsters exist.

After that, it didn't feel like a high priority. Who cares that your friend is a domme when they're also a goddamn vampire?

Now that the shock of that revelation has faded, I wish I'd found out more. Purely so I'd know what I'm getting into tonight if I go with Mona. A handful of late night internet searches about kink and BDSM means I won't be totally in the dark, but there's a big difference between reading the definition of domination and seeing it in action.

> Grace: Isn't Max going with you? No offense, but I'm not sure I'm the kind of friend that wants to see you two banging.

Mona's an exhibitionist. Honestly, I wouldn't have a problem seeing her naked because I already have, but I don't know if I could look Max in the eyes again after seeing his dick.

> Mona: Nope! He has to work tonight, so it'll just be me.

> Mona: Don't be scared. No one will bother you. You don't have to do anything except watch, and if that makes you uncomfortable, we'll go home.

> Grace: Who says I don't want to do something?

> Mona: With Blair? 👀

> Grace: What? No! Don't they have any sexy, mysterious doms with a firm hand and an even firmer dick?

> Mona: LOL I haven't noticed. Max already checks all those boxes for me. But we can ask around for you if you want.

> Grace: I'm joking.

> Grace: Maybe.

There's no fucking way I'm hooking up with anyone tonight, not with the iffy way my neck is still feeling. But I'm supposed to be the fun, adventurous friend so it's good to keep up appearances.

> Mona: I'll pick you up at 9? Or I can come earlier and we can get ready together.

I cringe at the idea of her coming over. My place is a mess, and it'd be too embarrassing for her to see it like this.

> Grace: Mind if we get ready at yours instead? I can bring over dinner.

> Mona: That sounds great! I'm so excited. It feels like it's been ages since we've hung out like this.

> Grace: Yeah, me too! 🤍

I'm still a little freaked out about the prospect of what I'll see at The Vault, but spending time with my best friend is the best possible outcome for the night. Much better than a date with a mediocre man.

4

BLAIR

Thumper is already in the parking lot when I pull up to The Vault. His pale, freckled skin glows like a beacon under the lamplight, and he mindlessly swats at the air as he frowns down at his phone.

It makes me uncomfortable, knowing he was waiting out in the muggy summer evening air, no doubt getting eaten alive by mosquitos. I'm supposed to be the bloodsucker marking his skin tonight. He's going to be itchy and covered in bites, which is a nightmare for a rigger.

I'd feel bad for him, but I'm not late. He's early. Also, he could've gone inside. Thumper is a member of the club, not my guest. Which makes his behavior more annoying.

He perks up when he sees me get out of my car, a bright, eager smile spreading his lips as he waves. He smooths a hand through his strawberry blonde hair, then wipes his palms on his pants. "Hey, Bella!"

I cock an unamused brow at him, and his smile falters for a second. "Sorry, I'm just excited to be doing this again. It's been a while," he says with a chuckle. I stare at him blankly and his eyes widen. "Mistress! It's been a while, Mistress. Not that I'm complaining! I'm just happy you messaged me."

"Don't make me regret it."

Thumper nods and his cheeks burnish a deep red. "Yes, Mistress."

That's better. "Why are you standing out here?" A mosquito lands on his arm and I slap it, eliciting a gasp from him. "You're getting eaten alive."

He gives me a sheepish smile. "Wasn't sure if I should go in without you."

I refrain from rolling my eyes at his eagerness. "Go inside. You're no good to me if you want to scratch your skin off."

"R-right. Of course, Mistress. I didn't think about that."

Thumper doesn't seem to be the type to think much at all, but I'm not mean enough to say the thought aloud. There's no purpose in pointing out how foolish someone is unless there's the possibility that they'll take the steps to learn and grow.

Like most men I've dealt with, he'll most likely smile and agree to my face, then keep doing the same shit again and again.

I roll my shoulders and sigh as I watch him turn and head inside the club. What did I expect? He's gotten too familiar with me and I don't have the energy to put him back in his place.

It's not his fault. I'm not a good match for him as a domme or a rigger, and I knew that. I'm the asshole for reaching out to him again. I should've canceled my demonstration instead of using him. But it's too late now, so I'll get through tonight and then try to see if I can play matchmaker with the people at the club tonight and find him someone more his speed.

It's for the best. These rigging demos are a favor I do for the club owner, but I could've been with a paying client tonight. I should tell Jeff I need to take a hiatus. Hanging out at the club while I'm not working is enjoyable, but I need to be practical.

Great. Another awkward conversation I'll get to have tonight.

At least I'll see Mona. Shame her partner isn't coming tonight— I would've used her as my bunny again, but she only wants to do that kind of play if Max is sitting in the shadows waiting to snatch her away as soon as the ropes come off.

I shake my head in amusement at their dynamic, but my stomach clenches unhappily. I'm full from the blood I had earlier, but something deep inside me isn't satisfied. It's hungry for the kind of connection they have.

My fangs threaten to distend, and I grit my teeth.

I don't need it. I'm content with my life. I'm enough on my own.

The pang fades into a dull throb that's manageable. I force the air from my lungs and head into the club.

THUMPER STRETCHES in the small dressing room that The Vault has set up for when they host burlesque performances, angling his mostly bare body toward me in an open invitation to watch him.

I suppress an eye roll. I don't outright tell my submissives that I'm a lesbian, but it's not a secret if you spend any time around me when I visit The Vault on non-demo nights.

His tall, muscular body is nice to look at from an aesthetic perspective. I mentally map rope placement that will best put his good looks on display for our audience. I'd originally planned on doing a suspension tonight, but shut that down when I asked if he has any new physical limitations, and Thumper gave me a cocky, dismissive smirk and gestured to his body as if to say, "who, me, the man with the perfect physique?"

Ugh. Men.

I would've called the whole scene off if he hadn't immediately sobered when I glared at him, unamused. Appearances don't mean shit. I refuse to hurt someone unintentionally because they were too flippant to take their safety seriously.

A crowd has already gathered in the room reserved for demonstrations and more elaborate scenes. Their collective pulses thrum in my ears, and as I lead Thumper to the space for our scene, I catch the scent of something warm and fruity, like a pie that was cooling in the sun. My fangs ache with the need to emerge, and I fight the urge to scan the room for the source.

I don't like it. I'm already not pleased with how the night is going and I don't need to be distracted on top of that. I swallow down the saliva pooling in my mouth and let my eyes glaze over, blocking out our audience.

Thumper is already flushed as I gesture for him to lower to the floor and sit on his heels. His pale skin looks good under the spotlight, no bug bites to be seen. It was wrong of me to slip a few drops of my blood into his drink back in the dressing room. He didn't consent to being healed, but I couldn't stomach the thought of dealing with both his cocky, overly friendly attitude and him squirming the whole scene because he's covered in itchy bites.

Once he's in position, Thumper looks up and has the audacity to wink at me and give me a lopsided smile. It makes me want to slap the idiotic look off of his face so he'll stop thinking we're friends.

But I don't get angry. Especially not for a man I don't care about.

I level him with a cool, stern glare and wait him out. He breaks quickly, dropping his gaze to the floor. Only once his head is bowed in submission do I unfurl my rope. From that point on, my thoughts melt into a pleasant blur, focused on the task at hand.

The purple looks good against his almost translucent skin, but dark blue would've been better—matching the delicate veins that spider across his body, singing to the baser parts of my mind. Tiny sun bleached hairs raise up everywhere my fingers and the ropes touch. A primal instinct inside him recognizes the danger I pose, even if he doesn't consciously understand.

If he knew what I'm capable of, he'd run screaming. But with each methodical weave and knot, I prove to both of us that he's safe. I'm in control.

At least I think I am until I catch that scent again. This time I can't stop my fangs from emerging, and it takes all of my composure to not abandon the remainder of the rope in my hands and leap up to hunt it down.

Pressing my mouth shut despite the prick of pain from my fangs digging into my lower lip, I turn my body away from the audience as I work on finishing up the binding framing Thumper's groin. My hands shake a little, one of my nails accidentally grazing the outline of the erection that's trapped in his tight purple briefs.

He hisses, and his eyes flash up from where they were glued to the floor to meet mine.

I freeze. My vision wavers, and for a second, I see a different set of eyes, pupils blown wide in terror as I loom over them, consumed entirely by the need to *feed*.

No.

My hands pull back from him like I've been burned, and I stand so fast I almost stumble in my heels. Thumper watches me, lust, not fear, blazing in his eyes. My stomach roils with the need to void any remaining blood from my meal earlier tonight, and I look away, stepping back on shaky legs to let the audience admire my work.

There's a smattering of applause and intrigued murmurs, but none of that matters. Because as soon as I break my focus from rigging, I find the source of my torment.

My best friend, Mona, stands at the front of the crowd, her golden brown skin burnished from the excitement of watching the demonstration and her warm brown eyes sparkling as she smiles at me. I barely register her friendly enthusiasm. Because by her side, looking like a gift from the heavens in a baby pink dress that hugs every dip and curve of her body, her cheeks flushed pink with vitality that I want to gorge myself on, is Grace.

5

GRACE

If looks could kill, I'd be dead right now. The blazing anger in Blair's eyes penetrates into my chest, and my heart slams against my ribcage. Blair always looks a little intimidating, with her blunt bangs, razor-sharp eyeliner, and general "don't fuck with me" aesthetic, but this is far beyond that. She's furious, her jaw clenched so tight I can see the muscles in her neck flexing. I have the ridiculous urge to run out of the room. Or maybe I'm the only sane person here. Because I know what she is and she's staring at me like she's out for blood.

Beside me, apparently oblivious to this entire terrifying encounter, Mona raises her hand and gives Blair a little wave. The effect is instantaneous. Blair's eyes snap from mine over to Mona, and any trace of her scorn vanishes. Her lips quirk for a moment before her cool mask slides into place and she walks back over to the bound man.

What the fuck was that about?

All the strange, throbbing awareness that'd been building between my thighs as I watched the demonstration is replaced by hot embarrassment. It's good that no one is looking at me right now, because I'm sure my entire face has turned beet red.

I should've stayed home.

I already feel supremely out of place. Mona failed to mention that the unspoken dress code at The Vault was black and red. I swear the bouncer did a double take when my barbie ass walked into the lobby. I guess I should've known that cute, pink, and sparkly doesn't match the vibe of a kink club, but I'd already picked this outfit out for my date.

That on its own I could've handled. Seeing the guy who canceled my date put on display and bound in rope while everyone can see the outline of his throbbing cock? That made things significantly worse.

I would've stormed out of the room, but didn't want to make a scene, so I swallowed down my indignance for the sake of my friends. Though, I'm not sure now if I can even call Blair that.

Why was she so upset about seeing me? Yeah, it's been a while since we've hung out, but I thought it was because she's busy with work and I'm busy being in pain. Was she avoiding me?

Sick dread washes over me in waves as the past few months rearrange themselves in my mind: Blair not coming to game night anymore because her work schedule shifted; Me inviting Blair out for drinks at Nightlight, and her never able to make it.

I stopped reaching out because I had a pain flare up and then kept meaning to set something up when I was feeling better, but forgot. Now that I think about it, she hasn't texted me at all since I asked if she wanted to come over and have a singles pity party with me when I was alone and sad on Valentine's Day.

That was four months ago.

Jesus, I'm oblivious. My ADHD makes it easy to forget about staying in touch with friends, but this is beyond that. This is her clearly not wanting anything to do with me.

And here I am, front row at her kink club demonstration. Fuck. No wonder she was so pissed.

"What did you think?" Mona asks, poking me in the side with her elbow and snapping me back to the present.

"I need to go."

Her brows shoot up in alarm. "What? Why? Don't you at least want to say hello to Blair?"

I let out a weird sound somewhere between a laugh and a whine. "You're joking."

Mona frowns and touches my arm. "Listen, I respect if the demo wasn't your thing, and I know it's probably a little awkward to see a friend in a kink setting like this. But it's not a big deal! She's still just our Blair."

Our Blair? She's not my anything, apparently.

Mona tugs on my arm, trying to lead me over to where Blair is coiling up her rope and talking to Isaac. I attempt to root myself to the spot, but she's surprisingly strong and I have to stumble forward to not fall flat on my face.

"I can't!" I hiss, pulling away from her grip.

It's too late. Blair looks up and there's a flicker of that heat again in her eyes when she sees me, but it's gone so fast I almost think I've imagined it. If I try to leave without saying anything to her, I'll be the asshole. Nevermind that she's the one who friendship ghosted me for no reason.

This must be retribution for when I asked Mona's now partner Max why he was staring at her from across the bar. Or for all the times I pushed Mona to have some fun. It's a terrible feeling. Crap, now I feel like a reject *and* a shitty person for putting Mona through that.

"Hey Bella! That was amazing, as always!" Mona says, tugging Blair's petite form into a gentle hug. Blair stiffens almost imperceptibly as Mona wraps her arms around her, but the tension melts a second later. Her eyes fall closed and a look of peace I've never seen before fills her face. Mona's hugs are the best, but this goes beyond that.

Holy crap. Does Blair *like* Mona? Could that explain why she distanced herself from me? She didn't want anyone in the way between her and her unrequited crush? But I'm no threat. I love Mona like a sister. Max is who she should be worried about.

Wait, what did Mona call her?

"Bella?" I ask aloud, and flush when all three sets of eyes land on me.

It takes a second to register the way Isaac gapes at me, just now realizing I'm here and he's been caught ditching our date to be with Blair. Or Bella, I guess.

"Grace!"

Both Mona and I look at Isaac at his exclamation, who drops his hands to cover his crotch. Mona turns back to me, eyes wide. "Oh shit. I forgot to tell you."

"Tell me what?" Please don't make this night any worse.

"When we're here, we use pseudonyms. So she's Bella," Mona says, gesturing to Blair. "And uh, I'm, um..."

"Grace," Blair finishes for her, an amused half-smile twisting her lips.

Hearing my name in Blair's husky drawl for the first time in months sends a shiver down my spine. It takes me a moment to understand she's not talking to me.

"You used your friend's name for your kink name?" Isaac asks, drawing my focus back to the conversation.

"Wait, *what?*" I turn to face Mona, who has a flush spreading all the way down her neck to her chest.

"I didn't do it on purpose! I needed one, and I panicked. Then everyone knew me as that, so I left it. I'm sorry!"

God, I wish I really had died when Blair glared at me before.

"It looks like you're already acquainted with Thumper," Blair says calmly, her eyes darting between us before focusing back on me.

What kind of name is Thumper? I frown and look at the mostly naked barista. As this conversation goes on, it becomes less and less likely I'll ever be getting another lavender honey latte from him.

Is it sad that I'm more upset about that than I am about him canceling our date?

You know what, who cares? He's a shitty person. I don't give a fuck that he ditched me for getting tied up by Blair. I don't care that Blair ghosted our friendship, either.

I don't!

I put on my best fake smile. "It's been a while, Bella. I guess you've been busy with... Thumper."

I should stop there, but I don't. Anger bubbles up inside me. "I get it. She's a great friend if you manage to get her to text you back. Would've been nice to know the two of you were together before he agreed to go on a date with me."

Fuck, I guess I do care.

Stunned silence follows my vitriol-laced words. And with that, my utter humiliation tonight is complete. "Hope you have a good rest of your night. I'll get a rideshare home, *Grace.*"

Mona looks stricken, and I internally wince. She doesn't deserve any bitchiness, but I'm too embarrassed to keep my temper in check.

I turn to walk away, but freeze in place when Blair speaks.

"No."

I glare back at the stern-faced vampire. A cold flame of an emotion I don't understand flickers behind her eyes and my heart leaps in my chest—wanting to run away at the same time I want to bare my neck to her. "N-no?"

"No, you're not calling a ride home. No, I'm not with Thumper. I wouldn't have asked him for a favor if I knew he had plans with anyone." She turns and levels her icy stare at him. "You'll need to find a new rigger. Our arrangement is done."

Isaac, or Thumper, sputters, his cheeks flooded with embarrassment. "Mistress, please, it was just a misunderstanding." He turns and looks at me. "I'm so sorry, Grace. I thought it would be okay. What I have with Mistress Bella isn't sexual."

I scoff. "Your boner earlier would suggest otherwise." God, why do I have such abysmal taste in men?

He opens his mouth to reply, but Blair interrupts him. "You can go." His expression falls, but he doesn't argue, standing and walking away, his posture laced with dejection and shame.

Good riddance.

"He's the guy you were supposed to go out with?" Mona frowns and I nod. A moment later, recognition flashes across her face. "Wait, he works at Cafe Celia's, doesn't he? Fuck, what about your lattes?" The amount of legitimate devastation on my behalf in her voice makes some of my anger crumble away.

"Guess that's why you never mix business with pleasure," I say wryly, shaking my head.

My amusement fades when I turn back to Blair. I swallow hard, trying to keep my tone even. "Is there a reason you didn't tell me we were done being friends? I think I would've preferred the finality of a dismissal like you just did to Isaac, if I'm being honest."

A rare furrow forms on Blair's brow. "I don't know what you're talking about."

I'd think she was gaslighting me, but she looks genuinely confused.

My brain decides that I'm going to compensate for her calm, measured reply with incoherent babbling. "You were so angry and... Why don't you come to game night? You never wanted to hang out. I texted, and you blew me off, so I stopped. Why did you glare at me like that? I didn't do anything wrong. I'm allowed to be here!"

I jab a finger at Blair accusatorially, but Mona snatches my hand out of the air before it pokes her in the chest. "Whoa, none of that." She says it like I'm a petulant child throwing a tantrum.

Which, fuck, maybe that's what I'm acting like. I cringe at my behavior and drop my eyes to the floor.

Mona touches my shoulder lightly. "I'm going to go to the bathroom. Let you two talk for a bit."

A surge of alarm pulses through me, and I want to beg her to stay. Again, I'm acting like a baby. *Calm down and talk to Blair like a logical adult.* I take a deep inhale as Mona walks away, working up the courage to look at the vampire.

"I'm sorry, Grace."

My eyes flash up to meet Blair's, stunned. "What?"

Blair's lips downturn slightly and she shifts in place, looking almost as uncomfortable as she did the night I found out she's a vampire. "I'm sorry. I've been really busy with work, but I should've checked in."

"Oh." It's hard to stay mad with such a direct, sincere reply. Or at least I think that until she continues, her voice tinged with uncharacteristic vulnerability. "I didn't know you cared."

What the hell is that supposed to mean? What did I do to make her think otherwise?

I suppress my scowl as best I can, but I can't fully keep a frown off my face. "Why wouldn't I care? We were hanging out all the time last year and then suddenly you were too busy. It sucked."

I hadn't processed that not seeing Blair had bothered me until I came here tonight. I didn't let myself think anything of it, because I didn't want to add another thing to the pile of shitty things going on in my life. It's like seeing her again tore the invisible wound open and now I can't stop gushing my feelings out like my lifeblood.

She nods solemnly. "You're right. I shouldn't have done that. If it helps at all, it's a fairly new concept to me."

"Someone caring about you?" I ask flippantly.

"Yes."

The unflinching honesty on her face knocks me back.

"Well, get used to it. I care about you! Mona cares, too." I cross my arms under my chest so I won't reach out and hug her. I have a feeling that wouldn't go well, even though I'm desperate to show her some affection after her admission. "That's what it means to be friends," I say with a teasing smile.

"Right. I'll do better." I almost miss the way her jaw clenches before she smiles at me because of how stunningly beautiful it makes her look.

Despite her smile, the air is still charged between us. It feels like I've missed something important. That while she apologized, I'm the one who screwed up.

Mona returns before I can stew in the discomfort from my lack of understanding for too long. "Well? Everything alright?" she asks, placing a hand on her hip.

Blair nods.

"Yeah. We're good," I say, even though I can't help worrying that's not true. I shake it off and melodramatically frown at Mona. "Can't say the same for us though, *Grace*."

She groans. "I'm sorry! I panicked! You can use my name as revenge if you want."

I laugh and shake my head, patting her shoulder. "That defeats the purpose of using a kink name, doesn't it? Besides, I want something cooler than Mona," I say, sticking my tongue out at her.

"Hey!" She smacks my arm lightly.

Blair laughs, and the sound makes strange butterflies kick up in my stomach. Relief that things might actually be okay between us, no doubt.

"Seriously, though, you need a name, even if you never come back after tonight," Mona says. She taps her chin, thinking. "What about Barbie?"

I roll my eyes. "Too on the nose."

"Sunny? Pinkie?"

"Now I understand why you couldn't come up with a name for yourself," I say, shaking my head at Mona's suggestion.

"Rose." Blair says the name decisively, and a warm, bubbling sensation spreads inside me.

"I like it!" Mona exclaims.

I'm blushing, and it only gets worse when Blair cocks a questioning brow at me. "Uh, yeah. That works."

"Well, *Rose*." The name from Blair's lips is an intimate caress that makes me want to melt on the spot from how much my cheeks flame. "Why don't we show you around?"

I nod, unable to untie my tongue enough to reply

6

BLAIR

Grace being here tonight makes this crappy night much brighter. And infinitely worse.

Now that I know the source of the scent, I should've realized she was here. No one smells as good as Grace. Like the fresh-baked berry pie my grandma left to cool on the windowsill, sun shining down on it as I stole a taste when she was out of the room.

I thought I was so sneaky, never getting caught. Looking back, I'm certain Grandma knew. She'd make a dramatic show of wondering who could've taken a bite, and then give me a big hug and offer me a slice while I struggled with the urge to confess.

I feel the same way when I look at Grace. Like she knows all my secrets no matter how hard I try to hide them.

She also makes me want to devour her, letting her sweet, tart flavor drip down my chin like the berries I picked from my grandma's garden. I lick my lips, and am disappointed to only taste the stale copper of my blood from when my fangs wouldn't retract. They're threatening to emerge again now, even though I can't smell her now that I'm not breathing.

Not needing oxygen to function comes in handy when I'm near Grace. I've trained myself to only suck in air through my mouth when I need to speak. I'm sure it's off-putting, but letting the scent of her sweet blood wash over me would be much worse. I pride myself on self-control, but even I have my limits. A few minutes smelling her nearby would break me. Maybe less than that.

"Alright, where should we start?" Mona asks, clapping her hands together.

"The bar?" Grace asks, letting out a weak laugh. Her cheeks are still washed a light pink that matches her dress. The dress that makes her stand out like a beacon in the dark, moody club and draws my eyes to the soft curve of her belly that's filled out since the last time I saw her. Fuck, she's gorgeous.

Gorgeous and unattainable.

Grace likes men. She's made that abundantly clear. She might get a small thrill from being around me, but most humans do. I'm a vampire. I make people squirm, and whether or not that's pleasurable, it doesn't change their sexuality.

I'm not a glutton for punishment, and I don't coerce people into sleeping with me. Thus, Grace is not for me.

"There's no alcohol at The Vault," I say. "Intoxication doesn't mix well with consent."

"Ah. Right," Grace says, nodding. A strand of golden hair falls in her face and my fingers twitch to reach out and brush it away.

"Are you looking to participate in anything tonight?" I ask, forcing my voice and expression to seem blasé.

Grace's brows shoot up. "With you?"

Mona cackles at her reaction. "Hah! You sound like me the first time Bella brought me here."

I didn't think it would be possible, but Grace's eyes go even wider and they flick back and forth between me and Mona. "Did you?! Are you telling me you two have... I thought there was a vibe, but you're with Max."

"Whoa, whoa," Mona says, holding her hands up. "Bella and I haven't slept together."

I smirk at her. "Oh, there was definitely a vibe. But, no, I only tied her up."

My buxom exhibitionist friend sputters, which makes me laugh. Mona and I share a mutual attraction, but we both know our interests aren't compatible. I don't fight for submission, and she craves the struggle.

"I feel like I'm the only person here that hasn't been tied up by you." Grace's comment is flippant, but it immediately puts the image in my brain.

Mona's eyes light up. "I'm sure she'd be happy to do something simple with you if you want to try it."

My fangs press against my gums at the thought of Grace bound for me, rope weaving across her body to accentuate every dip and curve that I'm obsessed with. I tense, trying not to show how terrible of an idea that would be. I'm supposed to be her friend. A friend wouldn't have any reason to not show a curious friend a basic tie.

"W-what? No... that would be...no!" Grace squeaks. She winces and gives me an apologetic smile. "No offense. I just..."

Grace's words are a bucket of cold water dousing the flame of hunger inside me. Of course she doesn't want that.

I nod. "It's fine."

It is. It's better to keep my distance.

Mona laughs, unaware of the sting of rejection I'm enduring. "Oof, sorry! I keep forgetting that you're not an exhibitionist. Or into any of this at all."

"I wouldn't say that I'm not into any of it... but yeah, not an exhibitionist. I tried it with the burlesque class student show and that was fun as a one time thing, but it did nothing for me. Maybe it's from having too many people ogle my tits in regular settings for it to have much of an impact." Grace laughs and places a hand above the swell of her breasts, drawing my eyes to the long line of her cleavage highlighted by the low neckline of her dress.

I look away quickly. She's my friend. You don't stare at your friend's breasts.

Mona leads us to a pair of the couches in a corner of the main club area. A few people are swaying to the thudding, moody music, and more than one eye the three of us appreciatively. I don't blame them. I know I'm attractive, and both Mona and Grace are stunning in their own right. I've ended up with two of the hottest, most unavailable women I've ever known as my friends. Maybe I'm more of a masochist than I think I am.

Mona sits on the far end of one of the couches, and Grace sits on the couch opposite of her, leaving it up to me to decide who to sit next to.

Great. If I sit next to Grace, I'll have to continue holding my breath, and even then, at such close proximity, I'll still catch her scent whenever I need to speak. But if I sit across from her, I'll be looking directly at her. I'm not sure which one is worse right now.

Grace is busy scanning the club from her new vantage point, so she doesn't register my hesitation. But Mona certainly does. She raises a brow at me, as if to say, "you good?" and then glances over at our blonde friend meaningfully.

I roll my eyes at Mona, pretending like she's making something out of nothing and not far too good at reading me, and sit down next to her.

I let myself breathe, and fortunately only get a hint of Grace's scent at this distance, with Mona's campfire and roasted marshmallow scent overpowering it.

I've never told my best friend that the reason I first spoke to her —other than that she looked painfully uncomfortable at the burlesque class we met at and I felt bad for her—was because her scent reminded me of the one camping trip my parents let me go on with my friend's family. It was the happiest and most relaxed day I'd had since my grandma passed away. And that's even considering that my father showed up in a rage to pick me up early because my mother found black lipstick under the sink in my bathroom.

No one ever explained why certain people have distinct scents to me now that I'm a vampire. To be fair, nothing was explained, since I was abandoned immediately after my creation. My guess is that there's something instinctual telling me that the person's blood will be good or bad for me. Avoid the ones that smell like rotting fish, bite the ones that smell delicious. Most people don't smell like much of anything to me, which is a relief. I wish that was the case for Grace.

"See anything you like?" Mona asks Grace, a hint of teasing in her voice.

Grace shrugs. "Honestly, it's tamer than I thought it would be.

Other than Blair's demonstration, it doesn't seem much different from a regular night club. Where's the whips and chains, and the people on leashes?"

"Oh, they're here," Mona says with a laugh. "Probably in the private rooms. Are you disappointed?"

"A little!" Grace replies, letting out a fake sigh.

"About which part?" I ask, unable to hold back my curiosity. It's a perfectly normal question to ask a friend who is at a kink club. I'm not being inappropriate. My brain isn't imagining what Grace would look like with a collar around her delicate throat.

Grace's smile immediately turns more shy. "Uh, I don't know…"

Mona scoffs. "Yes, you do! Tell us! I've told you all my kinky secrets, so it's only fair. Blair won't judge. She's a professional."

I should tell Mona to back off. No one should be pressured into discussing their kinks if they don't want to, and Grace has looked uncomfortable the entire time I've seen her tonight. But before I can intercede, Grace huffs and throws her hands up in defeat.

"Okay, fine! I'll tell you. But you have to promise not to make fun of me." Her cheeks are splotchy from the prospect of admitting things to us.

She looks like she's about to tell us she has a diaper fetish. If she did, she could probably find someone here to explore that with. But that's unlikely. Grace likes to act sexually liberated, but she's coming out of a marriage with the first man she dated. If I had to guess, her idea of extreme is wanting someone to spank her and call her a good girl.

"I've heard everything. You don't have to worry," I say, keeping my tone even.

"I promise," Mona adds, moving couches to sit next to Grace and give her a hand a reassuring squeeze.

"Well... I guess the best way to put it is that I want to belong to someone," Grace says, almost too quiet to hear over the club music.

My senses sharpen with interest at her words. I force myself to not lean forward in my chair or show any reaction at all.

When she doesn't say anything else, Mona pokes her in the side. "You can't just leave it at that! Belong how?"

"I don't know..." Grace looks down shyly, like she's trying to think of the words.

She knows exactly what she wants. She just can't get the words out.

I take pity on her. "Do you want a dominant that you submit to? Someone who gives commands and you follow them?"

"Y-yeah," Grace says, nodding without looking back up at either of us. Her posture is still tense.

"Do you want to be a servant? Someone's pet? A little girl for a daddy?" I prompt.

Her eyes finally raise from the floor. "I'm not sure." This time, her uncertainty sounds genuine.

"That's okay! You don't have to know exactly what you want," Mona says encouragingly. "Kink involves a lot of exploration and learning what you like and don't like."

"Yes, not everyone knows they want to be ravaged by their fake stalker right away," I deadpan.

Mona lets out a huff of protest at the callout, but it makes Grace laugh and relax. "It's all a moot point, anyway. I wouldn't know how to find someone to do something like that with. You can't just walk up to someone and ask them to dominate you. Or can you?"

If Grace were the one asking, it would work on me. "No." My reply comes out more forcefully than intended.

"I'd start with 'hello' first," Mona adds with a snort.

As if summoned by Mona's words and Grace's question, I sense someone approaching from behind me. My body tenses reflexively, ready to fight off any threats, but I force myself to stay facing toward my friends. No one here would try to harm us.

I search Grace and Mona's faces for any reaction to the person behind me. Grace pushes a strand of silky blonde hair behind her ear and perks up. Mona plasters on the kind of pleasant smile you'd give to a stranger.

"Pardon me for interrupting, ladies. Just wanted to say hello to Bella and introduce myself."

The voice is instantly familiar. *Declan.* The Vault's most eligible daddy dom. Of course. Grace is sitting there in her soft, sweet dress, looking every bit the perfect baby girl.

Wonderful.

I turn around in my seat and give the handsome human towering over me a cool nod. "Declan. Didn't realize you were here tonight. It's good to see you."

No, it fucking isn't.

Don't get me wrong, I have nothing against the man. Out of the other doms that frequent The Vault, he's the one that I respect the most. But that was until he came over here, like a shark scenting blood in the water.

My inner monster begs me to use my powers. I could compel him to leave without breaking a sweat. My fingers ball into fists at my sides, nails digging into my palm until the sting brings me back to reality.

Grace isn't mine. Declan is free to come introduce himself to her. She can do whatever she wants.

All of that logically makes sense, but it doesn't keep me from feeling like I've been punched in the gut when Grace gives him a dazzling smile, leaning forward to let the neck of her dress dip even lower.

"Introduce me to your friends?" he asks, his lips twisting into a smile as he notices Grace's reaction to him.

Friends. It's a good reminder. I push down my jealousy and make introductions.

7

GRACE

Men rarely make me flustered, but the guy that just walked up is a different breed. He's got to be at least six four, with a gray-streaked hair and a salt-and-pepper beard that indicates he's at least ten years my senior. His rugged, weather-worn light brown skin, and the fine lines that crease around his eyes when he smiles only make him hotter.

It's unfair. If I had the same amount of wrinkles and grays, men wouldn't glance my way. Nevertheless, the man is sexy in a way that makes me unsettled. I can't tell if the strange squirming sensation in my stomach is a good thing or not.

"Declan, this is my friend Grace," Blair says. Mona grabs my hand as I go to lift it to wave hello to the stranger. Shit, I really wish she'd picked a different pseudonym.

"Hi Declan! I think I've seen you around, but it's nice to get a formal introduction." Mona smiles brightly, catching me a little by surprise. Sometimes I forget how much her confidence has grown, and I still expect her to have her guard up around men. I know it was a defensive mechanism so she wouldn't have to deal with embarrassment if they didn't find her attractive, but I can't count the number of times a guy was obviously flirting with her and she was oblivious.

No, the Mona sitting next to me knows how hot she is. The man, Declan, smiles back and nods. "A pleasure to meet you, Grace. I've been an admirer since I saw you as Bella's rope bunny, but didn't know if the man you're usually here with would appreciate me stopping by to say so."

Mona giggles. "Yeah, probably not." Her left hand comes up to her chest and flashes the diamond ring adorning it. I still can't get over how pretty the engagement ring Max picked out is.

Declan clocks it with an easy smile, then turns his focus on me expectantly.

"This is Rose," Blair offers, when I'm unable to formulate words under the weight of this man's gaze. I'm sure I'm turning pinker by the second as he lets his eyes rake down my body and back up to my face.

His lips quirk into an amused grin. "Like Briar Rose?"

I blink back at him, my brain not able to process what he's asking.

"Sleeping Beauty. You certainly look the part, princess," he says with a wink that manages to come off as charming rather than creepy—not a small feat.

"Oh! Uh, no, I didn't even think of that. But that works! I do like to sleep a lot." Shit, I'm babbling.

Mona snorts. "It's true. Sleeping is one of her favorite hobbies."

"Mmm, I love a good nap. Especially when there's someone there to snuggle up with."

The genuine way he says that makes me laugh at how incongruous it is with his rugged appearance.

He raises a brow. "Something funny about snuggling, princess?"

"N-no!" I sputter. "I just wasn't expecting a strange man to come over and talk to me about his love for naps and cuddles at a kink club. But tonight has been nothing like I expected, so that tracks."

"Call me old-fashioned, but I like to get to know a woman a bit before I dive into more hardcore subject matter. But if there's something else you'd like to talk about, Rose, I'm all ears."

"I..." I feel like I'm diving into the deep end, but why the hell shouldn't I flirt with this sexy older man? I swallow down my nerves and give him a shy smile. "Maybe. This is all new to me, so I'm not sure what to ask."

"First time?" His eyes spark with interest, and the grin he gives me is filthy. "I've been told I'm a great teacher. What is it you're looking for, princess?"

I bite my lip, simultaneously feeling insane for considering diving into a kinky encounter with this man and thrilled at the potential that he could be what I've been secretly hoping for.

My eyes dart to Mona, who is watching the interaction with undisguised glee, then over to Blair, who looks... *bored*. There's a sharp pang in my gut when I notice her apathy that deflates my excitement. I thought she'd... I don't know. Tell me I need to learn more about kink before doing anything? Be protective of me as her friend?

It's silly. I don't need her approval or her guidance.

"I'd love someone to teach me, but I think you were right about getting to know each other better first." There. I'm being responsible without anyone helping me.

He nods, looking more pleased about my reticence than I thought he would be. "I like a woman who does her due diligence. Would your friends mind if I steal you away? Just to chat."

My eyes flit back over to Blair, who is completely inscrutable. Devoid of any sign that she approves or not.

I hate it. Why is she shutting herself off when she's the one whose opinion I'd trust the most in this moment? She's a professional domme, for fuck's sake. Why isn't she saying anything?

With nothing from my unhelpful vampire friend, I look to Mona. She may have been reckless when she first started exploring kink, but at least she knows more about it than I do. She raises a questioning brow at me, exchanging a silent "You need me to tell this guy to back off?", which isn't what I was looking for.

I want someone to tell me what to do! Don't they know I'm a disaster? My instincts can't be trusted—I married the world's biggest asshole because he told me I was the prettiest girl he'd ever seen.

Left to my own devices, I choose excitement over pragmatism. "They'll be fine without me." It comes out flirty, but inside there's another stab of discomfort at the statement.

Probably because it's true. Mona has her partner Max, and her new, much cooler best friend, Blair. Blair has Mona, and undoubtedly a never ending supply of interesting, kinky people at her beck and call. People that don't have to cancel plans because their body is defective.

Mona smiles, oblivious to my depressing thoughts. "Have fun, Rose." She grabs my elbow and leans in before I can stand, lowering her voice to a whisper. "I don't care how hot he is, or how cool Blair seems with it—stay in the public areas. Don't do anything without discussing boundaries and safewords."

I nod, my eyes widening a bit at her serious tone. "Of course. I'll be back in a bit—don't leave without me," I say, forcing a light laugh.

She pats my arm. "Never."

Mona's assurance bolsters me as I take Declan's extended hand. His grip is strong enough to help me up, but not crushing, and his skin is callused, indicating he works with them. He places a hand lightly on the small of my back as he leads me away, sparking arousal and nervous anticipation. Up close, he smells like leather and musk, the epitome of what you'd imagine a rugged, older, dominant man would smell like. Or at least, what I'd imagine.

If I'm being honest, it's a little disconcerting how well this man fits the image I've conjured when I've fantasized about submitting. Tall, older, toned body and rough hands, dirty smile, and hungry eyes. I don't normally get flustered around men, but he's putting me off-balance.

I like it. The only other person who's made me squirm like this is Blair, but that's different. She's a vampire and a gorgeous badass. Of course she makes me nervous.

We don't go far, only moving to the other side of the main room to a small table and set of chairs. Declan pulls my chair out for me, which seems oddly formal for a kink club, but it makes my stomach flutter.

He sits across from me and I realize he's positioned us so I still have a line of sight on Mona and Blair. He notices me figuring that out and gives me a warm smile. "In case you want to signal your friends to come save you," he says with a chuckle.

"Do I need saving?" I ask, returning his grin.

Declan laughs, the low rasp far too enticing. "You're safe with me, princess."

"That's what they all say."

He nods, unphased by my retort. "Fair enough. I'm just happy you're giving me a chance."

There's a moment of silence that stretches out after he speaks, his eyes assessing me, watching me squirm, waiting for what comes next. I lick my lips and he tracks the movement with focused interest.

"So, Rose, you said you've never done this before. That you might be interested in learning. What exactly do you want to learn, sweetheart?"

I can't stop the furious blush that floods my cheeks at the simple question. Telling this to my friends is one thing, but to a sexy, experienced older dom?

"You look beautiful when you blush," he rumbles. "Would it help if I ask some questions and you tell me yes or no?"

I worry my lower lip with my teeth and he reaches out and hovers his hand over where mine rests on the table. "Can I touch your hand?"

The question surprises so much, it snaps me out of my nerves a little and I giggle. "Sure. That's awfully polite of you."

He places his hand on top of mine and gives it a gentle squeeze. "Consent is crucial. I need to know that you're enthusiastic and comfortable with anything we do together. If we do anything together... that's still entirely up to you."

Shit, the blush is back with a vengeance. "R-right. Makes sense. Okay, ask your questions. I'm ready."

"Brave girl," he murmurs, raising the hair on my arms as the pad of his thumb strokes my wrist. He leaves his hand on mine, soothing me with the weight of it and his soft caress. "Let's start with the basics. Do you enjoy being submissive?"

"What do you think?" I ask with a weak laugh. He chuckles and gives me a look that can only be described as indulgent.

"I don't want to assume anything, princess. Do you like to be told what to do? Do you like the idea of pleasing me?"

My pulse spikes and a drop of sweat slides down the back of my neck. "Yeah." My voice is soft, but certain, and I'm rewarded with a nod and another gentle smile.

"How would it make you feel if I said you're being a good girl?"

"I'd like that," I breathe, unable to take my eyes off of him now. Is it normal to feel lightheaded talking about this stuff? Or is that because all the blood in my body is going to my face and clit?

He licks his lips and gives me a filthy smile that hits me right between my thighs. "What about if I told you that you were a naughty girl and needed to be disciplined?"

"That's good, too." I laugh again to play off how I'm burning up under his stare.

"You're being such a good girl, answering my questions, Rose." He squeezes my hand and I have to suppress another awkward giggle at how fucking hot and weird this whole situation is. "Should I keep going, or would you like to stop for now?"

The question takes me by surprise. Every guy I've been with would be asking me if I want to go fuck in the bathroom right now, not checking in to see if his racy questions are making me uncomfortable.

I'm honestly not sure if I want to keep going, so I choose a third option. "Can I ask you a question?"

His eyes go warm and soft. "Absolutely. Whatever you want, princess."

"Are you looking for sex or a relationship? If we did things together, would it be exclusive?"

He chuckles, but there's no derision in his expression. "All excellent questions. We'd need to negotiate the parameters of what our play would look like. I like to start with a short scene or two with no sexual or romantic expectations, for us to feel each other out, then check in and see where we're at."

"How would it not be sexual? Isn't that the point?"

Declan's mouth quirks at my interruption. "Not necessarily. Sex isn't always part of kink. I'd be lying if it wasn't a large component of mine, and I'd certainly get turned on playing with you. But the connection and the responsibility of taking care of my submissive is just as important to me."

Gosh, he takes this stuff seriously. I'm a little embarrassed about my naivety, so I cover it with a laugh. "You're saying you want to have sex with me, Declan?"

It's my first time using his name and his gaze turns hot. "Yes. I'd like to do a lot of things with you, princess."

Well, damn. My nipples harden, poking against the thin fabric of my dress. There's no way he can't tell that I'm turned on.

"To answer your other question, I'm happy to be exclusive during the experimentation phase, and beyond, if we're a good match. I prefer that, but don't require it from my submissives."

His responses are so well-practiced that it dawns on me that he's done this many times before. On the one hand, it's nice to know he takes things seriously and has a lot of experience.

On the other... it taps into my insecurities. Makes me feel like whatever happens won't really mean anything to him. I'll be one more woman in a man's list of conquests. Worse, he'll have a lot of people to compare me to. I won't be able to hide behind my appearance. He'll see all my inadequacies in bed.

My excitement cools rapidly as my crappy previous sexual experiences flash before my eyes like a highlight reel of disappointment. I've always imagined that being with a dominant would solve my problems in bed, but what if I'm wrong? What if I'm as broken and frigid as Zack said I was?

My vision wavers as my eyes grow watery. Fuck, I'm not going to cry in a kink club!

"You okay, sweetheart?" Declan asks, his brow furrowing in concern as he reaches to take my hand again.

I force a smile and nod. "Totally fine. Just thinking. It's a lot to consider!" I giggle to try to sell that I wasn't on the verge of tears a second ago.

God, I'm blowing it. I have a surprisingly kind and understanding man who is the dom of my dreams right in front of me and I'm too in my head to stick the landing. Fucking Zack. Fucking awful men who made me feel this way. This is what I want!

"I'm interested. You seem amazing and I want to try this."

Declan's face lights up. "That's fantastic. I'm excited to teach you, Rose. In case it wasn't obvious, that's one of my kinks," he adds with a wink.

"Guess I'll need a sexy schoolgirl outfit, then." It's a joke, but as soon as I say it, I realize that could be exactly what this man is into. A second later, I realize I'd probably be into it too.

"Such a tease. You look perfect the way you are, princess. A pretty pink confection." His gaze darkens, and he leans forward to brush a strand of hair out of my face. "Such a pretty girl. It makes me want to make you filthy."

Oh. Oh wow. That's... hot? Gross? Which somehow makes it hotter to me?

He shifts back in his chair and goes back to his relaxed smile.

"And now all of you is that lovely shade of pink. Stunning. I was wrong before. That must be why you chose the name Rose."

I shrug, trying to get my brain to cool down enough to reply.

Thankfully, he takes pity on me, no doubt able to tell that he's flustered me. "Why don't I give you my number? You can text me if you decide you'd like to meet up and try a scene. Or just get coffee and discuss things more."

I hand him my phone and he puts his contact info in. It feels weird to stay here if we're not going to do anything tonight and I've got his number, so I make a feeble excuse about needing to go to the bathroom.

As soon as he says goodbye, I make a beeline for Mona and Blair. Or rather, just Mona. Blair isn't sitting with her anymore.

Mona tells me that Blair is talking to some friends, then grills me for details, and by the time I'm done recounting how awkward I was and how hot and nice Declan was, she's practically squealing with excitement.

I wish I could say the same. Instead, I feel off. I wish Blair were here for the debrief. She'd know if the things Declan said were good or not. From what Mona has told me, Blair was practically her kink mentor. So then, why doesn't she care about me?

8

GRACE

It takes me less than 24 hours to cave and text. Blair, not Declan. I can't bring myself to even think about his offer yet because something in me says that I need her expert opinion before I jump into anything.

As soon as the sun sets, I press send on the message I spent the last forty-five minutes writing and rewriting. My first attempt was a rambling diatribe on how I was upset she didn't say anything at the club, how it's unfair that Mona got her help but I have to fend for myself, and how I need her to be the kink Yoda to my Luke. The second was an overshare about how I'm worried that I won't be enough for Declan and how I'm scared I'll never have good sex, and how I don't even know if there's any point in me trying kink because it'll probably be disappointing.

After all that nonsense, I settle on something simple and vague.

> Grace: I need your help.

I set my phone down and go back to unloading the dishwasher. Today has been a blessedly low-pain day, which means I'm doing all the stuff around the house that I've neglected. I have enough unproductive pain days that there's no such thing as a lazy Sunday if I'm feeling okay.

I almost drop the plate in my hand as my phone buzzes against the counter, and I scramble to set it down in the cabinet. In my hurry to see if Blair replied, I smack my shin into the edge of the dishwasher that's sticking out and curse.

Standing on one foot as I rub the spot I hit, I pick up my phone and check it.

> Blair: I'll be right there.

Wait, what?

I hastily text back a reply to stop her before she gets in her car. So much for my attempt at starting a casual conversation.

> Grace: No, no, I'm okay! I just didn't get to talk to you last night and I have some questions.

> Grace: Sorry, that was a bad way of wording it. Didn't mean to worry you. You're probably busy getting ready for work, so we can talk later.

> Blair: Ah.

A minute passes and there's no other reply. No prompting for what my questions are, or sign that she's willing to answer. Not even a confirmation that she's too busy to talk.

I go back to putting my dishes away, grumbling to myself about how it's rude to not say anything back and it would be better for her to just tell me she doesn't want to be friends so I can stop getting my feelings hurt when I try to talk to her. There's no way I'm messaging again. If she doesn't say anything else, I'll take it as a message that I should leave her alone.

I stew in my hurt feelings for the five minutes it takes to get another text, but they vanish when I read the message.

> Blair: Sorry, I was canceling my session tonight so we could talk.

> Grace: You didn't have to do that! It can wait.

> Blair: It's fine. I could use a night off.

> Blair: Ask away.

Blair's ability to make a decision quickly and stick with it boggles my mind. I could only dream of being that decisive. No, I struggle for a good thirty seconds to decide what to ask first.

> Grace: Thanks, I really appreciate it. I'm kinda freaking out.

> Grace: I met a dom last night. Which you already know. You were there. Duh.

> Grace: Anyway, he talked to me about some things and I feel like I'm in way over my head. It would mean so much to me to get your professional opinion.

> Blair: Did he make you uncomfortable?

Ugh, Blair is hard to read in person with her stoic demeanor, but impossible to read over text. There's no telling if that's a casual question or if she's being protective and about to go full vampire on Declan's ass for potentially bothering me. What's wrong with me that I'd like to imagine it's the latter?

> Grace: No! He was a gentleman. It was a little weird how un-pervy he was, to be honest. He said one thing that was suggestive, but that was after I flirted a bunch.

I'm not sure how much detail she wants or needs, so I leave it at that.

> Blair: So what's causing concern?

My thumbs hover over my phone. I'd spent so much time worrying about getting Blair's opinion that I didn't stop to consider what I actually want advice on. Declan's explanation of how things work with him was clear. He'd be happy to answer more questions, I'm sure.

Despite my earlier message drafts, there's no way I'm actually telling Blair about my worries about not being good in bed. That's way too pathetic to admit. Blair would never give a shit about what a man thought of her prowess—she'd demand that they give her what she needs.

Everyone assumes I'm the same way. I'm outgoing and confident, and I work hard to project an image that's fun and sexy. Someone like me should be amazing in bed. Appearances are deceiving in many ways when it comes to me.

> Grace: He's very experienced. It makes me nervous.

> Blair: An experienced dom is what you need, if you want to explore submission.

> Grace: I know.

> Blair: What's really the problem?

Shit. What am I supposed to say? I wanted your opinion and I don't know why. I was pissed you didn't seem to care at all last night about me trying this out when you helped Mona.

> Grace: I just wanted to know your thoughts. Find out if it's a good idea or not.

> Blair: You don't need my permission, and I can't make this decision for you.

> Blair: I'm not your domme.

> Grace: Yes, but you're my friend! And you helped Mona.

> Grace: Please, I need an objective opinion that's not influenced by horniness.

There's a long pause before Blair replies. Crap, I shouldn't have whined about this. I should've figured it out on my own. I'm embarrassing myself with how needy I'm being.

> Blair: I can't be objective about this.

My stomach clenches. I don't understand.

> Grace: Why not?

Another long pause.

> Blair: Declan is a good dom. One of the best in the area. If you want to experiment, he'll take care of you.

It doesn't escape my notice that she gave her opinion to avoid answering my question. But it's what I wanted from this conversation, right? Declan has her seal of approval.

> Grace: Okay. Great. I guess I'll text him then.

> Grace: Thanks for your help.

> Blair: That's what friends are for, right?

Somehow, that feels like a genuine question rather than a trite statement.

> Grace: Yeah. That and bitching about things.

> Grace: Speaking of which, we should hang out sometime if you're free. It'd be nice to catch up.

> Blair: I'm booked every night this week.

Right. I don't know why I expected a different response. That's the last time I ask. If she wants to be my friend, she has to put in some effort too.

I'm about to set the phone down and find something to distract myself from the sting of rejection when I get another text.

> Blair: I can do a week from today.

> Grace: That sounds perfect. My place?

> Blair: Yeah. I'll bring that candy you like.

> Grace: Hell yeah!

> Grace: I'd offer to get your favorite snack, but I'm not sure where to get blood.

> Grace: Unless you want some of mine.

Jesus, way to make things weird. My face heats as I conjure an image of Blair calmly brushing my hair to the side with her elegant fingers, and pressing her lips to my throat for a brief moment before sinking her fangs into my neck.

> Grace: Kidding!

Am I? It should be scary to think about Blair biting me, but instead it makes me shiver with interest. Weird. Didn't know I was into the whole vampire thing.

> Blair: Right.

I need to change the subject before I make things even more awkward than I thought possible.

> Grace: So, now that you have a night off, what are you going to do?

> Blair: Not sure. What do you suggest?

I guess I must secretly love getting turned down by Blair, because I immediately seize the opportunity to ask her to do something, knowing she's free.

> Grace: If you're not sick of me, we could go get a drink at Nightlight.

> Blair: I'm not sick of you.

> Blair: It's not too late for you? Don't you have work tomorrow?

I do. I really should stay home instead of going out for a drink.

> Grace: I don't go to bed at 9pm. I can hang out for a while.

Sure, I'm in my pajamas, but that's because I didn't bother getting dressed today.

> Blair: If you're sure.

> Grace: I am! See you there in a half hour?

That's enough time for me to make myself vaguely presentable.

> Blair: Okay.

Look at me. Going out two nights in a row. It's almost like I'm back to my old self. Maybe things are turning around for me.

9

BLAIR

I walked right into her trap. How was I supposed to say no to meeting up when I'd already told her I'd canceled my plans for the night?

Seeing Grace tonight will be torture. Not seeing her would somehow be worse.

When I realized my feelings for Grace had gone from a manageable appreciation of her appearance and scent, to full blown infatuation, I knew I had to back off. Not only was I counting the hours to when I could see her again and bask in her warm, goofy presence, but my inner monster was becoming ravenous at the thought of her. So I made excuses and stopped spending time with her.

I thought months away had been enough to cure me of my

craving for Grace. I finally wasn't thinking about her all the time. I filled my time with work and shored up my mental defenses. I thought I was safe.

And yet, last night I spent every moment until dawn trying to push the sight of Grace walking away with Declan out of my mind, where it incessantly replayed, each time a fresh stab in the heart.

It shouldn't hurt this much.

All the romantic, foolish notions drained out of me the night I was turned and abandoned by the person I thought loved me. I shouldn't have a heart left to crush.

So why does it feel like Grace has wrapped her fist around it, compressing it against my will and resuscitating my capacity to feel those emotions? I don't want them. They've only ever brought me pain.

This has to stop. The simplest option would be to tell her I can't be her friend. Cut her out and move on. But I'm weak. Losing Grace would mean losing Mona. I know where I stand in the hierarchy of friendships. Mona cares about me, but she's known and loved Grace for decades.

I don't want to be alone again.

Telling Grace how I feel would most likely have the same result—ending our friendship and making things too weird for Mona to want to spend time with me. Working to distract myself and making excuses didn't work, either.

There has to be another solution. Too bad I don't have time to think of it before I see her.

GRACE IS SITTING at the bar when I arrive at Nightlight, her golden hair a beacon under the dim Edison bulbs. She's talking to the owner, a mothman named Tomas, allowing me a moment to watch her unobserved. The predator in me freezes me in place, my vision heightening and my chest squeezing painfully as I drink in the sight of her.

She's a ray of sunshine in a tight yellow dress, blonde waves bouncing as she laughs at a joke Tomas makes, her smile blinding in its brilliance.

Grace is sunshine, and she makes me *burn*.

Tomas notices me first, raising a hand in greeting. I force myself out of my stupor and approach, cutting off my breaths before I get close enough to Grace to catch her scent.

"Good to see you, Blair. It's been a while." Tomas smiles at me as he wipes the bar top.

Slight guilt flickers inside me. I've never been friendly to the bartender, and yet he's been nothing but sweet to me. He even invited me to his New Year's Eve party. The one where I thought maybe Grace...

Don't think about that.

"Nice to see you." I don't miss the hint of surprise on Tomas's face when I give him a small smile. "How's mated life treating you?"

He lets out a dreamy sigh, and I know if he were shifted into his mothman form, his wings would be fluttering with delight. "Perfect. Better than I could've ever imagined. Last night Caleb got mad at me."

My brow furrows. "You like him being upset?"

Tomas's grin widens. "Yes. It shows that he trusts me enough to not hide his uglier emotions."

Grace clasps her hand over her heart. "Aww, that's the sweetest thing I've ever heard."

"I also have a fun time apologizing to him," he says with a wink and Grace snorts.

"What can I get you to drink? I have a new, uh, vintage that you might be interested in, Blair."

I raise a brow. Tomas stocks blood at his bar for the few vampires that have made Moonvale their home. Most of the time, what he gets is from a paranormal-owned company that sources donated blood from monsters looking to get some easy cash.

"Sure, that sounds good." Maybe having a drink will help me keep my composure.

"I'll have a soda water with lime," Grace says.

"No cider tonight?" I ask, and then immediately regret it. It's not that weird that I know her usual drink, but it's weird to ask someone why they ordered something non-alcoholic.

Grace doesn't seem phased. "Nope. I've been cutting back on alcohol."

"Ah." I keep my tone as neutral as possible, but I can't help wondering why. Not that her choices are any of my business.

She leads us to a booth and slides in, the hem of her dress sliding up to show off the tops of her thighs. I pull my eyes away even though they want to linger on her legs and sit across from her.

Grace gestures to her glass. "I know it's weird to invite someone to a bar and then not get a drink, but I wasn't sure what else was open at this time of night. Plus, there's something about this place that always relaxes me."

"There's a charm on the building."

"Huh? Really?" Grace's eyes go wide and she leans forward, lowering her voice despite no one being nearby. "Like *magic*?"

I smirk. "Yeah, like magic. It's meant to make the space welcoming and soothe stress."

"Wow! That's amazing." Her eyes sparkle with awe at the concept of magic.

It's adorable. Sometimes I forget Grace isn't aware of most of the supernatural elements that are woven throughout Moonvale. I wonder how she'd react if I told her that her favorite bakery is owned by an incredibly powerful fae. Or that currently, Nightlight has more monsters inside it than humans.

A pang of guilt sours my amusement at her excitement. She wouldn't be aware of them at all if it weren't for me.

The night Grace found out I was a vampire, and that monsters exist, wasn't my fault. I know that. I had to help Mona and Max. That doesn't stop me from blaming myself.

I was riding the high of post-performance excitement and seeing Grace on stage. I thought she felt it too, when she agreed to get a drink with me. The way she looked at me across the table, like the one we're at now, made me wonder if my feelings weren't one-sided. She said she wanted to ask me something. I'd decided I'd tell her about my attraction to her and if she reciprocated, broach the subject of me being a monster.

Then Mona called, needing my help, and that was the end of that delusion. Grace was terrified of me. She pretended not to be, but I could tell. She'd tense, her pulse would spike, and her pupils would dilate any time she saw me for a long time.

Once someone finds out you're a vampire who could easily rip their throat out, no matter how understanding they are, things change. Yes, Grace has become more accustomed to me, but you can't ignore base instinct. I'm a predator. And if she knew the things I've done, she wouldn't be here talking to me at all.

"Tomas is smart to put a charm like that on his bar." Grace takes a sip of her drink and grimaces. "Though I may need to ask him for some better non-alcoholic recommendations."

I hesitate to pry, but she's talking about it again, so it seems like she wants me to ask. "What prompted the choice to not drink as much?"

She looks down at her hands, cheeks burnishing slightly. "I'm trying to take better care of myself."

"Please tell me you're not on a diet." It's none of my business, but I detest the thought of anyone trying to force their body to be a certain size.

Grace laughs. "No! I mean, I've gained a lot of weight, but no. Diets aren't for me. I love food too much and don't want to ruin my relationship with it for the sake of making my stomach smaller."

"Good."

She leans forward to whisper again. "Would be nice though to be an immortal being who would stay the same no matter how much they ate. Or, uh, drank. It'd save on having to buy new clothes."

Her pulse ticks in her throat and I fight to not stare at it while she's discussing me feeding. When she leans back, I force a small smile onto my face.

"Staying the same has its issues." A lot of them, actually. I don't want to ruin the conversation by bringing some of the darker ones up, so I choose an innocuous one. "My hair, for instance."

"I love your hair! What's wrong with it?" Grace says it like she's affronted by the thought that my hair is a problem.

I try not to preen under the compliment, but it's difficult when she gives it so enthusiastically. "It never grows, and it will always be relaxed unless I curl it, because I died with it that way. Imagine being stuck with bangs for eternity."

"Oh damn. That sucks... not that they don't look incredible! You could have a bowl cut and still be hot."

I give her an incredulous look. "I doubt that."

She snorts and waves her hands at me dismissively. "You would!"

"Sure."

She narrows her eyes. "You would."

My heart thumps in my chest, creating a dull ache I want to rub away. I take a sip from my glass of blood to distract myself from the sensation.

It doesn't help much. Drinking blood can be as intoxicating as alcohol in some instances, and the zing of fae energy in the blood I ordered makes my skin tingle. But it tastes wrong with Grace sitting across from me. It isn't what I want.

Good thing I'm used to disappointment.

Grace purses her lips. "Hold on. I thought hair and nails kept growing even after you die. Why is that not the case for you?"

I wish I knew. I've heard of vampires that can channel the blood they drink into the energy needed to grow hair and nails, but I've never bothered to figure it out. It felt silly to worry about cosmetic things when I could be figuring out how to harness my ability to charm people and make sure I have a reflection so humans don't freak the fuck out when I stand in front of a mirror.

I shrug.

"Well, you look great. I stand by my assertion. I'd give anything to not have my body become any more decrepit than it already is." She follows up her statement with a soft laugh, but the humor doesn't reach her eyes. There's real worry and pain there.

Grace is hardly what I'd call decrepit. She's not even thirty yet. I wish I knew if it's the normal fear of aging or something else that's scaring her. I have no clue what to say to assuage her fears, and I'm not the right person to help her. She says she'd give anything to stay eternally young, and I know I'll get to the point where I'd give anything to stop living. I don't want to get into an argument over which is worse—living forever or getting old and dying. That won't go well.

Another reason why I need to put my infatuation with Grace behind me. Knowing that she'll be a drop in the bucket in the endless well of my life makes it unwise to get attached. I'm already set up for future pain because of my love for Mona, and she'll live twice as long as a normal human. Maybe longer with Max's magic. I can't handle more than that.

I settle for giving a vague compliment. "You look good."

She blushes, but shakes her head. "I know I look good. Appearances are deceiving."

I go still, the smile falling from my face. "What do you mean by that?"

She looks down at her drink, sighing, then takes a sip to stall, even though she visibly grimaces again at the taste. "My spine hates me. To put it more officially, I have degenerative discs in my cervical spine. The pain has gotten worse over the past six months, and I can't seem to figure out how to make it better. Not that it can ever get completely better. The best I can do is fight to stave off the inevitable for as long as possible."

"Shit." I don't know what else to say. "I'm sorry" would be trite. Waving it off or saying she'll be okay would be worse.

"Yep." She pops the "p" and goes to take another sip of her drink, but stops halfway and sets it aside. "I'm only letting myself drink on special occasions, because I don't want it to turn into my solution for the pain. My grandpa was an alcoholic. I can't..." She swallows heavily. "I don't want to be like that. I won't."

Her adamance strikes a chord with me. "I understand. The addiction part, at least."

Shit, I shouldn't talk about this. If I tell her who I truly am, she'll run away screaming.

Maybe that's for the best.

Grace looks at me expectantly, gaze filled with compassion. I'm compelled to speak even though it might ruin our friendship. "I'm a monster," I begin.

She shakes her head. "No, you're n—"

"I am." The words are clipped, and I have to clear my throat before I continue to get rid of the emotion that's clogging it. "Ever since I was turned, I've had a hunger inside me that will never be satiated. I feed to give my body the fuel it needs to function. But I will always want more. Every day, I have to choose to not give in to the predator that lives inside me. That will never change. I have to always be in control. If I let myself give in to that feral need, I..."

I want to confess my darkest sins, but I'm too much of a coward to say them aloud. Besides, she doesn't need to be burdened with the knowledge of my monstrous actions.

"Like you said. I won't," I finish. I stare into the blood in the wineglass in front of me. Facing down what makes me a monster and reminding myself I'm strong enough to resist the pull of my hunger. Unable to look at Grace and see her fear.

A warm hand rests atop mine and I jolt, inhaling sharply and getting a lungful of her tart berry pie scent. Grace squeezes my hand as I look up in surprise and meet her gaze.

Determination, not terror, blazes in her eyes. "We won't."

10

GRACE

I don't think she realizes it, but Blair's hands are shaking. I've never seen her like this. She's *terrified*.

I send as much calming energy as I can through where my hand holds hers. Her eyes search mine, looking for something. Maybe my own fear?

She won't find it. Yes, I was scared when I first found out that she was a vampire. Who wouldn't be? After I processed the shock, all I felt was awe. She saved Mona and Max's lives, for fuck's sake.

Blair is amazing. The coolest, strongest, smartest, prettiest person I've ever met. My chest aches for her. I want to pull her into a hug and tell her she'll be okay. She'd never let me, but the urge is still there.

"We won't," I repeat, patting her hand before pulling mine back. I give her a soft smile and cross my arms over my chest. "You know, it's kind of rude to make the conversation all about you when someone is telling you about their worries."

Blair's eyes go wide in alarm, but it wipes away the haunted look. "I didn't mean to—"

My cackling laugh cuts her off, and she glares at me, but the side of her mouth twitches. She can't fool me.

"Brat," she mutters under her breath, then takes a swig of her "wine".

"You love it," I tease.

Her tongue darts out to swipe away a bead of blood on her lip, and my pulse quickens. "It's annoying."

I scowl at her playfully and she finally cracks, grinning back at me. God, she's stunning when she smiles. No wonder she rarely does it. It's too powerful for us mere mortals.

We sit in comfortable silence for a moment and I realize how much I've missed this.

"You need to be careful," she says suddenly.

"What?" I ask, falling out of my peaceful daze.

"With Declan. If you have spine issues, you need to tell him about it before you do anything."

"Oh. Right! That makes sense." I'd completely forgotten that only a few hours ago, I was freaking out about his offer.

The mood between us shifts, the silence much less enjoyable. I squirm, wondering why Blair is so averse to discussing this stuff with me.

"Do you think I'm not cut out for it?" I blurt. She furrows her brow in confusion. "Kink. Submission."

"No."

Well, okay then. That explains the weirdness. She's an expert, and must be able to tell I won't be good at it.

I do a terrible job of hiding my stricken reaction by grabbing my gross drink and taking a swig. The bubbles from the soda water go up my nose, sending me into a coughing fit.

"Are you okay?"

I fight off another cough and nod. "Yeah. Totally fine. I'm great." I wipe away the tears that I'm blaming on the coughing and not my bruised feelings.

Blair's eyes narrow. "You're not."

"I mean, I'm a little disappointed." More like crushed. I try to sound casual, going to grab my drink again like a dumbass.

Blair reaches across the table and takes it away. "Stop torturing yourself."

"If I don't, then who will? You just said I'm not cut out for being a submissive," I say with a weak laugh.

"No, I didn't," Blair says, brow furrowing slightly.

I throw my hands up and stand in exasperation. "You literally told me 'no' when I asked you!" I catch Tomas raising a concerned brow from over at the bar and sit back down before I disturb the peace in the bar any more.

"I said 'no' when you asked if you weren't cut out for it."

"Oh." Damn double negative. "So... that means you think I'd be good at it?"

Blair shakes her head and lets out an exasperated sigh. "Yes, Grace."

"Then why don't you want to talk to me about it?" I ask. I shouldn't push, but I don't want this discomfort I sense between us whenever the subject comes up.

She doesn't speak for a long time. I don't let myself fill the silence, even though I'm dying to. Eventually, she takes a long swig of her drink, then folds her hands in her lap and looks at me calmly. "It's my job. I'd rather not talk about work stuff while I'm hanging out with friends."

"But you helped Mona!" I protest. I know I'm being childish, but her answer doesn't make sense.

It doesn't phase her. "She didn't have anyone else to guide her, and I was worried she'd do something dangerous." Blair sighs again. "You don't need me. You've met someone who is more than qualified to be your dominant. I'd rather keep things... separate."

It makes sense, though I still feel like there's something she's not saying. I don't particularly like it, but I need to respect her boundaries. Even I know that's kink 101. "Okay."

"Thank you." She nods and her stiff, formal posture relaxes. "Now, did I make things too awkward, or should I go see if Tomas can make you a drink you'll actually like?"

I smile. "Not too awkward. I appreciate the honesty."

I do. I'm just not sure why it still hurts, even though I have a reasonable explanation.

"WHAT THE FUCK AM I DOING?" I mutter to myself as I pull into The Vault's parking lot. The sense of dread about my trial session with Declan is now far outweighing any excitement I initially had.

When I got home from my drink with Blair a week ago, I texted the handsome dom. We agreed to meet up back at The Vault tonight. We talked through our session—or scene, as I learned it's called—ahead of time, and he answered all of my questions. I know what to expect, hypothetically.

It should've helped, but having it all laid out like that made me agonize about every step in the week leading up to our session. I spent far too long overthinking what I'll look like on my knees. I went through my entire closet, trying to find an outfit that looks good enough. I even practiced crawling in front of a mirror to assess how awkward and silly I looked.

The verdict on that was not good.

I'm a fairly adventurous person. I get nervous, but I do things anyway. So I force myself to get out of my car and walk to the entrance, attempting to chalk my anxiety up to new experience jitters, even though this feels different.

It doesn't help that my neck is bothering me. I slept weird on Wednesday night and spent all day Thursday and Friday trying to coax the muscles in my neck and shoulders to chill out and stop the sharp pain whenever I turn my head. I'm still in pain tonight, but am determined to go. I've already expended so much energy worrying and I can't bear to lose this opportunity because my body doesn't want to cooperate.

When I meet Declan in The Vault's lobby, my legs are shaking so badly I'm worried they'll give out on me. I curse my decision to wear heels instead of something more stable. He looks good, in a crisp black button down and well-tailored pants that are better suited for after-work drinks than a night at a kink club.

A broad smile stretches his lips when he sees me. "Rose. You look beautiful."

Normally when someone compliments me, I preen. Maybe do a twirl and show off the way the skirt of my dress flares up and give them a flash of my thighs. I'm not shy about my appearance, and I don't shy away from appreciation of it. So it shocks me when my face heats and I almost trip.

He reaches out to stabilize me, and I take his arm, laughing to try to play off my reaction as clumsiness instead of nerves.

"Thank you, Sir." I tack on the honorific he'd given me to call him, unsure if I should start right away.

His eyes fill with approval, which makes me want to sigh with relief that I didn't fuck things up immediately.

"I reserved one of the private rooms. Would you like to hang out in the main area for a bit first, or go there now?"

Waiting and worrying any longer might kill me. I give him what I hope is a flirty half-smile, but I'm off my game. "I'm ready if you are."

"I've been ready, sweetheart," he says, his deep rasp making my stomach clench.

Declan offers his arm and I take it in a vise grip, attempting to anchor myself to this solid man so I don't fall and eat shit in front of a room full of people. I already stand out enough in the pale blue a-line dress and matching pumps. Becoming a spectacle is at the bottom of my list of desired activities tonight.

He leads me to a small private room which doesn't match my mental image of what a kinky playroom would be. It looks like an office. Pale gray walls, a polished wood desk, a bookcase, and a large brown leather couch.

When Declan shuts the door behind us, I notice, with a mixture of relief and alarm, that there's no lock. Logically, I'm not worried about him harming me after Blair vouched for him, but there's always that instinctual fear that a seemingly nice man will turn into a monster behind closed doors.

No lock means someone could come help me. It also means that anyone could come inside.

My eyes linger on the door for too long, and Declan notices. "No one will come in uninvited."

"Right." I turn away from the door and scan the space again. "Maybe I should've gotten that schoolgirl costume."

Declan's mouth quirks. "You keep bringing that up. If that's a fantasy of yours, I'm happy to incorporate it into a future scene."

I flush and shake my head. "It isn't a specific kink of mine, but I know it's a lot of men's fantasy. So I'd be amenable, if you wanted me to do that."

He's moved over to a bar cart by the desk, pouring two glasses of water from a carafe set on top. "These scenes aren't about catering to what I want. It's about me giving you what you need, princess." His gaze drags down my body. "And thoroughly enjoying myself in the process. You're perfect the way you are."

He passes me a glass, and I drink down the contents gratefully, parched from nerves. I watch his throat work as he does the same. Goddamn, he's gorgeous. Being here with him feels more like a fever dream than anything that would happen in real life.

If Declan notices me checking him out, he doesn't acknowledge it. He takes my glass back and I almost jolt and drop it when his fingers brush mine. That he does notice.

He sets the glasses down on the cart and gestures for me to sit on the couch. The leather creaks as I lower myself onto it, and when I go to cross my legs, it sticks to my sweat-damp skin.

Declan sits down next to me and rests his hand on my thigh. He waits to see if I'm okay with that, like I'm a skittish animal he's coaxing. Which, I guess I might as well be. God, it's ridiculous how much anxiety is coursing through my system.

"Have we started, Sir?" I ask, my voice higher pitched than usual.

He squeezes my thigh. "Yes. Remember—green is keep going, yellow is you need to pause, and red is stop. Nothing we'll do tonight will prevent you from speaking, and when I ask you for your color, be honest. I won't get upset if something is too much. Alright, princess?"

"Y-yes, Sir." I can barely get the reply out.

Declan pats my leg and stands, grabbing a pillow from the couch and setting it on the floor by his feet. His eyes lock on mine.

"Kneel."

Oh fuck, this is it. It takes a moment for my body to respond, but when it cooperates, I almost fall on my face with how fast I scramble to get to the floor.

Once I'm in position, I clasp my hands together. In all my mental walkthroughs of how tonight would go, I couldn't figure out if I was supposed to look down at the floor or maintain eye contact. The internet was no help. I settle for staring straight ahead, and am greeted by the sight of Declan's thick, muscular thighs encased in his tailored pants. And his crotch.

My stomach sinks. There's no outline of his cock pressing against the fabric. He's not even semi-hard. He'd not aroused. I'm fucking this up already.

My head bows forward as I attempt to hide my reaction before I make things worse. I watch his feet as he steps back. My eyes close as I take a deep breath, trying to get myself under control. I listen as he circles around me, and can't stop my small flinch when he strokes a hand down my hair.

"Color?"

"Green," I reply automatically. Why wouldn't I be okay? All I've done is kneel.

"Good girl. You look beautiful on your knees, princess." He strokes my hair again, then places his hand under my chin and guides me to look up at him.

As I tip my head back, the pain in my neck flares, and I suck in a breath through my teeth.

Shit. I didn't tell him about my neck. I was going to if things worked out okay tonight, but was too embarrassed to bring up my pathetic body right away. I didn't think it would matter.

Declan's cool assessment as I force my eyes to meet his is a sharp contrast to his previous demeanor. I inhale, and this close, his cologne hits my nose like a slap to the face.

It's the same cologne Zack wears.

My stomach lurches. Memories of all the times my ex-husband fed me disingenuous compliments to placate me when I worried that something was off surge through my mind. Him telling me I'm beautiful. Saying he doesn't need anything else. All lies.

Just like Zack, Declan is looking down at me and he can see I'm not worth the effort.

The urge to cry or throw up roils inside me. I dig my nails into my palms as hard as I can, trying to focus on that physical pain instead of the absurd emotions washing over me.

This is supposed to be exciting. I'm supposed to be having fun. Why am I like this?

An eternity passes as Declan watches me, occasionally touching my hair or teasing his fingers across my shoulders, toying with the straps of my dress but never pushing them down. I told him I was okay with undressing, so I don't understand why I'm not naked. Doesn't he want to see me? My body is the one thing that men seem to like about me. It's the rest that fucks things up.

He must decide he's had enough of looking down at me, because he offers me a hand. "Get up and place your hands flat on the desk."

My palms are sweaty and I'm loath to touch him with them, but I stand and move to the desk. I might be flawed, but I can at least do what he asks.

I bend at the waist to place my hands on the desk, hoping it can bolster me through what comes next. This is what I've spent years fantasizing about. I need to get my shit together and relax so I can enjoy it.

"Very good, princess. Color?"

"G-green, sir." Fuck, did my voice sound as shaky to him as it did to me?

Declan smooths a hand down my spine, ghosting across my ass to the hem of my dress. He hooks his fingers under it and drags it up to my waist, exposing my panties.

My pulse spikes. What if I don't react the right way? He'll know how frigid I am if I can't even take a light spanking properly. He'll tell me he's changed his mind about being my dom.

Gnawing shame makes me lightheaded and queasy, and my cheeks burn despite the icy dread thrumming inside me.

Why do I bother? I'll never be enough. I'm broken.

"Rose, what's your color?" Declan asks, concern obvious in his voice.

It tips me over the edge. I burst into tears.

I don't give him my color, but he must know it's not the good, cathartic kind of crying. He quickly pushes my skirt back down and wraps an arm around my waist, guiding me up and over to the couch. He pulls me into his lap and presses me against his chest in a hug.

"It's okay, Rose. Let go. Let it out."

I sob deep, ugly tears that make my entire body shudder. He holds me tight as the tsunami of emotion crashes into me for god knows how long.

When I start to calm and realize that I just soaked a practical stranger's shirt with snot and tears, I stiffen. Declan rubs my back in soothing circles. "You did so well, sweetheart."

I push out of his hold and wipe my face with the back of my

hands. Thank god for waterproof mascara. How fucking embarrassing. "You're joking, right?" I ask, frowning at him.

Declan's face holds no judgment, only calm empathy. It makes me want to cry again. "No. Sometimes scenes trigger unexpected emotions, and that's okay. It's not uncommon to have a strong reaction your first time."

"But we didn't do anything!" I protest. Why is he being so nice?

He shakes his head. "You tapped into some really strong emotions. You let yourself feel them and trusted me to help you come down from them. That's not nothing."

"Maybe. But I failed the test," I say weakly.

Declan frowns and takes my hand in his. "There was no test, Rose. You don't have to prove anything. What happens next is up to you. I'm not going to rescind my offer to teach you because you cried. If you want to try again sometime, we can. If you want to pretend this never happened and run away, at least let me give you aftercare a little longer before you drive home."

"I... Thank you. I'll think about it." I smile weakly at him and he gives me another hug.

Pressed against his chest, I know it's a lie. I can't imagine a repeat of this with him. I'd be too embarrassed and worried I'd break down again. I never want to think about this disaster of a night again.

11

BLAIR

"Did I say you could move your hands?" I glare down at the naked man kneeling at my feet, and he winces as he pulls his hands back from where they'd been about to touch my boot.

His head bows at my chastisement, shaggy black hair falling into his eyes. "No, Mistress. But how else am I supposed to clean off the mess I made?"

I grab him by the chin and force him to look into my eyes. "You're a smart boy. Figure it out."

His eyes flare with heat from my harsh grip and the command, and despite coming all over my boot a minute ago, his abused cock twitches back to life. I'm mildly impressed at his fortitude.

G ended up breaking and removing his cage like I predicted. His punishment for touching himself without my permission is making himself come again and again until pleasure morphs into torture. He's made an absolute mess of my boots, and now it's time to add humiliation to cement his lesson.

"Yes, Mistress." He bends forward at the waist, hands dutifully clasped behind his back as he brings his mouth to the shiny patent leather and swipes his tongue through the splatter of cum.

"Good boy," I murmur, earning a groan of appreciation from my submissive.

It'd be easier to zone out while he goes to work, but there's a reason I'm in demand as a domme. I stay engaged the entire scene. I give my submissives the focus and attention they need. And while I may not derive any sexual pleasure from the man before me licking his cum off of my boots, it sure as hell satisfies the part of me that craves control.

With every man I have begging at my feet, I close up the wounds of my past. Dominic stole my life from me, preying on my desire to be wanted and special. With each scene, I remind myself that the only person I have to prove something to is me.

I guide G through the rest of his session, and by the time he leaves, I'm riding the high of a good scene. I have no more bookings tonight, so I clean and lock up my rented studio.

My body is thrumming with hunger as I head out onto the street, despite feeding when I woke up. The monster inside me scans my surroundings instinctively, honing in on a curvy blonde woman in a tight pink dress walking in my direction.

Her similarities to Grace don't go unnoticed, and the monster inside me is having a hard time telling the difference. All it feels is dark need.

I lick my lips, clinging to the shadows as I watch her approach. She's looking at her phone, oblivious to me or anyone around her.

Foolish behavior. Doesn't she know what lurks in the dark?

My pulse spikes and my fangs press against my gums with increasing insistence with each step closer she takes.

It would be so easy. A few words infused with my power of compulsion, and she'd follow me into the nearby alley. She'd let me sink my fangs into her neck with a smile.

Feast on her. Take what you need.

I hiss as my fangs emerge so fast that they nick my lower lip. The woman looks up, noticing me, and her brown, not blue eyes blow wide with fear. Now that she's close, I catch her subtle floral scent, and my monster recoils.

Not Grace. Not what I want.

I tear my eyes away, curling in on myself and pretending to look for something in my bag as she hurries past me. My hands shake as the adrenaline of my monster's urges gives way to disgust.

What is wrong with me?

I haven't felt like that in years. I don't attack people, and I don't force anyone to give me blood. Yet I see a woman who is vaguely similar to Grace, and I'm seconds away from surrendering to base instinct.

Fuck.

I scrub my face with my hands, attempting my breathing exercises.

I'm in control.
I'm more than my nature.
I didn't hurt her.
I'm in control.

When I get home, it's only a little past midnight. I spent the entire drive back from the city reminding myself that I'm okay and I didn't give into my urges, in order to not go into full-blown panic mode.

Dawn is still hours away. As much as I'd like to escape the turmoil in my mind, it's too early to go to sleep. I doubt that I'd find respite from my worries there, anyway.

I'd try to drown my thoughts out with work, but that didn't stop me from almost attacking someone tonight. It won't solve anything. I've let my control slip and I need to confront what happened to regain some semblance of composure.

I grab some blood from the fridge and heat it up to body temp, then sit down at the kitchen table to drink it like the civilized monster I'm attempting to be. Energy thrums through me as the blood works its magic, making me more awake and calm.

With a sigh, I close my eyes and look inward across the churning, vast ocean of my thoughts, and prepare myself to dive beneath the surface.

I'm hit with a wave of distress as I sink into my mind. My body tells me to fight. To find someone and drink them dry.

My thoughts do not control me. Not everything my mind tells me is real.

The feral panic happens every time I practice this exercise. I don't think the creators of the mental wellness workbook I found when I was searching for a way to cling to my humanity and sanity after I was first turned had vampires in mind. There's a layer of hunger and predatory nature like a barrier that resists me pushing through. But once I get past the initial haze, the choking miasma clears and I can breathe again.

My mind was a mess when I was alive, full of a discordant yearning for acceptance and love, and rebellion against the oppressive cage society placed me in. That chaos created the door that Dominic used to fill my mind with seductive lies. It let him prey on my hopes and fears.

I met my vampire sire on what I thought at the time was the worst night of my life. It was my 23rd birthday, and I'd walked in on my then boyfriend fucking my roommate on the couch of our shitty apartment. Looking back, it makes me laugh to realize I was much more hurt by her being with him than by his actions. Starting the trend of being hopelessly into women who wouldn't want me.

I went out and got drunk at the goth club I frequented. A man tried to get handsy outside the bathroom, and Dominic "saved" me. It was everything out of my deepest romantic fantasies—the broody, handsome man growling at the guy assaulting me and swooping in to steady me and make sure I was okay.

Ugh, I bet he paid the guy to bother me.

Dominic escorted me to a private booth, ordered me a drink, and coaxed me to confess my troubles to him. He swirled dark red wine in his glass and watched me with a hunger that made me dizzy.

No one had ever wanted me like that. It was love at first sight for me. It was a predator finding easy prey for him.

It only took a week for Dominic to confess he was a vampire. He "knew he shouldn't, but there was something about me that drove him mad with desire." He told me I was the first woman he'd ever met that made him feel alive again.

I was entranced.

I'm not embarrassed to admit that I was obsessed with Twilight at the time, despite its many problematic elements. Dominic was the real life Edward to my Bella. We were fated. None of my past mattered because it all led to him.

Thinking back, he may have even directly quoted some of Edward's lines to me. I was too far gone to see it.

He wanted to make our first time special, so we booked a room at a hotel. It was everything I'd imagined—champagne, rose petals, and candlelight. Dominic kept up the pretense until the very end. He fucked me, proclaiming that he wanted me to be with him forever. He told me how perfect I was. He asked in a hushed whisper if I'd be his for eternity.

It was perfect. I finally felt loved.

Mind fuzzy from the alcohol and buzzing from the overwhelming romance of the moment, I said yes.

As soon as I consented, a flip switched. He got off on the fantasy, too, but it ended once he'd "won" me. Fangs tore into my wrist. He took what he wanted and left me to wake up alone, terrified, and *hungry*.

It took me years to sift through the trauma of my turning to feel anything else. I examined each jagged fragment of my sundered life, searching for meaning or a lesson I could carry forward from the pain.

Some say that pain makes you stronger, but after experiencing so much, I disagree. It only changes you. Whether that means you rise from the ashes as something better or become consumed with despair is in your hands.

Now the pieces of who I was before Dominic are packed away—not fully discarded, but not on display. I'm not the person I was in life anymore. I won't let my mind be a gallery of what I've lost.

I cannot change the past. I am here in this moment.

Anchored in the present, I let my thoughts move on to what happened tonight. I replay my disturbing thoughts, reminding myself that they aren't what matters. That my actions are the important part.

I didn't hurt anyone. I didn't give in.

That has to be enough, because I'll never change. No matter how many self-help workbooks and mental exercises I do, the hunger will never go away. The violent creature that lurks inside me can be drowned out, but never silenced.

Why anyone would willingly choose to exist like this is beyond me. Being a vampire isn't living. It's fighting night after night to not become the monster your entire being is screaming at you to be. It traps you in unending darkness, haunted by the fear of what will happen if time wears down your humanity and you lose the fight against your nature.

In the brief instances I'm able to feel anything beyond loathing for him and what he did to me, I wonder if Dominic started out like me. Did he try to curb his impulses? Was it inevitable that with time he'd become a monster no matter how hard he tried to fight it?

I have to hope that he was always a cruel, selfish bastard, because the alternative means it's only a matter of time before I break, too.

Time will tell. I'll keep fighting for as long as I can.

I let out a heavy exhale as that determination bolsters me, then open my eyes.

My mind is more settled, but that doesn't address the root of the problem. It wasn't a random instance of my vampiric nature rearing its ugly head. It happened because the woman reminded me of Grace.

Dammit. I thought I was doing better when it comes to her. I thought I could handle being close again. We've texted casually, and I was taking on the friend role without as much struggle as before. Now that she knows I don't want to talk about kink, none of our conversations are remotely sexual.

That should be enough.

Yes, she's still the first person I want to hear from when I wake up at night. Yes, she's the one on my mind as I drift off to sleep. But I thought it was manageable, like a muscle ache that's annoying but one you can ignore.

Turns out I was wrong. My monster still craves Grace with a terrifying ferocity.

I could pretend I don't know why this happened tonight, but deluding myself won't help matters.

Grace set up a scene with Declan tonight at The Vault. Despite trying to keep myself ignorant of her kink exploration, Mona casually mentioned it when I spoke with her earlier.

On a surface level, I'm worried about Grace. She was so nervous, and I can't help feeling some guilt that I didn't talk to her about it more. I'm her friend and I could've helped prepare her better.

Beneath that, I'm seething with jealousy that Declan is teaching her about kink instead of me.

I want to be the one to coax her submissive side out, peeling back the layers of her doubts and defenses until she's laid bare. I should be the one that knows that hidden part of her, not him. I want to be the person who makes her gasp and cry out with pain and pleasure until she lets everything go and floats in the bliss of subspace.

I want Grace to be mine, and my monstrous side knows it. It saw someone who looked like her and begged me to claim her. It doesn't care that she's not interested in me. It only wants to take.

My fangs ache, and I press the heels of my hands against my eyes with a groan.

I hate this.

Grace is probably still there with Declan right now. I could go to The Vault and make sure she's okay. Friends do that kind of thing, right?

Or I could remember she's an adult and Declan has as much experience as I do, so she's in good hands. Better hands. He's perfect for her.

And I'm... I'm perfectly fine on my own. No matter what my vampiric nature craves and how much I enjoy being around Grace.

12

BLAIR

I wake up the next evening, determined to figure out how to get past my infatuation with Grace. I installed a dating app last night, thinking maybe what I needed was to find someone else. My last girlfriend and I broke up almost a year ago. Maybe that's why I'm stuck on Grace—I'm not giving myself opportunities to find anyone more suitable.

Though, when I check the Bewitch'd app, a quick scan tells me none of the messages I've received pique my interest. I don't enjoy wasting my time or anyone else's, so I don't bother responding.

There may not be any decent messages on the app, but there's a text from Grace. Of course there is.

I ignore it as I shower, dress, and eat, but the whole time I'm thinking about what her message might say. We're supposed to meet up tonight. I'm not sure if Grace texting me to say she needs to cancel or texting to confirm we're still on would be better.

When my brain spirals far enough to start worrying that maybe she texted because she needs help, I pick up my phone.

> Grace: You still good for tonight? I'm in pain, but I'd love to see you. As long as you don't mind me talking to you while lying on the couch with a heat pad.

> Grace: Ugh, that's not a very exciting way to spend your night, I know. I'd totally understand if you'd rather spend your night off not hanging out with my decrepit ass.

My chest tightens. I hate that she's in pain. She said it's gotten worse lately, but how long has she been hiding how she feels? Mona never mentioned Grace not feeling well when she didn't show up to things. She said she was flaking.

The idea that Grace believes it's better for people to think she's unreliable than to know she has a chronic condition unsettles me. It's far too relatable. I'd rather people think I'm a cold, distant bitch than know that I'm a monster that could easily rip their throats out.

How far does Grace's mask go? Is she hiding as much as I am?

> Blair: I'll be there.

I grimace at my reply. It sounds too cold.

> Blair: Is there anything I can bring to help you?

> Grace: Aww, you're sweet, but no. I just gotta ride it out.

> Blair: Okay. See you later.

I still have an hour to kill before I head over to Grace's place. I could fill the time with texting clients, or I could take a moment for myself. All I do is work and worry lately.

In theory, having down time is good. But none of my hobbies appeal to me right now. I don't want to read, because my mind wanders too much to focus on the story. When I started having enough money to spend however I wanted, I got into online shopping, but at this point I've bought enough clothes and gear that shopping feels wasteful. I could work on a costume if I had any burlesque gigs coming up, but I don't because I replaced those with much better paying sessions with clients.

Even my collection of half-finished DIY projects scattered around my house hold no appeal. When I bought the place, I made it my mission to turn it into the gothic home of my dreams. It's come along slowly, and what I've done looks great, but with how little time I spend at home, it's dawned on me how pointless the effort is.

The primary bedroom on the second floor is gorgeous, but I have to sleep in the basement. The vanity I've been refurbishing for the guest room won't ever be used because I don't have guests. I've been putting together my perfect little dream house, only for it to sit empty and ignored.

I'm aware that this is a self-imposed problem. I could let people visit. I've had girlfriends here in the past. Mona unsubtly asks all the time when I'm going to have her over. I can't explain why I've been isolating myself more lately, other than an instinct that it's becoming too dangerous. For myself or for them, I'm not sure.

Feeling restless but unable to pick something to do, I go out and check the back garden to see how the roses are fairing. On nights when my emotions are difficult to manage, being outside surrounded by their beauty and scent helps calm me.

The evening sky glows pink and red, matching the delicate blooms. Basking in the sunset's afterglow is a chance for me to experience the sky not shrouded in darkness, and I can pretend that I'm able to get a taste of some of the sun's light.

It looks like Nic's been by recently. Last time I came out here, there'd been a storm and some of the climbing roses had been knocked off their trellis, but everything is pristine now.

Ridiculous bear. I smile despite myself. It's hard not to like Nic. Despite all my skepticism, he's proven himself to be a truly decent, kind man. I haven't even had a session with him this week, but he still came by and fixed up the garden for me.

I should text him to let him know I appreciate it, but what comes out is more of a chastisement.

> Mistress Bella: You didn't need to do that.

> Nic: Do what, Mistress?

> Mistress Bella: You came over and fixed the garden. I didn't ask you to do that.

> Nic: Oh, that! It wasn't a problem at all. I was in the neighborhood and figured it might need a little TLC after the storm.

I'm not sure if he had an ulterior motive in helping, but the cynical part of me wants to assume that he only helped because he wanted something from me. He's my client. Of course that's what he wants.

At least I'm able to charge people for the privilege of my attention. If he wants me to praise him, he'll have to wait until our next session.

> Mistress Bella: Okay. Thank you.

There. If he wants something, he'll need to be direct. I'm not offering it to him.

> Nic: Anytime! I know it's harder for you to see what you're doing at night to fix things up, so I picked up some lights that are used for night gardening in case you'd rather not have me messing around in your backyard during the day. Just let me know if you'd like me to install them and I can pop over.

> Mistress Bella: What do you want?

I delete that message before hitting send, and try to not be so hostile. I don't want to lose him as a client for being a total asshole for no reason. Even if this is setting off major alarm bells.

> Mistress Bella: I didn't ask for that.

> Nic: I know you didn't.

> Nic: I didn't do it because you're my Mistress. I just wanted to help. You know how it is with shifters. Once our beast decides someone is part of our pack, we can't help but lend a hand from time to time.

His bear thinks I'm part of his pack? God, I knew I shouldn't have let him come do sessions in my home. I knew it was too informal and now...

Now what? Would it really be so bad to accept Nic's help?

For a second, I wonder if maybe it'd be okay to take his offer of support at face value. Blur the lines of our working relationship and accept that I'm someone he cares for outside of that. Accept that I'm oddly fond of him too and appreciate the help.

Maybe I could even attend one of his monster support group

meetings. I haven't been able to rid myself of this infatuation with Grace, and maybe another monster could enlighten me why.

As quickly as the thoughts come, I dismiss them. I can't do that. It's unprofessional. He's a paying submissive, not a friend.

> Mistress Bella: That's not necessary. If you want to do something for me, book a session.

He takes a minute to reply, and every second that passes, I hate myself a little more for shutting him down. I almost apologize and tell him I'd appreciate the help. Tell him that I'm so tired of doing everything on my own and it would be a relief to have someone to depend on.

I don't.

> Nic: Yes, Mistress.

With that boundary slammed back in place, I head back inside. Now I just need to find a way to shore up my barriers with Grace and everything will go back to normal.

13

GRACE

Dammit, why didn't I cancel?

I scurry around my living room, tossing things into a laundry hamper and narrowly avoiding tripping over a cluster of pillows that have fallen off the couch. There are piles of things strewn throughout my entire downstairs, which seems like a perfectly logical way to keep my house organized until someone is coming over and I realize how chaotic and messy it will look.

Bending over and picking things up makes my neck send out angry twinges of pain. It's been extra pissed at me since my failure of a foray into BDSM last night. It was already not great, but the stress really brought it up a notch.

It's incredibly frustrating how my body converts my emotion

into physical pain. My muscles tense when I'm upset, and that means more problems with my spine. Sometimes it feels like an unbreakable cycle. I'm in pain, which makes me unhappy and stressed, which causes more pain.

It sucks to feel like I can't let myself get upset or fully feel my emotions, because my body will punish me for it. I tried telling a therapist that once and she acted like I was being overdramatic. Needless to say, I didn't go back after that.

A knock on the door startles me, and I almost drop the basket in my arms. My body tenses as I catch it and my neck screams in protest. I shove the basket in the closet under the stairs and curse as I rush to answer the door.

Blair greets me on the other side, the perfect, polished foil to my bedraggled self. Her flawless brown skin looks warm and luminous under my dim porch light, while I'm sure it gives me a ghoulish pallor. Her hair and makeup are as pristine as ever, and I look like I just rolled out of bed with my tangled bun and splotchy skin. She looks way too nice to be coming over for a night of sitting on my couch.

"Hey!" I say, a little breathless from hurrying.

"Hey."

"Were you out earlier?" I ask.

She blinks back at me. "No. Why?"

I gesture at her perfectly tailored black jeans that hug the flare of her hips, and the lacy black top that shows off a sliver of her toned stomach and the line of her cleavage. She's in full sexy goth goddess mode. "You look ready to go out on a date."

She frowns, looking down at her outfit in concern. "I can go home and change." It's not a joke.

Crap, I'm making her uncomfortable and she hasn't even gotten in the door.

"What? No! It's not your fault you look gorgeous, while I'm a frumpy mess with a yogurt stain on my leggings."

"I wouldn't have noticed the yogurt if you hadn't pointed it out," she says. She doesn't deny that I'm frumpy or a mess, which somehow sets me at ease.

Who cares if I'm a mess? She's my friend and friends don't give a shit about that kind of thing.

I step back and hold the door open for her, but she doesn't follow me. It takes me a second to process why. "Oh shit, sorry! Come in."

She follows with a slight twist of her lips at my flustered invitation.

"I still can't believe that of all the vampire lore that's out there, not being able to enter a home without permission is one of the real things," I chuckle.

"Me either. It's annoying, but I'd rather deal with having to be polite than worry that some religious nut is going to melt my skin off with holy water. I had enough of my parents trying to cleanse me of my sinful nature when I was alive."

I grimace. "Ooof, yeah."

"Sorry, that was dark."

"No! I mean, it was, but I like knowing more about you. You can talk to me about anything." Blair has mentioned her terrible family before, but I wasn't sure if she'd want me to ask follow-up questions. She's hard to read and I don't want to be a dick.

She lets out a wry chuckle. "I'm not sure you'd feel that way if I told you all my secrets."

I cross my arms over my chest. "Try me." Blair thinks she's so scary, but I don't buy it. Yeah, she's a vampire, but she's not a mindless monster. She tries to hide it, but she's a gooey marshmallow at her core.

Blair rolls her eyes at me. "Let me get in the door before you start pestering me for my life story." She holds out a canvas bag to me. "Here. Brought you some snacks."

I'm sure my eyes light up with glee when I look in the bag. It's filled with every single kind of candy bar they sell at the grocery store, plus a bunch of different bags of gummy candies. She's so silly and sweet.

"Hell yeah!" I pull out a chocolate bar and rip it open, and take a bite. "Fmhank you," I say, mouth still half full of chocolate. I flush when I notice she's staring at my mouth in horror, and swallow quickly, giving a sheepish laugh. "Sorry, I'm being rude."

She blinks and the intensity she was looking at me with vanishes. "Don't apologize. I got it for you to enjoy."

"Obviously I do," I laugh, smiling and hoping I don't have chocolate on my lips. "Do you miss it?"

"Eating?"

I shake my head. "I mean, yeah, but I'm talking about candy specifically. It's what you always bring when we hang out."

"Oh." I don't think she's going to say anything else, but then Blair smiles slightly. "My parents never let me have it. When I moved out, I went through a phase where I'd eat candy after every meal, as my personal fuck you to their bullshit. I actually got sick of it after that, but I still think of it as one of my favorite foods from when I was alive."

"That's..."

"Pathetic?" She finishes for me.

I shake my head adamantly. "No! I love what it means to you. Makes it special. Like you're bringing me little pieces of sin and rebellion, wrapped up in a tidy package. What could be better than that?"

Blair laughs, a full throated, husky sound that brings me as much joy as the chocolate does. "Exactly."

I set the bag of candy down on my kitchen table, grabbing a few things to bring with me to the couch. "I always feel like a terrible host," I say as I settle in on the couch while she slides into the armchair across from me. "I can't even offer you something to drink."

Her eyes drop to my neck and my pulse suddenly won't stop thundering in my ears. God, I always have to make things weird. She swallows and gives me a calm smile. "Don't worry about it. I had something before I came over."

"Something or someone?" I ask, waggling my eyebrows.

Blair snorts. "You really want to know?"

"Of course I do! Tell me. Was it one of your clients?" I don't know why I care, but suddenly finding out where Blair got her blood is of the utmost importance.

She shakes her head. "Most of my clients don't know I'm a vampire."

"Oh right. Hmm... someone you met at The Vault?"

Blair shakes her head again, and I furrow my brow. "Someone you're dating? Do you have a secret boyfriend?"

A startled laugh bursts out of Blair. "No." She pauses and gives me a bemused look. "Grace, you know I'm a lesbian, right?"

"Wait, really?" My reply comes out embarrassingly high pitched, but it's only from surprise. "I thought Mona said that most of the submissives you work with are men, so I assumed you were bisexual."

"The key word there being 'work'." Blair narrows her eyes at me a little. "Is me being a lesbian a problem?"

"What? No!" I sputter. "That doesn't matter at all to me. Besides, men suck, so I get it."

Blair's lips twitch. "But not as much as I do, right?"

"What?" Where is that coming from? "You don't suck at all!"

"Yes, I do. Because I'm a vampire—nevermind." Blair shakes her head dismissively.

I erupt with laughter. "Blair, was that... a dad joke?"

She smiles back at me, even though she looks like she's trying to fight it. "Forget it."

I grin back at her. "Fine. But you have to tell me where you got the blood."

"I got it from a bag in my fridge. There are suppliers that ethically source blood for vampires."

"Ah, right." I don't know why I continue, but maybe it's because I can't help pressing now that she's relaxed. "That must be expensive. Probably not as good as from the source, either. Do you ever..."

"Bite people?" Blair finishes for me. "On occasion. Consensually."

"Oh! Cool."

"Is there a reason you care so much about my eating habits?" She asks the question evenly, but there's a flicker of concern in her expression. "I'm not going to bite you. I'm in control of myself. You don't have to worry."

Something in the way she says that makes me think she's reassuring herself as well.

I wave a hand at her dismissively. "I'm not worried! I was thinking that now that I know you feed from people, I have the potential not to be a terrible host when you visit."

Blair narrows her eyes at me. "Grace. You can't pick people up at the grocery store and have them sitting here for me to feed from."

I laugh so hard at the visual that she gets caught up in it, too. Warm pleasure suffuses me at the sound of her laughter. I love making Blair happy.

"I like the way you think, but no. No human buffet. I meant me!" I gesture down at myself with a flourish. "I have blood. As long as it doesn't hurt too much, I can give you some of mine in exchange for all that sweet, sweet candy."

I know I'm being silly, but Blair always seems worried that I'm going to be frightened by her nature. If I don't treat it as something momentous, if we talk about it out in the open, then maybe she'll see that I'm not afraid. She'll realize that I trust her a lot more than most people I've met.

If the idea of Blair biting me happens to make my stomach do a flip of nervous excitement, that's just a bonus.

"Grace..."

"What? It's not a big deal! You can do it now if you want. Just maybe not the neck, because I'm having a hard time turning my head without pain."

Blair stiffens, and I wonder if I've made some kind of vampire faux pas offering her my blood. All of my amusement drains as her singular focus bores into me.

"You're in that much pain?" she finally asks after what feels like an eternity passes.

That's not at all what I was expecting. "Uh, yeah. It's pretty bad after last night," I say with an awkward chuckle.

Blair's nostrils flare and the deadly look that flashes across her face sends an instinctual chill skittering across my skin as I see the part of herself that she tries so hard to hide. "I'll kill him."

"Wh-what?"

"He hurt you." Violence flares behind Blair's eyes.

I shake my head in alarm, wincing at the pain that follows the movement. "Whoa, whoa! He didn't! It was my fault. I didn't bring up my neck issue because I didn't think it would matter for the first time. But nothing happened! It was already not great, but then with all the stress and crying—"

Blair's hands tighten against the arms of the chair she's sitting in. "He made you *cry?*"

"Yeah, but it wasn't his fault! I got there, and I was in pain and nervous and he told me to get on my knees so I did, but then his cologne was the same one my ex wore, and the whole time all I could think about was how he was going to realize that I'm not worth the effort and that he'd been with so many other subs so there was no way I'd ever measure up. He told me I was doing well, but it was like it was my ex-husband's voice in my head, not Declan's—lying to me, pretending that I was enough while all the time looking for someone better. By the time he went to spank me, I was so upset I started bawling. I promise it wasn't Declan's fault. He was a total sweetheart, and he let me cry on him for god knows how long." I suck in a breath, then add, "Please don't kill him."

A long moment of silence passes. As the seconds tick by, I realize how much I overshared. "Shit, I'm sorry. You asked me not to talk about this stuff with you. I shouldn't have said all that. I just didn't want you to kill Declan for something that was entirely on me."

"Don't apologize. I overreacted," Blair says, shaking her head like she's upset with herself.

"Yeah, maybe a little," I tease. "I appreciate that you have my back, though, in case I do ever need someone taken care of."

Blair chuckles, and the murderous energy drains from her posture. "I'll always take care of you, Grace."

The utter sincerity of her tone threatens to take my breath away. An image of myself kneeling before her while she says that to me floods my mind and my cheeks heat.

"Thank you," I say softly, trying to hide my unexpected kinky thoughts.

"So, it didn't go well, then. With Declan."

I snort. "It was a disaster. He did everything right, was a total gentleman, and I... I was a fucking embarrassment. Not at all like any silly fantasies I had."

Blair's brow furrows. "Submission can be intense. You did nothing wrong."

"Declan said the same thing." I sigh. It's good to know that Blair agrees, and he wasn't saying that to get me to stop blubbering. "He even offered to try again if I felt ready, but I think last night was definitive proof that I'm not cut out for it."

"It's not a matter of being good or bad at it. Do you want to try again?" Blair asks.

"I..." I've always fantasized about submission. Thinking about it turns me on in a way I can't quite explain. The concept of letting go and being in the hands of someone else, being totally under their control and at the same time the complete center of their focus, takes my breath away.

"I thought you didn't want to talk to me about this stuff," I say. It's an obvious dodge of her question, but I'm also confused about why she's asking.

"I was being an asshole," she says with a sigh. "We can talk about it."

"Are you sure? I don't want to—"

Blair nods decisively. "I'm sure."

She doesn't elaborate. I'm still worried about making her uncomfortable if I answer her earlier question, but I have no choice but to take her at her word. "Last night was more than embarrassing. It was crushing. I don't think I'd be able to face Declan again."

"That's not what I asked. Do you want to try out submission again?"

"Well... yeah." I give her a teasing smile, trying to diffuse some of the tension. "Why, are you offering? It'd have to be pro bono because I'm sure there's no way I could afford your rates."

"I wouldn't charge you," she replies evenly.

My brows shoot up in shock. "Wait. You'd... You're really...?"

"It doesn't have to be sexual. I know you're not interested in women," she continues. Her face is an unreadable mask.

I shake my head, the thought that she'd try to take advantage of me like that utterly ridiculous. "I'm not worried about that! Blair, you're so sweet to offer, but I don't want to make you do anything that would make you uncomfortable."

"You're not," she replies with no hesitation.

"Blair..."

"You're not," Blair says again, more firmly. "The only thing that would make me feel uncomfortable is knowing that I can help with what you're struggling with, and not offering to help."

A strange wave of relief washes over me. I didn't realize it before, but I think I've secretly hoped that she'd be the person to teach me about kink ever since I found out she's a domme.

"Okay," I say with a soft smile.

"What?" She blinks back at me rapidly, probably expecting more of a fight.

She won't get one. The more I think about this, the more perfect it seems.

Blair is safe. I trust her implicitly. Maybe with her I won't have to battle fears that I'm not enough, because she's already decided that I'm worthy of being her friend.

Yeah, maybe it's a little weird to have a friend dominate me, but that's better than being triggered constantly when I'm trying to explore this part of myself.

"Yes. I want your help. I want you to be my domme."

14

BLAIR

This is not real. It's a very vivid, strange dream. There's no way I'm stupid enough to offer to train Grace as a submissive, and there's no way she'd agree to that.

I couldn't help myself when she started going on about how terrible and traumatic her first experience was. The visceral anger I felt at the damage done to her psyche by her ex-husband is still coursing through me. I wish I knew where he lived. I'd pay him back for making this breathtaking, brilliant woman feel like she's anything less than perfection. She'd never even have to know.

God, there's something seriously wrong with me. That's twice tonight that I've wanted to murder someone for hurting her. I'm losing control. I need to figure out a way to take the offer back. I need to...

My racing thoughts go fuzzy as Grace beams at me, genuine excitement sparkling in her icy blue eyes. She's looking at me like I offered her the world.

Fuck.

I can't take that away from her.

Grace grins. "So, when do we start? Now?"

I almost choke on my tongue, sending myself into a coughing fit. "N-no." I clear my throat. "Not right now. If I'm going to teach you, we need to set boundaries between the time we spend together as friends and any scenes we do."

"Right. Don't want to ruin our friendship." Grace's smile drops slightly. "No matter what happens, we'll still be friends? I don't want to fuck that up because I'm curious about kink and too messed up to try it with anyone else."

This is where I should tell her it's a bad idea.

I can't. The words refuse to come out. The monster inside me practically sings with pleasure at the prospect of dominating Grace.

I fight to keep my fangs retracted and nod. "I promise nothing that happens between us while you're learning will ruin our friendship." I don't know how the fuck I'm going to keep that promise when she's going to be placing herself in my hands so willingly, but I have to. "It's impossible to keep this kind of relationship completely separate, but we'll make it work."

Her smile falls back into place. "Hell yeah, we will."

We sit in silence for a while, and the entire time my mind is bouncing between terror and elation. Grace squirms around on the couch, repositioning the heating pad draped over her shoulder a few times.

She notices me watching her and gives me a sheepish smile. "Sooo.... Have you watched any good shows lately?"

I don't watch TV. She knows this. "No. You?"

"Nah. I'm waiting for the new season of In the Stars to come out. We should watch it together. You'll love it."

I scowl, and she laughs at my reaction. "Okay, more like you'll love to hate it. But isn't that the point of trashy reality shows?"

"I wouldn't know," I say drolly. The exasperated look I get in return makes my chest squeeze with amused affection. Teasing Grace has quickly become one of my favorite things, and she never fails to fall for the bait.

"Come on! Please? It'll be fun." She bats her eyelashes at me, and I struggle to keep my face placid. "Plus, if we're going to be doing... other stuff, it'll give us something to do that's reserved friendship time. I bet I could convince Mona to come too."

I do my best to ignore her mention of "other stuff" even though it makes me ache with the need to start right now. She continues to give me puppy dog eyes, and I pretend to think about it for a while. I don't want her to know that if she asks me for something, I can't say no.

Grace pouts. "Don't make me beg, Blair. I'll do it."

God, the thought of her begging causes a spike of arousal and hunger, and I fake a frown in a poor attempt to hide my reaction. "Fine."

"Yes! Okay, stay right there. I'm going to heat this up again and then we're watching some of last season to prepare you." Grace eases herself up off the couch and heads into her kitchen to put her heat pad in the microwave.

"I didn't agree to that," I call out to her.

She holds her hand up to her ear dramatically and shouts, "I can't hear you", even though the microwave isn't loud and she's less than 15 feet away from me.

I roll my eyes and cross my arms over my chest. Grace giggles and turns back to the microwave, her hand coming up to her neck to rub at it. When she thinks I'm not looking, some of her bubbly energy fizzles away, and I can see the discomfort and tension in her posture.

It makes me realize how good she is at masking it. Looking at her, you'd never know she's struggling.

When she returns to the couch, she gives me a sheepish smile. "Would it be okay if I lie down while we watch the show? It feels rude to do that, but it hurts less when I'm not sitting."

"It's not rude to take care of yourself. You don't have to hide your pain from me."

She sighs. "People don't like it when you complain or act uncomfortable."

I return her ridiculous words with a glare, though the truth of them is far too familiar to me. "People are assholes. You don't have to worry about that with me. You can be yourself—whatever that means at any given time."

Her eyes grow glassy and I worry that I've made her cry. She swallows heavily, then gives me a weak smile. "Okay. The same goes for you, you know."

"You don't want me to be my true self all the time. I'm a bloodsucking monster," I say dismissively.

"I'm not saying I want you to give into dark urges and drain all my blood," Grace scoffs. "I'm saying that you don't have to hide your feelings from me. They won't scare me away."

Yes, they will.

When she says it so earnestly, I almost believe her even

knowing that she's wrong. The urge to tell her I'm infatuated with her rise within me, but the words stick in my throat.

She's being a good friend. She doesn't mean those kinds of feelings.

"Thank you."

Grace smiles at my acquiescence, then grabs the remote and turns on the television. "Let's start with the first episode of last season, because I don't want you to miss the fight between the Pisces guy and the Gemini dude."

"Spoilers," I say in a mock stern tone.

"Oops, sorry!" Grace giggles.

She settles in to watch the show, providing a running commentary that she interrupts with apologies and then attempts to be silent, only to go right back to joking or pointing things out thirty seconds later. As much as I hate to admit it, it's fun. The show is absolute garbage, but Grace's reactions and pithy quips are a delight. It's even better when I let my guard down enough to attempt to joke back, because her bubbly laughter and amusement light me up inside.

We make it through three episodes before she starts to yawn, which I take as my signal to leave. I don't want to. I'd stay here watching this awful show all night if it meant I could be around Grace.

"I should go," I say, standing.

She lets out a groan of protest. "You don't have to go yet! It's still early."

I check my phone. "It's after midnight." Early for me, but late for someone who has to work in the morning.

"I can watch one more. We're at the episode where they do strip truth or dare. We can't stop now! Don't go." Grace pushes herself up from where she's nestled in on the couch and sucks in a sharp breath as she winces at the pain the movement caused.

Her pain draws me over to her side before I can stop myself. She startles at the speed of my movement, sucking in another breath. "Shit, you're fast!"

I grimace. "Didn't mean to startle you. I saw you in pain and wanted to help."

"You're sweet," she says with a soft, slightly sleepy sigh. "Unless you have access to cybernetic spine technology or some really good pain killers, there's not much you can do. Other than sit back down and watch one more episode with me," she adds with a cheeky grin.

It takes a moment for me to process what she's said, as I look down at her and get stuck on how fucking pretty she is right now, with her rumpled blonde hair and the sparkle of humor in her eyes that can't quite disguise the pain she's in.

"How do you feel about blood?" I ask.

"Uh, neutral?" she asks, confused by my non sequitur. "Why? Do you need some?"

This ridiculous, trusting woman extends her wrist to me in a clear offering. My fangs emerge and my senses heighten, focusing in on the thrum of her blood pumping through her veins. I make the mistake of breathing in, her sweet, tart scent slamming into me. I wasn't hungry before, but it's almost impossible to ignore my desire to take what she's offering.

I press my lips together, digging my fangs into my lower lip to use the sting of pain to anchor me to sanity. "No. I can give you some of mine."

Grace's comical look of disgust helps snap me out of the fog of hunger. "No thanks. I'm good." She shakes off a small shudder. "I hope that isn't rude. It's nice of you to offer," she says, patting my arm while giving me a bemused look.

She must not remember how my blood was able to heal Max.

Not that surprising given that was when she discovered monsters exist and I'm a vampire.

My lips twitch with a suppressed smile at her attempt to be polite. "It would help with your pain."

"It would?" Her eyes widen. "Oh shit, I forgot about that."

"It has healing properties. You wouldn't need a lot for it to provide pain relief."

I learned this trick by accident when an ex-girlfriend bit my lip while we were kissing and ingested some of my blood, then exclaimed that her cramps were gone. After that, she'd not so subtly beg me to give her some of my blood any time she was in even a little bit of discomfort. It's one of the reasons we broke up. Not because I was against helping her, but towards the end of the relationship, I felt like I was nothing more than a means to an end for her.

I should be more careful. By giving Grace my blood, I'm placing myself right back into the same situation that made me feel used. But I hate seeing her in pain, and the foolish, hopeful part of me that I try to smother most of the time tells me she won't treat me that way.

"I... No," Grace says, shaking her head both in denial and like she's trying to clear an unpleasant thought from her mind.

The rejection stings. "Why not?" I ask, before I can tamp down my reaction.

"It feels wrong."

I flinch and I step backward, her words like a slap across the face. I'm being ridiculous, but I can't stop the pain I feel from offering her something that could help and her refusing to take it. She doesn't know that I don't go around doling out my blood to anyone who wants it. She doesn't know that it's incredibly intimate for me to give it.

Grace grabs my wrist before I move any further away. My skin tingles at the contact. "Whoa! Not wrong, as in your blood is gross or me drinking it is objectionable. Wrong because I'm worried about what will happen if I take it and it helps."

I furrow my brow, not understanding.

She sighs and continues. "If your blood helps, I'll want it again. I'm worried that every time I'm in pain, I'll ask you for it. I don't want that... I don't want to be a burden. I don't want to use you." Her thumb strokes my wrist absently as she speaks, her eyes shining with sincerity as she gazes up at me.

Her concern makes any remaining reticence I have about her using my blood vanish. "You wouldn't be a burden," I say, swallowing heavily and fighting the urge to pull my wrist away before I beg her to touch me more. "I'll give you anything you need, Grace," I add in a whisper. I don't mean to say it aloud, but I've fallen under the spell of her touch and nearness.

"I'll... Let me think about it." Grace lets go, her voice so conflicted I can't help wondering if she's not just talking about using my blood.

I nod and step away. "You're tired. I'm going to head out, but I'll text you tomorrow night to see how you're doing."

She doesn't argue. Her smile is weak when she escorts me to the door. I think I've royally fucked things up with our friendship, but then she reaches out and pulls me into a hug.

I stiffen in shock as her sinfully soft, warm body presses into mine. I blink up at her in surprise, and she lets out a chuckle before releasing me far too soon. "Thanks for coming over, and for your offer. Both of your offers. They mean so much to me."

I stare up at her in a daze, head swimming from her embrace. "Of course."

When I get back home, I head back out into the garden and pray for the strength to follow through with my agreement with Grace without ruining what we already have or giving in to my monstrous side.

15

GRACE

Cool fingertips skirt over my shoulder, then across my back to ghost over the nape of my neck, sending goosebumps skittering across my bare skin. I hold completely still, struggling to keep my breathing calm. The fingers continue their path to my other shoulder, then up to rest lightly on my jugular. The dull press of a pointed nail into the vulnerable spot makes me gasp involuntarily, and a husky, rich laugh from beside me follows in its wake.

"So responsive," Blair murmurs, the rest of her fingers wrapping around my throat and tilting my chin up oh so gently to meet her eyes. Their usual dark brown is replaced with a supernatural red, and her fangs gleam in the low light as she smiles down at me.

My pulse leaps, and I swallow heavily as the ache between my legs builds. Wet arousal drips down my thighs, and I fight the urge to squirm and create some kind of friction to relieve the need coursing through me.

I can't move. I need to be good for her.

"Such a good girl," she murmurs, echoing my thoughts. She lowers herself down in front of where I'm kneeling, the hand on my throat sliding down my sternum to rest on the swell of my breasts. "What do you want, Grace?" she asks, her blazing eyes still locked on mine.

My answer falls from my lips immediately. "You."

Blair moves in a flash, dipping her head to scrape her teeth against my throat as her hand cups my breast. I moan as she sucks on the delicate skin, her mouth and tongue and teeth all a teasing hint of what she's going to do.

She pulls back and I whimper at the loss. "Say it again. Beg me."

"I want you. I need you. Please."

She lets out a pleased hum. "I'll give you anything you need." A second later, there's a bright flash of pain as her fangs sink into my neck.

I WAKE UP GASPING, with one hand on my neck and the other wedged between my thighs. I'm soaked, and so close to coming I could cry, the pleasure from the dream still searing into me. It wouldn't take more than a few circles of my clit... if I can just get the image of Blair back into my mind.

The fingers working between my thighs freeze and my eyes pop open.

Holy shit.

I almost came while thinking about Blair.

I grab my phone from the bedside table, wincing at the pain in my neck that must've been what woke me up. Pulling up my text thread with Mona, I send her a message.

> Grace: Sex dreams don't mean anything, right?

It's just after 7am, so she should be awake soon. I stare at my phone screen as my mind races.

It felt so *real*. When I said I wanted Blair, it was a bone-deep urge. I've never had a sex dream like that before.

> Grace: You don't think I'm like you, do you? You had all those dreams about Max and they ended up happening.

Another minute passes, and as the shock wanes, embarrassment about my overreaction takes its place. Weird shit happens in dreams all the time. I once dreamt that I starred in a Broadway musical adaptation of an alien smut book I read.

> Mona: Who did you have a sex dream about??

> Grace: It doesn't matter. I was being silly.

> Mona: Tell meeeee.

> Mona: Don't be embarrassed if it was me. I had one about you before. Well, it was a hybrid of you and our math teacher, but I think that still counts.

> Grace: Which one?

> Mona: Mrs. Thembold.

I snort. Our Calculus teacher was at least 65 and dressed like she was 80.

> Grace: Ewww, Mona!

> Mona: Don't kink shame me!

> Mona: And stop trying to change the subject. Tell me who you had a dream about.

I have the strong urge to pretend I have to go get ready for work and don't have time to talk anymore, but we both know that I'm up earlier than usual.

> Mona: It was Blair, wasn't it? I knew it! I've been holding my tongue, but I see the way you look at her. Plus, every time I've tried to bring up you having a crush on her, you did that thing with your face that tells me you're hiding something.

My phone drops out of my hands as I shove the covers down and sit up, suddenly overheated. What is she talking about?

> Grace: What face? I don't make a face!

> Mona: Girl, you've been doing that thing where you look down and up really fast since we met in middle school.

It's annoying how well she knows me, but she's wrong this time. I haven't had a crush on Blair. Yeah, I think she's really pretty and I get excited whenever I see her, but that's not the same thing as liking someone.

Is it?

I snatch my phone back up and type out a hasty reply.

> Grace: Well, maybe I do that. But this isn't the same. I don't have a crush on Blair.

Mona doesn't respond for an agonizing few seconds.

> Grace: I don't!

> Mona: Okay. You don't. You're the only person in the universe who doesn't, but if you say you don't, I believe you.

A lump forms in my stomach, the same one I get whenever I'm dishonest with my best friend.

> Grace: I like Blair a lot. She's really cool and interesting. I enjoy spending time with her and I'd have to be blind to not think she's hot. That doesn't mean I have a crush on her.

The dream memory of her lips at my throat flashes in my mind, and there's a dull throb between my thighs, serving as a strong counterpoint to my statement.

> Grace: Shit. Do I have a crush on Blair?

> Mona: Yeah, babe.

> Grace: What does that mean?

> Mona: What do you mean, what does that mean?

> Grace: I'm straight. I like men.

It's true. I've spent my entire life being low-key obsessed with guys. Growing up, I would spend hours writing in my journal about my crushes and my dreams for my future, where I'd marry the perfect guy and have a fairy tale life. As I got older and my gangly body filled out, I loved knowing men were attracted to me. It's a double-edged sword and I've been harassed more times than I can count, but there's an annoying part of me that craves attention and validation from men despite that.

It's not like I'm scared of being gay. Yeah, my dad was a little conservative and prejudiced when I was growing up, but he's come around on that. He even puts a rainbow flag up next to his American flag during pride month, because he wants the gay couple across the street to know he supports them. So I wouldn't have to worry about familial fallout from coming out.

When Mona told me she was bisexual, I was happy for her because it meant she'd maybe not end up with another trash boyfriend. She seriously has had the worst taste in men—Max aside.

Hell, I even had a moment where I wished I liked women, so I didn't have to deal with toxic manchild bullshit. But for better or worse—mostly worse in my case, given my terrible marriage and dating track record—I'm solidly into men.

So, then why does the mere thought of Blair right now send my pulse racing?

> Mona: You can like men and not be straight. Trust me, I know.

> Mona: I feel like this would be better to talk about in person. Take the morning off and come over.

> Grace: I can't take the morning off just because I had a sex dream about Blair!

That, and I'm now questioning everything I thought I knew about myself.

> Mona: Yes, you can. It's called a mental health day. Your asshole boss can deal.

> Mona: I know you. You're freaking out and won't be able to focus until you work through what's going on in your head.

> Mona: I'll get Max to make us pancakes.

I really shouldn't. I save my wellness days for when I'm in severe pain, or at least that's what I tell myself. Since I can work from home, I usually force myself to work even when I feel awful. But Mona's right. I won't be able to concentrate.

> Grace: Pancakes sound good. I'll grab coffee from Celia's and be over around 9:30.

Wait. Shit. I can't go to Cafe Celia's. What if Issac is there? The last thing I need right now is an awkward interaction with one of Blair's submissives.

> Grace: On second thought, I'll skip the coffee. Too awkward.

Mona: You'll be safe. Isaac doesn't work on Monday mornings.

> Grace: How the hell do you know that?

Mona: I told Max about him standing you up for that date and he may have used his skills to find out Isaac's schedule so we wouldn't run into him. He offered to dig up some dirt to get him fired so you could go whenever you wanted, but I figured that once the situation was a little less fresh, you'd miss Isaac's lattes.

> Grace: Your fiancé is amazing. And a little scary.

Mona: He is 😊😊

Mona: See you in a bit!

"Okay. Enough stalling. Tell me about Blair." Mona pokes her fork out toward me accusatorially.

I swallow my mouthful of pancakes, my eyes darting over to where Max is cleaning up in the kitchen.

"He has earbuds in and is listening to a podcast. He can't hear us."

I narrow my eyes and raise my voice to test the validity of her statement. "Do you remember that time that you stole that boy's underwear from his gym locker?"

Mona's eyebrows shoot up in alarm. "That was a dare!"

"Yeah, but it wasn't a dare that made you keep them in your bottom drawer for two years," I say even louder.

Mona reaches across the table and smacks my arm, but there's zero reaction from Max. He's either the best actor in the world or he can't hear.

I rub my arm, playing up the mild sting. "Ouch! I'm delicate."

"Baby. You'll have to get used to it if you're going to do anything with Blair."

"She told you?!" I ask, my brows shooting up in alarm. We only had the conversation about Blair being my domme last night. Did she immediately text Mona after?

"Whoa, hold on. What?"

Oh. She was teasing me. Shit. "I, uh, nevermind."

"Grace Lynn Ashbrook! Don't give me that crap. What's going on?"

"Fine! Blair came over last night to hang out and I accidentally overshared about my disaster of an attempt at a scene with Declan. She offered to teach me how to be a submissive instead."

Mona's eyes grow comically wide and her mouth hangs open. "And you agreed?"

"Well, yeah. Should I not have? I know she only offered because she feels bad for me, but she's a professional. If anyone can help me get past the nonsense rattling around in my head, it's her."

That and the thought of Blair dominating me makes me shiver with anticipation.

"She definitely didn't offer because she feels bad for you. Blair doesn't do anything she doesn't want to. And trust me, she definitely wants to do you." She cackles at her own double entendre.

"Mona!" I say, my cheeks heating at the insinuation. "No, she doesn't. She's being a good friend. That's it. She told me it doesn't have to be sexual."

She rolls her eyes. "Yeah, right. Max is your friend, but you wouldn't let him dominate you, would you?"

My eyes dart back over to the handsome redhead who is obliviously scrubbing a pan. Max is really sweet and attractive, but no way. Beyond the fact that he's obsessed with Mona and would never so much as look at me, it would feel wrong. "What? No! That'd be super weird."

Mona snorts at my reaction. "Relax, it wasn't an offer. Merely illustrating a point."

"There's a difference between your fiancé being with me like that, and our friend doing it."

"Why?" Mona asks, baiting me.

I throw my hands up in exasperation. "Because it's too intimate!"

Mona takes a casual sip of her coffee, her lips twitching in amusement as she sets the cup back down. "If trying out kink were something nonsexual to you, it wouldn't freak you out so much to think of doing it with Max. Or me, for that matter."

"You'd be a terrible domme," I say, trying to ignore her annoying logic.

Mona laughs and nods. "Yeah, probably."

I shove a bite of pancake into my mouth and glare at her. I

thought coming over here was supposed to help me, but I'm even more worked up now.

"Don't give me that look. Stop trying so hard to ignore what's staring you in the face. You have a crush on Blair."

"I don't—"

She holds a hand up to cut me off. "You do. There's nothing wrong with that. If you don't want to do anything about it, then don't. Just because you had a sex dream about her doesn't mean you need to do it in real life."

My eyes drop to my cup of coffee, staring into the liquid like I can divine what to do from the shapes in the foam.

Mona continues, her voice softer. "If you do want to do something about it, that's okay, too."

I look up to see she's watching me with gentle compassion that reminds me why I love her so much. She's my rock when I'm freaking out. If she's pushing me on this, it's because she cares.

"Is it? How do I know if it's real attraction or a passing blip brought on by admiration and post-divorce sadness? I've never wanted to… Sure, I think women are sexy, but I've never fantasized about being with them like I do men. Well, other than that dream last night. And yeah, maybe I like to watch lesbian porn, but that's because I don't like how violent most straight porn can get." I'm rambling now, and the more I talk, the more I confuse myself. "You know what I'm trying to say," I add feebly.

"I do." Mona nods. "I hate to break it to you, but that's how I felt at first when I started figuring things out."

The concerned way she says it is like she's diagnosing a disease, not talking about her bisexual awakening, and it amuses me enough to ease some of my stress. "Yeah, but I'm not…"

"You don't have to pick any label the second you have a crush on a woman. Chill. Let's look at this in a different way. Forget straight, gay, bi, whatever exists. Step back for a moment and think about when you first met Zack."

I grimace at the mention of my ex-husband. "No thanks."

Mona reaches out and squeezes my hand. "I know he's a total bastard, but you loved him. How did you feel when you first met?"

"Like I was about to make the worst mistake of my life," I grumble.

"Grace." Mona says my name like a chastisement.

"Ugh, okay." I let myself go back to that time. I've actively tried to rewrite my history with Zack, so what he did doesn't hurt so much. But Mona is right. I loved him. I hate it, and I wish I didn't, but I can't change that. "I felt nervous every time I saw him, but in the good way that makes you a little giddy. I wanted to spend all of my time with him. I'd get this fluttering feeling inside me whenever he looked at me. I..."

Shit. I know where Mona is going with this, and it terrifies me. "I dreamt about him. I'd think about him having his way with me." Mona nods encouragingly, and I continue. "Little did I know he would have zero interest in taking control like that," I say with a wry laugh, trying to push down the way my thoughts are racing.

She chuckles but says nothing. Silence stretches between us and a wave of emotions wash over me.

Nerves.

Excitement.

Worry.

Hope.

"I like Blair."

"Shocking." Max's wry voice startles me, and I turn to see that he's done with the dishes and pulling out his earbuds.

"I thought you said he wasn't listening!" I scowl at Mona and she holds her hands up in surrender.

"I didn't think he could hear us, I swear!"

"I wasn't listening," Max says with a chuckle. "My podcast just ended, and I wanted to give my fiancée a kiss before I headed upstairs for a bit."

I glare at him in disbelief, but his easy, calm smile stays in place. He's good at bluffing. "Sure, sure."

He bends down and kisses Mona's cheek, and the way she lights up at his casual affection makes my heart ache. I thought I had something good with my ex, but it was never like that, even at the beginning. I can't help being a little jealous of how in love they are with each other.

Max gives me a knowing look as he stands back up and heads out of the kitchen.

As soon as he's gone, Mona turns back to laser focus on me. "You like Blair." I can tell it's taking everything inside her not to say "I told you so". "What are you going to do?"

"I don't know. Probably call off the lessons she offered," I say with a sigh.

"What?! Why?" Mona exclaims in horror. "You like her! You want to try out kink and she's more than willing."

"I..." It takes me a second to come up with the right words to explain the mixture of hope and worry roiling inside me. "What if she touches me, and I realize that I don't actually want her that way? I don't want to treat Blair like an experiment. She means too much to me." I rest my face in my hands and sigh.

"Aww, honey..." I hear Mona's chair scooting backward, then feel her hand on my arm a few seconds later. "Come here," she commands, pulling me up into a hug.

I accept it willingly. Mona's hugs are the best. I'm tall enough that my chin slots easily onto her shoulder and I let her soft, loving hold comfort me.

When I pull back, she grips my arms and holds my gaze. "Talk to her about this."

"I can't…"

"You don't have to tell her you're crushing on her right away. Just… you've already agreed to have her teach you about kink, so why not ask for everything you want to try in that context? That way, you can safely figure out if you like it or not without hurting her feelings."

"You think that would be okay?" I'm not sure it's a great idea, but I can't ignore the spark of excitement at the prospect.

"Yeah. Oh! I know!" Mona lets go of me and claps her hands together, then grabs her phone. "There are a bunch of different online kink checklists. I'll send you one that looks good, or you can ask her for one, since she probably has them for work. Then you both can fill the form out and say what is and isn't on the table, without the awkwardness of directly telling her you want her to fuck you face-to-face."

I want to argue, but it's a good idea. "Alright. Yeah. Fuck, I can't believe I'm doing this."

"Hell yeah, you are. You're adventurous and amazing. If it doesn't work out, it'll be okay. Blair isn't the type of person to stop being your friend because you're not comfortable with something. But…" A salacious grin spreads across Mona's face. "If it does work out, you have to promise to tell me everything."

I laugh. "Deal." I pull her into another hug. "Thanks for this."

She squeezes me back. "Anytime." A heartbeat passes and she groans. "God, I hope Max wasn't lying. I'll never hear the end of it if he heard about that thing with Stephen's underwear."

16

BLAIR

My phone rattles against the concrete driveway with an incoming text notification, drawing my attention away from the vanity I'm in the midst of staining. I keep forgetting to turn off notifications for anyone except close contacts during my down time. I should ignore it. Whatever it is, it can wait until I'm done with the task at hand. The whole point of me working on this DIY project was to get my mind into the blank space I go to when I'm concentrating on a repetitive task.

I stretch and continue, the dark cherry stain looking almost black under the light of the moon. Crafting in the dark isn't the smartest idea, but my vampiric vision is much better than what it was when I was alive. It's nights like these, where I'm outside at 2 am refinishing furniture, that I'm glad for the tree cover and private driveway. Getting the money to afford this house wasn't easy, but it was worth everything I did to get it.

Before I was turned, I was broke, spending my days working a shitty receptionist job so that I could spend my nights at various goth clubs and bars throughout the city. After I was turned, I only had my ancient car and a handful of possessions because I'd given up my apartment, thinking I'd be moving in with the love of my life.

Once I survived the initial blood-soaked haze of my acclimation to vampirism—the horrific memories of which are still clear despite how mindless and feral I felt at the time—I had to figure out the practicalities of being a monster. Even if I hadn't lost my job because I'd spent three weeks in a violent feeding frenzy, I wouldn't have been able to go to work because the sun would burn me to a crisp. I had no friends to call on, because Dominic had deftly pulled me away from the few I had remaining after my boyfriend cheated on me with my roommate. I certainly didn't have any family that would help.

So I took what little money I had to my name, rented a room at an awful motel on the outskirts of the city, bought a slutty white dress and matching heels, and signed up for a sugaring website. I could've tried bartending or worked the overnight shift at a warehouse, but I was done with having nothing. Being a sugar baby made me more money than I'd ever seen in my life, even though I despised every minute of it.

It's also how I found out I had the power to charm people into doing what I say. One too many men grabbing me without my permission, and I snapped. Yelled at a man to get his hands off me. He listened placidly. I told him to give me all the money in his wallet. He smiled and passed me a wad of bills.

I did that for three years, robbing rich men blind while convincing them they wanted to do everything I asked. Feeding on them if the scent of their blood didn't repulse me. I reasoned that they were going to give me the money anyway, so I was just cutting out the steps in the middle, where I had to fawn over them and pretend I liked their jokes and their wrinkly dicks. I could've probably kept doing it as long as I moved around, but I loathed it. I gave nothing to those men, yet I still felt dirty.

Luckily, I met my first monster client, Aven, who changed my trajectory for the better. Unbeknownst to me, they were a fae, and when I tried to charm them, they were shocked but unaffected. Aven laughed and patted my hand and explained that it would take a lot more than a neonate's powers to affect them. They could've destroyed me on the sugaring sites, or honestly killed me for daring to try my tricks on them. Instead, they took me under their wing. They taught me the basics of paranormal society. They introduced me to kink. They even told me about the burgeoning monster community in Moonvale.

I still wonder sometimes where Aven is. They vanished, leaving no sign they ever lived in their fancy loft apartment. No one knew who the hell I was talking about when I asked where they went. At first, I thought I was crazy and they were a figment of my imagination. Then I learned that fae love to do bullshit like that. Aven was my weird, kinky fairygodperson, and I guess they decided I could make it on my own. Maybe I'll see them again in a few hundred years when the whim strikes them.

My phone buzzes again, pulling me out of my memories. I know I should ignore it, but there's a spike of worry that something is wrong and if I don't look, I won't be able to help in time. To be fair, it's not an unfounded worry with what happened with Mona last year.

I set down the brush and wipe my hands off on a rag, then unlock the screen. It's an unknown number. Probably spam. Still, I check it in case it's one of my clients and they got a new phone.

> Unknown: Put to death, therefore, what is earthly in you: sexual immorality, impurity, passion, evil desire, and covetousness, which is idolatry. On account of these, the wrath of God is coming. (Colossians 3:5–6)
>
> Unknown: It's not too late. Repent and come home.

Mother. If only she knew how much of an impure, deviant sinner I am now.

How the fuck she keeps getting my number, I'll never know. My grip on my phone tightens so much I'm afraid I might crack the screen, but I swallow down my rage and block the number. There's no point in replying.

There goes any sense of calm I was going to get tonight. I sigh and drag the vanity and supplies back into the garage. No doubt to be neglected for another month or so.

As usual, the house is dark and quiet, and I don't bother turning on the lights as I make my way to the kitchen to grab some blood from the fridge. I warm it up a bit in the microwave in my faded mug that says "I hate Sundays" with a satanic version of Garfield that I've kept as a reminder of my past self's questionable sense of humor. I take it with me into the living room and turn on my rarely used tv, putting on a random home improvement show where a smiling redhead calmly informs people how hideous their perfectly nice homes are and how they need to spend thousands of dollars on renovation that almost always end up making the place look worse.

It does little to help calm me down, but at least it redirects my anger from my mother and shitty family to an innocuous source that I'll never encounter. I'm grumbling about the lifeless beige clean mom aesthetic they redid a nursery in with when my phone vibrates. I scowl at it, ready to tell off any client bugging me on my night off or block yet another fake number from my mother, but it's neither.

> Grace: Hey.

It's almost 3am on a Monday night.

> Blair: Why are you awake?
>
> Blair: Are you okay?

> Grace: I'm fine. Sometimes I can't sleep.

I frown at my phone.

> Blair: Because of pain?

> Grace: Yeah. Not tonight though, thankfully. Just too many thoughts that've been rattling around in my head.

> Grace: Anyway, since I've been awake, I filled out a checklist.

I'm missing something.

> Blair: What kind of checklist?

An attachment pops up to a file, and I open it.
Oh.
It's a kink checklist. Looks similar to one I use with new clients.

My undead heart races, pumping the blood I just consumed through my system as I read. As a vampire, I don't sweat unless I actively make myself do so, but I swear my palms are getting damp from nerves.

The checklist is categorized by types of activity, with colored bubbles to indicate levels of interest and experience levels.

I laugh when I see she's typed in a note at the top.

I didn't bother filling out any of the experience information because other than my disaster with Declan and one guy using nipple clamps on me and asking me to call him daddy, I have none. I'm a blank slate. Do with me what you will.

I don't think she'd say that if she knew what I want to do with her. Grace's effervescent beauty begs the vampiric side of me to consume every part of her. I'd be greedy, taking every piece of her I could until there was nothing left but her true self laid bare at my hands. Not because I want to ruin her, no. She's already been torn apart and left to cobble the jagged pieces of herself back together in a way I'm all too familiar with. No, I want to bask in the radiant warmth that she exudes straight from the source, with nothing else in the way.

I sure as shit can't tell her that. She'll think I'm crazy. Maybe I am. I'm the one that offered to teach her, knowing how much my monster hungers for her.

I shake the thought away and continue to read the form. It starts with a bondage section, and blindfolds, light bondage, ropes, shibari, and cuffs are all marked as interested. Gags are a maybe. Mummification and more intense bondage are no's.

Nothing unexpected. I already have some rope that would match the signature pink she loves to wear. I'm sure I can handle tying Grace up without it becoming too much of an issue. I teach shibari and have done so many demonstrations that the process has become almost second nature to me. I'll be able to focus on the beauty I'm creating with my ties, and the sensations that it evokes for Grace, instead of everything I'd want to do with her once she's bound.

At least I hope I will.

She's left another note in this section.

I can't do anything that will mess with my neck too much. I'd be happy to try a collar and leash, but you probably couldn't tug on it very much.

Fuck me. Grace wearing my collar as I gently lead her around is now all I can think about. Knowing how eager she is to please, I doubt I'd have to tug at all. I'd issue a command, and she'd follow.

The idea makes me ache with unfulfilled need. My clit is begging for me to reach between my thighs and give myself some sort of relief. I close my eyes and try to breathe through it, startling when my phone vibrates in my hand.

Focus, Blair.

> Grace: Are you reading it?

> Blair: Yeah.

> Grace: If you have a better list for me to fill out, I'll do that instead.

> Blair: This one looks fine.

> Grace: What part are you up to?

> Grace: If you have any questions, I can answer them.

> Grace: I put some notes because I felt like things needed explanations.

I smile down at my phone as I read her influx of messages.

> Blair: I've read through the bondage section.

> Grace: And? What do you think?

I think the idea of her bound and at the mercy of my commands is making me wet, but I'm not going to tell her that.

> Blair: It all makes sense. Give me a minute to read the rest, okay?

> Blair: I promise I won't judge anything you've put on here.

> Grace: Okay.

I go back to the checklist. The next section is impact play. Again, there's a note at the top.

This one is hard for me to know what to put. A lot of them sound interesting in theory, but I'm not sure how I'll react to them. I'm already in pain a lot, so I'm not sure if I want to add to that. But we can try if you want!

Despite what I just said, I message her.

> Blair: Some people with chronic pain like impact and pain play. It helps them feel in control of the pain and their bodies. Plus, the endorphins that come with it are no joke. But it's not about what I want, it's about what you're comfortable with. If we did it, we'd start gentle and be very cautious.

> Grace: Oh wow, okay. Let's try it.

Great. Now I'm imagining marking her pale skin as she begs me for mercy. My clit throbs at the thought.

I read through the next few sections, and it turns out Grace is interested in more things than she isn't. She has a strong inclination towards servitude, and an aversion to intense humiliation, which doesn't surprise me at all. I laugh when I see that she's written "duh", followed by a vampire emoji and a winking emoji next to blood play.

Then I get to the bottom, where it lists sexual activity. I'd planned on sending her a modified checklist that didn't include it, so it wouldn't make her uncomfortable. I brace myself for facing the reminder that she doesn't want me that way. The shock I feel as I read what she's put takes my breath away.

Kissing- Interested
Breast play - Interested
Fingering (Giving and Receiving) - Interested
Oral (Giving and Receiving) - Interested
Face sitting (Receiving) - Interested
Vibrators - Interested
Dildos - Interested
Strap-On Dildos (Penetration) - Interested
Edging - Interested
Forced Orgasm - Interested
Orgasm Denial - Interested

I stare at the checklist in disbelief. There must be some kind of misunderstanding.

> Blair: Did you fill this out as a general thing? Or did you put what you're comfortable doing with me?

It takes over a minute for her to reply. My stomach clenches as I wait for her answer.

> Grace: With you.

Holy shit. I feel like I'm dreaming. There's no way she wants that.

> Blair: You don't have to do anything you're not interested in.

> Grace: I know.

> Grace: I didn't mark anything as "interested" that I didn't want to try.

> Grace: But I know you also need to consent to things and set your own limits. So can you fill out the form and send it back to me? Then we'll be on the same page.

I'm at a loss for words. I blink down at my screen, dumbfounded. My hands shake as I type my reply.

> Blair: Okay.

> Grace: Are you okay?

> Blair: Of course I am.

I'm not. With a simple checklist, Grace has turned my world upside down.

17

GRACE

Blair is coming over tonight, and I'm freaking out.
The chronic pain gods were merciful for once, and I woke up this morning feeling pretty good, but that gave me more mental space to worry about other things.

What should I wear?
Does what I eat affect the taste of my blood?
Should I shave my pubes?
Would it be too weird to give her a little thank you gift?
Should I get waterproof sheets to prevent bloodstains?
Is this whole thing way too weird?
What do I do if I cry again?

I wish Blair were awake so I could text her. Poor Mona has

fielded my frantic questions as best she can, but there's really not much she can do once the anxiety beast takes hold of me.

Few people know how much I worry. I'm adventurous and outgoing, so I couldn't possibly be anxious. Just another imperfect facet of myself that I've grown excellent at hiding.

I won't be able to hide it from Blair. She reads me far too well. I don't want to hide it from her. Isn't the whole point of this BDSM thing that I need to be honest and trust her?

Still, I wish she'd told me what to wear. I've torn my entire closet apart looking for an outfit that somehow conveys both "this is totally casual and no big deal" and "I want you to put me on my knees and order me around". Everything either looks like I'm trying too hard or not trying enough.

I've had to take two showers because I keep getting super sweaty. It feels pointless because I know the second she gets here I'm going to be a sweaty, gross mess, no matter how hard I try to stay calm.

I should've asked if she wanted to drink my blood tonight. I have anti-anxiety meds I could take, but then they would be in my bloodstream, and I don't know if she'd want to ingest that. I wonder if that's how vampires do drugs...

When I'm finally dressed and as put together as I can manage, I pace around the house, trying to burn off some of this agitated energy so I won't be a ball of nerves when she arrives.

God, I'm so nervous. But that's not all of what's making me want to jump out of my skin. I'm also really damn excited. Blair sent me her list of interests and boundaries that seem to align very well with mine. I made her promise me she didn't fill things out that way to make me feel more comfortable and told her I didn't want her to do anything she didn't like. I swear I could hear the laughter in her text back, thanking me for my concern but reminding me she doesn't do anything she doesn't want to.

Which means she wants to have sex with me.

I know that's not a big deal. I'm sure Blair has had casual sex with plenty of women, and I know that I'm attractive. Lots of people have casual sex and it doesn't mean anything. I can't seem to get the hopeful, romantic part of my head that's harboring my crush from hoping this might be more than that.

I honestly don't know if casual sex is something I'll be okay with. Just like I don't know if I'll like sex with a woman, or any of this kinky stuff when it happens in real life. But I'll regret not finding out, and I don't want to go through my life wondering what could've been if I'd been brave enough to try.

I wasted way too many years of my life with comfortable mediocrity. I want to find something that makes me truly excited. And god, I really think that could be Blair.

The sex dreams every night that feature her certainly seem to agree.

By the time Blair arrives, I'm so anxious and excited I'm not sure if I want to cry or beg her to make me come. I scurry to the door, then take a deep inhale to collect myself and plaster on what I hope is a calm smile, and open it.

I don't know what I was expecting, but the second I see Blair, some of my nerves evaporate. She didn't suddenly turn into a different person the second we scheduled this first scene. She's not going to put on some intense domme persona because she doesn't need to. Blair is plenty intimidating and powerful in her default state.

"H-hey!"

"You look surprised to see me. Expecting someone else?" Blair says with a wry tilt of her lips.

I laugh and shake my head. "No. Just... this is so silly, but I thought maybe you'd look different."

"Do you not like what I'm wearing?" Blair gestures down to her black top and tight jeans that hug her hips perfectly. God, how is she so casually hot? It's not fair to us mere mortals. She's wearing what she'd normally wear to come over, which makes me feel a lot better about my choice not to answer the door in my sluttiest dress.

"You look perfect. You always look perfect." My cheeks heat at the little eyebrow raise she gives me in response to my words. "Don't give me that look! You know how hot you are."

That makes her laugh. "Alright."

She hovers in the doorframe as I turn to head inside. "Oh shit, I always forget. Please, come in."

Whatever supernatural weirdness bars her from entering my home falls away at my words, and she follows me as I head to the living room.

"Would it work if I told you that you could come whenever you want?"

"I don't need your permission for that," she says deadpan.

My face flames even more. "I meant come in! Into my house. I wouldn't presume to try to dictate...that. That's your job." I clear my throat. "I assume anyway." Fuck, I'm so awkward.

"Ah." There's restrained amusement in her tone. "Yes."

"Yes, it would work to let you in, or yes, you're going to tell me when I can come?" I blurt.

She grins. "Yes."

I roll my eyes at her annoying reply, but my pulse speeds up at the thought of the latter. "Alright, then you have permission to come into my home whenever you want."

"Thank you. That means a lot to me." There's a hint of genuine relief in her voice that makes my chest squeeze.

The urge to hug her overwhelms me, and I tug Blair's smaller frame against my body, even though I know she probably won't like it. There wasn't a section on the form to list if you're interested in hugs, but I can ask for forgiveness after.

"You don't have to thank me," I whisper. She's slightly stiff as I hold her against me, but after a few seconds, her arms come up to wrap around my waist. This close, I catch a hint of her soft, lightly floral scent and I resist the urge to suck in a deep breath so it envelops me. There's something so simultaneously sexy and comforting about the way she smells. "You're always welcome. Anyone who thinks otherwise is an idiot."

I let go when she starts to pull away and give her a sheepish smile. "Was that okay? We're not in a scene yet and I thought it might be good..."

She nods. "Hugs are okay. I just wasn't expecting it."

"Well, get used to it because I hug the people I care about." And ever since I realized how much I like Blair, I care about her a lot. God, I hope I don't fuck everything up. What if we try this and it ruins things? Maybe it'd be better to stay friends without anything else in the mix.

Blair frowns and places a hand on my shoulder. I almost jolt at the contact, despite having just hugged her, and she squeezes, her nails digging into the sleeve of my top. "Tell me what's freaking you out," she says, a clear command.

"Everything?" I say with a laugh.

"Be more specific."

"I don't want to ruin things," I murmur.

"Grace, if you don't want—"

I shake my head. "I do! I want to. But you matter a lot to me, and I feel like I'm using you. If I can't handle it or it doesn't work, I don't want to lose your friendship."

Her eyes lock on mine. "You won't."

"You can't say that for certain!" I'm unsure why I'm arguing.

She sighs. "You have to trust me for this to work. That includes the kink, but also to make sure that neither of us gets hurt to the point it's irreparable."

"I don't want you to get hurt at all," I mutter.

"You don't get to decide what feelings I open myself up to, Grace. I've been through more than you can ever imagine. If I say I can handle any pain or weirdness that arises from us trying this out, I can."

Shit, she's right. "Okay. Same, by the way. If it ends up not working, I'll be an awkward mess for a bit, but that seems to be my default state for all of this. We'll be okay once that blows over."

Saying it aloud makes the stakes of this feel a lot more real, but also more manageable.

"Then we're on the same page." She releases her grip on my shoulder, and I try not to sag at the loss of contact. I didn't realize how much it was bolstering me.

"So... when do we start?" I ask, clasping my hands behind my back.

Blair scans over me, her eyes leaving a burning trail of awareness across me. "Now."

Oh wow, okay. I thought maybe there'd be more preamble, but she probably knows I'll pester her with questions if she gives me more time. We've talked for hours about this leading up to tonight. She's already answered everything I needed to know. I'm as ready as I can be.

God, I hope I don't fuck this up.

18

GRACE

"Starting now until the end of the scene, you will not speak unless I ask you a direct question, or if it's to use your safeword. Do you understand?"

The authority in Blair's voice is staggering. "Yes." I'm not sure if she wants me to add something like Mistress after, but she doesn't seem displeased by my reply, so I leave it off.

"Good. Tell me your safeword."

"Calico." I spent way too much time overthinking what I should use, and I don't love what I settled on, but there's no judgment in Blair's expression.

"If you don't use your safeword, I'll explicitly tell you when the scene is over."

I'm not sure if nodding is allowed, so I hold still. I'm pinned by her gaze, my body tingling with trepidation and excitement for what's coming. Will she make me undress? Will she touch me? Will she have me touch her?

"Go get a glass of water."

It's so out of left field that I almost slip up and ask her why. Why the heck does she want me to do that? Is she going to pour it on me? I swear I see a hint of a smirk forming on her lips as she watches the confusion cross my face.

I go to the kitchen and do as she asks, then return to stand in front of her. "Drink it."

I fight the urge to furrow my brow at her order, and bring the glass to my lips and start to drink as quickly as possible.

"Slower."

This time I can't hold back my bemused reaction. I slow down and drink at a normal pace, with Blair watching my every movement.

When I'm finished, she nods. "Good. Go fill it up again."

This is so weird. I hesitate, mind failing to determine what the point of any of this is. I grumble a little to myself as I'm filling the glass again.

"Did you say something?" Blair's tone is sharp and I freeze at the warning.

"No, Mistress." This time, it feels appropriate to add the honorific at the end. I hurry back with the water, my legs a little shaky this time from the small surge of adrenaline I felt at almost disobeying Blair's command.

"Hand me the glass."

I keep my eyes downcast and pass it over, cheeks burning even though I have no clue why.

She circles around me, glass in hand. She isn't really going to pour it on me, is she?

"You're doing very well, Grace." Her casual praise pours over me like honey, leaving me feeling warm all over. She takes a small sip from the glass, her lips closing over the spot I marked with my lipstick. The strange intimacy of the action makes my breath quicken.

Why is this turning me on?

She moves away and sits down in my armchair, then takes one of my throw pillows and places it on the ground on the side of the chair. She gestures down at it. "Sit here, facing the same direction I am."

I follow her instructions, moving beside the chair and sinking down to sit on the pillow. I can only barely see her in my peripheral vision, but I don't dare to turn my head to look at her.

"Very good," she purrs. "Hold this with both hands, keeping it a level that won't hurt your neck." She hands the water glass back to me and I take it. It's absurd how my hands tremble as I do, but I can't help it.

A minute passes, and I'm on edge the whole time, waiting for her next command. Another. I shift slightly, trying to get more comfortable on the thin pillow. My eyes dart to the side as I freeze, wondering if she'll reprimand me for moving without her order.

She reaches out and takes the glass from me, and I think we're finally moving on to something else, but she just takes another tiny sip and hands it back to me. I didn't even know vampires could drink water.

She doesn't look uncomfortable. No, Blair is entirely at ease. She sits back in the chair and pulls out her phone. "Eyes front."

I look away, feeling a sting of chastisement despite her not sounding upset. The odd sensation blends with the heat that's been slowly building inside me. My nipples harden, pressing against the thin fabric of my shirt. I flush. Can she see that this is turning me on? Is it weird that I want her to know?

I startle when she reaches out and runs a hand over my head, petting me like I'm my safeword's namesake. The dull heat flares to life even more at this small touch and I almost gasp.

I want her to do it again. I want to feel it everywhere.

She lets out a low chuckle, no doubt reading my thoughts from the way I unconsciously lean into her hand.

"So beautiful. You're doing so well."

The words are so genuine, it takes my breath away. She pets me again, then removes her hand and goes back to whatever she's doing on her phone. Her praise is like a weighted blanket, quieting my mind.

I don't know how long it goes on like this, Blair occasionally sipping water then handing it back to me, with small touches in between. I'm floating in a strange feeling of warmth and anticipation, with barely a thought for the dull ache that's building from sitting on the floor.

"How do you feel, Grace?" Blair's voice feels distant, and I have to pull myself out of my reverie to formulate a coherent reply.

"Good." I turn my head and smile at her, my heart stuttering at the matching one I see on her face. She looks so pleased, and I made her feel that way.

"Wonderful. Let's stop there for tonight."

I blink back at her, confusion seeping back in. "What?"

Blair gives me an indulgent smile. "It's been almost an hour."

My mouth falls open. "No way. Really?" It felt like maybe twenty minutes max. I look down at the glass in my hands to see that it's empty.

Her lips curve up. "You're a natural." She stands and offers me a hand, which is good because my legs are stiff from sitting on the floor for so long.

"But I didn't do anything," I protest. I don't get why she's praising me for sitting on the floor and zoning out.

She narrows her eyes. "You submitted to my orders. You let go enough to lose track of time. I wouldn't call that not doing anything."

"I guess I expected more..." Touching? Sex? I mean, I'm ridiculously turned on for someone who just spent the last hour being a living cupholder, but it's not at all what I was anticipating.

Blair cocks a brow at me and I change course. "I wasn't lying when I said I'm interested in the things I picked on the list. I know I'm not experienced with them, but that doesn't mean I don't want to try them. With you." After she seemed confused by my interest in sex, I feel like it's necessary to tack on that clarification again.

She nods. "I know. And I want to do them with you."

The surge of pleasure I get from hearing her confirm she wants me like that is a little embarrassing. But what can I say? I like being desired. Being desired by the hottest woman I've ever met, who could probably have anyone she wants, is a heady rush.

A soft smile spreads across my lips. "Then why didn't you do them?"

"Patience, Grace. You had a shitty first attempt at trying out kink. I wanted to give you a chance to experience the feeling of submission without any elements that would make you worry you weren't doing a good job."

That's... kind of brilliant.

I snort. "You think the only thing I wouldn't worry about screwing up is drinking a glass of water and sitting on the floor for an hour?"

She smirks back at me, sitting down on the couch and gesturing for me to join her. Even though we're out of the scene, it's natural to follow her lead. Once I'm seated, she reaches out and places her hand on my thigh. It's a casual gesture undoubtedly meant to comfort, but fuck me, if it doesn't kick up a flutter of excitement in my stomach.

I fight against the blush threatening to darken my cheeks as she leaves her hand resting there and speaks. "Some people would've fought against my commands. You didn't. Your list told me you want to submit and serve, and you did that beautifully tonight. We have plenty of time to explore the rest."

"Y-yeah," I murmur, losing the battle against showing how her praise affects me.

Her hand on my thigh squeezes almost imperceptibly. If I weren't so aware of her touch, I wouldn't have noticed. I wet my lips, and she tracks the movement with intense focus.

"Tell me. How did it make you feel?"

"Wh-what? It was good."

She shakes her head. "Good could mean anything. Good is what you tell someone when they ask you how your week's been and you don't want to take the time to detail how it sucked."

I laugh, but she's right. It was more than good. It was... "It made me feel strange. At first I was tense because I was confused. Which, by the way, what was up with the water?"

"You never remember to drink enough water. I thought it'd be good to start the scene off with some hydration." She shrugs, a twinkle of amusement behind her eyes.

"I thought maybe you were going to dump it on me. Or make me drink until I had to pee my pants," I grumble.

Her brow furrows. "You said no watersports or humiliation on the checklist. Why would you think that?"

"I don't know!" I say, throwing my hands up. "I always think about the worst-case scenario. It's kinda like that weird feeling you get when you're up high and looking over the edge of something that tells you to jump."

"The call of the void."

"Huh?"

"That's what that phenomenon is called."

"Oh wow, really? That's pretty metal."

"Yes." She squeezes my thigh purposely this time, refocusing me. "Now, let's go back to my question."

"Right. Sorry." There's a flicker of embarrassment about the way my mind likes to chase random conversation topics rather than stay focused, but I can't always help it. "After I realized you weren't going to do that, I felt a little awkward. Shocking, I know." I pause for a beat, gathering the courage to be fully honest. "Then I felt… warm. Every time you said something nice, it was like you were caressing me the same way you did when you stroked my hair."

Blair turns to face me more, and as she scoots a little closer, her hand slides up my thigh. I'm not sure she's noticed, but that's all I can think about now. "That's exactly how I hoped you'd feel. Was that everything you experienced?"

The loaded question and the way her eyes lock on mine make me feel like I'm going to spontaneously combust. I can chicken out and say that's all I felt, but I think she already knows the truth.

"No." My heart thumps so hard I think it's going to burst out of my chest. "It turned me on. It made me wish you'd touch me other places."

"Fuck," Blair whispers, the curse so soft it sounds involuntary. Her eyes drop to my lips. I shift closer, and she leans in.

She's going to kiss me. I want her to kiss me. I don't think I've ever wanted anything more in my life.

19

BLAIR

Grace's blood sings to me, drawing me closer. The lure of her mouth is even stronger. Fuck, I want to touch her everywhere she'll let me. Soft caresses and rough grasping. Pain, pleasure, teasing, and torture. I want to give her all of it.

My mind is so clouded with desire that I almost do it.

But I can't. She's riding the high of our first scene. No matter how insignificant she thought it was, it impacted her. When she comes down, she might regret asking for more right away. We're not mistress and submissive right now—we're Blair and Grace. I shouldn't blur that line.

But god, I want to.

Her breath hitches as I lean in, and I linger for a few seconds, then pull back with a reluctant smile. "I'll remember that for next time."

Her eyelids are half-closed and her lips are still slightly parted, and I feel like an asshole for not giving her what she wants. Grace flushes as she realizes I've moved away, and her posture stiffens.

"R-right. That'd be good. When will next time be?"

Her eagerness is adorable. "I have work most nights this week. Saturday is monster night at The Vault, and I haven't been to the last few ones, so I was planning on going."

Grace's smile flickers. "Of course. You should definitely go. That'll be fun."

She absolutely doesn't sound like she likes the idea. We agreed on exclusivity while I'm teaching her, outside what I do for work. Like I'd want to do this with anyone else in my free time, when I could be doing it with her. Is it wrong that her apparent jealousy feels good? I don't want Grace to doubt me, but I like that she wants me for herself.

"I'd like for you to come with me," I clarify.

"Oh!" She perks back up immediately. "Yeah. I'd love to if I'm allowed. Not sure how that works since I'm not a, uh, a monster."

"You're allowed. As long as you know about our existence and are accompanied by a monster member of the club, you're good."

Grace's eyes sparkle with delight. "Whoa, cool! Does that mean I'll get to see other kinds of monsters while we're there?"

I chuckle, glad the thought seems to intrigue rather than frighten her. "Yes. Though I hope that most of the time you'll be too preoccupied to gawk at them."

"Right." Her cheeks are as pink as her shirt now. I love it. Grace's smile broadens. "I don't know, depends on what kind of monsters are there. I've read some pretty hot minotaur smut."

I pretend to consider, bringing a hand to my chin. "There's a minotaur that goes, but sadly for you, he's taken. No beef for you."

She giggles at my terrible joke and the bubbly sound makes me wonder if her blood tastes like champagne. I'd happily get drunk on it. Hell, I'm already intoxicated from listening to her.

"That's alright. I've always been partial to vampires," she says lightly.

"Is that so?" I do my best to not sound relieved, though the idea of her preferring someone else, someone less dangerous, has crossed my mind.

She grins mischievously, letting me know I'm in for a joke as terrible as the one I made. "Yeah. I love sparkly things! You do too, right, Bella?"

I groan. "You had to bring that up, didn't you?"

Grace's grin widens. "Uh, yeah. You're a vampire and your kink name is Bella. I'd bet anything that you were obsessed with Twilight."

"I have a dark sense of humor, in case you hadn't realized that yet," I say drolly.

Everyone who knows I'm a vampire and that I use Bella as my pseudonym asks the same thing. Each time I play it off as something ironic. Which it is, but it's also a reminder to myself. I let myself get caught up in the romance of stories like Twilight, ignoring every single red flag for the sake of chasing the feeling of being unique and wanted. I don't care what anyone says, looking back on it now, Edward was a predator beyond his vampiric nature. The power and age differential between him and Bella allowed him to prey on a teenage girl. He was a true monster, and while it was only a silly story, it helped groom me for mistreatment by an actual vampire.

"Hmm, I get the sense that there's more going on there," Grace says, not buying my answer. Am I that easy for her to read?

I sigh. "I'm Bella because I was obsessed with Twilight, and that obsession plus general lack of support and affection at the time made me end up how I am now. It's a reminder not to let romantic fantasy cloud my judgment."

Grace's brow furrows. "Hold on. You weren't, uh, turned into a vampire voluntarily?"

Right. I guess it'd make sense that she'd assume I chose this. A dark laugh escapes me. "Technically, you could argue I did. Though, I don't think a person who has been groomed and misled their entire relationship can give real consent."

"Oh god, Blair..." Grace reaches out and touches my hand, her eyes full of concern. I've spent so much time and energy rebuilding myself after I was turned that the intensity of her reaction takes me by surprise.

"It's fine," I say, shaking off her sympathy. "I've accepted what happened and what I am now."

She frowns. "That doesn't mean it was okay."

I don't like her feeling bad for me. I want to reach out and smooth the furrows forming on her brow. "I know that," I sigh. "Trust me, I know. I'm past it."

"Alright." Grace says, sounding like she doesn't quite believe me. She pulls her hand back and I want to grab it and hold on to it so I can stay connected to her. "Doesn't seem to me like someone who has moved on would use a name that reminds her of her trauma," she grumbles.

"You're right." Grace looks surprised that I admit that so freely. "What happened irreparably changed me. What I meant by moving past it is that my trauma doesn't control me. It doesn't define me."

Grace nods, and I think that's the end of that discussion, but her eyes drop to her hands in her lap and she speaks, much softer this time. "How did you get to that point? How did you figure out how to not let it define you?"

It's not a hypothetical question. There's worry and a tinge of shame behind it. "Is this about your ex-husband?" I ask.

She lets out a wry laugh. "No. I mean, I know I have a lot of baggage from that mess and it'll take me a while to figure that out. I was thinking about my neck. I... It's a struggle to accept that it's never going to get better. I know it's nowhere near as traumatic and life changing as what happened to you. I'm not saying it is. I just don't want it to define me, like you said, and I haven't been able to figure out how."

The sadness and worry in Grace's eyes makes me wish I had the answer. "I..."

Grace shakes her head, her expression morphing into a tight smile. "Sorry! I didn't mean it like I expected you to know. I'll figure it out. I'll be fine."

"It's okay to not be fine," I say, but it doesn't seem to get past the guard she's put back in place.

"Yeah. Well, with all that said, I still don't know if Bella's the right fit for you."

"Really?" I ask, cocking an intrigued brow.

She's back to her cheeky smile, any hint of vulnerability hidden away. "Yeah. You're more of an Éowyn."

I give her a confused frown. "Who is that?"

Grace gasps in horror. "What?! Haven't you seen Lord of the Rings?"

"Ah. I didn't realize you were as much of a nerd as Mona is. My bad," I deadpan, delighting in the scowl Grace gives me in response.

"Not 'as much of a nerd'! I'll have you know I'm the one who got her into LOTR."

"LOTR?" I ask, even though I can deduce what she means.

"That's it, forget teaching me kink. We're getting together and watching the movies instead. I seriously can't believe that you don't know what I'm talking about." Grace throws her hands up in exasperation. "'I am no man'?"

I give her a blank look. It sounds vaguely familiar, but I enjoy seeing her all worked up.

"Ugh, fine, stay Bella." She crosses her arms across her chest, looking at me like my lack of Lord of the Rings knowledge is a personal affront.

I shrug. "I like being Bella." Grace gives me a disbelieving look and I let out a sigh. "The world tells women that the most important and precious thing they can experience is the love and desire of a man. Bella embodies that mentality. So every time I use her name and take back my power, it helps me remember that's bullshit."

"Oh. Well, in that case, I guess it's okay," Grace says softly. "Still, you're watching those movies with me."

"Fine," I say with an exaggerated sigh. That's two things I've agreed to watch with Grace now. Soon my life will be consumed by spending time with her. The thought makes me far more happy than I'd like to admit. "But I'm still teaching you," I add.

"Yes, Mistress," Grace says coyly, looking at me through her eyelashes. "If you don't have anywhere to go, we could start now."

"I don't have any other plans." That's not entirely true. I have client emails and texts to reply to, but that can wait. If Grace is asking me to stay longer, I'm not leaving. Especially since no small part of me feared that she'd be weirded out after our first scene and then avoid me for a while. Everything about tonight has been a pleasant surprise.

"Okay! Let me go change into something more comfortable."

I raise a brow at Grace, and she flushes, then lets out something between a giggle and a snort. "Don't worry, I don't mean it that way. I'm gonna put on some pajama bottoms because these pants are cute, but uncomfortable."

I try not to read too much into the fact that she wore them to look nice for me, appreciating the view of her ass in said cute pants as she heads out of the room to go get changed. While she's gone, I pull a small insulated mug from my purse and take a few swigs. I need something to help me keep my composure, because after the scene, it's much harder to resist the urge to pull Grace close and sink my teeth into her.

She's back before I know it, settling in on the couch right next to me. Grace grabs a blanket from the back of the sofa and drapes over herself, then gives me a questioning look. "You want to share?"

I'm about to point out that I don't need to worry about feeling cold because I'm dead, but stop myself and nod. She hands an edge of the blanket to me, scooting closer so there's enough for both of us. Her thigh presses against mine, her body heat seeping into me. I'd hold my breath, but it's no use. With Grace this close, her sweet, tart scent envelops me.

We watch the first thirty minutes of the movie, but I can't focus on the fantasy world on the screen. Grace makes comments and glances over at me occasionally to see my reaction, and I do my best to appear interested. I'm sure the movie is fine, but the woman sitting next to me is much more compelling.

When I can't take it anymore, I scoot away and pull my mug back out of my bag, bringing it up to my lips with a slight tremor in my hands. I drink the remaining contents, but it doesn't do much to quench my thirst or calm my instinct to devour Grace.

She watches me wipe my mouth and put the mug back in my purse with keen attention. "You're thirsty? Even after all that water?" Grace teases, but there's a hint of a rasp in her voice.

"Yeah." My voice is thick with restrained desire, and I clear my throat. "It's draining to consume anything other than blood, though water usually isn't too bad. If anything, it made me thirstier."

Grace's eyes fall to my mouth, and she swallows heavily. "Do you need more?"

She shouldn't ask me that. It sounds too much like an offer. I always need more. In Grace's case, I'm certain I could drain her dry and still want more of her. "Yeah," I say quietly.

The hobbits and whoever else is with them are forgotten, a dull drone in the background that can't hide the rapid beat of her heart. She extends her wrist toward me, and time slows.

Bite her.

Taste her.

Consume her.

I jump up from the couch, moving away from her outstretched hand like it's a poisonous snake about to strike.

"Are you okay?" Grace asks, brow furrowing. "Did I do something wrong?"

"No!" *Shit.* "I, uh, I remembered I have a meeting with a client tonight." It's a flimsy lie, but I have to get out of here while I'm still in control.

She doesn't seem to question it, and the blood in my stomach roils unpleasantly from lying to her. "Oh crap, okay." Grace turns off the video, and stands, walking me to the front door, where she gives me a shy smile. "Thanks again for tonight."

"It was my pleasure," I say, doing my best to keep my mouth as closed as possible so my fangs don't show.

"See you on Saturday?" She says it like it's a question and she's worried I changed my mind.

I give a curt nod. "Yes. I'll text you the details." Her arms lift slightly, no doubt preparing to give me a hug. I dodge backward out of the door gracelessly, and give her a wave and a tense smile. "Goodnight."

Her smile flickers, but then it's forced back in place. "Night!"

Fuck, I hate the way she's looking at me, masking her confusion and disappointment. I can't keep doing that to her. When I get home and my mind is clearer, I'll do my best to explain. She'll undoubtedly call our arrangement off, but my impulses tonight have shown me that's clearly for the best.

20

GRACE

After a night of fitful sleep spent dreaming about Blair telling me she changed her mind, she's not interested in me, and deciding that she'd rather not talk to me at all, I'm terrified when I wake up to see a voice memo from her.

She's only ever texted me before, so that's got to be a bad sign. Oh god, the dreams were prophetic. I knew Blair seemed off when she left. She didn't have to go meet with a client, she just wanted to get away from me.

I hug the blankets tighter around my body as if they'll insulate me from whatever hurt is coming my way, and press play.

"Hey Grace."

Blair's voice is as sexy as the rest of her—even and melodic, with a hint of a rasp.

"To start, you didn't do anything wrong, and this isn't a message telling you I'm not going to be your domme."

The relief I feel is palpable. Warm tingles replace the dread that had pooled in my gut. She knows I'd freak out, so she said what I needed to know right away.

"I think you'll be the one to change your mind, though, after I tell you this."

The resignation in her tone makes it clear she thinks that will be the case. But what could she tell me that would make me change my mind? We've already talked through everything. Last night went really well, aside from her running away mid-movie.

"I've told you before that being a vampire means I have urges that can be difficult to control. The desire to feed is always there, and I've learned to manage it so it doesn't become a problem. But... it's very difficult with you, Grace. Last night, I wanted your blood. Not just a taste to satisfy a reasonable thirst. The monster inside me told me to consume you. That's why I left so fast. I can't hurt you. I won't."

My breath halts at her grim, determined words. What does she mean by consume?

"You've given me your trust, and I'm terrified I'll break it. I..." She takes in a shaky breath. Her voice is tight as she continues, like she's choking back a sob. "I killed someone. The night after I was turned, I woke up alone and disoriented. My sire, the man who made me into a vampire, the person I thought loved me, was nowhere to be found. I was scared, but more than that, I was *hungry*. Someone knocked on the door, and I didn't think, I just... the instinct to feed overwhelmed me and I grabbed them. Drank from them until there was nothing left but a cold, lifeless body in my arms and the horror at what I'd done."

Oh god. Tears slide down my cheeks, and the hand holding my phone shakes as I listen to Blair's grim confession.

"What I did is unforgivable. You don't want me to get close to you. I'm a monster, Grace." A muffled sobs burst from her and the memo cuts off abruptly.

I stare at my phone, stunned by the devastation in Blair's voice. My chest aches knowing she's had to bear the weight of pain and shame from such a horrific experience.

I have to do something.

I dial Blair's number, heavy tears plopping down onto the phone screen as I hold it up to my ear. It's after sunrise, but I can't wait. I'm not even sure what I'm going to say, but I need to talk to her now.

After five rings, she picks up. "Grace?" Blair's voice is a hoarse croak. She must've been asleep.

"Was that the only time?" I ask, the words coming out of me in a rush.

There's a moment of silence before she replies. "Yes, but—"

"You haven't killed anyone else?" I ask, needing to confirm what I already suspected.

"Not since that first time, no. I attacked more people in the weeks after I was turned, but didn't drain them. I regained control. But Grace, it's always there, inside me. You're not safe with—"

I don't let her finish. I'm not letting her torture herself more. I can't imagine the trauma and horror of realizing you've accidentally killed someone. Of course she's riddled with guilt. I don't know how I'd cope after that either. But there's one thing I'm certain of.

Blair is not a danger to me.

"You are *not* a monster." I surprise myself with the forcefulness of my tone. "You said it yourself. You were alone and confused and you had no one to help you. It's a miracle you didn't kill anyone else, and even if you had, it wouldn't have been your fault. That death isn't on your hands. It's on the hands of the bastard who turned you and then abandoned you."

You'd think I'd be more shaken. That I'd be horrified to know that Blair's vampiric nature has caused her to kill. But all I feel is certainty. Something deep inside me tells me I can trust her.

"You've never told anyone about this before, have you?" I ask, softening my voice. There's no way Mona would've heard her story and not had the same reaction as me.

Blair lets out a shuddering exhale. "No. I didn't want to scare people away. Besides, I thought I had it under control. But every time we're together, the monster inside me begs me to feed from you. I've never felt such a craving like this before. Not even that first night."

My mind latches on the last part of her statement. The intensity of her desire for my blood should scare me, but instead something hot builds in my core. "How is it different?" I need to know.

"It's... fuck, Grace." Blair lets out a sound that's a mix between a groan and a dark laugh. My body floods with more heat. "It's like you're the most decadent dessert in the world, and all I've eaten for ages is stale bread. You're temptation incarnate."

"Oh." I'm so flustered that it takes my brain a second to reboot.

Blair mistakes that reaction for something other than arousal. "I know it's frightening to hear that a vampire wants your blood that desperately."

"You know you can eat dessert in moderation, right? If we follow your metaphor, a dessert like that usually gets savored. It's too rich to eat all at once."

"I..."

"I'm not scared of you, Blair. What you're describing doesn't sound like monstrous hunger. It sounds more like a craving you need to sate. I bet that if you do it once, you'll realize that's all it is."

The thought cools my arousal. I'm a craving. Once she has me, will she move on to something better like everyone else?

"It's not safe. What if you're wrong and I lose control? I can't..." Blair's voice cracks as she trails off.

"You won't. You have the strongest willpower of anyone I've ever met." If I knew where she lived, I'd be on my way over to her place and busting down into her basement to show her right now that she won't hurt me.

"I can teach you about kink without drinking your blood," she says feebly, and that's the first thing she's said in this conversation that I don't believe. If we keep doing this, it will happen eventually.

"I don't want that. I want it all, Blair." I pause, trying to figure out how to convince her. "We could... Oh! We're going to that monster night at the kink club. Surely someone there can be on standby to intervene if you lose control? You're a badass, but I bet a burly monster could pry me from your clutches if need be."

There's a long pause, followed by an almost inaudible sigh. "Okay."

"Really?" I expected her to argue more, despite my sound logic.

"Yes. I don't want to fight this... I want to give you what you need." She doesn't say that she'll also be getting what she wants, but it's evident in the rasp of her voice. "I can ask Max. He owes me."

"Wait, hold on, *Max?*" My best friend's fiancé isn't exactly who I imagined when I made the suggestion. I was thinking more like that minotaur she mentioned. I can't have Max there when I'm doing this sort of thing. It'd be too weird!

"Yes. As a half-succubus, he can sense strong emotions, so he'll be able to tell if I'm about to lose control without needing to be in the room with us."

"Oh shit, I forgot about that. No wonder he's so good at reading people. It makes sense, but I don't know if I'll ever be able to look him in the eyes again. "Won't that be too awkward?" I ask.

Blair chuckles, some of the casual ease of her normal tone finally returning. "I've stood guard enough times for him and Mona during some of their more... intense scenes. He has no room to judge anything we do. Also, he's a private investigator, so he's probably seen and heard it all."

"Alright..." I'm still cringing at the thought, but I don't want to argue when she's gone from proclaiming she's too dangerous to agreeing to try feeding from me despite her fears. If this is what it takes, I'll deal with my embarrassment. "We need to make sure Mona is alright with it, too."

"I'll talk to them both." Blair pauses for a long moment, then continues. "I'm sorry, Grace," she says, her voice thick again. "I didn't want to burden you with my trauma, but I needed you to know what I am."

"Nothing you've told me is a burden." A tear slides down my cheek at how lonely and in pain Blair must've been since she became a vampire. From what she's said about her life before that, I don't know if she's ever felt safe enough to trust someone with her emotions.

"You matter to me. That includes the painful, difficult parts of you that you hide. That's what it means to be..." I almost say friends, but she feels like much more than that to me now. "That's what it means to truly care for someone unconditionally. You take everything that makes someone who they are—the light, the dark, and all the murky things in between—and you accept them."

"I..." Blair's voice cracks as she trails off. Her breath shudders audibly on the other end of the call. It feels like there's a myriad of things she wants to say, but what comes out is a soft, achingly vulnerable, "Thank you."

I'm crying hard now, tears streaming down my face both for Blair's pain and for the sudden recognition of my own. It was easy to say those words to her and know their truth, but I've never been able to apply them to myself. I accepted the conditional love doled out sparingly by my ex-husband, even though in the core of my being I knew that wasn't genuine care. I'm mad at myself that it took five years and him asking for a divorce so he could be with the woman he was cheating on me with to see it.

I sniffle and wipe at my tears with the hem of my sleep shirt. "Alright, now that that's all settled, I should let you get back to sleep." It's a sunny day already, and I don't know a ton about vampires, but it's probably very difficult for her to be up right now.

"Okay," Blair replies, her exhaustion apparent in the croak of her voice.

"Talk to you later. Sweet dreams." I don't want to hang up, but I know I need to.

"For once, they might actually be sweet," Blair murmurs with a sigh before hanging up.

21

BLAIR

We're going to The Vault tonight. I've arranged everything with Max and Mona, who both readily agreed to help. Max, because he knows he literally owes me his life, and Mona because she's obsessed with the idea of "her two best friends being together". Her words, not mine. It makes my undead heart squeeze whenever she says I'm her best friend. I've never been anyone's best anything, outside my professional life.

I told her about my fear of harming Grace, and while I tried to leave out the more gruesome details of my past, she came right out and asked me what happened that would make me worry. That was the second time telling someone I'm a murderer, and both times I didn't get the reaction I anticipated. Grace was the epitome of kindness and empathy, and Mona... she rolled her eyes at me and told me I was being ridiculous.

I'm beginning to realize she might be right. It's difficult to feel like anything other than a monster, when I dream about that horrific night far too often, but it's hard to argue when I'm two for two with people I trust telling me that's not the case.

I've built what I thought was an impenetrable exterior both to shield myself from getting hurt again or letting myself hurt others, and now that it's cracking, I feel off-balance.

I'm *feeling* more in general. My confession and subsequent call with Grace was the first time I'd cried in over five years. It's easier to laugh freely when Mona makes a joke. I even send Nic an apology for my rude rebuffing of his offer to help with my garden, and am flooded with unfamiliar warmth when he readily accepts it and I find the next day that the lights are installed and he's left a note wishing me a good weekend. If I'd seen him in person, I might've hugged him.

Me. Hugging someone. *Voluntarily.*

I don't know what to do with this version of myself. I worry that if I don't find a way to shore up my defenses again, I'll lose all the control I've worked so hard for. Letting people in and allowing my emotions to lead me has never ended well, and yet, I find it much harder to shut myself off again now that I've received a taste of care.

If I'm not careful, I'll become as ravenous for that feeling as I am for Grace's blood.

I'm still not sure letting myself bite her is a good idea. After some negotiation—me suggesting we wait a little longer before I bite her, and Grace insisting that it be the first thing we do tonight to get the fuss over with—we've settled on doing it toward the end of our scene. That way, if it's too much for me and I need to change my mind, Grace will still get more of the experiences she's eager to explore.

For all my skill at being a domme, I'm finding it difficult to refuse Grace anything she asks.

God, I'm already so far gone for her. I can feel the hurt and disappointment that'll happen when Grace decides to move on to someone else coming from miles away, like a train barreling towards me, and instead of stepping off the tracks, I'm voluntarily tying myself to them.

THE VAULT'S parking lot is crowded when I pull up to the club. I drove here alone, since Mona insisted Grace ride with her and Max. I'm not sure if it was for moral support or to grill her on everything that was going on between us. I hope she doesn't freak Grace out too much with her enthusiasm.

The bouncer lets me in with a quick nod hello, and I linger for a moment in the short, dark hallway that connects the entrance area with the club's main room. I can already hear the dull thrum of moody, bass-heavy music through the door at the end of the hall, and the vibrations send goosebumps skittering across my skin.

I frown at the unusual, involuntary reaction. Since I died, my body doesn't respond to stimuli in the same way it did in life unless I dedicate energy from the blood I've consumed to make it happen. I haven't felt the hairs raise on my arms since I died.

Is that a good or bad sign?

I inhale as deeply as I can and hold the air inside me for a long moment before exhaling with a powerful sigh.

It'll be okay.

I'm in control.
Grace wants this.
I want this.
Max and Mona will keep her safe in case something goes wrong.

I open the door at the end of the hallway and let the blast of moody club music wash over me as I walk inside, the energy of the space transforming me from Blair to Mistress Bella. My shoulders roll back, and my hips sway as I take purposeful strides in my black stiletto boots.

I'm aware of the appreciative eyes that land on me, but I don't pay attention to the monsters lounging and mingling in the large, open room. Mona stands and waves from the same set of couches we sat together at before, though she didn't need to. I knew where they were the second I entered the room, my instincts honing in on Grace's presence immediately. Grace turns her head as she follows Mona's movement and we lock eyes.

Time slows and my vision tunnels, my heightened senses so focused on the blonde across the room that I almost stumble in my heels. It feels like everyone in the room can sense the tension stretched between us in this moment, taught as a bowstring.

And then Grace's lips curve into a shy, excited smile and it breaks. I smile back, knowing that it goes against the stern domme persona most people here expect of me. I don't care what any of them think. All I care about is her.

Grace and Max join Mona in standing, the bubbly blonde giving me a small wave as I approach. Mona's demonic fiance nods in greeting, but I can barely acknowledge it because…

Fuck, she's gorgeous.

Grace has on a hot pink dress that clings to every curve of her body. It's clear she's not wearing a bra from the way the fabric molds to her breasts, the neckline dipping so low that if she were to lean forward, you'd see a hint of her nipples. It makes me want to bite and suck at the generous swell of her tits until she's breathless and aching for more.

My eyes fall to the gentle curve of her low belly. God, I don't know if there's anything sexier than seeing the outline of her softness just waiting to be unwrapped and worshiped. There's no panty line, which means she's bare underneath, and fuck if that doesn't make me want me to have her sit back down and spread her legs so I can feast on her pussy right here in the middle of the club.

Who am I kidding? I'm greedy. The only one I want to witness Grace come undone is me. Even letting Max monitor our scene makes the possessive part of me bristle, though it's necessary.

I wet my lips and resist the urge to grab Grace and haul her off right now to the private playroom I reserved for tonight.

"Bella!" Mona pulls me into a hug, snapping me out of my lust-addled thoughts. Her campfire scent is a balm to frayed nerves I didn't even realize I had. With her mouth close to my ear, she holds me in place for a moment. "You've got this," she whispers, before squeezing me and pulling back to give me a meaningful look.

"Good to see you, Grace." I direct the words to Mona, but Grace answers.

"Good to see you—shit, that's so confusing." Grace crosses her arms in frustration and glares at Mona. "You need to change your kink name if I'm going to come here more often."

Max lets out a soft chuckle, and slides in next to Mona, wrapping an arm around her waist and squeezing her hip. "I agree. Let's pick something else... maybe Siren?"

Mona's golden brown cheeks darken as he practically purrs the name idea at her. "Yeah, that could work."

"There we go. Problem solved," Max says, giving her a heated smile that makes her flush even darker.

I hope they can stay focused when I need them to monitor me and Grace later. I swear those two are always seconds away from tearing each other's clothes off. Or rather, Max tearing Mona's off while she pretends to beg him not to.

"You look perfect, Rose," I say softly, while our friends are distracted.

"So do you," she whispers back, her eyes dropping down my body, then back up to my face, with a shy smile that spreads slowly into a wider grin. "How the heck do you even get into something like that?"

I wore something more suited to my domme persona tonight, both because we'd be out in public and because Grace seemed a little disappointed I didn't give her the full experience of Mistress Bella for our first scene. My black latex catsuit is high-necked and full coverage, with only my arms bare.

I laugh at her question. "A lot of patience and lube," I say, loving her flustered reaction. "Not nearly as sexy as it sounds," I add. "But at least I don't have to worry about sweating since I'm a vampire."

"Speaking of vampires... I thought you said it was monster night, but I haven't seen anyone who looks, uh, non-human," Grace says, her eyes scanning the room, a flicker of nervous curiosity.

"Oh, don't worry, you're surrounded by them," Mona says with a cheerful laugh.

Grace's brows shoot up, and she scoots a little closer to me. "Wait, really?"

It makes my breath hitch, both from the hit of her delectable scent and from her instinctual reaction to go to me for protection. I'm one of the most dangerous monsters in here, and yet she feels safe with me.

I don't understand it, but god, I fucking love it. My fingers twitch with the urge to draw her against me and whisper that she has nothing to worry about. That I can handle any threat that dares come her way—which they won't, considering I'm with her. My reputation of not tolerating bullshit is well established at The Vault, both with regular and monster patrons.

"Yeah," Mona says with a laugh at Grace's surprise. "They stop letting people in after 11, and then do a quick security check to make sure everyone is good to let down their glamors or shift. Things get pretty wild then, but you'll most likely be otherwise occupied." She waggles her eyebrows at me and Grace.

"If you'd rather wait a while so you can see—"

Grace shakes her head emphatically. "No! Uh, I mean, it'd be cool to see that, but I'd much rather... get started. With you." She adds the last part with a small, nervous smile that makes my chest squeeze.

I nod. "Then, we'll get started." This time I do reach out and touch her, just the tips of my fingers resting against the small of her back. I expect her to tense at my touch, but some of the tension in her posture melts.

Fuck, she's already so responsive to me and we haven't even started. I don't know how I'll make it through tonight without completely losing myself to my obsession with this woman.

"You two ready?" I ask the couple next to us and they nod in unison. No going back now. A burst of nerves explode in my stomach. "Rose, will you go ahead with Siren? Maybe she can give you a tour of the private playroom area. I need to talk to our demon friend for a second."

Grace tilts her head a little in a silent question and I do my best to not show my tension in the smile I give in return. When Mona leads her off, I follow her with my eyes until Max softly clears his throat.

"Right," I say, looking back at the redhead, who's giving me a questioning look.

"You're scared," he whispers, and despite no one being close enough to overhear us, I still stiffen. "Sorry, I know it's not my place to dive into your emotions, but Mona loves you and I like you even though you're not a fan of me, so I need to help if I can."

He's wrong. I didn't like or trust him at first, and it took a long time seeing him treat Mona with nothing but adoration and respect to accept that he's not a bad guy. But I like Max now. Not nearly as much as Grace or Mona, but he's tolerable. For all his abilities to sense emotions, I'm surprised he hasn't noticed the change yet.

I don't correct him. I've had too many soft emotions lately. I don't need to pile a fondness for Max onto them.

"You are helping. I wanted to double-check you know what to do in case..."

Max nods. "I do. If you want, you can try to charm me to be certain that it still doesn't work."

As someone who is half succubus and has studied a good amount of magic, Max is almost entirely resistant to compulsions. Still, it's a good idea to make sure. I tap into the power in my blood and lock eyes with him, channeling the full force of my mental domination into it. "Kneel."

His lips twitch. "Nope, nothing."

"Good." That still doesn't address my concern that he won't be able to overpower me enough to pull me away from Grace if I go into a frenzy while feeding from her.

I don't have to say it. Max picks up on my worry immediately. "Someone I know from a monster group I'm a part of is here tonight. He's a minotaur. I could ask him to stand guard with me. His partner is a human, and she's friendly with Mona, so they could hang out while we monitor you. That way, if something does happen..."

A minotaur could definitely restrain me. As for the rest, I get what he's not saying. Max is trying to prevent me from terrifying both of my friends if things go horribly wrong.

A surge of affection and appreciation for the considerate demon bubbles up inside me.

Max gives me a surprised smile, and he looks like he might try to give me a hug, so I hold my hand up to stop him. "Thank you, Max. That'd be good."

He smiles and nods. "Okay. I'll go grab him," he says, but lingers in place like he's debating saying something else.

"What?" I ask, my tone a bit too sharp.

"It's going to be okay," Max says solemnly. "Grace cares about you, and I don't have to be an empath to know you'd do anything for her."

I want to protest that there's no way he can know what I'll do when the monster inside me gets a taste of Grace's blood, but his adamance is mildly reassuring.

All the pieces are in place to keep Grace safe. Now all that's left is to let myself take the risk, knowing that in one night, I could destroy my fragile hope for something good if I'm not strong enough to stay in control.

22

GRACE

"Don't be too nervous. A little nervous is good, though. Hell, I felt like I was going to barf the first time I came here and Blair tied me up for a demo and I didn't even have more than a tiny crush on her. Sorry, is that weird to bring up right now? I swear she only has eyes for you and I love her, but as a friend. She's amazing and you're amazing, and I'm so happy for you two. Don't worry about the sex stuff. If you overthink too much, then you won't give yourself the chance to actually feel whether you like it. As cheesy as it sounds, try to let your body guide you. You have to promise to tell me what it feels like to be bitten. Speaking of which, if you need anything at all, I'll be out here with

Max. Not that you'll need it! Everything will be great. You'll have so much fun, I—"

I grab Mona's shoulders. "Mona. Calm down." She's been a nonstop stream of reassurances and encouragement since she led me to the hallway lined with doors on each side, and paused at one with a solid red wood door at the far end. It looms ominously in front of us, but I barely have the capacity to think about that because of how much my best friend is freaking out.

"Sorry," she says with a sheepish laugh.

I give her arms a squeeze. "It's okay. I get it. I'd be the same way if the situation were reversed." I'd probably be even worse.

Mona nods, her expression growing serious. "I love you and want you to be happy. It's... it's been a long time since I've seen you excited about anything like this."

"Yeah, divorce will do that to you." I let out a humorless laugh.

"It's been longer than that. That bastard never deserved you, and I could kill him for how he crushed your heart."

I shrug. She's expressed a similar sentiment before, but unlike in the past, I don't feel the same seething rage and hurt. The pain of the past is still there, but it's muted to a dull ache. The romantic part of my heart has started to bud again, despite my fear that nothing would ever grow there again after Zack destroyed it. And it's because of Blair, and my faith that she'll keep it safe. Even if she ends up not being the one to help me tend and grow it back to full bloom, I trust she won't do anything to make it wither again.

"He doesn't matter now," I say, hoping that the words are the truth.

Mona smiles softly. "No. He doesn't." Her eyes light up a moment later. "Oh! They're coming." She tugs me into a crushing hug and gives me one last "it's going to be great" before releasing me.

I turn and see Blair and Max, accompanied by two other people I don't recognize—a tall, muscular Black man with a glinting nose ring, his hand placed possessively on the back of a significantly shorter, curvaceous White woman with faded pink hair.

"Oh! I didn't know you'd be here tonight, Ari," Mona says with a warm smile to the woman. There's no one nearby, so I'm guessing we're using real names, not kink pseudonyms.

The man who looks like he's in the gym at least two hours a day gives her a dazzling smile. "Wouldn't miss it. Ever since you showed her this place, she hasn't stopped talking about it."

The woman next to him rolls her eyes. "More like I told him once and then he kept suggesting we come together."

"If you keep rolling your eyes at me, there definitely won't be any coming together tonight, baby girl," he says, giving her hip a squeeze.

"Ariana, Wesley, this is my best friend, Grace. Wesley and Max are in a monster support group, so Ari, Caleb, and I started our own group for people with monster partners. Mostly to talk about how ridiculous they are," Mona says with a laugh.

"Oh, that's really cool! Nice to meet you both," I say, my friendly mask sliding in place atop my nerves. I almost miss Blair stiffening as Mona speaks, and I can't tell if she's uncomfortable with these newcomers or there's something about what Mona said that bothered her.

"Nice to meet you, Grace," Ariana and Wesley say almost completely in unison, and I laugh at how in sync they are with each other.

"I didn't realize there were that many monster-human couples in the area. But then again, I didn't realize there were enough monsters to warrant an entire night at a kink club. Or a monster support group!" I say, attempting to make small talk while trying to figure out why Max and Blair brought them over to talk to us.

Blair tenses again at the mention of the support group. Huh. I wonder if she didn't know about it and is upset that she wasn't invited to be a part of it.

Max nods. "One of the reasons I moved to Moonvale was the large monster population. It gets bigger every year."

"Really?" I ask, trying not to sound too incredulous. Sure, Moonvale is nice enough, but it's nothing that special.

"My dad thinks it has something to do with magical ley lines in the area, but it could just be that once a few monsters realized it was a safe place for them to live in peace, word got around," Max says.

"Yeah, I heard from a friend that it was a good place to live. Moving to Moonvale was the best decision I ever made," Wesley adds, giving Ariana a besotted look.

Blair clears her throat. "We'd like to get started. Wesley agreed to help Max in case we need his... assistance."

My face heats at her mention of the scene and the idea of this stranger and his partner waiting outside the room as well.

"He's a minotaur," Blair explains.

"Oh! Wow, that's so cool!" I blurt, then flush even more.

Wesley chuckles. "Thanks! I like to think so."

Ariana rolls her eyes again, then squeaks as he pulls her against him and gives her ass a rough pinch.

"What did daddy tell you, baby girl?" He smacks her ass and then lets her go. Mona and I exchange a look, her amused and me wide-eyed at their dynamic. "Now be good and keep Mona company for a while."

Mona lifts a questioning brow at Max and he gives me a sympathetic smile. "I thought Grace might not want everyone lurking outside the door."

Bless that sweet, broody redhead. I love Mona, but the thought of her being so close while I'm doing... whatever Blair wants us to do, was weirding me out. I didn't bring it up because I didn't want to hurt her feelings, but I don't get off on the idea of people watching or listening to me like she does.

"That makes sense," Mona says, unbothered. She pulls me into yet another hug with a whispered, "good luck" and then heads off with Ariana.

I do my best to hide my relief until she's gone. "Thank you," I say to Max, then turn to Wesley. "You too. I apologize if you overhear anything... embarrassing."

The beefy man waves a hand at me. "I'm happy to help. Plus, I've got these," he says, pulling a pair of earbuds out of his pocket. "Max will let me know if I'm needed."

"Good," Blair says, giving him a wary look. It's obvious that he has no interest in anyone but his "baby girl", but her protective vibes send a little thrill through me.

And just like that, the distraction of meeting new people is gone. Nervous excitement slams back into me as Blair gives them a nod, then opens the red door beside us and gestures for me to go inside.

I step into the dark space, unsure what to expect, and my heart leaps up into my throat as Blair follows behind, closing the door and flicking on the lights.

My breath hitches as she steps closer behind me and rests a hand on my back while I take in the room. The first thing I notice is the large, black X-shaped cross against the far wall with hot pink cuffs dangling from the top points. In fact, that's really all I can see, as a vision of me spread and restrained against it floods my mind.

Blair doesn't say anything, and the silence in the room is so heavy and full of potential it makes it hard for me to breathe.

When I'm able to look away from the cross, I see the table with a bright pink flogger that matches the cuffs, and a lighter pink wand vibrator neatly laid out on it. It all looks like what BDSM Barbie would use.

"Did you get those just for me?" I ask, stepping toward the selection, a smile curving my lips as I turn to look at the woman behind me.

Blair chuckles. "Yeah. I'm appreciating pink a lot more lately."

A pleased flush washes over me. It might as well be her saying that she's appreciating me. "I love it," I say softly. I truly do. Maybe it's silly to be so touched by her picking things out to match my favorite color, but I can't help it. "It even matches my dress!" I add brightly in an attempt to disguise how besotted with Blair I'm feeling right now.

"I noticed. It's a shame that you won't be wearing it during our scene."

The mood shifts abruptly with her words, my body flooding with awareness of the powerful, dominant vampire here with me and the promise of what's to come.

"Are we starting?" I murmur.

"In a moment. First, how is your neck tonight?"

I shrug. "Not too bad, thankfully."

"Does it hurt to hold your arms above your head?" Blair gives me a concerned look.

I reach up to test it out, though usually that doesn't cause me pain. The hem of my dress rides up my thighs as I do and Blair's eyes dart down with a flash of heat, before dragging back up to meet mine. I keep my arms up, pinned in place by her gaze.

"No pain. I won't be able to turn my head to the left much right now, but otherwise I should be okay."

Blair nods, and I lower my arms, resisting the urge to smooth my dress out. She's going to see everything soon. When I was getting dressed, I felt bold. Now I'm second-guessing my choice to not wear underwear.

Will she think I'm too eager? Will she like the way I look naked?

Blair saw me in pasties and a thong when I was part of a burlesque student performance with Mona, but that was almost forty pounds ago. I like my body's new fullness, but will she?

"What are you thinking so hard about?" Blair asks.

"Ugh, stupid bullshit I thought I didn't care about," I groan.

Blair cocks a brow at me.

I let out a sigh and continue. "I was worrying you won't like what I look like naked because I've gained weight. Which, I know, is ridiculous. I'm hot. I think Mona is objectively one of the sexiest people alive, and she's plus size. But there's that annoying voice that says, 'what if you're wrong and Blair thinks you're gross?' I guess I shouldn't be surprised, because I had the same voice before. It just said different mean things."

I expect Blair to say something reassuring or passionately proclaim I'm a goddess, but she snorts. "Some things are universal, aren't they?"

"Huh?"

"I have that voice, too," Blair explains. "Between the shame from growing up as a closeted queer goth in a born-again Christian home ingrained in my brain, and the hateful bullshit that society puts on me as a Black woman, I'm not immune to self-doubt."

"Whew, okay," I say, then my eyes widen. "I'm not relieved you've had to deal with that shit, sorry! It's just nice to know you're human like me. Or, uh, you know what I mean."

"I do. And in case it doesn't become abundantly clear to you tonight, I think you're the most beautiful woman I've ever met."

Oh. My insides melt at her words.

There's a few moments of silence, Blair waiting to see if there's anything else I want to get off my chest. But I'm still stuck on her saying I'm beautiful, so I stay quiet.

"Are you ready to begin?" she asks, her voice pitching a touch lower than usual.

I am. "Yes," I breathe.

"Alright. Since we're alone in here, I'm going to use your name. You may call me Mistress, or Mistress Blair. You may speak freely for this scene, and that includes telling me immediately if your neck hurts, you start to feel pins and needles or numbness in your limbs, or feel any other discomfort that isn't intentional. Use your safeword at any time if you need to stop. Do you understand?"

"Yes, Mistress." We've discussed all of this prior to tonight, but the reminder helps ground me.

Blair nods. "My safeword is 'sparkle'." Her eyes hold mine as if daring me to crack a joke, and I can't hold back my snort.

"Sorry, Mistress."

Her lips twitch as she suppresses her smile, and it seals my certainty that no matter what happens tonight, we're going to be okay. That our friendship doesn't completely disappear when the scene begins, but serves as a bond that will allow us the comfort and trust needed to explore my desire to submit.

And hopefully my desire to find out if we could be something more than friends.

23

BLAIR

I don't normally give a safeword. A lot of dominants use them, but it never felt necessary. At least not until tonight. I control my scenes with my clients. If I need to stop, I stop. If they need me to do something different, they tell me. It's simple.

Nothing with Grace is simple. What was meant to be an offer to teach her the basics of kink and work through her anxiety has turned into her wanting sex and my bite. When I look at her, her hot pink dress a vibrant beacon in the dim playroom, every inch of her body calling out to me, my thoughts and emotions are the most complex they've ever been during a scene.

I have countless hours of experience, yet this is more thrilling than the first time I tried my hand at domination.

I shouldn't smile back at her when she appreciates the humor in my choice of safeword, but there are too many cracks in the veneer to hide the way she makes me so damn happy.

I walk in a slow circle around Grace, giving myself a chance to appreciate how fucking stunning she is without her being able to witness the fierce desire that's already brewing inside me. When I return to face her, I've gotten control of my expression.

"Take your dress off," I command, though there's no bite to my tone.

Grace flushes and nods, her hand going to one strap of her dress. She pushes it off her shoulder and gives me a nervous smile. "I'm, uh, just to warn you, I didn't wear any underwear. It doesn't look right with the dress."

"I noticed," I say evenly, my eyes watching the strap of her dress as if I can will it to slip further down her arm and bare more of her to me.

"R-right. Okay. Wanted to make sure." Her eyes hold mine as she pulls the other strap down and slides her arms out. With nothing to hold it up, the top of her dress falls down, and god, her breasts are perfect. Full and rounded, far too big for me to hold in one hand, but that won't stop me from trying, with tight pinkish brown nipples that beg for me to suck them until she gasps my name. I could spend an eternity teasing and worshiping those breasts alone.

Grace's tongue darts out to wet her lips, drawing my eyes back up to her face. Her pupils are blown wide when my eyes meet hers and I wonder if she feels the tension and need between us half as much as I do. And if she does, if it's because of the kinky situation or if part of that excitement is because she's with me.

I don't care that she sees me staring brazenly at her tits as her hands return to her dress. She's mine tonight. I can look however much I like. After all, this might be my only chance to do so if the monster inside me fucks this up.

She hesitates for a second, eyes darting to my face, then back to the floor. She smiles softly, something passing through her mind that must reassure her, and then pushes the fabric down over her hips in a slow drag, bringing her eyes back up to meet mine.

I wish I could say that I hold her gaze for more than a moment, but I can't resist looking down to watch as she reveals the rest of her body to me. Every inch of her bare skin she exposes stokes the heat flaring inside me. Every part of Grace's body is tempting in its sumptuous curves. The flare of her hips and strong, thick thighs that I want to sink my fingers into as I feast between them. The way her stomach creases at her belly button then fills back out into a soft low belly that might be my new favorite part of her. Though, god, all of her... fuck, it's too much.

Seeing all of Grace reminds me of the secret, confusing thoughts I had as a kid when I saw a pretty woman on TV. The tingles I felt when my friend kissed my cheek on a dare. The feelings I prayed to God about every night my entire childhood. I thought I was praying for them to go away, but I realize the truth now. I was praying for her.

Grace's hands glide back up her bare thighs and hips in a light caress after she releases the fabric to let it fall to the floor.

I swallow hard, fighting to keep my expression from broadcasting the goddamn awe I feel right now. She's the one who's meant to serve me tonight, but all I want to do right now is fall to my knees and worship her.

Neither one of us says anything, and I realize a little too late that the usual confidence in her posture has wilted.

That won't do. "Stand up straight. Arms at your sides. Don't hide from me."

Grace startles like she didn't even realize she was shrinking in on herself, then unwraps her arms from her waist and rolls her shoulders back.

"Much better," I say, taking a step to close some of the gap between us. I purposefully rake my gaze down her body and then back up to lock eyes with her. Her breath hitches slightly when I smile to reveal my fangs, which emerged the second I got closer and couldn't resist dragging her scent into my lungs. "Perfection."

"Thank you, Mistress," she whispers, her eyes never leaving mine. They shine with vulnerability and a hint of doubt.

"You know that, don't you? You came here tonight wearing that skintight scrap of a dress because you wanted everyone to see how perfect every inch of you is."

Grace shakes her head. "N-no. I didn't wear it for them."

Pleasure sizzles inside me. "Then who did you wear it for, Grace?"

"You," she says, her cheeks pinking again.

"What did you hope I'd do when I saw you in it?" I ask, taking another step toward her. She's close enough now that I could reach out and touch her. I'll wait a bit longer before I do. I want to linger in the tension between us until we can barely stand it.

"I..." Grace's eyes fall to the floor as she hesitates, but I give her the space to decide what she wants to say. I'm worried if I push her right away, she'll give the answer she thinks I want to hear, not the truth.

Her eyes slowly rise back to mine and she chews her lower lip for a second before giving me a sheepish smile. "Don't laugh, but I kept envisioning you seeing me across the room and immediately dragging me away because you needed to get me alone. I knew you wouldn't because you're far too good a friend to ignore Mona like that."

She told me not to laugh, but I can't stop from at least smiling at her assessment. "I think she would've understood if I hadn't controlled myself. I don't think anyone would've blamed me if I spread your legs and tasted you right then and there. The only reason I didn't was because I know you wouldn't enjoy that."

Grace's breath hitches at my words. "Besides, this is for me," I murmur, finally reaching out to touch her, a light graze of my fingertips along the side of her arm. My predator's senses sharpen at the feel of her, and my fangs ache to pierce her delicate skin as fine hairs on her arm skin raise in the wake of my touch.

Not yet.

My voice is thick when I speak again. "Come with me." I take her hand in mine, leading her over to the St. Andrew's cross. She follows willingly, and the way she squeezes my hand makes my chest ache. I resist the urge to use my free hand to reach up and rub at the sensation.

I guide Grace to turn around and get my first view of the back of her. A smile spreads across my face when I see the familiar heart-shaped birthmark right on the center of her left ass cheek. I first noticed it when she was practicing her burlesque routine for the class we took with Mona, and I've wanted to trace it with my tongue ever since. It's adorable and somehow makes her even sexier.

Sensing my eyes on her ass, Grace looks over her shoulder with a slight frown. "I know, I know. My ass is as flat as a pancake. I'd hoped that when I gained weight I'd get a bigger butt, but no."

"I wasn't thinking that," I say sharply as I lift one of her wrists and secure the padded pink cuff around it, testing to make sure it's not too tight.

"O-oh." I can tell she wants to ask what I was thinking, but senses that the time for nervous chatter and worrying is quickly passing.

I move to her other side, skimming my hand across her back and playing with the ends of her silky blonde tresses. I've wondered since I met her if it was her natural color or not, and now that I can see the thatch of blonde pubic hair peeking out between her pressed together thighs, I have my answer. I love that she didn't remove it, because it's fucking sexy.

I lift her other arm and secure it with a cuff as well, which positions her body to press against the cross. Her spine is still fairly straight, so I'm hopeful it won't cause an issue.

"Are you okay? Can you hold this position for a few minutes?" I ask, unable to resist stroking a hand through the ends of her hair again. It's so damn soft. As tempting as it is to see the golden locks wrapped around my fist, that's a no-go for someone with her neck issues.

"Yes, Mistress," Grace answers breathily. She's sinking into the scene now. Her pulse speeds up to a rapid flutter as I run my palm down the center of her back, then glide further down across her ass, where I circle the adorable birthmark there with a fingernail.

"This is what I was thinking about. How this cute little birthmark is going to look against your skin when it's red from my flogger," I say, palming her ass cheek before removing my hand and moving over to pick up said flogger.

I test it a few times, idly hitting it against my palm to draw Grace's attention. I love this part. The space before impact play begins, where the submissive anticipates what's to come. Their muscles tense. Their breathing speeds up. It calls to the bloodthirsty predator in me, reveling in the sensation of knowing I've caught my prey and there's nothing they can do but submit.

I smile when the muscles in Grace's back tense as I step behind her and trail the ends of the flogger up and down her back. I wait for her to relax into the sensation before moving on.

"Spread your feet wider apart and relax your chest forward onto the cross," I order.

She's eager to obey, widening her stance to a more stable one and presenting her ass to me for my strikes. God, I can see how the curls between her thighs are already glistening with arousal. She's turned on and we've barely done anything. I can't wait to see how worked up she'll be soon. I want her wetness dripping down her thighs so that when I finally bite her there, the heady tang of her desire will mix with the taste of her blood.

I move the flogger down to stroke across her butt, avoiding getting too close to her inner thighs, which has her squirming. "Don't move," I say, putting a small amount of bite into my tone.

"S-sorry, Mistress," Grace murmurs, going stock still.

"Good girl." I stroke her hip with my free hand, using the touch and praise as a distraction as I ready my first hit. I remove my touch once she's relaxed again, and then bring the flogger down lightly on her right ass cheek in a soft thud.

"Oh!" Grace gasps, more out of surprise than from anything else.

I pull back and gently strike her other cheek, aiming for the birthmark. She gasps again, the sound making me grin. Oh yes, this is going to be so much fun.

I build her up, adding in an occasional hit with more force before backing away to tease the tails of the flogger across the red blotches blooming across her ass. I learn what elicits shocked inhales and what makes her let out soft hums of pleasure-pain. I could play with her like this for ages, but the scene isn't over yet and I don't want to keep her in one position for too long for fear of hurting her neck. I put the most force I've allowed myself into my final strike, and Grace *moans*.

"Mmm, looks like you enjoy some forms of pain," I murmur, bringing my free hand down to rake my nails across her sensitive skin.

Grace whimpers and nods slightly. "Yes...fuck, it feels good, Mistress."

My clit throbs at her words, my body aching with the need for release.

I give her ass a light slap before backing away. "That's enough for tonight. We'll experiment with that more another time," I say as I undo the cuffs.

Grace rolls her shoulders and turns around to face me. Her eyes are shining with arousal and she gives me a slight frown. "We-we're done for tonight?" she asks, disappointment clear in her tone.

A wicked grin curves my lips. "Not at all, sunshine. We're just getting started."

24

GRACE

The heat of Blair's words and the filthy look she gives me are tempered by my visceral reaction to the pet name. I grimace before I can stop myself.

"What's wrong?" Blair asks, her brow furrowing as her dominant persona falters.

"Sorry!" I give her an apologetic smile, trying to shake off the sudden shame and sadness that hit me from hearing one innocuous word. "That's what Zack used to call me. I loved it at first, but towards the end it felt like he was mocking me with it."

"Fuck," Blair murmurs, and I don't think she intended to let the curse slip out. She evens out her expression and nods. "I won't use it again."

"Thank you," I reply softly. My nakedness feels difficult to ignore now that the reminder of my ex-husband has reared its ugly head. I want to cover myself with my arms and shield myself from the embarrassment of Blair seeing how pathetic I am, getting upset at such a silly thing.

I'd hoped tonight would be different from my other sexual experiences. I'd thought maybe because Blair is a woman, and I trust her implicitly, it wouldn't be a problem. Sadly, I'm still me. Am I even going to be able to relax and enjoy myself or has my past tainted my thoughts enough that they're forever spoiled?

"Enough." Blair's sharp word cuts through my thoughts. My eyes lift to meet hers instinctively at the command. "You're not here with him, or anyone else who may have hurt you. You're here with me. We're not done yet. Unless you want to use your word."

I blink back at her in surprise. Her adamance is a sobering splash of cool water across my spiraling thoughts. I nod. "No, Mistress. I don't."

"Good. I'm going to bind you to the cross again. Tell me if it causes any strain or discomfort."

I nod again, and start to turn to face away toward the cross, but she stops me with a hand on my shoulder. "Stay facing me. I want to watch every expression that crosses your face with what we do next."

A wave of heat washes over my exposed skin at the dark promise her words contain. I want to ask what we're doing next, but the words won't come out. Not when she gets close enough that her body presses against my side, and her cool fingertips play along the sensitive skin of my wrist for a moment before she re-cuffs me to the cross. Her face is so close to mine, our height difference minimal with me barefoot and her in heeled boots. All I'd have to do is lean forward a little and my lips would be on hers.

God, I want to kiss her, but I'm terrified to cross that line. What if she pushes me away?

It's a ridiculous fear, given the way she's been looking at me all night, but I can't shake the worry that I've misinterpreted her intentions. That, yes, she's attracted to me and probably enjoys dominating me, but she doesn't want that kind of intimacy. Blair does this for her job, and gets men she has zero interest in to cling to her every word, coming back time and time again because she's so damn good at being their dominant. For all I know, it's the same with me. Any attraction I think she feels toward me could simply be the combination of a well-crafted persona and a friend's desire to help me get out of my head.

Blair moves to my other side and cuffs my other wrist, and I let my gaze fall to the floor rather than continue to stare at her mouth, silently begging for her kiss.

"Spread your legs wider," she says as she returns to my front.

My face flames furiously at the command. "Wh-what?"

"Step your feet further apart. I'm going to bind your ankles as well." Blair says it casually, like she's done this a million times. Which she probably has. I can't tell if it's reassuring or makes me jealous of the people she honed her craft with.

"Right. Of course." It's considerably harder for me to get myself to do than any of her other orders tonight because she's watching me with such intense focus and when I step apart, she'll be able to see so much more of me. I won't be able to hide how wet my thighs are from her flogging me and tying me up. There's a thrilling surge of nerves unlike any I've experienced before, forcing myself to do what Blair ordered even though it's embarrassing, and it only heightens when she sinks down to the floor to cuff my ankles to the cross.

The wicked smile she gives me as she looks up after finishing the task makes my breath hitch. I'm fully exposed to her, and she's not shy about looking her fill. After a few moments, Blair stands and takes a step back to take in the full picture. She watches me, gaze wandering over every inch of my body in an unhurried drag.

I'm not usually shy about being naked, but it's a little different when you're strapped to a cross and being stared at like you're a feast by the most intimidating woman in the universe. Who happens to be a vampire.

Fuck, why does that make it even hotter?

My breaths are shallow, and every rise and fall of my chest feels exaggerated by the position I'm held in. I'm completely at her mercy. Blair could do anything to me right now, and god, I want her to. I know she'd stop if I use my safeword, but that's the opposite of what I want. My body aches for her to do something to relieve the overwhelming need that's coursing through me. Why isn't there a word to make her give me more?

"Please," I whisper.

Blair's eyes snap to mine. "Please what?"

"Please, Mistress," I say louder.

Her lips twitch with a suppressed smile. "That's very good, but I want to know what you're begging me for."

"Anything," I say, the word coming out on a shaky exhale.

This time she doesn't hold back her grin, the dirty, knowing look making me want to whimper. "Anything? There's a lot I could do with you right now." Blair steps in closer and strokes a finger down my cheek.

The touch makes me shiver, and I suck in a sharp breath as she collars my throat with one hand. She doesn't apply any pressure, but she doesn't need to. I already feel unable to breathe with her hand on me like this.

"I'll take whatever you want to do to me," I say, when I'm able to think past the mind-fogging anticipation.

She leans in even closer and her lips ghost against the shell of my ear. "That's right. You will," Blair says, her voice taking on an edge that makes my pulse spike.

Kiss me.

Bite me.

The hand on my throat slides down to my sternum, Blair's fingertips brushing my breasts as she trails her palm between them. My back arches reflexively, begging for her to touch them with more than an idle tease. She doesn't give in to my body's demand, instead continuing her descent down my body to slide across my stomach and down to my low belly. She licks her lips, resting her hand there and giving the soft flesh there a gentle squeeze.

"I love this. It's so sexy," Blair murmurs, her tone softer than before. Almost reverent.

I let out a weak laugh. "That's what you think is sexy? Not my tits or my pussy?"

"Those are incredible, too," she says, matter-of-fact. "Every inch of your body deserves to be worshiped, Grace."

Fuck me. More of my arousal slides down my thighs, and with the way my legs are spread, it'll be dripping on the floor soon. I squirm against my bonds, unsure if I'm trying to hide myself or beg for more of her touch.

Blair lets out a low, throaty chuckle at my movement. "So desperate." She removes her hand and I can't hold back my whine. "Maybe I should make you wait a little longer. Teach you some patience."

I open my mouth to protest, but close it again as heat flares in her eyes. She set a trap, and I almost fell into it. I don't want to be a brat. I don't want to fight Blair. I want to submit.

"Yes, Mistress. I'll be patient for you."

"Mmm, such a good girl," Blair purrs, stroking a hand through my hair. Her praise wraps around me, teasing my body as much as her light touches.

"Thank you, Mistress," I whisper.

She watches me for a few agonizing minutes, peppering gentle touches that never stray to anywhere my body begs for. When Blair finally touches my low belly again, then slips down through my damp curls to rest right above my pussy, I gasp.

My body is lit up, more turned on than I've been in my life. Blair holds my gaze as we hang on the precipice, silently asking if I want to take the leap.

I falter.

Fuck, I want this so badly, but years of past sexual experiences slam into me, like they always do when things get to this point.

"You don't have to..." I drop my gaze in shame.

Blair freezes immediately, the pads of her fingers resting on my mound, her hand cupping me without any pressure. An inch lower and she'd be touching my clit. She'd feel how wet I am from her overwhelming presence.

Her other hand grips my chin and lifts it, her touch careful but insistent as she forces me to meet her eyes.

Blair's stern gaze bores into my soul and finds me... Shit, I don't even know. Maybe she thinks I'm pathetic. After all, I'm the one who keeps falling out of the scene. I'm the one who keeps sending mixed signals.

I'm hot and cold all over and I could pass out from how badly I want her to touch me more. When I spoke with Mona, I was worried I wouldn't enjoy being with a woman, even with the crush I'm harboring. That fear has mostly evaporated, but in its place is the sadder reality that even if I enjoy her touch, it'll be pointless.

"If you don't want me to touch you here, use your safeword." Blair doesn't reassure me that she wants to touch me, only searches my face while I decide.

It's maddening. I hate not knowing for certain. It only makes things worse.

I shouldn't have asked our scenes to include sex. It was incredibly selfish of me on multiple levels. Blair told me multiple times this didn't have to include sex, and I assumed it was because she didn't want to make me uncomfortable. What if she said that because she didn't want to have sex with me?

I take a deep breath and force myself not to shut down from embarrassment. I should've told her about my issue before we started the scene, and I definitely should've asked point-blank if she wanted to have sex with me or if it was a favor as part of her lessons. "I... I don't want you to stop. But I only want you to touch me if you want to. And I need you to know..."

Fuck, this is so embarrassing. I squeeze my eyes shut, unwilling to see her inscrutable face when I admit my shortcomings.

Her fingers tighten their grip on my chin to the point of pain. "Look at me when you're speaking, pet."

Pet? I gasp at both her harsh grip and the name, and my eyes flutter open. "Yes, Mistress."

"Good girl. Now, speak." Her command is so absolute I almost think she's using some kind of vampiric power on me. But no, that's just Blair.

My knees threaten to buckle at the intensity, but I obey. "If you touch me, I...I won't come."

A flash of pain passes across Blair's expression before she can hide it.

My eyes widen in alarm. Shit, I'm screwing everything up. "Not because it's you! But because I can't. I mean, I can, but I never come with a partner. And before you say that men are trash and that you could do better, it's not like some of them haven't tried." I let out a weak laugh. "Believe me, they did."

To the point that it made things infinitely worse. Zack may've been an asshole but he tried using my favorite vibrator on me, and he even attempted to go down on me for over an hour. Multiple times.

I'm the one that's defective. I'm the frigid bitch who can't get off unless she's alone. I'm the person who makes sex a problem.

I've learned that anything sexual is better if I don't bother trying to get off. This would've been so much simpler if Blair had bossed me around and used me for her pleasure so that I didn't have to worry about this exact moment, where all the focus is on me. Now I'm having to face the thing about myself that'll ruin this otherwise thrilling night.

God, I'm so stupid. Tears well in my eyes, and I have no way of wiping them away while I'm bound. All of my faults and weaknesses are laid bare.

Blair stays silent for a long moment, waiting to see if I'm done talking. There's no sign of judgment or disappointment on her face, only the same blazing intensity that makes me shiver.

"Then don't come," she says.

"What?"

A predatory smile twists her lips. "I'm going to touch you, and you're not allowed to come."

The idea is absurd. Why would she bother? "I...I don't understand. Why would you do that?"

"Because I want to. Because right now, you're my pretty little pet and I get to do whatever I please with you. And yes, I will do what I *want* to do." She emphasizes the word "want" as she holds my gaze, before releasing my chin and stepping back, her gaze a hot brand on my exposed skin.

"Your body belongs to me, Grace," she continues, moving back in to run a fingertip down my sternum, my nipples pebbling at the faint touch. She strokes down my stomach and wets her lips when she reaches my small thatch of pubic hair. "It's my right to feel how wet you are for me," she murmurs, leaning in close enough that I feel her cool breath on my throat.

I stifle a gasp as she slips two fingers between my thighs. Blair lets out a dark chuckle as she finds how slick I am. "Remember—you're not allowed to come. Do you understand?"

"Y-yes, Mistress." I gasp again as she circles my clit. She says it like it's even a possibility and I find myself tempted to believe her. It won't, but the threat of causing her ire if I miraculously come from her touch is setting me ablaze. "I won't come."

25

BLAIR

It's taken me until this point to fully immerse myself in the scene. But when faced with Grace's heartbreaking worries, I sink into my dominant role to stop myself from tracking down every single person who contributed to her insecurities and rip out their throats. I've been hungry for Grace this whole time, but the ache to seek vengeance has made my monster bloodthirsty.

Orgasm denial is one of my favorite things to do as a dominant. It shows that you can read the cues your submissive gives you, and know how to take them as close to the edge as you can before pulling back. Making them so desperate that they'll beg for release. Holding their pleasure in your grip and deciding if they're worthy of the relief you can grant.

This isn't all that different. Grace says her partners have tried to get her off, but from what she's said in the past, I'm confident they tried out of a sense of obligation or they wanted her to come to supplement their ego.

I'm not like them. I want everything from Grace, not just that fleeting rush of pleasure from an orgasm. I want to catalog every single sigh and moan. The way her body responds to even the most minute changes in my touch. I want her body to sing for me, and it doesn't fucking matter if that ends in either of us coming.

I would happily spend eternity learning Grace. She's worth all the time in the world.

Could I make her come, despite her protests? Yes. She's coiled up so tight now that the right touches would shove her over the edge, but brute force isn't my style.

I want her to fight it until she can't hold back. I want tears to run down her cheeks as she trembles to keep it at bay. And then I want her shocked pleasure and dismay as she shatters.

God, even those thoughts have me on edge, my body as primed for release as Grace's. I suppress the urge to slip my hand between my legs and rub my clit through the slippery latex.

I wore this catsuit for a reason. Anything easier to get in and out of, and I might've pivoted tonight's scene by placing Grace between my thighs and making her mouth too occupied to say all the nervous thoughts that've been pouring out of her. It's a good thing I enjoy the ache of denying myself as much as I enjoy denying my submissives.

The soft, shuddering sigh Grace releases as I slip two fingers further between her thighs is the sweetest music. I spread my fingers apart to skirt around her clit and rub across her labia, enjoying the tease and slicking my fingers on the wetness I find there. She's soaked, which I already knew by her glistening thighs, but feeling it for myself is worlds better than looking.

Heady pleasure and satisfaction flood my mind. Her pussy is dripping because of me. Maybe I'm no better than a man, inflating my ego with how easily I can arouse Grace, but it feels like more than that. There's a pang in my chest that accompanies the pride, a desperate urge to connect with this woman who draws out all my dark and vulnerable pieces.

Can she feel it too? Does she crave that same connection?

When I move closer so I can get the right angle to touch Grace the way I want, her warm breath comes out in stuttering exhales. I bask in her soft gasps as I explore her slick folds, never giving her clit more than a small graze.

Standing with my body pressed to hers, I'm close enough to sink my fangs into Grace's throat. Her pulse flutters rapidly, triggering the monstrous side of my brain to see her as prey.

She's at my mercy. She told me she wants me to bite her. I could do it now.

I close my eyes and cut off my breath. *Not yet.*

The choked moan Grace makes as I finally circle her clit snaps my focus back to what matters. I have to give her what she needs before I allow myself to let go.

"How does that feel?" I ask, sliding my free hand up to cup her breast, eliciting another soft moan.

Grace watches me with hooded eyes. "Good, Mistress. It feels so good."

I rub her clit, searching her face to see what motion makes her eyelashes flutter. "That's it, isn't it?" I ask, as I repeat the motion, softly rolling her clit between two fingers.

"Wh-what?" Grace replies, already having a hard time focusing on anything other than my steady stroking of her clit.

I lean in and press my lips to the shell of her ear. "This is how you touch yourself. When your needy little pussy is weeping at the thought of me making you mine."

"*Fuck*," she gasps, "Y-yes, Mistress."

"You really think that I wouldn't know how to make you come again and again?" I pull back and level her with my gaze. "I'm in control, pet." I hope the reminder will continue to keep the worries about her ability to orgasm at bay. "Your only job is to take what I choose to give you, and thank me for the privilege of receiving it."

I give her nipple a rough pinch, hard enough that she cries out and her hips buck against my hand. "What do you say, pet?"

"Thank y-you, Mistress."

"Good girl." I remove my hand from between her legs, and lock eyes with her as I lift my fingers and lick her wetness off of them. I fight a groan at her taste. Fuck, I need more.

I brought the vibrator tonight to aid in my torture, but something shifts in my brain as her sweet, tangy taste coats my tongue. I drop to my knees between her spread legs and lap at the slick arousal dripping down one thigh, then move to the other.

"Blair!" Grace gasps, squirming as my tongue trails along her inner thighs until I reach her glistening pussy. I grab a greedy handful of her ass, pressing her hips forward and holding her in place as I flick her clit with my tongue.

"Oh my god, this can't be real," she says, and I look up from my place buried between her thighs to make sure she's okay.

The sight I find is pure debauchery. Grace's trembling, flushed body bound to the cross as her mouth hangs open with panting breaths, eyes shimmering with a mixture of disbelief and desire.

"This is fucking real," I say, my voice rough. I don't wait for a reply before going back between her thighs to eat her pussy like a starving woman.

I experiment until I find what makes her legs shake, and repeat it again and again, working her cunt with my tongue and lips until she's moaning my name in a constant stream. I press two fingers inside her and she cries out, hips bucking wildly.

"Fuck, Blair, I'm going to..."

I pull my mouth from her immediately. Grace gasps in confusion and frustration. "I told you. You're not allowed to come."

The stunned way she looks down at me tells me she didn't think I was serious.

"You're not really going to... Ah!" Grace jolts as I rub the fingers still inside her against the front wall of her channel.

She'll learn that I never joke about that sort of thing.

"Do you want to use your safeword, pet?" I ask.

"N-no. Oh god."

I lick my lips and grin up at her before giving her clit a flick with my tongue, and she gasps again. "Are you sure?" I ask.

"Yes, Blair. I mean, Mistress! Please. I'll be good."

I know she will be, and that makes her inevitable failure to follow my command that much more exciting.

I bring Grace to the edge again with my tongue and fingers, stopping when she warns me she's about to come. Then I do it a third time with only my fingers so I can watch the agonized expressions of pleasure cross her face as I build her up.

When tears begin to slide down her cheeks, leaving dark mascara trails in their wake, and my fangs ache so badly that I'm trembling, I quickly undo the cuffs on her ankles and wrists, then guide her over to sit on the couch.

I stroke her tear stained cheek with my thumb, and Grace holds my gaze, her eyes pleading. She whimpers as I kneel between her thighs one last time, knowing this is the time she'll break.

I let my fangs graze against her inner thigh, a warning of what's to come, before sucking her on her clit.

"Blair, please, please, I can't, please," Grace babbles, her hands gripping the edge of the couch. She's such a good girl, not reaching out to hold me where she needs me despite all my torture.

"You've done so well for me, Grace," I say, pulling back in a feeble last effort to clear my mind before I give my monster what it's screaming at me to take.

She must see the need in my eyes, because she nods. "I want it. Please. Do it," Grace says between gasping breaths. We both know she doesn't mean her orgasm.

I lick her inner thigh once, then strike. My fangs pierce into her tender flesh with ease and I barely register Grace's gasping cry of pain and pleasure as my bite triggers her release, because the second her blood hits my tongue, my vision whites out.

I was wrong.

Oh god, I was so wrong.

This is nothing like the night after I was turned. That was feral, dark hunger.

This is... *Fuck*. How will I ever go back after knowing that this exists?

I groan against Grace's thigh as a pulsing ecstasy like nothing I've ever felt floods my body. I can't tell if I'm coming or having an out-of-body experience as I swallow my first mouthful of Grace's blood. She tastes exactly like her scent. Sweet and tart decadence. Nostalgia. Sunlight and safety.

I take another pull, greedy for more of the euphoric bliss that is drinking from Grace.

She groans, and her hand comes down to thread in my hair and tightens. Shit, she needs me to stop.

Not yet. Please, just a little longer.

It's a monumental task to release my bite, but I do it. There's no frenzy or anger from the monster inside me at my withdrawal, only pure, desperate longing.

I try to pull back to look up at Grace and make sure she's not horrified by the reality of being bitten by a vampire, but the hand in my hair holds me in place and she spreads her thighs open a little wider with a breathy whine.

Oh.

I lick at the twin puncture wounds, nicking my tongue to use a drop of my blood to close them, then move to lave at her clit with firm strokes.

"Blair. Oh shit, B-Blair, that's so good...*f-fuck*," Grace says, her voice hoarse and trembling.

I press two fingers inside her, working her g-spot as I lavish her clit with my tongue until she's close to coming again.

"More. Do it again. Please," she gasps. I wait for her to fall over the edge from my fingers and tongue this time, biting her other thigh right as she starts to come.

God, I swear I can taste her orgasm in her blood as her pussy clenches hard against my fingers and continues to pulse in time with each drag I take from her. Her pleasure slams into me and my own unstoppable release overtakes me. My fingers dig into the back of Grace's legs as I moan against her thigh over and over, the sweet tangy mixture of her blood and pussy the most exquisite thing I've ever tasted.

Only when Grace shudders and her tight grip on my hair releases do I remove my fangs. This time I lick the wound, but don't use my blood to make it vanish. I don't want to remove the evidence of how she begged for my bite.

I sit back on my heels, head still swimming with pleasure. Grace looks down at me, equally dazed. In the afterglow of this life-altering experience, I'm at a loss for words. All that's running through my mind is the pleading hope that she felt more than just an orgasm. That she wants me even a fraction as much as I want her.

That, and immense relief that my fear was unfounded. I didn't lose control.

No, I was more myself than I've been since I died. It scares me how much I *feel* right now.

As all of those thoughts swirl in my mind, I watch Grace's face for a sign of how she feels. When the post-orgasmic fog fades, a smile spreads across her lips.

"Holy shit, Blair," she says with a shocked, throaty laugh.

Holy shit is right. I smile back. "I thought I said you weren't allowed to come."

Grace laughs harder and shakes her head at me. "Sorry, Mistress. Kinda hard not to come when your domme has an orgasmic vampire bite."

"Hmm, I'll forgive it just this once."

She grins at me and offers me a hand up off the floor. I take it, the small thrill at the connection making my palm tingle.

"Is, uh, the scene over?" Grace asks, shifting to close her legs.

Right. She's probably going through a myriad of emotions and feels exposed being naked after something so intense. It's jarring to be reminded that this was a scene, but I hide my reaction with a smile.

"Yes, but stay right there."

Grace raises a brow at me. "Okay."

I go to a cabinet in the back of the room and grab the pink blanket I stored inside for tonight, then return and sit next to her on the couch after draping it over her shoulders.

She gives me a shy, breathtaking smile as she touches the soft fabric, but doesn't make a move to cover herself. Instead, she slides closer to me and holds one end of the blanket out for me. I blink in surprise before taking it. Once it's draped over me as well, Grace nods. "Right. Okay. So, uh...Sorry, I..."

My heart sinks. Shit, is it already time for her to tell me that she had fun but she doesn't want to do it again?

"Don't apologize. We don't have to do this again. I'd never push you to do something that made you uncomfortable."

"No! Why the hell do you think that? Ugh, I'm just... I don't know what to do... This is new for me and I don't want to ruin things...but, fuck it." Grace swallows hard. "Can I please kiss you?"

My mouth falls open and my mind goes blank. "What?"

This is a dream. There's no way she wants that.

"I want to kiss you. I've wanted to kiss you since I saw you tonight. If that's too weird, I understand, but I—"

"Yes," I say, cutting her off before she has the chance to talk herself out of it.

Grace's blood thrums with excitement in my undead body, the roar of its potent energy almost deafening.

"You sure?" Grace asks, her eyes falling to my lips.

"Kiss me, Grace," I murmur, hoping that I won't break whatever spell is woven between us.

She cups my cheek and pulls me closer. Her warm breath ghosts across my lips as she pauses for an excruciating moment of uncertainty. I think she's going to change her mind. That she's come to her senses and realized who she's about to kiss. But then her lips crash into mine and she's kissing me, and I finally put a name to the sensation I felt as I drank her blood.

Grace feels like home.

26

GRACE

Tasting my blood and arousal on Blair's lips is odd, but after a second, I barely notice it. Feeling her mouth against mine after all we've done tonight is its own form of blissful release. It's silly, but I was worried it would be harder to kiss a woman, given how much smaller Blair is than the men I've kissed, but my lips slot against hers with ease, like they were formed with this very purpose in mind.

I start out a little too forceful, needing to dive in full force to get over the hurdle of my anxieties, but melt at the way her soft lips mold against mine. She's warmer than I expected, maybe from my blood now coursing through her.

Why does that thought excite me? That I'm literally inside Blair now, heating her as much as she makes me burn for her.

My hands have a mind of their own, one holding her face like it's worried she'll break the kiss too soon, and the other wandering down to stroke along her bare arm, then in to palm her breast over her catsuit.

I can feel how hard her nipple is through the thin latex, and we both gasp as I brush against it with my thumb. I seize the opportunity to deepen the kiss, feeling wild and reckless and needy despite coming harder than I ever have a few minutes ago.

It's impossible to remember why I was worried about this. Blair's tongue in my mouth as I caress her breast is a revelation.

Blair groans against my mouth, her hand flying up to cup the back of my head as our tongues slide together. The strange coppery taste is stronger now, but I'm starting to like it. It's a reminder of what we've done and what Blair is. I'd probably laugh at the absurdity of being bound and bitten by a sexy vampire if I wasn't totally lost in the feeling of her mouth on mine.

When Blair pulls back from the kiss, I'm gasping and eager for more. I shake my head and tug her in back to me, and she laughs against my mouth. I nip at her lower lip and her laughter turns to a curse.

"*F-fuck*, Grace," Blair rasps.

The raw need in her voice makes me shiver. She's always so in control that breaking through her composure excites me. Knowing I'm the person who's making her sound like that is intoxicating.

When my tongue slides into her mouth again, there's an unexpected flash of pain as I scrape against something sharp that wasn't there a moment ago. Right, her fangs.

Blair immediately pulls back, her dark eyes filled with concern. "Shit, I didn't mean for them to come out. Are you okay?"

"I'm fine," I say, shaking my head. There's a bit more of the metallic taste in my mouth, and I test my tongue with my finger, looking to see how much it's bleeding. There's hardly any blood, but Blair eyes the small amount of crimson on my fingertip with barely restrained hunger.

I absently bring my finger back toward my mouth to clean the blood off, but Blair's hand darts out lightning fast and grabs my wrist. My pulse quickens as she guides my finger to her mouth and sucks it between her lips. Her eyes flutter shut in pleasure as she swirls her tongue around the pad in a way that's shockingly erotic.

I whimper involuntarily, my clit giving a needy throb. Fuck, how can I be so desperate for her again?

Blair hums slightly as she pulls my finger back out of her mouth and gives me a slightly sheepish smile. "We should probably stop before I lose control and bite you again."

"I don't have a problem with that." I barely recognize the husky, seductive rasp of my voice.

Blair groans. "You're not making it easy for me to do the right thing."

I lean in, pressing my breasts against hers as I drag my lips against the column of her throat. "Who says stopping is the right thing?" I whisper.

"F-fuck." God, there's that unexpected break in her voice again. Does she really want me that badly? "I..."

Whatever she's about to say is cut off by a soft knock on the door. Blair immediately stiffens and shifts to put me behind her, guarding me from whatever threat may come bursting into the room.

"I'm so sorry to interrupt. Do you think you need us anymore, or are you good?" Max's voice calls from the other side of the door.

"We're good. Thanks for checking. Now fuck off," I call back before Blair can answer.

There's a faint rumble of Max's laugh before he replies. "Roger that."

I laugh as Blair eases back out of her protective posture. "God, I forgot he was out there. Do you think he could, uh, hear when I...?"

Blair smirks. "When you screamed my name as you came?"

I groan, flushing with embarrassment. Of course he heard me. "I'll never be able to look at Max again without cringing."

She shrugs. "When you're a part of a small kink community like this, you're bound to end up knowing what everyone looks and sounds like when they come."

"That's not helping! Now I'm thinking about how awkward it will be if I see Max railing Mona."

"Not if. When," Blair says with a wry laugh. "Mona's an exhibitionist, remember?"

I tug the blanket around myself, eyeing the door warily as the reality that we're in a kink club comes crashing in.

"Next time, maybe we can do this somewhere a little more private?" I ask.

"You want a next time?" Blair asks, dodging the question.

Two can play that game. "I don't know. What do you think?"

"Grace," Blair says with a concerned frown.

"Yes! I want a next time. Quit being ridiculous."

Her eyes widen at my adamance.

Oh shit, was she trying to let me down gently? "Wait, do *you* want a next time?"

"Yes. Quit being ridiculous," she says, echoing me with a slight smirk.

I can't decide if I want to smack her or kiss her until we're breathless again.

Who am I kidding? I want the kissing.

Blair must see the way my expression shifts because she stands up from the couch and crosses her arms under her chest. "In order for there to be a next time, we need to stop now. I drank as much from you as I safely could, and I don't want to risk taking more if we continue tonight."

I resist the urge to pout, and when I wobble a little as I stand, I know she's right. Now that the high of our activities is wearing off, I realize I'm a little lightheaded.

Blair steadies me, and if I lean a little more into her hold than is necessary, she doesn't comment on it. "Sit back down for a minute. I'll get you a drink."

I allow her to guide me back down onto the couch and watch as she crosses the room to the same cabinet she got the blanket from. "A drink?" I ask.

She digs through a small insulated bag and I laugh as I see what she pulls out. It's a juice box.

"What, no cookie?" I ask, unable to keep the amusement from my voice.

"I forgot it, but hopefully this will be enough," she says, completely sincere.

My chest squeezes with affection. If you were to look at Blair in all of her stern, goth goddess glory, you'd never imagine that such a sweetheart lurked beneath the surface. She's so goddamn kind and caring. What did I do to deserve someone like Blair in my life?

I have the sudden urge to wrap my arms around her and never let her go.

Instead, I sip the juice dutifully, and the pleased smile she gives me in return makes the urge to kiss her rise again.

When I'm done, she takes the box and puts it back in her bag, then grabs my dress for me. "Do you want some privacy while you get dressed?"

I furrow my brow. "What? Why would I want that? You've already seen me naked."

"Sometimes people feel vulnerable after a scene. I don't want to assume anything about what you do or don't feel comfortable with."

"Ah, right. Well, I don't care." I stand and let the blanket fall off me as I take the dress from her hand.

Despite my bravado, I'm more than a little self-conscious about Blair watching me wriggle back into the tight dress. She busies herself with gathering up all the things she brought with her tonight, which is good because putting the dress on is decidedly less sexy than taking it off. I have no idea how she brought all that stuff in here without me noticing, since she didn't have that bag with her when she arrived. Did she put it in here ahead of time? Thinking about her putting in that much effort to prepare for tonight makes my stomach flutter.

When I'm back in my dress and heels and she's slung an entire duffle bag with the gear over her shoulder, my nerves kick up. What happens when we leave the privacy of this room? Will she want to go hang out with other friends? Watch some scenes in the main room?

Oh shit, I forgot, most of the people out there are monsters! I freeze midway through the door out into the hallway as Blair holds it open for me.

"Breathe, sweetheart," she says, placing a hand on the small of my back. "I can take you home right away if you're not ready to experience the full offerings of a monster-filled kink club."

"Are you sure? What about Mona and Max? I don't want to be rude and leave without saying goodbye."

She rubs a circle on my back and I lean into her touch, letting it soothe me. "They'll understand. Besides, I'm sure they're occupied." She drops the hand from my back and laces her fingers with mine. "Come on, I'll take you out through the back. We'll save the monster fuck fest for another time."

I laugh, tension bleeding from me. "Thanks," I say, squeezing her hand.

Blair guides me down the hallway through an unmarked door that eventually leads out into the cool night air. We loop around the building to get to the parking lot out front, and she keeps my hand firmly in hers until we reach her car, where she releases it to open the door for me.

Again with the casual kindness and care. Before Blair can move away, I grab her arm and hold her in place, and softly press my lips to hers. I have to bend down a little now that I'm back in my shoes, and that makes the butterflies kick back up in my stomach again.

Everything with Blair feels new and exciting. I know no small part of that is discovering that, yeah, I'm not straight like I assumed for most my life, but it goes beyond that. I don't think I'd feel this way kissing a random hot woman. I'm melting at even this brief kiss because of the overwhelming sense of rightness that washes over me when I'm with Blair.

This is special. This is important. Fuck, I hope I don't ruin it somehow.

When I pull back, I give Blair a smile, hoping she understands how I feel. "Thanks," I whisper.

She nods, looking a little dazed before returning my smile with one of her own. "You don't have to thank me. I'll do anything for you, Grace."

It's said with calm casualness that almost disguises the flare of serious intention of her words. It's a confession and a promise. One I'm not sure I merit, but I'll do everything I can to be the kind of person who deserves the favor of the breathtaking woman before me.

27

BLAIR

The drive back to Grace's house is quiet. My mind races with things I want to say, but worry will overwhelm the blushing blonde confection in the passenger seat, who keeps reaching over and squeezing my hand.

I don't like that she feels compelled to reassure me. It's my job to be the solid, steady one. I should be squeezing her hand. Letting her know that I'm happy to talk about anything that happened tonight if she has questions. Telling her she was a fucking revelation, both in and out of the scene.

Instead, I'm staring at the road, trying to fight back the surge of desire at the memory of Grace kissing me not once, but twice. Neither time was part of a scene. It's... I don't understand...

"I thought you liked men," I say, the words spilling out suddenly to break the silence as we sit at a stoplight. *Shit.* What's wrong with me?

Grace giggles. "I do."

"So, why do you keep kissing me?" I ask, glancing at her out of the corner of my eye.

"Isn't it obvious?" she asks with another laugh, squeezing my hand again.

Her question feels like a trap. I want her kisses to be because of genuine attraction, not because it's a novelty. "This is an experiment. Like the rest of the kink we're exploring."

"No," she sighs, the humor evaporating from her voice. "I mean, yes, but also no."

"Explain." I'm even more confused now.

"I want you, Blair," she says softly. "It's true I like men. I've never had these feelings toward a woman before, and I wasn't sure if I'd actually enjoy being intimate with a woman. But I'm ridiculously attracted to you and I knew I'd regret not trying. I'm sorry if that was wrong of me."

"Ah." Everything that happened tonight reshapes in my mind with that vital piece of information.

Grace is attracted to me. Grace was willing to try something to see what that attraction meant. It was more than a scene. She wanted to know what it'd be like to be with me, not just a domme.

Before I know it, I'm pulling into her driveway and still haven't managed to formulate a response that is anything other than "thank god, I want you so much it aches".

"I'm sorry. I didn't mean to upset you," Grace whispers when I cut the engine, startling me from my thoughts.

I shake my head adamantly. "You didn't. Shit, please don't

worry. I'm... So I'm certain, you wanted to try being with me, even though you weren't sure if you'd like it?"

"Y-yeah. I knew I shouldn't have done that but—"

"And the verdict was that..." I swallow heavily as I think about how she came undone beneath my tongue and fangs. "You didn't hate it?"

Grace lets out a choked laugh. "Yeah, Blair. I didn't hate it. In fact, you could say that I loved it."

I feel simultaneously relieved and ridiculous for even needing to ask. "So did I."

"Good. Now, that's not to say that I won't be awkward as fuck when I try to eat your pussy, but I trust that you'll be patient with me."

A snort bursts out of me. "Grace, I'll let you take as long as you need to learn how to eat me out. But only if that's something you're interested in. I get plenty of enjoyment from giving you pleasure. Not all relationships need to be an equal balance of giving and receiving, as long as everyone is enjoying themselves."

"Oh, I definitely want to try!" Grace flushes, then goes silent for a moment, worrying her lower lip with her teeth. "Do you, uh, not enjoy receiving?" she asks gently.

I reach out and free her lip from the abuse with my thumb. "I didn't say that. If you want to use that pretty mouth of yours on me, I'll make sure to put it to good use next time."

Grace's breath hitches. "O-okay."

With the way she's looking at me, I'd have her going down on me right here in the car if it wasn't for the infernal latex catsuit.

We get out of the car, tension stretched tight in the air as I walk Grace to her door. I shouldn't have risked getting out and escorting her, because it's making it infinitely harder not to grab her and pin her against the nearest surface while I lavish her pretty pink-flushed skin with my lips and teeth.

Grace fumbles through her purse for her keys, her tongue darting out to wet her lips as she finds them and looks up at me. She hesitates before unlocking the door, and I swear I can hear the blood rushing through her veins as her heart beats faster. It calls to me, insistent, but without the same terrifying potential of losing myself to the mindless, insatiable monster.

"Do you want to come inside? Maybe, uh, spend the night?" Grace asks with a shy flutter of her lashes.

God, yes.

I swallow down that instinctive, foolish reply, and brush a lock of hair away from her face. Her breath hitches at the touch as she waits to see what I do next. Every fiber of my being wants to go inside and spend the rest of the night with Grace in my arms. But it's not possible.

"I can't," I sigh, pulling my hand away and clasping it behind my back so I'll stop touching her and making this harder than it needs to be.

"Says who?" she asks with a frown.

I sigh again, wishing I didn't have to address the reality of my situation. "The sun. It'll be dawn in a few hours."

Grace's eyes widen. "Oh! Shit. Right. I didn't realize how late it was. I almost forgot about...that."

I didn't.

As wonderful as the night has been, the curse of my vampirism is never forgotten. It breaks my heart to see the disappointment on Grace's face as she realizes the romantic end to the night she'd hoped for isn't going to happen. I don't want her to go to sleep sad. Or worse, rethink her desire to try for something more with me after being reminded that even the simplest parts of being in a relationship are much more difficult with a vampire.

"Next time, we'll go to my place," I blurt, panicking with the need to see her smile again.

She perks up. "Wait, really? I've always wanted to know what your place looks like! Even Mona hasn't seen it."

It's been a long time since I brought a woman back to my place. Since Paloma, my ex who had me install the mirror over the bed, which was... shit, three years ago? And I only invited her over out of a begrudging sense of obligation and months of pestering.

That makes me sound like a complete asshole, and maybe I am. But I don't like having people in my space. It's the one place in the world where I don't have to have my guard up. Maybe it's a vampire thing, needing a lair or a secure sanctum. Or maybe it's years of living in places where I never felt safe. Not wanting someone to come in and destroy the peace that I've worked so hard to build. Either way, the last person I let inside my house after that ex was Nic, and at least with him I can attempt to keep up the barrier of a client relationship without seeming like a jerk for not allowing him to explore.

So then why am I returning Grace's grin with a small smile instead of finding an excuse to retract the invitation?

"It's really not that exciting," I say with a shrug. Even though it definitely is. Exciting and dread-inducing.

"Uh, yes it is! I bet it's all sexy and gothic like you. Lots of dark velvet curtains, moody candlelight, maybe even some hidden passages, or gargoyles! Maybe a hedge maze?"

"You make it sound like I live in a castle, not a two-story Victorian in Moonvale."

"You don't need a castle to have those things!" Grace's eyes sparkle with humor as she laughs at her own silliness. God, she's captivating when she laughs. "Okay, maybe not a hedge maze..."

"I'll have to hire a gargoyle to come sit on my roof when you visit. Though we'll sacrifice some privacy if we do that because they have excellent hearing."

"You're joking!" Grace says, mouth falling open a little.

"I'm not," I say, resisting the urge to laugh at her shock at the confirmation that gargoyles exist.

"Whoa. Alright, it's decided." She nods her head emphatically.

I raise a brow in confusion. "What is? Hiring a person to sit on my roof?"

"No! Next time there's a monster night at The Vault, I want to go and, uh, observe. I can't keep hearing about all these different creatures and then never see them for myself."

"Sad you didn't get to see any minotaur cock in the flesh?" I ask, crossing my arms over my chest. It's a joke, but also a nagging fear. What if she realizes she's not happy with what I have to offer? After all, she's said herself that she's never wanted to be with a woman before me.

Grace shakes her head adamantly. "No! I mean, would I maybe like to see for curiosity's sake? Sure. But I'm more interested in seeing the monsters in general. Not their, uh, cocks."

Despite her denial, I make a mental note to shop for monster dildos when I get home. I'm not letting worries about Grace missing dicks paralyze me while I have her standing right in front of me, flushing so prettily. If she wants monster cocks, she'll get them. I told her I'd give her anything.

"I'm happy to take you back to *observe*."

Grace's cheeks burnish even more and she covers her face with her hand. "God, it sounds so dirty when you put it like that."

"I like it when you're dirty," I murmur, reaching out to pull her hand off of her face.

"Sure you can't come in? Just for a bit?" Grace asks, looking at me through her lashes.

I shake my head. "I shouldn't." I kiss her palm before releasing her hand, and take a step back, even though it hurts to let go.

"Right. Gotta get back to your coffin before the sun comes up." She smirks at her joke, but a moment later her eyes go wide. "Wait, you don't sleep in a coffin, do you?"

I grin, flashing my fangs at her. "You'll have to find out for yourself."

"Such a tease," she says with a bubbly laugh that makes it hard for me not to press my lips to hers and taste her amusement for myself.

She does it for me, kissing me for the third time tonight. There's no heat, only pure tenderness and affection that leaves my head a little fuzzy when our mouths part. "Goodnight, Blair," she murmurs. "I had an amazing time with you."

"So did I. Goodnight."

She unlocks her door and steps inside, giving me a small wave before closing it. I stare at the door for a moment, thinking of what an understatement that was. I didn't have an amazing time. I had the best night of my life.

28

BLAIR

"So, how did it go?"

Mona swirls a spoon through her mug as she waits for me to answer. I can tell she's dying to know, and the sadist in me enjoys making her wait a little. Besides, the knowing grin she gives me as she looks up tells me Max must've spilled at least a few details.

"It went well."

Her lips flatten into a line and her eyes narrow at me in an almost comical look of disbelief. "Blair."

I look back at her, keeping my expression blank. "Mona."

She sets the spoon down with a loud clatter, then throws her hands up. "Come on! You were in there for over an hour. You took her home. There's got to be more than 'it went well.' Tellll meeeee."

I break, chuckling at her frustration. "I would've thought you'd already know details with Max listening in."

"No!" Mona sighs dramatically. "Max wouldn't tell me anything other than that you both were safe. Though he blushed a lot when I tried to get more details, so it had to be good, right?"

"You haven't talked to Grace about it?"

It's been two days since our night at The Vault. Plenty of time for Mona to pester Grace for all the juicy details. Unless Grace didn't want to talk about it. We've been texting back and forth, and nothing indicated she was feeling awkward, but maybe I misread her.

Fuck, I hate this nagging doubt. I've purposely built my life so I have as little uncertainty as possible. Worrying like this means I'm losing the emotional control I've spent so long developing.

"Whoa, what is that look?" Mona asks, her playful smile falling as she sees the thoughts crossing my mind show up in my expression. "Grace told me it was incredible, but was too shy to give me details."

The relief I feel is absurd. I already know that's how Grace feels. She told me she loved it. We've planned a time for her to come over and try another scene. I need to chill out and stop worrying about nothing.

"If she doesn't want you to know the details, I don't think I should share them."

"Ugh, you're all impossible!" Mona's spoon clatters to the ground as she accidentally knocks it off the kitchen table with her frustrated gesticulating. The commotion startles the lump sleeping under a blanket on her lap, and a spectral blue pug face peeks out from underneath to give her a disgruntled look.

"Sorry, angel," she coos, and he gives a little huff as if to say "please chill out" before settling back down.

"Even Nugget agrees that it's none of your business," I say wryly.

"Fine, I'll stop." Mona sighs. "I confided in you about all kinds of things, so I don't get why you won't tell me anything. I don't need to know how many times you made her come or anything. I'm not a creep."

"You're not?" I ask, deadpan.

She scowls at me, and I crack.

"Only two," I say, staying expressionless as I sip from my thermos.

"Only two, what?" Her brow furrows in confusion before she understands what I said. "Ahh, really?!" Mona claps her hands in excitement, and this time the pug on her lap wriggles completely free of the blanket and jumps down off her lap to find somewhere quieter to nap.

Mona beams at me. "Fuck it, I know it's weird to be happy my friends are getting off, but that's so exciting! I don't think Grace has ever had an orgasm with a partner... oh, shit, I shouldn't say that."

I smile at her concern. "It's okay. She told me."

"Oh, thank god. I'm glad you know. And that you showed her she was wrong. Twice! All the horrible things her ex-husband said to her about being frigid and awful in bed really fucked with her head."

My grip on my thermos tightens and my spine goes rigid.

"He told her that?" I ask, unable to keep the icy rage from spilling into my voice.

Mona blanches. "Uh, yeah. The bastard said it was part of why he cheated. Why he wanted a divorce. Can you believe it? If I ever see him again, I'm kicking him in the balls. Repeatedly."

"Does he have the same last name as Grace?" I make my tone even again, but I'm not fooling Mona. The monster inside me is screaming for blood.

"Blair, you can't murder him!"

"Yes, I can. I've told you before. I won't get caught."

Mona rolls her eyes. "Okay, you *can* murder him. But you're not going to. That's not who you are."

She says it with such confidence that it snaps me out of my singular focus on tracking down Grace's ex and ripping his throat out. "It's not?"

"Girl, you spent years torturing yourself for accidentally killing someone. There's no way you'd go through with murder, no matter how angry you are on Grace's behalf. The guilt would eat you alive. Earlier, you looked devastated when you thought you'd squashed a spider on my porch."

"No, I didn't." I definitely did, but I thought I'd hid it well. Another sign that my cold facade is crumbling the more time I spend with Mona and Grace.

"Sure, whatever," Mona says with a teasing smirk. "The point is, you're too good of a person to do it. So bluster if you want, but I know the truth."

I don't bother denying it. She's right.

I'm an imposter. I pretend to be tough and badass and cold, but inside I'm the weak little girl who sobbed as her parents washed her mouth out with soap and called her a sinful devil worshipper after they found her secret stash of Halloween candy.

People are cruel, and I'm not strong enough to actually do anything about it.

I'm a vampire, for fuck's sake. I shouldn't be bound by morals. I should've gone to my parents' house and paid them back for every time they punished me for failing to live up to their insane expectations, but all I do is block my mother's texts when she manages to find my phone number. I should've spent the last ten years hunting down the bastard who turned me, rather than catering to men's desires for money. I should be able to defend the people I care about.

Instead, I'm sitting here in Mona's kitchen trying not to cry as I think about the poor little spider who'd worked so hard on making her web that I almost carelessly destroyed.

"Please don't tell anyone," I murmur, swallowing hard against the ridiculous tears.

"Oh Blair, I didn't mean that as a bad thing. Shit." Mona stands and rounds the table to where I'm sitting and the next thing I know, she's using her surprising amount of strength to tug me out of my chair and crush me against her chest. "Not having the capacity to intentionally harm means you're a fundamentally good person."

I let out a humorless laugh. "It makes me weak," I mutter against her shoulder.

"Fuck that. Weak people hurt others. It takes strength to uphold your morals even in the face of shitty people."

"I hate that he hurt her like that," I say thickly.

Mona must understand that I'm not referring to just Grace, but also my past self, because she hugs me even tighter. "I know. I do, too. But she's not alone now."

Unlike in the past, I don't bother fighting her embrace. Yet another sign of how I'm losing control. I let Mona hold me, rubbing my back until the urge to cry passes. A few drops of blood tears slip free despite my best efforts, and when I pull back, there's a dot of crimson on Mona's cute white top.

"Shit, sorry," I say with a grimace.

Mona glances down. "Oh, no worries. You cry blood? That's so cool."

Her bizarre reaction pulls a choked laugh from me. "You're ridiculous."

"You're only now realizing this?" she asks with one of her goofy snort-laughs. "So are you, by the way. But your secret is safe with me. I know you need to keep your stern, sexy dominatrix street cred."

"Thanks," I reply with a weak smile. "I'd hate to lose out on work because people found out I cry over spiders."

"Aha! I knew I saw that."

"You see way too much. It's annoying," I deadpan.

Mona grins, unbothered. "That reminds me! I had a dream about us hanging out with Grace. We were watching the premiere of that reality show, and I went to the bathroom, but when I came back I caught you making out and she was touching you under the blanket. It was nice!"

"And you claim you're not a creep?" I ask, raising a brow at her cheery declaration.

"I'm not!" She shoves my shoulder lightly. "I only brought it up because it made me happy to know that you'll still be, uh, having fun together a month from now. That's when the premiere get-together Grace is planning is, right?"

Mona discovered her latent magical abilities last year, which manifested as dream visions. "You think it was a premonition?" My chest squeezes at the thought of spending a month with Grace.

"Oh, definitely. I'm learning what's likely to be a random dream versus a portent. You're lucky it warned me ahead of time so that when it happens in real life, I'll know to stay in the bathroom longer. So you two can have more time alone." Mona winks at me, and my cheeks heat.

I resist the urge to press my hand to my face. I'm not seriously blushing, am I? How is that even happening without me controlling it?

Something is seriously wrong with me.

I almost ask Mona if she thinks she'll be able to see further in the future. What will things be like between me and Grace in six months? A year? Do I even dare to hope for something that's more than a passing phase? Or worse, something that will ultimately ruin me if it turns out to be real?

Focus on the present. That's all you can control.

"How generous of you," I say, rolling my eyes.

"Speaking of generous... twice?" Mona waggles her eyebrows at me.

"It would've been more if I hadn't made her promise not to come."

Mona lets out a squeak of titillated surprise. "Oh damn, that's really hot."

"You think twice is generous?" I ask, crossing my arms and giving her a teasing look. "Is Max not doing his job right?"

"What? No! Max is amazing at his... job," Mona says, flushing.

"What's that about my job?" the man in question asks as he wanders down from upstairs, stooping over to rub Nugget's belly and earning a sleepy groan from the pug, before coming over to join us by the kitchen table.

"Oh, nothing!" Mona waves his question off, then stands so she can kiss the confused look off his face. "Blair was telling me about how well the other night went."

"Ah. Right." Max clears his throat, a red flush that matches his hair creeping up his pale, freckled neck and onto his cheeks. "I didn't, um, give her any details. In case you were concerned about that."

I fight the urge to chuckle at how worried he is. If we were closer,

I might even beg him to tell me the emotions he felt coming off of Grace during our scene. Not that he would tell me. Max only reveals the secrets of the people he's getting paid to observe for his job.

"I wasn't," I lie.

Of course I was concerned. I hated that not only was someone listening in on our private moments, but that someone had a line into my thoughts. Max surely knows now how much of my strength and calm are an illusion. I want to believe that he wouldn't use it against me, but I can't be certain. What if he decides that I'm too dangerous to be around his fiancée?

Mona wraps an arm around Max's waist, giving him a loving squeeze. He bundles her closer, leaning down to kiss her hair. The love they share is palpable, and tonight it makes my chest expand uncomfortably, as if it's making space for something similar. It's far too close to the way I felt back when I was infatuated with Dominic. When I believed I could have a fairy tale romance. Now it highlights the void where those hopes and desires once lived.

I don't want to fill back up with futile dreams. It's easier to be empty. Yet my mind can't help but wonder how it would feel to have Grace hold me the way Max holds Mona. God, what would it feel like to truly feel safe in someone's arms?

I clear my throat and stand. "I should go. Need to get to a session with a client." I have three hours until I'm meeting X in my city studio, but I don't know if I can sit here with these thoughts any longer.

We exchange farewells, and it's clear as I leave that Mona wishes I'd stay longer, but she's kind enough to not press me. Which is good because I might end up crying more blood tears onto her shirt.

When I get out to my car, I check my phone to confirm the

AFTERGLOW

session is still on before I drive all the way into the city. Under my messages from X, there's a new one from Grace.

> Grace: I can't wait to see you on Friday. Is it silly that I miss you even though it's only been a few days?

A lump of emotion clogs my throat. She misses me. When was the last time someone told me that who wasn't a client angling for more of my services?

> Blair: Do you miss me or the way I made you come?

> Grace: You. Duh.

> Grace: That other part was just an added benefit 😊

> Blair: Just checking.

> Grace: Well, stop it. How many times do I have to tell you I have a huge crush on you and can't stop thinking about you?

I laugh, imagining the glare that would accompany Grace's words if she were saying them in person.

> Blair: At least a few more times.

That's the truth. I know myself. All of this with Grace seems far too good to be true, and it will take a long time for the alarm bells to stop ringing. When you've been burned like I have, it's easier to expect and prepare for the worst, so the fallout won't cause as much pain.

> Grace: I'm really into you, Blair. I keep getting all these weird fluttery nerves whenever I think about seeing you again. It's like when I met my ex but times a thousand, and so much better because I'm 99.9% certain you're not an asshole and you won't hurt me.
>
> Blair: I won't.
>
> Blair: I'm glad you don't think I'm an asshole. Mona said something similar earlier, so clearly I need to work on my scary vampire bitch energy.
>
> Grace: Haha I do like that side of you. It's sexy. But it's even hotter because I know you're secretly the sweetest person I've ever met.

I grin down at my phone, the same fluttery feelings she described having surging in my stomach.

> Blair: Ugh, sweet?
>
> Grace: Deal with it.
>
> Blair: I'll need to show you how wrong you are when I see you.
>
> Grace: I like the sound of that, Mistress.
>
> Grace: I know you're working tonight, so I'll leave you alone. For now. Who knows when the urge to bother you again will strike?

Please don't stop. Hearing from Grace is the best part of my night.

> Blair: You're not bothering me.

> Grace: Tell me that when you wake up tomorrow night with five rambling voice memos about my theories on alien life and the feasibility of space travel.
>
> Grace: I got sucked down a video rabbit hole. Or maybe I should call it a wormhole.
>
> Grace: Anyway, have a good night! Give your client hell, or uh, whatever they're into.
>
> Blair: I will. Goodnight.

Before I head out on the road for work, I do a quick search for podcasts on space exploration. I settle in for the drive, a ridiculous smile still tugging at my lips as I think about how surprised Grace will be when she's the one waking up to messages from me about her current fixation.

29

GRACE

Fuck. No. Come on, not today.

I hiss as the muscles in my neck seize up, followed by the telltale sharp pain that means I'm fucked. I'm halfway into the dress I was putting on for my night at Blair's house, the fabric still bunched above my chest after I'd gotten it over my head. When I try to pull it down, my neck screams at me again and I wince, dropping my arms, leaving my stomach and ass out.

"God dammit, now I can't even put on clothes?" I ask my reflection in my standing mirror, frustrated tears already welling in my eyes. Fat teardrops spill down my cheeks as I blink and grip the back of my neck, and I set off toward the kitchen to grab my heating pad. I know they tell you to do ice at first, but that's always made things worse for me.

I catch my reflection in the microwave's chrome exterior and see that there are big black streaks across my cheeks. Great, now my makeup is fucked, too.

Why now? My neck pain hasn't been bad for almost a week. So much so that I temporarily forgot how much of a bitch my body is.

The times where there's no warning are the worst. When I've been lifting heavy things and looking down at things a lot, then yeah, I understand why my spine might get angry. But when I've been careful and have done all of my exercises and self-care techniques and I still end up jacking my neck up trying to put on a damn dress? It's maddening.

There's only an hour until sundown, and I still need to pack an overnight bag to leave in my car in case things go well and Blair wants me to stay after our scene. After a few more hesitant, testing turns of my head that result in more sharp pain, I know there's no way I'm going to be better enough to drive, let alone do whatever kinky things Blair has planned for us.

With more tears spilling down my cheeks, I grab the heat pad and head back to my bedroom, phone in one hand and my neck braced in the other as I lie down flat on the bed. It's hard to even do that, because it fucking hurts. I know when I try to get back up, it'll take all my mental fortitude to face the pain of moving.

I lift my phone up to my face, and at least that doesn't hurt to do. Gotta take the small wins. I know from experience that one of the few things I can do while I'm incapacitated like this is hold my phone to read. Not a book or an e-reader, though. Too heavy. And texting is pushing it because of the way it positions my arms, so as much as I hate calling people, it's the better option right now.

Dammit. I don't want Blair to hear me crying over not being

able to make it. It's too pathetic. I take a minute to gather myself so at least I'm not actively shedding tears when I press the call button and take a deep, shaky breath as it rings.

Blair answers after three rings. "Grace? What's wrong?" Her voice is slightly hoarse.

"Crap, sorry. I didn't mean to wake you up."

"Don't be sorry. You can call me any time. Are you okay?" A hint of panic is evident in her question.

There's a pang in my chest knowing that she cares that much, and it makes the guilt that I'm having to call at all even worse because I don't like that I've made her worry. "Uh, yes and no. I'm in no imminent danger or anything like that. But I can't come over tonight."

"Oh. Okay."

Those two words are even and emotionless, a stark contrast to the undisguised concern from a moment ago. If I didn't know Blair, I'd think she didn't care at all. But the detachment is so practiced that it sets off alarm bells in my head and I scramble to explain before she builds her walls back up.

"I hurt my neck!" I blurt. "I was getting ready to come over and my stupid piece of shit spine decided that halfway into my dress was the perfect time to show its displeasure with me. I won't be able to drive over."

I leave it at that. It's too vulnerable to admit that I'm currently immobile on my bed, unable to move my head at all without pain.

"I'll come over there," Blair says, concern bleeding back into her voice.

My place is a disaster zone right now. The thought of her seeing me in my natural habitat with no ability to make it more presentable makes me panic. "You don't have to do that! I won't be up to doing, uh, anything, so I don't want you to waste your evening on me."

Blair scoffs. "I don't give a shit about if we do anything. Please let me come over and make sure you're okay."

"My place is a mess. I'm a mess. You don't need to…" I trail off as annoying tears fill my eyes.

"Grace." The way Blair says my name is a reassuring caress. "I won't come over if you'd rather not see me, but your messy house or appearance isn't a reason not to let me check on you."

A tear runs down my cheek. I've always dealt with my pain on my own. I hate the thought of being a burden. When my neck pain first started, I didn't tell my ex-husband because I didn't want to add to his list of reasons why I was defective. Who wants to be with someone who can't do things as simple as putting on clothes?

"I don't want you to be alone," Blair adds when I say nothing. I'd brush it off if I sensed any pity in her tone, but all I can hear is genuine care.

I really shouldn't let her see me like this, but god, it would be nice to not suffer alone for once.

"O-okay," I say, hating the way my voice breaks.

"Okay," Blair repeats. "I'll be there as soon as I can. Do you need me to bring anything with me? I was going to make you dinner at my place, but I can bring the ingredients with me if you feel up to eating."

"You… you were going to cook for me?" I ask, stunned by the idea. I don't think anyone I've dated—not that I'm even sure that's what we're doing—has cooked me dinner. Even when I was married, it was a fight to get Zack to help with our meals.

"Yeah. It's been a while, but I doubt I've forgotten how to use a stove."

A small smile twists my lips. "Well, that's good, because I may have. I'm terrible about cooking myself actual meals."

"All the more reason for me to cook for you," she says, matter-of-fact.

"That's really sweet of you, but I don't think you're going to want to stay that long once you see the state of my place and find out how pathetic and boring I am right now."

"I don't expect you to entertain or impress me," Blair says evenly. "If I want to leave, I will. But I've been waiting all week to see you again and I frankly don't give a shit what that entails."

Butterflies kick up in my stomach, and my smile widens. "Okay, okay. Come over and make me dinner. Maybe do some laundry while you're at it," I add with a laugh.

"Sure," Blair replies.

"Wait, what?" I squeak. "No! It's a joke."

Blair chuckles at my alarm. "We'll see. I'm going to hang up so I can get ready to leave once the sun goes down. Don't try to get up and hurt yourself more."

"But the door is locked. And I need to get dressed."

"Can you do either of those things right now without it causing more pain?" Blair asks.

"No, but—"

"Stay where you are. I'll figure it out."

I'd protest more, but my neck chooses that moment to throb with pain as I dare to move my head a miniscule amount. "Alright."

"Be there soon," Blair says, then hangs up.

I can't decide if I want to groan with embarrassment that the woman I'm hardcore crushing on is about to see me at my lowest or squeal with delight that she's so damn sweet. I settle for sighing and closing my eyes, willing the heat pad to work some magic so I can get up and make myself presentable before Blair gets here.

A soft touch on my arm and the slight dip of the mattress rouses me from my unintentional nap. My eyes blink open in confusion and alarm, and I wince as my reflexive movement to swat away what's waking me up sends pain shooting through my neck.

"Whoa, hey, it's me," Blair says, her cool palm resting atop my shoulder.

"Shit, sorry, I didn't mean to fall asleep," I say groggily.

Her face comes into focus and I can't help smiling. Blair's makeup is as polished as always, the crimson of her lipstick set off beautifully against her rich brown complexion, and her winged eyes taking on a reddish hue in the dark of my bedroom.

"You're so pretty," I murmur, not meaning to say the thought aloud, but pleased when I see her lips twist into a smile.

"So are you."

My heart flutters until I realize that I've still got my dress bunched up around my tits, too pathetic to have even pulled a blanket up to cover myself up. "Yeah, I'm really killing it with my whole pooh bear look," I say with a weak laugh.

"I have no complaints." Blair drops her eyes to look at my exposed tummy and underwear before meeting my gaze again with a hint of a smirk.

I flush, glad for the relative darkness of the room. "Noted."

Hating that I'm laying here instead of getting up to greet her, I roll onto my side, and cradle the back of my neck with one hand to prepare myself for the arduous task of sitting up.

"Can I help?" Blair asks, brow pinching.

"I don't think so. Just gotta psych myself up for it." I inhale deeply and push up with my free arm, grimacing through the pain as I bring myself up to a seated position.

"It's bad." She says it as an assessment, not a question.

"Um, yeah. It's not great right now." My eyes lower, unable to meet hers as embarrassment overtakes me. I feel the urge to wave off my feeble state, even though it's impossible when I'm in this much pain.

The furrow between Blair's brows deepens as she reaches out to rest her hand on my thigh. "Do you have anything you can take for it?"

I sigh and give her a sheepish look. "Yeah. I should've taken my muscle relaxer before I decided to lay down, but my brain doesn't work well when I feel like this. It won't help with the pain much, but it will at least tell my muscles to stop freaking out."

"I'll go get it for you. Tell me where it is." Blair shifts to get up but then freezes in place, a hesitant expression filling her face. "Unless..."

"What?" I'm confused by her hesitation.

She shakes her head. "You said no before, and I don't want to pressure you."

I still don't know what she's talking about, and when she sees the blank look on my face, she explains. "My blood. It could help with the pain."

"Oh! Right."

Blair gives me a weird look. "You didn't remember that?"

"Shit, I'm sorry I forgot. That night was so intense, and you told me about your past right after that, and..." My words falter as shame about not remembering something makes my skin prickle. "Like I said, the pain makes my brain a little wonky sometimes. That, and the ADHD." I try to laugh, but it sounds forced.

Blair grabs my hand and squeezes it. "Hey. I'm not upset you forgot. It surprised me, but not in a bad way."

"Oh. Of course." Great, now I'm embarrassed that I got embarrassed. I force myself to push past it with a smile.

"I'm only offering because I want you to have the option. My blood won't magically cure the degeneration of your spine, but it can provide some relief. If you want it. It's alright if you don't. I don't want to 'fix' you, Grace. You're perfect the way you are."

"Hah! So perfect I can't even get dressed without hurting myself," I say, the compliment making me squirm. Blair doesn't seem the type to lie about that to make me feel better, but I can't understand how the hell she'd feel that way now that she's seen me like this.

Blair surprises me when she snorts at my reaction. "Okay, maybe not perfect. You know what I mean. Yes, I'd love to help you not be in as much pain because I care about you. But I'm not offering because I think your neck issues are a burden."

How does she know what to say to quiet the voice inside me that had that exact worry?

"That means so much to me. And I..." I hesitate, unsure of what to do. Resisting the offer of something that could help me feel better was much easier when it wasn't so acute. I don't want her to think I'm using her, but fuck, it'd be nice to get some relief. "Is it addictive?"

"You won't suffer from withdrawal or negative side-effects if you stop using my blood, but it's potent. I don't suffer from chronic pain, so I'm not sure how hard it would be to stop taking something that was helping you. If you'd rather not risk becoming reliant on me for that, I understand. But if it helps, my blood is yours, no matter what happens between us. I won't withhold it if this..." Blair gestures between us. "Doesn't end up working out."

"I couldn't ask you to do that," I protest.

She shakes her head. "Well, it's a good thing you're not. I'm offering."

You'd think I'd leap at the chance to get rid of my pain. Who would voluntarily stay like this when it could be avoided? Nevertheless, it feels like a monumental decision. If I take Blair's blood, she'll be obligated to take care of me, and no matter what she says now about not minding, it *will* become a burden if things don't work out between us. It comes down to if I think I'll be strong enough to face this pain again if she's not a part of my life.

For once, I trust in myself to weather that if the time comes. Either that or I'm delusional and worn down from the pain, but I'll pretend like it's me knowing my own strength.

"Alright. Yes. Please. I'd like to try it." I search Blair's face for any sign of if that was the right decision or not, but she keeps her expression infuriatingly even.

"Okay. Do you have any straws?"

My brow furrows at her non sequitur. "Why? Am I going to poke one into you like a juice box?"

Blair laughs and shakes her head. "I figured I'd mix some of my blood into a drink for you so you won't taste it as much, and I don't know if it's hard for you to drink from a glass right now."

"Can't I just, uh, drink it from you?" I ask hesitantly, unsure if there's a reason she'd rather I not do something that intimate.

Heat flashes in her eyes, and when she smiles, her fangs have emerged. "I would love for you to drink from me, but I'm worried that might make me too... excited. I don't want to risk fighting the urge to bite you."

"Oh." A furious blush spreads across my cheeks at the memory of how her teeth sinking into my thighs made me come. I haven't worked up the courage to ask her if that's a general effect of being bitten by a vampire. If it's not, then it means I've discovered a new, very specific kink. "I, um, I wouldn't mind if you did. I've heard orgasms are good for pain relief."

Blair licks her lips, her eyes falling to my throat. My pulse quickens as tension rises in the air between us. I may be in pain whenever I move my neck, but I'd have to be dead to not experience a surge of arousal from the way she's staring.

After a few seconds, she clears her throat and shakes her head. "Let's stick with a blood cocktail to begin with. If you're feeling up to it after, then we can see if my bite provides any additional relief."

30

GRACE

Blair flicks on the bedroom light, and heat burns across my cheeks at my current state of undress now that I'm no longer protected by the darkness. She helps me wriggle my dress off down over my hips and belly so I don't have to sit around in something uncomfortable. It should be a decidedly unsexy and embarrassing experience, but Blair's cool fingers on my bare skin as she coaxes the fabric off of my body have me shivering. When she kneels so she can tug it the rest of the way off and kisses my low belly before she rises, my knees go weak.

I really hope her blood helps with the pain. Having her here being all effortlessly alluring will make sitting around like a pathetic lump even more tortuous than usual.

She helps me into a robe, and my breath hitches slightly when she wraps her arms around me from behind to tie it closed.

"Sorry, did I hurt you?" she asks, stepping back.

"N-no. I'm good. Thank you for your help," I say, turning around to face her and hoping my shy smile doesn't give away how turned on I am right now.

"Okay. Tell me if I do anything that hurts," she says, some of the commanding tone she uses as a domme slipping into her voice.

I give her a sheepish smile. "Right now, pretty much any movement I make hurts. So even if it does, it's not your fault."

Blair's brow furrows in clear concern. Or maybe she's finally realizing how pathetic I am.

"It's fine. I'm used to it!" I let out a forced laugh, and drop my gaze to the floor, which pulls a hiss of distress from me as the movement sends pain jolting through me.

She threads her fingers through mine and gives my hand a squeeze. The absurd urge to cry builds at that gentle sign of reassurance, and I blink rapidly against it.

"Let's go make your drink so you can have that right away. Then, if you're hungry, I'll make dinner."

She's so calm in the face of my pain. There are no trite apologies or hopes it'll get better soon, which is one of the many reasons I avoid telling people about my spine issues. Blair's silent acceptance of my physical problems being part of me makes me feel more seen and cared for than I have since the chronic pain started.

"Sounds perfect. Thank you," I say, squeezing her hand back.

We head down to the kitchen, and I fight against the urge to apologize for the piles of stuff littering my entire downstairs. Blair said she didn't care, and she doesn't bat an eye at any of it. Though I still cringe as she pulls a glass from my open dishwasher with the clean dishes still waiting to be put away, then goes to my fridge to assess what I have available.

"I don't have a ton, and I'm not sure if any of it would pair well with blood," I say with a weak chuckle. The thought of drinking her blood is a little gross, but not enough to stop me from wanting to try it. Maybe I'm weird, but I think I'd enjoy it more from her directly, my lips on her skin and her body pressed close to mine.

Blair grabs a can of seltzer and an unopened bottle of cranberry juice I didn't even know I had. "I've never made a blood cocktail before, but from what people have told me, my blood doesn't taste unpleasant. If you hate it, we can order something stronger to cover it better." She looks endearingly nervous about what I'll think of her blood.

"I won't hate it!"

Her lips quirk at my adamance. "Okay."

She pours a few ounces of cranberry juice and a splash of seltzer into the glass and swirls them together with a spoon, then gives me another nervous look. "I'm going to, uh, add some of my blood now. If you want to look away."

It's odd seeing Blair visibly worried, and if I didn't think it would hurt like a bitch, I'd give her a hug. I smile at her brightly. "I'm not bothered by the sight of blood. At least not in smaller amounts."

"Right." Blair nods and brings her wrist to her mouth and doesn't even flinch when she bites shallowly into her own flesh.

"Oh!" I don't hide my surprise that she isn't just pricking her finger. I guess I need more blood than I'd imagined.

My stomach does a slightly queasy lurch, but I can't help watching as she brings her hand over the glass and rivulets of crimson flow down her deep brown skin to splash into the liquid below. After a few moments, Blair brings her wrist back to her mouth and licks the puncture marks until the skin starts to knit back together before my eyes.

"Whoa, that's wild," I murmur.

Blair's eyes meet mine, her blood-stained lips tilting into an apologetic smile. "It's unsettling, I know."

"No, it's amazing. I forget how... *magical* you are sometimes."

"That's one way of putting it," she says drolly.

"You are, Blair!" I argue. "You're giving me your blood to help get rid of my pain. You saved Max's life with your blood, for fuck's sake. If that's not magical, then I don't know what is."

Blair chuckles, stirring the drink again to incorporate her blood. When she's satisfied, she passes it over to me. "Drink half and see how you feel. If it's not enough, have the rest."

I bring the glass to my lips with feigned confidence, giving her a smile. Blair has been so worried about me not being able to tolerate the taste that I don't want to show any sign of discomfort. Still, I'd be lying if I said I wasn't hesitant to down the bizarre cocktail.

I'm prepared to chug it, but the second the liquid hits my tongue, I slow down. The taste is a little odd, but it's inconsequential because my body suffuses with pleasure as I swallow it down. It's like sinking into a hot bath at the perfect temperature after a long, hard day. A stifled moan escapes my lips as tension melts from my body, and I reluctantly set the glass down when I've drained half of it.

"Fucking magical," I whisper in awe. The pain is muted, barely more than a twinge as I reach out and pull Blair toward me, driven by the urge to kiss her now.

I bend down and bring my lips to hers, sighing as more relief floods through me when our lips meet. Blair arms fly up from where she held them stiffly at her sides to grip my hips, and I part my lips in invitation for her to deepen the kiss. She takes it, the taste of blood on her tongue sparking my senses, sending prickles of pleasure dancing down my spine.

I slide my tongue against hers, wrapping my arms around Blair in an attempt to anchor myself to her. Her fangs scrape against my lower lip and I moan against her mouth, hips pressing forward, mindlessly seeking some kind of friction to ease the ache building between my thighs.

"Fuck, baby," Blair murmurs as I pull back to suck in a breath, before claiming her lips again.

Hearing her call me "baby" has me grinding my hips against her again, heedless of how our bodies slot together in an unfamiliar way. I don't care that it's different. I need her more than anyone I've ever been with.

Blair presses forward, backing me up gently until I bump into the countertop behind me, and wedges her thigh between my legs. I gasp into her mouth as she raises her leg and grabs my hips again, encouraging me to grind against her thigh. The flimsy barrier of my soaked panties and her skintight jeans make the position we're in feel dirtier than it would if we were naked.

Blair catches my lower lip with her fangs again, almost drawing blood this time. I arch forward with a gasp, and she pulls off of my lips to bring her mouth to my ear. "That's it. Use my thigh to give that needy pussy what it wants."

I rub against her and the friction feels amazing, even though I doubt I'll be able to come this way. For once, I'm too wrapped up in the moment to give a shit if what we're doing leads to me coming or not. I just want more.

Blair's mouth trails down the side of my throat, carefully dragging her fangs across the delicate skin. I shiver and rock against her thigh again. She groans and laves her tongue across my pulse point.

"You're making a mess, dripping all over my jeans. Such a dirty girl, Grace."

"F-fuck," I whimper, cheeks burning with embarrassment at how needy I am, but arousal stoked higher because of that prick of shame. Maybe I'm into humiliation after all.

"You like being my dirty girl, don't you? Show me how much you like it." Blair grips my ass and grinds me against her thigh again, helping me build up a rhythm.

My mouth drops open with a silent moan as she sucks my neck. "Do it. You can bite me. I want you to."

I want it so bad I could scream. Not because it might make me come, but because I want the connection. When Blair bit me before, it was like everything else melted away and it was only us, tethered together through pleasure and something else that I'm scared to name. Something that's way too early in whatever this is between us to be thinking about.

Her grip on my ass tightens, but she rips her mouth away from my neck, eyes burning into mine with barely restrained hunger. "I shouldn't," she rasps. "You're still under the effects of my blood. I need to make sure your pain is under control, not add to it."

"I'm fine. Please, Blair. I want you."

She shakes her head, eyes screwing shut. "You want to come because of how my blood makes you feel. That's not the same thing as wanting me."

Frustration cuts through my arousal. I want to grab Blair by the shoulders and shake some sense into my stubborn vampire.

"Fine. Don't bite me," I say sharply, pushing against her shoulders to create space between us. Her expression hardens as she steps back, no doubt thinking her assumptions about me were correct.

I don't give her more time to live in that delusion. I sink to my knees before her and look up into her eyes. There's a twinge of pain as I do, but it's nothing I can't ignore. God, her blood really is magic.

"What are you doing?" she asks, brows knitting together in confusion.

"Showing you how much I want you," I bite back, fingers fumbling with the button on her jeans.

Blair blinks down at me, eyes wide in shock. "What? No. Get up. You don't need to prove anything to me. Forget I said anything. I'll bite you if that's what you want."

I roll my eyes at her. "I'm not proving anything other than how fucking dense you're being."

I tug down the zipper and hook my fingers under the waistband of her jeans and underwear with determination. "I'm going to eat your pussy until you get it through your thick, undead skull that I want this. That I'm obsessed with you and can't stop wondering what you taste like. So use your safeword or shut the fuck up, Blair."

31

BLAIR

The challenge blazing in Grace's eyes would knock the breath from me if I hadn't stopped breathing the moment she started undoing my jeans.

Fuck, she's hot when she's pissy, and even hotter down on her knees, tugging my jeans and underwear down my legs while glaring up at me.

In all the ways I imagined Grace putting her mouth on me, it was never like this. How did we go from giving her my blood for pain relief to her grabbing my thighs, her pink manicured nails digging in enough to hurt a little as she pushes them apart?

Does she like taking control? She didn't list it as something she wanted to try when she filled out the kink questionnaire. No, Grace is only doing this because she's right—I'm a stubborn, dense fool who keeps waiting for the other shoe to drop and I find out this isn't real for her.

Grace presses a tentative kiss to my inner thigh, and my head swims from desire and the unmooring sensation of not being the one setting the pace for sex.

It's too much. I need to regain control for both our sakes.

I gingerly thread a hand through Grace's hair and tighten my grip, not wanting to yank her head back and aggravate her neck issue, but needing her to feel the prick of pain in her scalp.

She gasps and pulls back, tilting her head up to give me a petulant look.

Grace isn't a brat. She's pissed for good reason. I don't want her to be in that kind of headspace the first time she does this. Maybe I'm selfish, but I want it to be something she'll remember with eagerness to do it again, not the memory of being angry at me. I'm already worried enough that she'll hate it.

"If you want to negotiate a scene where you're in charge, we can do that when our heads are clear. Until then, I say when you've earned my pussy, pet."

Grace's breath catches and her pupils expand at the shift in energy between us. She licks her lips. "I've been good. Please don't make me wait any longer."

I pretend to think, even though my clit is throbbing, seeing that she's serious about wanting to go down on me. I release her hair and stroke her cheek, then graze my thumb across her kiss-swollen lips. "Pets don't get to make demands. They take whatever they're given."

"Yes, Mistress," she murmurs, the flame of frustration in her eyes shifting into yearning submission.

As much as I want to fist Grace's hair again and hold her mouth against my pussy, I'm still concerned about her neck. She's not in pain now, but that doesn't mean I want to make things worse once the effects of my blood wear off. If she had a fresh injury, like a cut, it could heal that easily, but it doesn't undo a disease that causes degeneration. It's not a cure.

I gesture to the abandoned blood cocktail on the counter. "Drink the rest of that. When you're done, go upstairs, take off your robe and underwear, and lie down on the bed."

Grace's mouth falls open, and her brow pinches, but no protest escapes. She stands and grabs the glass, bringing it to her lips. Watching her throat work as she downs the liquid reminds me of our first scene together, but this time I won't be going home afraid of what my monster will do to her if I give in to my desire.

This time, I'm letting myself have what I'm desperate for.

She sets the glass down and wipes her lips, then turns to head toward the stairs, but I grab her arm. "You know what to say if you need to stop. Use it if you don't enjoy something we do when we get into the bedroom or if it bothers your neck. I promise I won't be upset. If I'm not allowed to be stubborn about this, then neither are you."

She nods, and I let go of her arm, watching her cross the living room to the stairs and giving myself a moment to get my head on straight before fully diving into this impromptu scene. I pull my pants and underwear back up over my hips, smiling at how adamant Grace was when she tugged them down. As I'm putting the bottle of juice back in the fridge, I pause when I see the ingredients I'd brought for dinner sitting in there.

I didn't come over tonight for sex. I came because I wanted to take care of Grace in any way she'd let me. I'd planned on making dinner and tidying up while she rested, and the thought of being able to help her like that made me happy.

But then she had to kiss me like she couldn't live without my lips on hers.

I'd write it off as a side-effect of my blood, but I know from experience it doesn't have that effect. I've given people my blood before and it makes them feel relaxed and floaty, but never forced arousal. That kiss was all Grace.

Now she's waiting for me upstairs, naked and ready for my command. Her dinner will have to wait.

I head upstairs, and even though I expected Grace to be naked, I freeze in the doorway at the sight. She's turned off the overhead light and put on the bedside lamps, casting a warm glow over the pale pinks and creams of her bedroom, a perfect compliment to her flushed bare skin and rosy nipples. She's sprawled on her back, her blonde hair fanned across the pillow, looking like an angelic offering to my monster. Her soft stomach rises and falls with rapid breaths as she hears me in the doorway, but she stays still, waiting for me to use her as I see fit.

Every inch of her is tempting. I could worship and tease her gorgeous breasts, or pepper kisses and nips across the soft dips and curves of her stomach and hips. I already know how divine her pussy tastes, and the thought of experiencing it again as she begs for me to give her more makes my mouth water. But she wanted to try eating my pussy, so that's what she'll get. To start, at least. Who knows what my monster will want when I'm overtaken by pleasure?

"Such a good pet, waiting patiently for me," I murmur as I move over to the bed.

"Thank you," Grace says breathily, her head turning so she can look at me. There's no sign at all of discomfort or pain, and pride surges inside me.

I helped her. I took away her pain. I may despise my vampiric nature, but without it, I wouldn't have been able to give this to Grace. It makes my monstrous side slightly more bearable.

A shy smile curves her lips as I peel my shirt off over my head. I didn't bother wearing a bra tonight, and the cool air of the bedroom makes my nipples stiffen. Or maybe that's from Grace's eyes on me. Does she like what she sees?

Unwilling to let myself get caught up in that question, I tug off my jeans and underwear unceremoniously and step out of them. It's not a particularly sexy thing to do, but when I meet Grace's gaze after, she's staring at me like I'm something special.

"You are so fucking gorgeous," she says, her eyes darting all over my body like she can't decide what part she wants to look at the most. "I knew that already, but... damn, Blair. How are you so perfect?"

"I'm not," I say with a shrug, trying to play off how much her praise affects me. I turn to show her the scar on the back of my leg from when I fell climbing a tree as a kid. My body heals injuries on its own now, but it doesn't remove the marks of the life I lived before becoming a vampire. "See? Not perfect."

She laughs, the sound breathy with her excitement. "How is showing me your amazing ass supposed to convince me otherwise?"

"There's a scar." I move closer and point directly at the puckered, jagged line.

I don't expect her to bring her hand up to trace it reverently, her warm fingers ghosting across the back of my thigh, doing more to turn me on than anything I've done with past partners.

"Nope. Still perfect."

The look Grace gives me when I turn back around is laced with a multitude of emotions. Many of which I'm scared to name, afraid that recognizing them will shatter what little remains of the barrier protecting my heart. I almost stumble backwards under the weight of it.

I swallow down my urge to panic at the mirroring cacophony of emotions inside me and focus on the heat pooling between my thighs. Pleasure is simple and infinitely safer than feelings. It follows my command.

I get on the bed and straddle Grace's waist. Her body tenses for a moment, but then she visibly melts as my weight settles atop her. I can't resist the urge to lean down and kiss her, consuming her little gasps of pleasure like I need them to sustain me.

She lets out a needy whine that almost makes me bite her right then and there when I pull back to let her catch her breath.

"What would you do to earn a taste of my pussy, pet?" I ask, my eyes locking on hers.

"Anything, Mistress," Grace gasps.

"Anything? Such a needy little thing, aren't you?"

"Yes," she replies with no hesitation.

Heat flares inside me and I rest a hand on her throat. Her pulse hammers beneath my fingers, calling to my monster. "Open your mouth and stick out your tongue. Take what I give you like a good girl and maybe I'll consider it."

Her eyes grow hooded at my touch and order, which she immediately obeys. Fuck, she really is a natural submissive.

I nick my lip with my fang and let my mouth fill with a mixture of saliva and blood as she waits, mouth open and pretty pink tongue presented to receive whatever I do. I lean forward, hand still lightly pinning her in place by the throat, and spit.

Her eyes flare wide in shock and she makes a garbled sound, but she keeps her mouth open.

"Swallow," I command.

Grace follows my order, and I feel her throat work under my

palm. Without my prompting, she opens her mouth and sticks her tongue out again.

It drags a low, dark laugh out of me, and my clit sparks seeing how much Grace wants to please me. "Mmm, you liked that, didn't you, dirty girl?"

Grace nods, her eyelashes fluttering at my words. She's stunning like this. There's no worry that she's not doing a good job. Only the beauty of her submission.

I lean forward and claim her lips again, the taste of my blood in her mouth making me moan. Enough playing around. I need some relief from the desire burning inside me before it immolates me.

When our lips part, Grace is panting. Her hands fist into the sheets beside her and I realize that she's keeping herself from touching me because I didn't give her permission. Her restraint is so goddamn sexy, it makes my head spin.

"Such a good girl. You've earned your reward," I murmur. "Since you won't be able to speak, tap my thigh twice like this if you need to stop."

I demonstrate what I mean, and she nods.

"Thank you, Mistress," she whispers, her voice threaded with a mixture of relief and desire.

Lifting off of Grace's stomach, I move up until I'm kneeling above her face. I grab hold of her headboard to steady myself as I lower down until my pussy is just out of reach of her mouth.

"You want this pussy?" I ask, my eyes locked on to hers where they peek out from between my thighs.

"Yes, Mistress." Her breath ghosts over my slick labia. I'm so fucking wet, I'm already dripping on her face.

"Go on, lick it. *Once*." I lower down so that she can reach me and she doesn't hesitate. Her tongue swipes a searing brand from my entrance up to my clit.

"How do I taste, pet?" I ask, backing off enough that I can see her expression better. I know I shouldn't care, but I can't help wanting the woman I'm obsessed with to not be completely repulsed by the taste of my pussy. It's her first time doing this and if she doesn't like it, we can stop.

But Grace surprises me, licking her lips and smiling up at me. "You taste like... sex. Like the desires I never knew I had until we met, hidden, but craved once I knew what it could feel like. I love it."

Fuck me. She might as well have told me she loves me from how my entire being burns at her words.

I lower myself back down and guide her hands to grip onto my hips, which she squeezes with a grateful hum of approval. My thighs are going to get a workout from trying not to put too much weight on her neck, but I couldn't care less. "Such pretty words from an even prettier mouth. Show me how well you can put that mouth to work."

32

GRACE

I extend my tongue as Blair grips the headboard and rocks her hips forward, dragging her pussy across my chin and mouth. Her taste and scent surround me, musky and sweet. I've tasted myself out of curiosity in the past, and it was inoffensive, but nothing I'd seek out. It certainly wasn't the same as Blair's arousal coating my lips.

This is intoxicating. Why I ever worried that I wouldn't be into eating pussy is a mystery now that she's grinding hers against my face, guiding my outstretched tongue wherever she needs it.

It helps that I don't have to think about what I should do because she's using me exactly how she wants. And god, why does it feel so good to be used by her? The picture we must paint dances around in my mind, sparking even more arousal to life. Me willingly pinned in place by Blair, licking her pussy like I need the taste more than air as she lets out small gasps of pleasure.

"That's it," she sighs as she slows her grinding for a moment when I circle her clit with my tongue. I do it again and this time she rocks her hips in tandem with my movement, pressing my tongue more firmly against the underside of her clit. "Keep doing that until I tell you to stop," she orders, her voice edged with a hint of desperation.

Pleasure and pride suffuse my body as I obey and her restrained gasps turn into shuddering, soft moans. I'm making her feel good. There's nothing to worry about in this moment except doing exactly what she needs to chase her release.

I'm Blair's willing pet, but I feel *powerful* as her thighs start to shake and she grinds harder against my mouth. All that exists is her wet heat coating my face, the soft give of her thighs as I hold her close, and the burning desire to make her come.

"Fuck," Blair curses, and a moment later, her hand drops from the headboard to grip my hair. I can tell she wants to tug my head up to force it harder against her pussy by the tight sting of her hold, but even when she's lost in pleasure, she doesn't lose her concern for my well being.

"You love eating this pussy, don't you? You want me to soak your pretty face."

I let out a muffled groan against her and she jolts, her grip on my hair tightening enough that she might pull some of it out. I fucking love it. I groan again and redouble my efforts, flicking her clit with my tongue in short strokes that make her cry out.

"Fuck, don't stop. God, baby, your mouth is so perfect. You're going to make me come," Blair gasps, sounding shocked by how quickly we got to this point.

More pride bubbles up inside me and I moan, doing as she commands. I'll never stop unless she asks me to. I could do this for the rest of my life.

"Yes, ah, fuck, Grace!"

Blair coming with my name on her lips is almost enough to make me come too. Her clit pulses under my tongue, but she hasn't told me to stop, so I keep licking her through her release.

She sags as she comes down from her peak, letting her full weight rest against my face, and the sensation is so arousing that I moan. There's not room for me to work my tongue against her much like this, but I keep trying.

"Stop," she commands, but there's no sharpness to her tone. No, Blair giggles as she releases her grip from my hair. My stoic vampire *giggles*.

Damn, as much as I love having her smothering me with her pussy, I'd give anything to see what she looks like when she laughs like that.

She grants my wish, raising off of me and moving down so she's straddling my waist again. My breath hitches when I see her face.

Blair beams down at me with an expression of pure, unguarded happiness. If this is what she looks like after she comes, I'm going to beg her to let me make her come as many times as she'll let me. Her fangs glint in the low light as she grins, and her breasts rise and fall with her shallow breaths, drawing my eye to them.

Unthinking, I reach up and thumb her nipple, reveling in the way her eyelashes flutter at my touch. I grow bolder, cupping her breast and giving it a gentle squeeze. "You're so beautiful," I murmur, in awe of the radiant goddess allowing me to touch her.

Her eyes open at my words, and the reddish gleam of them in the dark captivates me. I expect her to chastise me for touching without her permission, but she places her hand atop mine to mold in against her breast. She guides me to squeeze it, letting out a breathy sigh as I thumb her nipple again.

I need to be closer. I need to feel her against me.

I drop my hand, and Blair gives me a questioning look, her expression shuttering slightly. She doesn't have long to shut down though, because I use my arms to push up to sitting and mash my lips against hers. It's an inelegant and awkward move, and my mouth is messy and wet from her, but Blair doesn't seem to care. She kisses me back with equal fervor, gripping my back to hold me close.

I gasp when she drops her head to kiss and suck along the side of my neck. She teases me, grazing me with her fangs, but I resist the urge to ask for her bite. I don't want her to freeze up like she did down in the kitchen.

She trails her lips down to the top of my breast, then back up to the other side of my throat, her kisses a hot brand against my skin. I'm so tense I'm almost vibrating with the need for something more. Anything to give me some relief from the ache I feel between my thighs.

"Do you have a vibrator?" Blair asks, lifting her lips off of me to give me a wicked grin.

"Uh, yeah?"

"Where?"

"In the nightstand, but I'm okay, I don't need—"

Blair silences me with a forceful kiss, then disentangles herself from my lap and goes to the drawer.

My cheeks burn as she digs through the small assortment of toys, which is ridiculous considering she was sitting on my face less than five minutes ago. There's something incredibly intimate about her seeing what I use to get off, and the embarrassment only serves to make the heat pooling in my core more intense.

Blair grabs my curved pink g-spot vibrator with the external clit stimulator that stays in place without needing to hold it, giving me a look of triumph. "Perfect. Lube?"

The toy isn't very girthy, and I'm so wet right now. I'm already squirming at the thought of her putting it inside me. "I don't need any," I murmur.

Blair's filthy grin makes my stomach clench. "Spread your legs for me, baby. Show me how much your pussy is dripping for me."

Baby, not pet. I don't know if she's picked up on the way she changes what she calls me sometimes, but I have. I love being her pet, but she calls me baby when she's turned on the most. When her guard is lowered, and her softer self bleeds through her domme side.

I sit back against the headboard and let my thighs fall open, and Blair shakes her head. "Wider, baby. Show me that needy pussy."

I flush but obey, opening my legs wide and dropping a hand to spread my labia apart for her.

"Gorgeous. Has anyone ever told you that you have the prettiest pussy?"

Her question takes me by surprise, startling a laugh out of me. "Um, no?" Plenty of guys have been eager to get between my thighs, but no one has ever commented on what I look like. I always thought it was one of those things where they liked being inside me, but didn't think the outward appearance was particularly appealing.

"Well, you do. I bet it'll look especially pretty once I fill you up with this," she says, circling the rounded end of the toy around my entrance. "Maybe we'll work on finding out what else we can stretch this dripping cunt out with. See if you can be a good pet and take my whole hand someday."

"Oh fuck," I curse, the concept making my pussy clench. I

marked fisting as something I was only slightly interested in on the kink survey, but hearing her put it like that makes it shoot up much higher on my list of things to try. At least in theory. I have a feeling in practice, it won't be realistic at all for me.

"Mmm," Blair purrs as she dips the tip of the toy inside me without applying the pressure needed to slip it in past my entrance. "I thought you might like that. Don't worry, sweetheart. I'll give you everything you need. Even the things you didn't know to ask for."

"Thank you." My breath catches as she presses the toy a bit harder, the tip only making it in a few centimeters. Nerves spike inside me as she pulls it back and presses it in again, but still meets resistance. I flush. "Sorry, I know I'm really wet but it can take, uh, more force for me."

It's something I've struggled with my whole life. I know a lot of dudes act like the tighter the pussy, the better the sex is, but that's never been the case for me. I've always struggled with being so tight that it's hard for a guy to get his cock inside me without a lot of force, lube, and unpleasantness on my end. Zack complained the first dozen times we had sex that he couldn't get it in, and then once he got over that, he got frustrated that he came super fast because I was "too tight". It took me years to venture into trying internal toys because even then, there's always been discomfort if I don't take my time easing them inside me.

Blair frowns, and there's a flash of anger behind her eyes that I don't think has anything to do with me. "We're not in a hurry. I won't need to force anything."

"O-okay," I whisper, trying to get myself back into the moment again. I let out a frustrated exhale and close my eyes for a moment. I can't let shitty past experiences ruin my sex life anymore. I'm sick of always worrying I'm not enough or too difficult.

My eyes pop back open as Blair turns the vibration on, and teases the toy across my labia and around my clit. She does it again and again, occasionally catching the tip of the toy against my entrance before skirting it back over my labia and clit, stoking my desire back to life. Now, each time the tip dips toward my opening, I can't help letting out a whine of need.

"Shh, be patient. I'll give you what you need when I'm ready," Blair chastises, moving the toy away again and up to brush my clit. Reframing it as her wanting to take her time, as her not being ready, rather than me needing a ton of warmup, makes something tighten in my chest. She understands me so well. She's so good and kind to me, I could cry.

When she finally presses the toy inside me, it slides in with barely any resistance, but she pulses it inside slowly, in and out a few centimeters at a time until it's all the way in, the rumbling vibration against my g-spot making me gasp.

A moment later, Blair presses the button for the vibration in the external part of the toy resting on my clit and grins as I cry out. "There we go," she purrs, moving back and sitting back on her heels to stare at the toy buzzing between my legs. "Exactly as I thought. You look beautiful taking it for me."

"Oh god, I need... I can't..." I gasp, unsure of what I'm asking for. I'd take anything. Her lips on mine. My hands on her body. For her to wrap me up in her arms so I won't fall to pieces when the orgasm threatening to shatter me takes hold.

Blair pulls me against her so I'm straddling her lap, the new position pressing the toy against my g-spot in a way that makes me see stars. She kisses me, her mouth on mine as hungry and desperate as I feel.

When I pull back for air, the heat in her eyes makes me moan. "You're going to come for me, Grace. Once like this, then as many times as you can while I drink the ecstasy from you. Come for me. Now."

More stars explode across my vision as she grazes my throat with her fangs, using her other hand to turn up the vibrations. I can't do anything but take what she gives, my body obeying even this command.

I break. My pussy clenches hard against the toy and I cry out something desperate and unintelligible as my orgasm hits me. I writhe in Blair's lap, clutching onto her. "Oh god, please. Oh fuck, fuck, *please*." I don't even know if I'm begging for the too-bright pleasure to abate or for it to go on forever.

Blair decides for me. "Such a good girl. Give me another," she rasps. There's a sharp flash of pain as she sinks her fangs into my neck, followed by more blinding bliss.

I give her everything I have as I come again. My pleasure. My blood. The yearning hopes that fill my heart every moment we're together.

33

BLAIR

It's late by the time I've wrung every ounce of pleasure I can out of Grace. She's smiling and sated, melted into a puddle on the bed as I kiss the bite on the top of her breast before finally forcing myself to pull back. There's a deep yearning in my gut to lie down next to her and hold her as she drifts off to sleep, but if I stay any longer, I'll risk not making it home before sunrise.

"I have to go," I whisper, stroking her arm because I can't seem to stop touching her.

"I know," she sighs, giving me a sweet, sad smile as I trace the bite on her forearm, one of many that I scattered across her supple body. Arousal thrums inside me that some of them are already bruising her skin, since I didn't immediately heal the wounds. Grace looks so fucking good covered in my bites.

"I don't want to," I add, though I'm sure that's evident from the way I can't will myself to get off the bed.

"I know," Grace says again, threading her fingers through mine and giving my hand a squeeze.

"I'll call you as soon as I wake up tomorrow night. I don't know how long the pain relief from my blood will last, and I worry we were... overzealous after seeing the immediate effects."

Grace nods, pushing herself up to sit beside me on the edge of the bed. "It was worth it. Even if I'm in pain later, I'll at least have had the chance to enjoy tonight with you."

"I would've been happy just to take care of you. You know that, right?" I ask. I grimace as I remember the ingredients for dinner still sitting in her refrigerator. "Shit, you didn't eat. You must be starving!"

"I ate plenty." She waggles her eyebrows at me.

"You did, but my pussy isn't a replacement for a meal," I deadpan, and she giggles. I glance at my phone to check the time. "Do you like eggs? I'll make you something quick before I go. Tomorrow night I can come over and make what I'd planned—shit, wait, no. I have work... I'll cancel."

"Don't cancel!" Grace protests. "I'll be fine on my own, and I'll make sure to use up the stuff you brought, so it doesn't go to waste. Your work is more important than cooking me dinner."

I narrow my eyes at her. "That's debatable."

She laughs and shakes her head at me. "Seriously. You've worked hard to get to the place you are with your job. You have clients that...rely on you." A soft flush raises on her cheeks. "I know it would ruin my week if I thought I'd get to have a scene with you, and then it got canceled at the last minute. You should've seen how much I cried when I thought I wouldn't be able to see you tonight because of my stupid neck. Don't make those poor men cry, Blair. At least not in a way they won't enjoy."

Even though she's joking, I can tell she's earnest. We haven't broached the subject of what I do for work and how she feels about it. If it bothers her, me dominating people who aren't her when we're...

Fuck, we haven't even talked about what exactly this is between us. My stomach twists, but I shove that concern aside. It's far too late to bring up that weighty subject now.

Still, a part of me needs to know what she thinks of my job before I fall too deep into this... *thing* between us. "You don't mind that I'll be with someone else?"

"Honestly?" Grace asks, and I nod, the knot in my stomach twisting tighter. "I thought it would weird me out more than it does. After being with someone who cheated on me for over a year while I obliviously assumed things between us were fine, it should bother me to know you're spending your nights with other people, right?"

"There's no should or shouldn't, Grace. They're your feelings, and whatever they are, they're valid. Though, I'd be remiss to not remind you that what I do with clients isn't romantic or arousing for me. I get satisfaction from it, but it's work."

"That's what makes it feel okay," she says, her tone thoughtful. "Plus, you're fucking incredible at what you do. It's weird... but I kinda like the thought of you going out there and domming the shit out of your clients. It makes me wish I could be a fly on the wall and see how they bend to your will."

My eyebrows raise in surprise, and I scan her face to see if she's being sincere. Voyeurism definitely wasn't on her list of kinks. "You'd want to watch me?"

Her cheeks flush even darker at my scrutiny. "Uh, yeah. It'd be sexy. Seeing what you're doing to someone else and knowing how it feels to be under your control..." She clears her throat and lets out a breathy laugh. "If you hadn't looked like you were going to murder me and it wasn't with the guy who was supposed to be on a date with me, that night at The Vault watching you tie someone up would've been really hot."

"Oh yeah?" I stroke my fingers across the bite on her thigh, savoring the way she subtly parts her legs to invite more of my touch.

"Y-yeah. I mean, it's like anything else where I'd have to try it to find out, but in theory... yeah."

I need to stop touching her. If I don't stop, I'm going to bury my face between her thighs again and end up having to spend the day trapped in her closet because I didn't make it home in time to not get burned to a crisp by the sun. "Some of my clients would love the chance to be watched by a goddess like you," I murmur.

It's an intriguing thought, bringing Grace with me to observe a scene with a client. She'd get to witness some kinks we haven't explored yet, and it's absolutely true that many of my clients would leap at the chance to be dominated in front of a beautiful, unobtainable woman. Still, the possessive part of me doesn't want to share her like that, at least not so soon after I've finally had her in my arms. And definitely not while things are so nebulous between us.

"I'm not sure if any of them have earned that privilege yet, though," I say, forcing myself to remove my hand from her thigh while I'm still capable of rational, non-lust fogged thoughts.

"That's okay," Grace says with an easy smile. "I'm happy the way things are. More than happy." Her expression flickers, and a moment later a look of horror replaces her smile. "Shit, I hope you don't think I want to watch because this isn't enough. That I need to see dicks in order to be happy. This is more than enough! This is the best thing I've ever experienced in my life."

Warm affection swells in my chest at her worry, and I kiss her. It's brief and a lot less than I'd like to do to show her what her words mean to me, but it'll have to do for now. "Same."

I want to tell Grace that being with her is a revelation. That I've slept with dozens of people, dominated many more, and no one has come close to making me feel the way she does. That I don't think anyone else ever will. Instead, I settle for kissing her again and hoping she can feel it through my lips.

Work keeps me busier than I'd like over the next few weeks, but I do as Grace asked and keep the sessions I'd already booked. She's right. I owe my clients the courtesy of showing up for them, even if I'd rather spend the time somewhere else. Although, I've started easing many of my regulars into the idea that I won't have as much availability going forward, whittling my future schedule down so that I have more free time.

Some of my clients complain, and I take them off my schedule entirely. I'm not playing games with that nonsense, and have plenty of others who are happy to take what I can give them. Nic sees right through me when tell him I'll only be available to see him once a month for the foreseeable future, his eyes going watery as he congratulates me for finding something special that will require extra time off work, and asking if he can give me a hug. I refuse him, of course, but that doesn't stop the fluttering feelings from bursting forth inside me at the concept that I have something to care about outside of my job.

Those damn flutters seem to be a daily occurrence lately, but I've stopped trying to fight them. The time I have to spend with Grace feels precious with my packed schedule, and it's a waste to use it on freaking out about what we're doing together. For the first time since I was turned, I loosen the reins on my self-control, and see what it's like to not constantly consider the consequences of my actions.

When I'm with Grace, I take my stoic mask off completely. I smile brighter, laugh more freely, and make my insatiable hunger for her abundantly clear. I let myself fulfill Mona's "prophecy" when we get together to watch the season premiere of In the Stars, even knowing how much more prying into my relationship with Grace that will invite from Mona.

Living like this, without trying to control and restrain my emotions, is intoxicating. My blood might help Grace with her chronic pain, but she gives me *life*.

But like everything else in my wretched existence, that delusion of happiness comes crashing down.

It's early in the evening, only an hour after I've woken up for the night, and I'm buzzing with excitement because my client texted to cancel our session tonight. I know for a fact Grace doesn't have any plans other than pretending that she's going to do her laundry instead of playing that ridiculous vampire dating sim on her phone that she downloaded as a joke, but became obsessed with. Her current running joke is complaining that I never do any fun vampire things like kidnap her and keep her chained in my lair, duel a rival werewolf gang to win her, or use a compulsion to make her in my thrall.

I've planned a scene where we can roleplay that first one, and I'm grinning as I finish arranging for her to come over to my "lair" tonight, when there's a firm rap on the front door.

I glare toward the offending noise, mentally willing whoever is there to go away. Solicitors are always coming over here despite my many signs warning them off. Too bad I can't put one up that says "beware of vampire who drains the blood of trespassers."

There are two more sharp knocks in quick succession, and I set my phone down with a disgruntled sigh. Why can't anyone get the message to leave me alone? I force my fangs to retract and head to the door, yanking it open with a scowl.

My menacing look falters as I see who is on the other side.

They laugh and roll their eyes at my posturing. "*Finally.* I thought maybe you'd died in there."

34

BLAIR

"A*ven?*" I ask, blinking in confusion at the fae standing before me.

"None other." They grin, flashing their razor-sharp teeth at me and holding their pale, pearlescent arms out with a dramatic flourish.

A moment of stunned silence passes as my brain attempts to process that my fae kink mentor I haven't seen in years is here on my doorstep.

"Well, are you going to stand there slack jawed, or are you going to invite me in?" they ask, rolling their milky green eyes at me as their opalescent wings twitch behind them in agitation. It's a good thing I have a long driveway and tree cover surrounding my property, because explaining the literal fairy standing on my porch to neighbors would be difficult.

I open the door wider and they stride inside, letting out a low whistle. "Damn, Blair. You've done well for yourself. Got yourself your own godsdamn gothic manor and everything."

"It's just a house," I say, brow knitting together.

What are they doing here? What do they want? With fae, you never know what to expect. It could be anything from swinging by for a friendly chat, to coming to con me out of everything I own because I said something in passing that made them mad. Things are finally going well, so it'd be my luck that Aven is here to seek vengeance for a long held grudge. Shit, is that why they ghosted me?

Aven spins around and startles at my stormy expression. "Whoa, why are you looking at me like that? Aren't you happy to see me?"

"I... I'm confused," I say hesitantly. "You vanished without saying anything, and now you're here at my house, four years later."

"Oh! It's only been four years? It's felt more like decades with how tedious all the fae realm nonsense I was dealing with was. Though, time is weird between here and that plane, so maybe it was decades for me... Anyway! I'm here now," they say cheerily.

"So you're here because..."

"I wanted to say hello to my favorite vampire protégé! I was visiting with an old friend and imagine my surprise when she mentioned a vampire named Blair living in town who helped her out with some nasty demon trouble. Nice work, by the way! Your compulsion skills must've improved tremendously in my absence. Do you want to try them out on me again and see if you can make me... what was it you tried to do the night we met?" They clap their hands together. "Oh! Right. Give you all the money in my wallet."

"I'm good, thanks." I'm still on edge, but there's no sign of malice in their demeanor. No, they're exactly as talkative and friendly as they were before. I guess it really is a social visit.

"Don't tell me you're upset I didn't say goodbye. Is that why you're not more excited to see me?" Aven asks with an exaggerated pout that twists the uncanny beauty of their face.

From what I remember of Aven, they were never a fan of hiding the truth, so I answer honestly. "I was hurt at the time. But I'm past that. It's good to see you now that I know you're not here to exact revenge."

"Oh gods, no!" They clasp their chest with their hand melodramatically. "I save that for people far less interesting and beautiful."

I suppress an eye roll at their flirtation. Nothing ever happened between us beyond their training, but they enjoy hitting on me, anyway. "Come in." I lead them into my living room, which they scan with the same excitement as the entryway. "Want something to drink? I have someone coming over in an hour, but I'd love to catch up before then."

Aven cocks a brow at me as they sit down and cross their long legs and flick out their skirt with a flourish. "Someone's coming over? I thought you didn't like people in your space."

I can't contain my snort. "If you knew that, why did you show up uninvited?"

They grin back, delighted at my reply. "Darling, I'm not 'people'. I'll take a glass of wine, if you please."

"I have water, cold brew, some kind of sparkling juice, and blood," I say drolly.

"So your *guest* doesn't warrant getting a nice bottle of red? Interesting..." They give me an assessing look. "I'll take the juice, then."

"She doesn't drink wine," I say with a shrug. I've offered to get

Grace more beverage options, but she insisted she was happy as long as she has her coffee. The juice was my feeble attempt to get her something else just in case, and it's sat in my fridge unopened for a week.

"Screw the juice. Tell me more about this woman that's coming over to your house and making you smile like that," Aven says, curiosity glittering in their milky eyes as I take a seat across from them.

"She's..." What do I say? We still haven't had the conversation about what exactly we are. I think we're both afraid of messing things up or scaring the other away by putting a name on it. "She's a close friend."

Aven narrows their eyes.

"And my submissive," I add.

"A human?" I nod, and Aven gives me a dirty grin. "This friend must be very special to get an invite to the elusive Mistress Bella's home."

"She is. I'm fond of her." Aven's discerning gaze bores into me, making me feel like I'm cheapening what I have with Grace by not being open about my feelings for her. A lump forms in my throat.

"How adorable! Human pets are such a fun diversion. It's been ages since I've had one. At least a century. Ooo, maybe I'll get one to spice things up for a bit. They're always so eager and vibrant. Probably because of their ridiculously short life spans."

I stiffen. It's clear Aven isn't trying to offend me, but hearing them speak like humans are disposable playthings, that they think that's what Grace is to me... I clench my fist at my side to contain my anger, nails digging hard into my palms to ground myself. "She's *not* a pet."

I may call Grace 'pet'. I may act like she's an object for me to use. But that's what it is—an act. I would never actually want to keep her like a doll to be put on a shelf when I grow bored. She's my partner. She's who I want by my side for as long as she'll have me.

"Oh!" Aven looks genuinely taken aback, their eyes going wide. "My mistake! Well then, when are you turning her?"

They ask with such nonchalance that it takes me aback, and I can't hide the way my stomach clenches painfully at their words. "What?"

Their brow furrows. "You love her, yes? Better to do it while she's still in her prime. Humans wither so quickly, and I doubt she wants to be a haggard old woman for eternity." They shudder melodramatically.

For all that I don't need to breathe, I'm suddenly suffocating. The blood I drank when I woke up whooshes in my ears, drowning out Aven's voice as they continue to discuss the merits of turning someone sooner rather than later.

Grace is going to die if I don't turn her.

Of course she's going to fucking die. What did I think was going to happen? I knew this. I pushed it to the recesses of my mind, too reckless to listen to the warnings in my gut.

The pain of considering the future loss lances through me. Beside it is the grim, hopeless certainty that there's no universe in which I'll make Grace like me. I can't condemn anyone to this existence, let alone the most brilliant, vivacious woman I've ever met. She deserves life, not some facsimile where she's burdened with unending hunger and darkness.

I can't do that to her.

I won't.

"—and then you have to consider how they're going to change once they're turned. You'd be surprised how many people's personalities suddenly become absolute shit after they've been granted immortality. Not you, of course."

I shake my head. "I'm not going to turn her."

Aven immediately stops their pontificating on the subject, eyes narrowing at me. Their mouth opens and closes a few times until they finally let out a low sigh. Any hint of humor or playfulness has vanished from their voice as they speak. "I wasn't going to say anything, but that's for the best. I forgot how wise you are for a neonate."

"Why do you say that?" I ask evenly, trying not to betray the way my body is tensing, like I'm getting ready to fight off an unseen force. Except death isn't something I can fight, unless I want Grace to end up a monster like me.

"Oh, a multitude of reasons. Some I'm sure you've already thought of, if you've decided against turning her. As I was saying, people change when death is no longer a threat. A few for the better, but the vast majority for the worst. When you've lived for as long as I have, you've seen some of the kindest souls twisted by the ravages of time. It takes extreme mental fortitude and a sense of self-preservation above all else in order to make it through the centuries without losing yourself." They tap their chin thoughtfully. "You've been a vampire for what, a century?"

"A decade."

Their eyes widen, and they shake their head, letting out a rueful laugh. "Gods, you're so *young*. Fate must truly have been guiding me when I decided to stop by for a visit. I'd hate to think that your attachment to mortal mentalities would lead you to make an impulsive decision that would haunt you for eternity."

They sigh, the sound heavy with the weight of centuries worth of living. "I'm sure your human is very special to you right now, but letting yourself get too attached is unwise. It may not feel like it yet, but a human lifespan is exactly that. A momentary flash. Blink and they're gone."

Blink and they're gone. I do just that, and when my eyes open again, cool, wet tears are sliding down my cheeks. I can't speak past the lump in my throat that's choking me.

"Oh darling, shit, I'm so sorry," Aven says when they see my tears. "It gets easier with time, I promise. You learn how to protect yourself from the pain."

All I've done since I was turned is learn how to protect myself, and yet here I am, sliced open by the harsh realities of my vampiric condition that I promised myself I wouldn't ignore, yet immediately did when Grace walked into my life. I swipe away my tears, bitter anger and frustration with myself for being so fucking weak churning in my gut.

I startle as Aven's weight settles on the couch beside me and their hand rests on my arm. "Truly, I'm sorry."

A long silence stretches between us as I attempt to compose myself, but it's no use. All the pieces I painstakingly put back together after I became a vampire are falling apart, and all it took was a simple reality check. "It's fine," I finally manage to bite out.

Aven squeezes my arm, and there's a slight tingle of warming magic infused in their touch. Something to calm me, no doubt, and as much as I don't like them doing it without my consent, I'm grateful for the numbing clarity that seeps in past the overwhelming emotion.

"I'm not saying these things to be cruel. I care about you, Blair. You have what it takes to be an immensely powerful and relatively well-adjusted vampire, unlike most who are turned. I don't want to see that ruined by something as... *fleeting* as love."

They pause, a haunted look crossing their face.

Aven's voice is much softer when they continue. "I've been there, and it almost broke me. You don't deserve to be broken again."

Not after everything you've already been through in your short years."

"What happened?" I ask, even though I dread knowing the details for fear they'll be too similar to my situation. There's still a kernel of pathetic hope in my chest saying that Aven is wrong. That I could handle things differently than them. That the way I feel about Grace isn't the same.

"The first time? I was young like you and absolutely infatuated with my human lover. Shit, what was her name?" They shrug and continue, unbothered by their failure to remember. "Anyway, I granted her fae immortality so we could be together forever. This was back before the fae purposefully forgot that magic because of the absolute havoc it wreaked. Turns out, she'd been manipulating me. She saw an opportunity in me and when she became immortal, I was no longer necessary."

"That's awful. Grace isn't like that, though." I don't know why I'm arguing. I won't turn her, but I hate their implication that she's using me for what I can give her as a vampire.

"I'm sure she isn't," Aven says evenly. "Though, if she were, I wouldn't blame her. Being a mortal must be terrifying. They're so easily hurt, and no one wants to die."

I do.

I don't say it out loud, but I never fucking wanted to be immortal. I accepted it in the moment because I was naive and lured in by a manipulative bastard. What Aven is describing confirms just how hellish living forever will be.

I don't want to watch people die over and over. I don't want to feel this gnawing, violent urge that presses against the edges of my mind, waiting for the moment I lose control. I don't want to face the ravages of time.

Oblivious to my despair, Aven continues. "You'd think I would've learned my lesson, but us fae are egotistical little shits. The second time I thought I knew everything and that it would be fine. I loved Seamus, and he loved me. Truly. We had about a century before that love faded. That's the problem with love. No matter how much you tend to the bloom, unlike us, it *will* die. Like I said, living this long changes you. Seamus became someone I didn't recognize by the time he left me. That loss was even worse than the first." Aven laughs humorlessly. "And now I have to see him at every other fae gathering. Ugh, he's like a wart I can't get rid of no matter how many times I cut it away."

"I'm sorry for asking," I say, sensing unhealed pain in the way Aven holds themself stiffly.

"Oh nonsense! It's nice to find a use for all this hard-won wisdom. Most of the time, I have to sit back and watch as people ruin their lives again and again."

"I guess it's a good thing I don't have it in me to turn someone," I say ruefully. "I care about Grace too much to manipulate her affection for me into an eternity of being a monster."

"Well then, I'll stop babbling about the downfalls of making your lover immortal." Aven stands up and claps their hands together. "I should go before your human arrives. I won't presume that you'd want her to meet me, especially if she's not going to be sticking around for long."

I want to scream at them to stop being so callous, but they're saying what I need to hear. Still, I can't stop myself from asking one more question.

"Have you ever loved someone who stayed mortal?"

Their smile flickers. "Yes."

"And how did you cope?"

"I didn't. At least not the first time. But once was enough to learn to never get attached to mortals. My advice? Play with them, have your fun, and then move on to the next one. It's better for everyone involved."

I nod, swallowing hard so I don't cry again, but a tear escapes anyway.

Aven reaches up and wipes it away with their thumb, the crimson liquid stark against their unearthly pale, shimmering skin. "You're strong. You'll get through this. Shed your tears and keep moving forward. That's all any of us can do."

I have nothing to say. My thoughts flicker back and forth from petulant rejection of their words to grim acknowledgement of their veracity and what needs to be done. They reverberate so loudly in my head that I want to reach inside and claw out every emotion and all the hope inside me until I'm empty, because at least then I wouldn't feel this way. I wouldn't have to feel anything at all.

"It was good to see you, darling. I'll check back in soon to make sure you're okay." Knowing them, that means at least another five years.

Maybe by then the ruins of my heart will have mended. Maybe by then I'll have learned the lesson that the universe keeps beating into me again and again.

When I let emotions lead me, I end up utterly destroyed.

35

GRACE

I'm going to ask her tonight. It's been almost two months and I'm driving myself crazy, not knowing what it is we're doing. It's time to stop being scared and find out for certain.

Fortunately, I'm ninety-nine percent sure that Blair will laugh and kiss me, then agree to anything I propose. I'd have to be blind to not notice the adoring way she smiles at me every time we're together lately. She's told me again and again that she'll give me anything I need. I just have to be brave enough to ask for it.

By the time I arrive at her doorstep, my palms are sweating and I'm vibrating with a potent blend of nerves and excitement. She hasn't given me any details about what we'll be up to tonight since it's so last minute, but it's only my second time coming over to her place. I have a small overnight bag over my shoulder, in case she wants me to stay over.

The first night I came over to her house, I had work the next morning, and she didn't want me to be exhausted the next day, so she sent me home at a reasonable hour. We didn't even make it to her bedroom. But today is Friday, which means I can stay as long as she wants. *If* she wants.

Crap, now the nerves are starting to overwhelm the excitement. I shake out my arms, flicking the excess energy out toward the ground and inhaling deeply, then ring the doorbell. I half expect Blair to be lurking on the other side, waiting for me to arrive, but she takes almost a minute to answer.

My heart skips a beat when I see her, like it does every night we get together. I'll never get over how breathtaking Blair is. Tonight, she's forgone her usual makeup in favor of a clean face, but if anything, that only emphasizes the beauty of her high cheekbones and flawless umber skin.

Affection for her bubbles up inside me, and I wrap my arms around her, pressing a kiss to her lips before she has a chance to say anything.

Blair stiffens in surprise, but after a second, kisses me back with a soft groan that makes my belly flutter.

I give her a sheepish grin when I pull back. "Sorry. I'm happy to see you tonight. In case you couldn't tell," I add with a chuckle.

Her lips quirk. "I might've noticed."

She guides me inside, then holds out a hand to take my purse to hang it up on a hook near the entryway. Her eyes flick to the overnight bag on my shoulder, and I clutch at it, suddenly very self-conscious about my presumption about how tonight will go.

"I, uh, brought some stuff. Just in case," I say, flushing.

I expect her to tease me or ask for details, but she nods and hangs it up beside my purse. Guess I was worrying for no reason.

"Come in," Blair says, leading me into her immaculate gothic living room that looks ripped from the pages of a dark academia novel. It's hard not to feel a little self-conscious about how nice her place is compared to mine. Especially since she's seen my condo in full-blown disaster mode.

"I know I said this last time, but your place is so cool. You did all the decorating yourself, right?" I ask, trying to hide my feelings of inadequacy. Blair told me she doesn't care what my place looks like, and she didn't run screaming after seeing it, and me, at our worst.

"I did. Well, the garden was here when I moved in. But other than that, it's all me. The upstairs still isn't done yet, otherwise I'd give you a full tour."

"Ooo, can I at least see the garden? It's beautiful out tonight. Maybe we could sit out there for a bit?" I almost stumble over my words, worried that she can tell I'm acting weird or know what I'm going to bring up.

An indecipherable look flashes across her face, but she nods. "Yeah. That's a good idea."

I thread my fingers through hers and for a moment she gazes at me with such sheer longing that it takes my breath away. I'm caught under her spell, ready and willing to go to my knees and do anything she asks of me. I'm desperate for her command.

I wet my lips and step closer, heat crackling between us.

Shit, no. Talk first. Then we can have lots of passionate, earth shattering sex after.

Squeezing Blair's hand, I shake off the lust as best I can. "Lead the way," I say with a smile.

Blair guides me through a set of French doors at the back of her living room, and we emerge out onto a dark cobblestone patio and backyard garden surrounded by hedges. She flicks a switch near the door and I gasp as everything is illuminated by soft fairy lights. Roses ranging from delicate pinks, to deep blood reds cover the hedges and climb across the overhead trellises where the lights hang.

"It's like something out of a dream," I murmur, stepping further out into the rose garden and letting the gentle fragrance wash over me. "This is beautiful."

"Not half as beautiful as you," Blair says softly, coming to stand beside me. There's a strange, almost wistful look in her eyes when I turn to smile at her.

"I bet you say that to all the women you take out here," I say with a teasing smile.

Blair doesn't smile back. "I've never brought anyone out here before. The only person who's seen it other than you is a stubborn client who does landscaping and refused to take no for an answer about helping set up lights out here."

My stomach does a flip at the knowledge that I'm the first. "Why not? You've had other women spend the night, right?" We've spoken a bit about her dating history, and she's had at least one partner for long enough that they slept over.

"I…" I watch Blair's throat work as she swallows heavily, and the butterflies in my stomach kick up even more.

Maybe I won't have to ask her what's going on between us. Maybe she'll confess the reason she feels comfortable with me out in her garden is that she wants me beyond the sex and kink.

Disappointment tamps down that fluttering anticipation when she clears her throat and looks away. "It never came up. Most people care more about going to the bedroom than seeing a garden."

"Thankfully, I'm not like other people," I tease with a soft laugh.

295

Blair's eyes shine in the dim light as she holds my gaze. "You aren't."

This is it. I need to say how I feel. I need her to know what she means to me.

Instead, I chicken out, looking away toward the roses as my cheeks burn. "This space is special to you, isn't it?"

"Yeah." I think that's the only response I'm going to get, but then Blair continues. "I enjoy coming out here. The flowers are beautiful and, against all odds, they've managed to survive, even with my subpar gardening skills. There's something about being out here, surrounded by them, that calms me. Helps me sort through my thoughts."

"I can see why. It's very peaceful out here."

She nods and a moment of silence passes between us as I imagine Blair coming out here to sit under the moonlight and find calm amongst the roses. As I picture it, I realize something that increases the yearning tenderness in my chest tenfold.

Maybe I'm reading into something that isn't there, but it doesn't feel like a coincidence.

I move closer, so that there's only a few inches between us. Emotion threatens to clog my throat as I struggle to find the courage to ask my question. "Is this why you said I should use the name Rose?" I ask, voice barely above a whisper as I look down into her eyes.

Blair tenses, and for an agonizing second I worry I was horribly wrong. I take a step back, my eyes dropping to the ground.

"It is," she finally says, her voice raspy with emotion.

I look back up to find she's closed the distance between us again. My breath hitches at her proximity and the desperation etched onto her face.

For all that Blair proclaims that she's a predator, a monster that should be feared, all I see in her eyes is longing. An ache to be wanted. Hunger for affection. If she'll let me, I'll give her everything. I'll let her drain my heart dry.

"I love you," I whisper, overcome with the desire for her to know exactly how I feel. To show her I can give her what she craves.

"Wh-what?" she asks, eyes blowing wide in disbelief.

"I love you," I say, louder this time. I'm ready to burst with how much I love this woman.

"I..." Blair's gaze flicks away and everything deflates inside me in that moment of hesitation.

"Oh." I stumble backward as if she slapped me, tears blurring my vision.

"Grace, wait," Blair says, reaching out to grab hold of my arm before I'm able to move any further away.

I smile feebly through the tears pouring down my cheeks. "It's okay!" I squeak. "Sorry, I shouldn't have said that. It wasn't fair of me to tell you that. I know that this is..." I swipe at my face and shake my head. "That this isn't that kind of relationship for you. You've just been teaching me and I got caught up in things."

"That's not it."

I force my eyes up to meet hers despite the storm of devastation ravaging me right now, a glimmer of hope flickering at her words. "It's not?"

She shakes her head, her jaw tight as she fights to keep her composure. "I care about you. This has meant so much to me."

The unspoken "but" hangs in the air between us.

"You're breaking up with me," I say, a surreal numbness flooding my body. It feels like I'm not even here anymore, like I'm watching this moment unfold from the outside. Me, the lovesick fool who's come to the crushing realization that she'll never be enough, and Blair, the vampire breaking the news as gently as she can to the idiot who fell in love with her domme.

"I... I can't bear to lose you," she whispers.

That snaps me back to my body. "What the hell is that supposed to mean? You don't want to stop having sex with me? You don't want to lose my friendship? I'm so tired of not knowing what is happening between us! Yes, I know I should've asked before I fell in love, but you said nothing to make me think I shouldn't."

"I know. I'm sorry. You did nothing wrong. You're perfect and I... I care about you too much. If we keep going, I'll never recover."

"I don't understand! What do you mean you'll never recover? I'm telling you I love you. I want to be with you. You make me feel seen and safe and alive, and I don't want anyone else. I won't leave you, if that's what you're scared of."

She shakes her head, a single bloody tear rolling down her cheek. "Yes, you will."

"No, I won't! If this is about you being the first woman I've dated or some bullshit worry that I'll wake up one day and suddenly be straight again, it's not going to happen. I would gladly never see a cock again if it means I can stay with you."

Blair grimaces like she has a foul taste in her mouth. "That's not it, but you still—"

"I mean, maybe if you go on murderous rampages or have a complete personality change, we might have to have a talk, but otherwise, this is it for me, Blair. *You're* it for me." I choke back a frustrated sob. "If you don't want me that way, t-tell me."

"I want you more than anything!" Blair protests. She's crying as much as I am now, crimson droplets wetting the neckline of her shirt.

I angrily swipe away my own tears. "Then what is the fucking problem?" I bite back.

"You're going to die!" she shouts, voice laced with pain.

Her words ring out in the night air between us, my confusion and anger shocked away by her sorrowful proclamation.

"You're going to die, and if we keep doing this, if I let myself love you, it will ruin me," Blair says, the heartache in her words making my chest ache with the need to hold her in my arms and take away her worries and pain.

There has to be something I can do. I can't bear to see her like this. I'll find a way to stay alive. Maybe there's some kind of magic or...

"Make me a vampire," I blurt.

Blair shakes her head with a sigh. "I can't do that."

"Yes, you can. It doesn't have to be right away, if you're worried it's too soon. But I want to be with you, and we have the solution staring us in the face. We can be together."

"You don't understand. You don't want to be like me."

For the first time in my life, I don't feel worried about a decision. This is the solution. I love Blair. I'd do anything for her. She needs me. What else is there to consider?

"I'm not going to pretend that I have a burning desire to live forever, and drinking blood for every meal will take some getting used to. Oh, and not being out in the sun. Good thing I'm not a huge fan of sunbathing—it gives me a headache and I always get burned no matter how much sunscreen I wear," I say with a soft laugh.

Blair's expression grows even more fraught with worry. "Grace... it's not just that. I can't turn you into a monster. Being a vampire is a curse. I care too much about you to use your love for me to selfishly destroy your life so I don't have to be alone."

"You're not! I'm an adult, and I can take more time to think through the consequences, but please don't make this decision for me." I reach out and grab hold of her hand, needing to reassure her.

"This could be a good thing. You said that your body froze in the state that it was in when you were turned. If you make me a vampire, then I won't have to rely on your blood for the chronic pain." A surge of hope wells up inside me as I follow that train of thought. "My spine won't get any worse."

Blair stiffens and tugs her hand free from mine, a scowl twisting her face. "No."

The denial makes my blood run cold. "What?"

"If you want someone to keep your physical issues from getting worse, if you're tired of 'relying on me', find another vampire. I won't turn you," she says, voice deathly calm.

Indignance flares inside me as she shuts herself off, the transformation of her demeanor horrifying. "Blair, come on! That's not what I'm saying, and you know it. How could you even think that?"

"What else should I think when you won't listen to me when I'm telling you that becoming a vampire is a fate I wouldn't wish on anyone? I was okay with you using me for your experimentation, and I was happy to give you my blood, but I won't let you use me for this."

I don't recognize this woman staring at me with such cruel, shocking disdain. Every tender moment and vulnerable confession we shared, every hope that what we were doing together meant something, turns to ash as devastated rage consumes me.

"*Fuck you*," I say, spitting the words. "You want to push me away because you can't handle the potential for pain? Fine. I'm leaving."

Apologize! Take me into your arms and tell me you didn't mean it. Say that we'll figure this out together. Tell me you love me.

Blair's jaw clenches and her hands ball into fists at her side, but she stays silent.

Hot tears spill down my cheeks. I want to scream at her. I want to shake her until her stony facade crumbles away again, and she's the Blair that made me feel safe and happy again.

I don't. I may be an idiot for thinking she wouldn't hurt me, but I still have a shred of dignity left.

"I *trusted* you." My voice breaks, and I have to grit my teeth to fight back the sob that's threatening to burst out of me before continuing. "You promised me that this wouldn't ruin our friendship, but I can't be friends with someone who thinks so little of me. I'm done."

I turn on my heels and storm back inside, anguish threatening to tear me apart with each step. My traitorous mind tells me to turn back and beg Blair to listen, but somehow I get my purse and overnight bag and make it to my car without giving in. I watch Blair's front door for a heartbreaking moment, willing her to appear and race out to stop me, then blink away my tears and start the car, leaving behind any hope I had for something good as I drive away.

36

GRACE

I somehow end up at Mona's house instead of my condo, parked in her driveway and sobbing too hard to get out of my car or even send her a text to let her know I'm here. The entire drive over, I kept replaying Blair's words in my head, screaming out a slew of replies and arguments as if she could hear me. Praying that if I lanced the festering pain enough times, it would make me feel better. But I've only deepened the wounds, my heart carved open, unable to stop the anguished tears from rolling down my cheeks and my ragged, heaving breaths.

I cover my face with my hands, curling in on myself. Something shifts in my spine, and I have a moment to recognize what's happening before my muscles seize up.

"*Fuck!*" I slam my hands down on the steering wheel as I scrunch my eyes shut against the oncoming pain. I accidentally hit the horn and a blast echoes out into the quiet suburban street, a perfect compliment to the shrillness of my shout. I'm too far gone to care that a neighbor is going to call the cops on me for disturbing the peace, or that I may have woken up Mona's neighbor's newborn.

Does it really matter? Does anything fucking matter?

I grip the back of my neck to brace it so my wracking sobs don't throw things out of alignment even more and cover my face with my other hand.

A knock on my passenger side window startles me and I look, the pain flaring in my neck as I turn my head. "Fuck," I curse again, scrabbling to wipe the tears from my eyes so I can see who is out there.

A blurry Mona stands beside my car wearing a thin, lacy green robe, arms wrapped around her waist in a feeble attempt to conceal her state of undress.

"Grace?" Her voice is muffled through the car door, but her confusion is clear in her tone. I hit the button to disengage the safety locks, and a second later, she's opening the door and peering inside. "What are you doing—" Her expression shifts to horror when she sees my ruined state. "Honey, what happened?"

An indecipherable, tortured sound tears out of my throat, but I'm unable to provide a reply.

Why did I come here? Shit, I don't want Mona to see me like this. She already knows how much of a failure I am, but this is a new level. She'll see how truly broken and pathetic I am.

"Shit, it's okay. Just stay there, I'm coming in," she says, climbing into the seat beside me.

"S-s-o-rry." I'm barely able to get the apology out through my shuddering breaths.

"It's okay, shhh, I'm here," Mona murmurs, reaching out to pull me into a hug over the console. I flinch backwards and hold my hands up, knowing the movement will only make my neck worse.

Mona's eyes go wide in alarm at my reaction. "Grace, are you hurt?!"

An anguished bubble of laughter rips from my chest, as painful as my tears. "Y-yeah, is it tha-at o-obvious?"

"What's wrong? Do you need me to call an ambulance?" she asks, panic lacing her words.

"N-no." I shake my head like a dumbass and grimace as my muscles seize up tighter.

Mona frowns. "I thought you were going over to Blair's house tonight. Does she know you're hurt?"

Something inside me crumples even more than I thought possible when Mona says Blair's name, and my chest heaves as I sob harder.

Mona's expression turns murderous. "Did *she* hurt you?"

I startle at her reaction, and it chases away some of the tears. "Wh-what? No! I mean, yes, b-but, n-no!"

"Then why are you sitting there like you can't move and don't want me to touch you? You can tell me." Mona's eyes blaze with rage as she reaches out to clasp my hand. "I swear to god, if she hurt you and left you to fend for yourself, I will... well, I won't be able to do anything, but Max will go fuck her up for me."

"Please, d-don't! This isn't her fault." At least the neck pain isn't. Not directly. Although, I doubt I would've thrown my neck out tonight if it weren't for my heartbroken sobbing. "I have an issue with my neck."

Understatement of the year. Embarrassment twines with my

broken heart, making me wish I could leave my body so I wouldn't have to endure this godawful night any longer.

"Huh?" Mona asks, her brow crinkling. "What kind of issue?"

I sigh, swiping away the snot that's streaming down my face with the back of my hand, then grimacing.

Not missing a beat, Mona wriggles out of her robe and hands it to me to wipe my hand off with.

There's a momentary pause of shock on my part when I see what she has on underneath. Or rather what she doesn't have on. She's in the tightest, sluttiest dress I've ever seen her wear, a chain necklace dangling between her breasts, drawing my eyes to the way a hint of her nipples peek out from the neckline. One strap is ripped, barely hanging on by a thread, and she flushes, attempting to tug it back up onto her shoulder.

I quickly avert my eyes and shove the robe back toward her. "I'm n-not going to g-get my snot on your pretty robe," I say with a frown.

Mona rolls her eyes and keeps it held out to me, unrelenting. "Screw the robe. I couldn't give two shits about it. Tell me what's going on."

"O-okay." I reluctantly use the lacy fabric to blot at my tear and snot covered face and hands, attempting to even my breathing enough so that I won't undo the effort by crying again. "I have a neck issue."

"You said that already. What does that mean?" Mona asks, tracking my hand as I bring it back up to brace my neck.

"I have degenerative discs in my neck. Sometimes it makes my neck go out, and then I'm in a lot of pain. I don't want to hug you because moving at all at the moment is dicey." I twist the fabric of the robe between my hands, bracing myself for Mona's inevitable pitying expression.

Instead, there's a flash of unexpected hurt on her face. "How long have you had this issue?"

"I mean, I've had it my whole life, but I got the official diagnosis when the pain got bad a few years ago."

"What the hell, Grace? You've been dealing with this for years and you didn't tell me?" Mona asks sharply.

Guilt makes my stomach clench. She's not pitying me. She's upset I didn't tell her. Why do I keep upsetting people tonight? Fuck, maybe I am as selfish and awful as a person as Blair thinks I am.

The tears burst forth again, and I have to fight through them to reply. "Please don't be m-mad at me. I'm sorry. I should've t-told you, but I didn't w-want to complain."

"Shit, Grace, it's okay. I'm not mad!"

I can't look at her face. I need to leave. No one deserves to be saddled with someone as broken and selfish as me. "You should be. I'm a terrible f-friend. I keep fucking everything up, I-I know. Just give me a m-minute and I'll go home."

Mona grabs my hand as I fumble for the car keys. "You're not a terrible friend. You're my best friend and I love you. You're not going home like this. Don't be ridiculous."

"I love you too," I say, the words a stinging reminder of what happened when I said them earlier.

Mona has stuck around longer than anyone I've met, excluding my dad, but it scares me to think that some day she'll decide I'm not worth the effort and move on. She's become best friends with Blair, and she has an amazing partner in Max. What value do I bring to things? Surely it's only a matter of time before she cuts me out like everyone else has.

"It's okay if you decide that y-you don't love me," I say. "I don't want you to be o-obligated to be my friend because we've known each other since we were kids. I'll be o-okay."

Mona's face twists in a mixture of concern and disbelief. "I'm not going to stop loving you because you didn't tell me about your neck. Why would you think that?"

"B-because no one wants to stay. First my mom, then Zack, and n-now her. Why wouldn't you be next? There's obviously something w-wrong with me."

"Oh, Grace," Mona's devastated expression is a match for my own as she realizes what I'm saying.

I know how excited she was about me and Blair getting together, and there's a moment where I feel bad for her that we've broken up. Even though the only thing I did wrong was fall in love. "I'm sorry. I know you w-wanted it to work between us."

"Who gives a fuck about me and what I want? You have nothing to apologize for. You're in pain and upset and that makes it hard to recognize when thoughts aren't true, but please believe me when I say that I will always love you. There is nothing wrong with you. You're my favorite person in the world, and not to brag, but I have excellent taste."

A weak laugh bubbles out of me, but I shake my head. "What about Max?"

"Eh, he's a demon, and he's got an unfair advantage being my partner, so I'm not counting him. Besides, you've been around longer. You stayed by my side through the horrors of middle school and when I went through my emo phase."

"I still think you looked good with that black eyeliner," I say, a fraction of the ache in my chest easing.

Mona reaches out and takes the robe I'm clutching out of my death grip, and blots my face with it gently. "Can you come inside? Or will it hurt too much to move?"

"I can come inside, but it's really o-okay. I don't want to bother you and—"

"Grace, shut up and come inside."

I give her a watery, appreciative smile. "Okay."

She opens her car door and gets out, holding the tear-soaked robe over her chest and using her other hand to tug down the hem of her dress to make sure her ass isn't completely hanging out.

I ease myself out of the car and join her, and she lets go of the skirt to take my hand, giving it a gentle, reassuring squeeze. We head inside her house, and she helps steady me as I kick off my heels.

A low voice echoes from the dark staircase, startling me. "Mmm, you thought you could get away from me, pretty girl, but I've found you now. You've got nowhere to run, and once I catch you, I'm going to fuck you until—oh!" Max rounds the corner, and startles backward when he sees Mona isn't alone, his hands not fast enough to stop me from getting an eyeful of his dick. "Shit!" His bright red face is a stark contrast to the darkness in his voice before, and I can't help letting out a surprised laugh.

"Sorry, baby. It wasn't the neighbor's car, it was Grace."

I give a feeble wave.

"She's going to spend the night," Mona says, barely containing her amusement at her fiancé's flustered state.

"Sorry for interrupting," I say with a sheepish smile.

"N-no, it's okay! I'll be right back," Max says, scurrying back up the stairs in a flash of pale, freckled skin and a surprisingly juicy ass.

I look over at Mona and raise my eyebrows.

She shrugs and laughs. "What? You know I'm a freak."

"Not that," I snort. "Just... *damn*." I spread my hands apart to indicate Max's impressive size.

Mona giggles and that's what makes her flush, not me walking in on their kinky roleplay. "Yeah."

Max returns a moment later in low slung sweatpants and a soft fluffy robe, which he passes over to Mona. His face is still bright red as we head into the living room, but he gives me a concerned smile when our eyes meet.

"Okay, so what's the most comfortable for you? I can move Nugget off the couch if you need to lie down," Mona says, going into caretaking mode. "Do you have any meds or things that will help?"

My stomach lurches as I think about dealing with my pain. About the sweet, strange taste of Blair's blood, and the blissful relief it provides. How last time, she let me drink it directly from her wrist, which led to me exploring every inch of her body with my lips and tongue.

Fuck, it hurts.

"I have muscle relaxers, but they're at home. Also, heating pads and a TENS unit. So it's probably better if I go home and let you enjoy your evening."

Mona and Max exchange a look, and he nods. "I'll go grab them. Are your keys in your purse?" Max asks, no hesitation in his offer.

"Yeah, but it's okay—"

He shakes his head. "We're not letting you go home like this. Anything else that would be helpful to have?"

"I..." I go to argue, but Mona glares at me. "Maybe my pillow? I, uh, already have an overnight bag out in my car." A fresh wave of sadness hits me and I fight against crying again.

Max looks at me like he can feel my pain, and I realize after a moment that he can. He can sense how devastated I am. He knows the depth of what happened tonight before Mona does. "I'm so sorry, Grace," he says gently, which makes me lose the battle with the tears again.

He heads off, leaving me and Mona alone. I sit on the couch, and a moment later, the blankets at the other end come to life and move over toward me, Nugget's small glowing face peeking out as he climbs into my lap with a sleepy snuffle. I bury my hands in his soft fur, grateful for his affection. It's still beyond surreal that there's a ghost dog sitting in my lap, but his weight is as solid and comforting as it was when he was alive.

"Someone else who loves you," Mona says with a gentle smile as she sits in the chair across from me.

I scoff. "He loves everyone."

Nugget circles around in my lap before settling in with a contented chuff.

"Yes, but you're a top favorite." Mona's smile flickers and there's a long silence while I pet Nugget before she speaks again. "You don't have to tell me what happened, if it's too hard to talk about right now. Just know that I'm here if you do, and I promise not to judge."

"I don't even know where to begin," I say, looking down at the spectral dog in my lap since it feels too difficult to meet Mona's eyes without crying again.

"Did you..." Mona hesitates, then continues much softer. "Did you break up?"

"Yeah." I want to make a quip about how you can't break up with someone if you never defined what the relationship was to begin with, but I can't get any other words out. I blink rapidly, carding my fingers through Nugget's fur like petting him can anchor me through the heartache.

"I'm so sorry," Mona says, her voice wobbling, sounding like she's on the verge of tears too.

I look up to see the devastated look on my best friend's face. "Why are you sorry?"

"I pushed you to explore things with Blair. I thought you were perfect for each other and I wanted you both to be happy."

"It's not your fault. I thought so too, but I guess we both were wrong." My stomach churns as I think about how happy and excited I was a few hours ago. How did things go so wrong so fast?

A tear slides down Mona's cheek, making the churning turn into a painful clench.

"No, stop, don't cry!" I say, vision becoming blurry. "If you cry, I'll start again, and you did nothing wrong."

Mona sniffs and wipes her cheek before steeling herself with a shaky exhale. "Okay. Sorry. I'll keep it together."

There's another long silence as we both attempt to pull ourselves together. Eventually, I find myself answering her unspoken questions, knowing it's probably killing Mona to not know what's going on.

"She broke up with me. In case that wasn't clear." I let out a humorless laugh. "I told Blair I loved her and she said she couldn't be with me anymore because..." I swallow heavily. "Because she doesn't want to get too attached when I'm going to die."

Mona's brow furrows. "What? What kind of reason is that? She's a fucking vampire. Can't she do something about it?"

I grimace, feeling a dull echo of the blow that came from Blair's words. "I told her she could turn me. She took that really poorly. Said that she didn't mind me using her for sex, but drew the line at being used to become a vampire. I..." Tears pour down my cheeks again and I exhale, my chest shaking as I fight off a sob. "I told you from the start that I worried I was using her to explore things, but I didn't think she saw it that way. Not after everything... but I guess that was me all over again, letting my heart get tangled up with someone who didn't feel the same way."

"No!" Mona's exclamation is so loud that Nugget startles

awake. She lowers her voice, but there's still a harsh bite to it as she continues. "That's complete bullshit, Grace. You did everything you could to make sure you weren't taking advantage of her. She wanted to do it. She agreed to be with you. Don't put that on yourself. Fuck her for making you think it was your fault."

I grab a tissue from the side table and blow my nose. "You don't have to take my side. I know you're friends with her."

Mona scowls. "I don't give a shit about Blair right now. My best friend is in excruciating pain and had her heart broken. Blair made her choice and she can handle the repercussions of that on her own."

"I appreciate that, but just because I'm not her friend, doesn't mean you have to cut her out of your life. She needs you, too."

As upset as I am, I can't cut off my feelings for Blair. I care about her. I know she's upset, even if she doesn't love me. She doesn't have anyone else besides Mona, and it would be selfish for me to claim our mutual friend for myself.

Mona's indignant expression softens. "Fine. If that's what you want. But I'm still really pissed at her."

"Thanks," I say, giving her a weak, unconvincing smile. "I'll be fine," I add, wishing that I could convince myself with that lie.

"You will be. But right now, you're not. And that's okay."

I want to believe Mona, but the hollowness in my chest and defeated exhaustion make it seem impossible. I don't know that I'll ever recover from loving Blair.

37

BLAIR

> Mona: Are you okay?

I stare down at the text from Mona, my phone sitting on the kitchen table while I sip a mug of lukewarm blood. She knows what happened. Grace must've told her.

Are you okay?

Not "why the fuck did you do that to Grace?" or "I hate you and our friendship is over." No, that would be too easy. Anger is simple to deal with. You weather it and move on.

Compassion, though? It's unbearable. I don't deserve it. I don't want it.

I down the rest of my drink, the stale, unpalatable taste a grim reminder of what I've lost tonight.

It's for the best. Think about how much worse other blood would taste after years of feeding from Grace. You did the right thing.

The thoughts do nothing to alleviate the way my hands shake as I bring the mug to the sink and almost shatter it when it slips out of my hands. Dammit, the blood should've helped calm me down. Why am I still on the verge of going feral?

I leave the mug in the sink, bypassing my phone on the table as I head down to my bedroom on unsteady legs. There are many hours before dawn, but I can't stand being awake with these thoughts any longer tonight. I hope that sleep is merciful and claims me quickly.

DARKNESS. A pungent smell of iron and sweet berries filling my nose as I come to consciousness. Wet, sticky blood covering my palms.

No, not just my hands. Slicked over my arms up to my elbows.

A wheezing, shallow inhale. "Blair," a weak voice whispers.

I look down in my lap at the woman resting there. Blonde tresses spread out over my legs like a halo, the tips painted crimson by the blood flowing from a jagged wound in her chest.

Not resting. Dying.

"Oh god, Grace, no," I gasp, my blood-slicked hands trying to staunch the bleeding, but more pours out.

Her skin is so pale it's almost white, and her eyes beg me to do something. To stop the pain. To save her.

"Fuck! No, please, you can't die," I beg, tearing into my wrist with my fangs and shoving it to her mouth. She attempts to swallow, but it's too late. The life behind her eyes vanishes, and all I'm left with is her rapidly *cooling corpse and the endless tears streaming down my face. If only there were enough of them to drown me so I could join her.*

> Mona: Please call me. Or message me. Anything to let me know you're alright. It's been two days.

I SWIPE AWAY the message notification. I drink as much blood as I can choke down, then head back down to the basement to climb back into bed.

My head pounds, mirroring the sluggish pulsing of the blood I consumed through my body, both sensations making me feel like I'm going to be sick. I curl into a ball on my side, pressing my face into the cool pillow and fight for sleep to claim me again, even though it will be worse than being awake.

HE THRUSTS INSIDE ME, *and I hiss against the burn, trying to hide how much it hurts. This is how it's supposed to be. He loves me. He wants me so badly that he can't control himself. Isn't that what I always craved?*

The painful stretch of his cock forcing me open and the bruising grip on my wrists as he pins me to the bed is proof that I'm wanted.

It doesn't matter that the weight of his body on top of mine makes me shudder. It doesn't matter that I'm not turned on. All that matters is that I'm finally loved.

"You love this, don't you?" he growls, licking a hot stripe up my neck that makes me clench unpleasantly around him.

"Yes," I murmur, even as tears well in my eyes.

He kisses me, sloppy and frantic, his fangs scraping my lower lip. "Be with me. Forever," he pants, slowing his thrusts. "I cannot bear the thought of eternity without you."

An eternity of love. Of having this handsome man cherish me. What more could I possibly want?

"I..."

His hand lands on my throat, his gleaming red eyes boring into my soul. "I'll die without you, Blair. Living without you would rend my soul in two. Say yes."

Warm fuzziness floods my mind and I nod. "Y-yes."

When his fangs rip into my wrist, the searing pain almost makes me black out, but I don't make a sound. Because all that matters is him. This is my happy ending. The end of the pathetic, confused girl and the start of my life as someone worthwhile.

Time blends together as I cycle between nightmare-filled sleep, where I relive hazy memories of the worst moment of my existence, and forcing myself to get up and eat enough to not lose the ability to function at all. I've canceled all of my sessions, claiming illness, since none of my current clients save Nic know I'm a vampire.

I keep waiting for the numbness to kick in. For the self-sufficient badass version of myself I built after I was turned to come on board and get things back to normal.

Where the fuck did she go?

I'm a raw nerve, pain and heartache shocking through me, whether I'm awake or asleep. I despise this version of myself. Even more than I hated the foolish romantic who let herself get taken in by Dominic's lies, because I know I'm capable of being strong and unaffected, and of moving past heartbreak, yet it seems entirely insurmountable this time.

It's pathetic. I wish Aven had shown up a month earlier, because it's clear they were too late. The damage from falling for Grace was already done.

What good were all those years of teaching myself to be strong and self-sufficient, learning to guard myself from the mistakes of the past? They certainly aren't helping shore me up against the battering storm of my emotions and my monster's anger at giving up Grace.

Loving Dominic cost me my life, but loving Grace has ruined me. I wish I could use my powers of compulsion to force myself back to a state of normalcy. I don't want to feel anymore.

> Mona: Blair, enough. I know your address and if you don't get back to me by tonight, I'm coming over.

MY EYES ARE SO PUFFY from crying after my latest nightmare that it's hard to read my notifications. I have ten missed calls, four voicemails, and at least a dozen texts, all from Mona.

A series of heavy thumps on my front door startle me, and I miss my mouth with the mug of blood, splashing the liquid over my chin and down to add another stain to the wrinkled, oversized shirt I've been living in for the past week.

Shit. Is Mona here already? I should've messaged her back, but I couldn't face it. And now she's here, and she's going to see how much of a pathetic mess I am.

More loud knocks echo through the entryway and I groan, knowing Mona is stubborn enough that she won't go away or stop until I answer.

I head to the front door, my legs lead weights I have to drag to move at all. I yank it open. "Mona, I'm alive, but I can't—"

I do a double take when I see it's not my friend scowling at me on the other side of the door, but Nic, my bear shifter client and occasional landscaper.

The burly man is at least one and a half times taller than me, his wide shoulders and thick torso taking up most of the doorframe. Though his soft, open posture makes him unintimidating despite his size. He gives me a warm smile, which flickers as he takes in my current state.

"Sorry for disturbing you when you're expecting company, Mistress. I can come back another time," Nic says, rubbing the back of his neck with a meaty palm.

"Why are you here?" My voice is a croak after almost a week of disuse. I clear my throat, but it doesn't help.

"It's supposed to be unseasonably cold tonight, so I thought I'd stop by and put some special covers on the roses to help protect them from the temperature drop. But when I got back there, I saw..."

My stomach lurches, remembering the destruction I wrought on them the night I broke things off with Grace. I couldn't stand the sight of them. Something in me snapped and the next thing I knew, my arms and hands were bleeding from dozens of thorn pricks and the garden was littered with petals and torn off blooms.

"Is everything okay?" Nic asks, reaching out hesitantly to place his hand on my shoulder.

Something about his gentleness makes any shred of composure I have left break. I step into him and fling my arms around him, burying my face into Nic's chest as an ugly sob tears from my chest.

Immediately, his arms wrap around me in response, and he rubs circles on my back.

"No. I'm n-not okay," I say through shuddering tears, and he squeezes me tighter.

"Let it out. I've got you," he says, his low voice a soothing rumble.

And because I've got no pride or defenses left, I do.

AFTER COMPLETELY SOAKING Nic's shirt with blood tears, we end up inside with him bundling a blanket over my shoulders before he passes me a mug of warmed blood and takes a seat on the couch across from me. I'm too weak to care how unprofessional it is to have a client here while I'm having a mental breakdown. Service is Nic's primary kink we explore, but there's nothing remotely sexual about how he's taking care of me tonight.

It should feel far too vulnerable letting this giant man into my house without controlling the encounter with the strict rules of a scene, but I've already cracked myself open and poured out my pain onto his chest. There's no coming back from that. Resisting the care he's offering wouldn't help anything.

"Can I get you anything else, Blair?" Nic asks softly, surveying me with kind, worried eyes that make my chest ache.

Blair, not Bella or Mistress. "How do you know my name?"

A faint flush creeps out above his wiry beard, staining his light brown skin, and he rubs the back of his neck. "I, uh, I didn't find out on purpose. I run that monster support group, and Max mentioned a vampire named Blair in passing. I figured there probably wasn't another intimidating vampire woman in town. I'm sorry, I should've asked before using your real name. I just felt weird using your, uh, professional name right now."

"It's okay," I sigh. Another boundary destroyed—not that it matters at this point.

He visibly relaxes. "Forgive me if you don't want to talk about it, but what…uh, what inspired the sudden landscaping changes?"

I swallow heavily, fighting against the urge to cry again. When I speak, the words that come out of me are unexpected. "They were going to die, eventually. It felt silly to keep taking care of them, knowing I'd watch them wither."

Nic blinks at me, his brow furrowing. "You killed them so you wouldn't have to see them die? Roses are perennials, so they'll come back again next year."

I nod. "I know." A tear slides down my cheek.

Nic tracks it, his confused look softening to understanding. "This isn't about the roses."

I nod again, unable to speak through the weight of the sadness crushing my chest.

Nic hums softly, considering the situation. "Can I share a story with you?"

"Sure, why not?" I say blithely. Listening to whatever the shifter wants to say has got to be better than crying again.

"Alright." Nic sighs and shifts to better settle in on his chair, then closes his eyes for a second like he's preparing himself for something difficult.

"What kind of story is this?" I ask.

He gives me a sad smile. "One that might be helpful for you to hear. One I don't talk about much, but not because it isn't important."

"How cryptic," I mutter.

Nic snorts and nods. "Alright, alright. It's a story about my wife."

My eyes widen. I never assume that a client not wearing a ring means anything, and it isn't my place to pry into people's personal lives. But kind, dependable Nic, being married and hiding it, shocks me. "You're *married*? Does she know about your sessions with me?"

"I was," he says with a sad smile. "She passed away a little over ten years ago."

"Oh." Shit, what am I supposed to say to that? "I'm sorry for your loss," I add feebly.

"Thank you. To answer your other question, she wanted me to move on after her. We had time after her diagnosis to talk about that kind of thing. Well, more like argue about it. A lot." Nic laughs, shaking his head at whatever memory flashes through his mind. "Mary made me promise that I'd at least find someone to help with my... needs. She knew how much I need to take care of someone. I don't think she imagined it would take on the exact form that we explore in our sessions, though," Nic chuckles. "I didn't realize that's something I'd want until I had my first experience with you."

"Nic... that's..." A surge of complicated emotions washes over me now that I know why he sought me out.

"I know, I know. I didn't fulfill my promise to her like she'd really have wanted, but... it's the best I could do. She wanted me to fall in love again, have kids since she passed before we could..." He clears his throat, wiping away a tear before giving me a cheeky smile. "We both know that's not what our relationship is, Mistress."

"Good, because for a moment there I was worried I'd have to let you and your dead wife down," I say with a matching smile. The first one I've been able to make since that awful night with Grace. That realization immediately wipes it away.

"Anyway, her approval isn't what I wanted to talk about. I wanted to tell you about Mary, because she was the best godsdamned thing that ever happened to me. I loved her with every fiber of my being, and when I found out our time together was going to be much shorter than we'd expected, it almost destroyed me. She was my heart. My everything. Hell, she still is, even with all the things I've done to surround myself with friends and people to care for. It hurt worse than anything I've ever felt, losing her."

"How can you stand it?" I ask, fist clenching around the blanket I'm holding as I struggle not to weep. "How did it not ruin you?"

Nic gives me a rueful smile. "It fucking hurts. I won't pretend otherwise. Yes, it's gotten easier over time, but the ache will always be there. Surrounding myself with people who care about me and continuing to take things one day at a time is what lets me keep going."

He's sitting here smiling at me, as if it's simple. As if the emotions tormenting me are manageable with enough can-do attitude. "I... I'm not as strong as you," I say, shaking my head.

Nic frowns. "What? You're the strongest person I've ever met."

"No, I'm not." Frustrated tears spring forth and I swipe them away. "I'm scared of the pain. I don't understand how you can sit here and tell me about the woman you loved so calmly." Panic constricts my chest. "I can't do it. I can't face being with her when each passing day is a reminder of the time we have left rapidly slipping away. Knowing that I'll mourn her for an eternity."

"You really think the alternative is better?" Nic asks gently, then lets out a heavy sigh. "You can't stop yourself from loving someone, so what's the point of being miserable for even longer?"

He levels his steely gaze on me, and he's staring into my soul when he speaks again. "You let yourself love her. You cherish what time you have together. Because it would hurt infinitely worse to not have loved her at all."

38

GRACE

I'm headed back to Mona's house again tonight. She's invited me over every night, an unspoken understanding that I shouldn't be on my own. When my ex-husband left, I tried to handle it alone, which was a mistake. I cried for hours every night, looking at pictures of the woman he'd cheated on me with, watching videos from our honeymoon, and endlessly picking apart each moment of our marriage trying to find an answer for why he didn't love me.

Looking back, it's hard not to cringe at my past behavior. It wasn't my fault that he broke our marriage. He didn't deserve my love, and I wasn't happy with him. Yet I beat myself up over and over, deepening the wounds on my psyche that he'd started. Wounds that I thought were healing in Blair's arms.

Fuck. Don't cry.

I'm not doing that this time. I'm not torturing myself, because I don't deserve it. I never deserved it. So I'm going over to Mona's house every night she'll have me until I feel safe enough to be alone with my thoughts. Maybe distracting myself and not allowing myself time to think isn't a healthy coping mechanism, but it's got to be better than self-flagellation.

I only wish I didn't have to be alone at all. When I'm lying in bed trying to sleep, I can't keep the tears at bay as I torture myself with memories of Blair. There's no one there to stop me from opening up our text history and typing out a message telling her how much I miss her and how she was wrong about what I want from her, then promptly deleting it.

I bet Mona would let me sleep at her house again if I asked. The night I showed up devastated and dealing with a bad neck flare up, she put me in her guest room and laid next to me on the bed, letting me talk to her for hours and holding my hand until the comforting weight of Nugget pressed against my side and exhaustion pushed me to sleep. I'm sure she'd be willing to snuggle me in bed again and hold my phone hostage, but I can't ask her to do that. She's already doing more than enough.

If my neck has taught me anything, it's that sometimes you have to deal with pain and no amount of crying or outside help will make a difference. You have to keep going knowing even if it hurts so fucking badly that you can't think straight. And when it's absent, you know that reprieve is only temporary. It's also taught me what I can endure. I'll grit my teeth and breathe through the misery of Blair's rejection and my love for her, even if it never gets better. I'll find ways to distract my mind from the pain.

What else can I do?

With that cheery thought, I grab my purse and head out the door to go to Mona's. And immediately proceed to almost trip over a small package sitting on my doormat, barely catching myself before I tumble down the stairs.

I frown down at the box, resisting the urge to kick it in retaliation. I didn't order anything recently, so I have no clue what it could be. I bend down to pick it up and on closer inspection, there's no shipping label or indication of what's inside.

"What the hell?" I mutter, using my house key to cut through the packing tape. Inside, the small white box is insulated, with a disposable ice pack like the ones I got when I tried that home meal kit delivery service. Even more perplexed, I remove the ice pack to reveal four small vials filled with dark red liquid.

Blood.

"You've got to be fucking kidding me." I dig through the box looking for a note or something, but find nothing. My stomach clenches painfully and anger rises, hot and insistent.

"Fuck you. I don't want your pity," I hiss down at the vials, resisting the urge to raise my voice in case my neighbors catch me screaming at a box. I want to shatter them on the concrete steps, but then I'd have to deal with the broken glass and explain why there are bloodstains on my porch.

Getting an impersonal blood delivery from Blair is a slap to the face. A reminder that she thinks I cared more about what I could get from her than anything else.

"Fuck you," I mutter, resolve settling in my chest as I carry the box to the garbage bin on the curb, then toss the whole thing inside.

She wants to treat me like I'm not even worth a goddamn note? Fine.

Good.

Anger is as good a distraction as anything else. I'm done worrying about the heartbreak crushing me. Let it burn her out of my system.

WHEN I PULL into Mona's driveway, there's already another car parked in front of their garage. Some of the rage that was fueling me on the drive over sputters out as I worry about whose car that could be. I'm not really in a place to talk to strangers tonight. I wanted to have an anger-fueled bitch fest with Mona, not make small talk.

I pull up my text thread with Mona.

> Grace: Hey! Do you have someone over?

> Mona: Yes. Max's sister showed up for a surprise visit a few minutes ago. I'm sorry, I would've warned you, but she literally just appeared at the door with an overnight bag and invited herself to spend the weekend here.

> Grace: Yikes. Does Max like this sister?

> Mona: Define "like".

> Grace: Ooof. Yikes indeed.

> Mona: Samantha loves to give him shit and flirt with me. It's harmless, but because he's the baby of their family, it's hard for him to see the humor in it sometimes. Even if they love each other.

> Mona: I know you're probably already running away, but if you can bear it, maybe come in and have dinner with us? She's friendly and it'll be nice for her to focus her flirting on someone that won't piss Max off.

Ugh. I look down at my ratty hoodie and bleach-stained leggings, then assess how bad the dark circles under my eyes are in the rearview mirror. Not exactly how I'd want to look when meeting someone new, but fuck it. Mona and Max have been saints helping me through my bad neck flare up and my post-breakup funk. Playing interference with his sassy sister is the least I can do.

> Grace: Sure. I'll warn you in advance, though, that I'm in a really pissy mood, so I may not be an amazing guest.

> Mona: That's okay. Be as surly as you need to be. Knowing Samantha, she'll probably like it.

> Grace: She sounds...interesting.

> Mona: Oh, just wait.

I dig some lip balm out of my purse and put it on, then pull my hair back into a ponytail to try to hide how oily and limp it is from not washing it in a few days. It doesn't do much to improve my look, but it's not like it even matters. I don't need to impress Max's sister. I just need to be a distraction.

Mona meets me at the door before I have a chance to ring the doorbell, a frazzled smile plastered on her lips. "Grace!"

I raise a brow at her. "Want me to kidnap you? If we're fast enough, we can hop in my car before they notice."

She snorts and shakes her head. "Thanks, but Max is a P.I. He'd find us before we got very far."

"True," I sigh. "Alright then, I guess we'll stay."

"Come on in. They're in the kitchen arguing over god knows what." Mona rolls her eyes as I follow her inside and through to their living room and kitchen area.

"Come on, Maxie! Don't be so sensitive. I was teasing."

"Telling me my haircut makes me look like a loser isn't teasing!" Max's eyes flick to me over his sister's shoulder, who is facing away, and he sighs and gives me a strained smile. "Hey, Grace, good to see you."

I give a little wave, and his sister turns around to see who he's talking to.

My eyes widen when I take in the grinning woman next to Max. Damn, hotness runs in their family. Samantha looks strikingly similar to her brother, but with white-blonde hair and lighter eyes.

I tug at my hoodie, suddenly much more self-conscious about my appearance.. It gets worse when she gives me an obvious quick once over. Nothing like looking like shit in front of someone ridiculously attractive to really put your confidence in the toilet.

I force a smile, pretending that I don't look like I crawled out of a dumpster in comparison to her. "Hey Max!"

"Dude, you didn't tell me we were having hot company," Samantha stage whispers to her brother.

He rolls his eyes at her. "That would've required some advance notice about you coming to visit," he murmurs back, then raises his voice. "This is my sister, Samantha. Samantha, this is Grace. Mona's best friend. She's here because she was invited. Unlike you."

His frustrated comment rolls off of her as she steps forward with a wide grin, extending a hand out to me. "A pleasure, Grace."

I take her hand and she gives it a shake, her fingers sliding along my palm in a tease as she lets go. I flush, taken aback by the unexpected flirtation. "Uh, nice to meet you."

Mona laughs. "At least she didn't kneel and kiss your hand."

"She did that when she met Mona for the first time because she can't resist the opportunity to fuck with me," Max explains.

"Ah." My eyes flick to Samantha, who doesn't look chastened at all. No, she's grinning even wider, her violet eyes sparkling with delight.

"You should've seen the look on his face," she says conspiratorially, leaning toward me.

Mona pats a glowering Max on the shoulder, and I resist the urge to laugh at how easily his sister gets to him. It's funny, but makes me glad I'm an only child.

"We were thinking takeout for dinner," Mona says, attempting to redirect the conversation. "Are burgers okay?"

"What, no home cooked meal for your sister you haven't seen in ages?" Samantha teases, crossing her arms under her chest and cocking her hip to the side with a pout.

"I saw you last weekend," Max deadpans.

"Burgers sound perfect!" I exclaim. Mona gives me a grateful nod.

"Hmm, if Grace wants burgers, then who am I to argue?" Samantha says, winking.

The flirtation shocks me again. It's like there's a palpable wave of her attraction that hits me whenever she does something flirty. And the way she's watching me only makes it weirder. It's feels supernatural...

Probably because it is. Shit, it's easy to forget that Max is part demon. That means Samantha is too.

Normally, I'd shake it off, but I'm still riding the adrenaline of my rage earlier. I'm not in the mood to be magically flirted with. "What are you doing to me?" I ask bluntly.

"Oh shit, sorry!" Samantha's smile flickers, and the sensation ends. She looks genuinely apologetic as she holds her hands up in appeasement. She gives Max and Mona a questioning look. "Does she know?"

"Yes, she knows about monsters. She knows I'm part-succubus, about Mona's magic, and her girlfr—"Max winces and cuts himself off. "Shit, I'm sorry."

"It's okay," I say, surprising myself with how calmly the words come out. Inside, the cold flame of anger blazes to life. "I was seeing a vampire. Now I'm not."

Samantha gives me an assessing look. Can she sense emotions like her brother? If she can feel the rage in me, she doesn't react. "Her loss."

I nod, her comment bolstering the indignation inside me.

Yes. It fucking was. I'm a goddamn catch and this hot succubus recognizes that within five minutes of knowing me.

"Right, so I got a lot more of our Mom's succubus abilities in the genetic lottery, compared to magic Max here," Samantha says, flipping her icy blonde hair off her shoulder with a flourish. Even that small movement has a touch of magic to it, drawing my eye to the elegant slope of her shoulder. "I wasn't doing anything intentionally. Sometimes my seductive powers, uh, leak out of me, for lack of better terms, when I'm attracted to someone. I'll focus on keeping it tamped down if it's bothering you. I didn't mean anything by it."

Her candor and the compliment mingle with my determination to move past Blair. Maybe I should tell her I don't mind. Encourage her to flirt with me. What's wrong with getting some appreciation?

Those thoughts last for about five seconds before my gut twists, recoiling at the idea of smiling and flirting back. It feels wrong. The only person I want looking at me with desire is...

No. Dammit! I don't owe Blair anything. I tried to give her my fucking heart, and she didn't want it.

I swallow the surge of pain down and give Samantha a smile. "I've never heard of leaking as being seductive, but I guess there's a first time for everything," I say, with a forced chuckle.

A peal of laughter erupts from her, making Samantha so beautiful it's almost hard to look at her. "Gorgeous and funny. You have suspect taste in men, but not in friends," she says to Mona.

"It's not too late for me to kick you out," Max mutters, and Samantha's supernatural charm vanishes as she turns and smacks his arm.

"Please tell me you're not going to be like this the whole weekend," Mona says with an exasperated sigh.

Samantha freezes, and both she and Max have twin sheepish looks after her frustrated comment. "Sorry, Mona. I'll behave," she says, a little too saccharine to be entirely believable.

DINNER ENDS up being surprisingly enjoyable. Samantha eases off her teasing, turning her focus on chatting with Mona about past D&D campaigns, and asking me about myself. She's not flirting as hard, but every so often I get another spike of desire off of her when she looks my way.

"So, did you really drive all the way out here to bug me all weekend, or is there some ulterior motive for your visit?" Max asks when the conversation lulls.

Samantha snorts. "Hey! I've been nice all dinner. I didn't even make fun of you when you choked on a fry."

"How magnanimous of you," Max says drolly. "But seriously, why the sudden appearance?"

His sister looks like she's about to give him a rude comeback, but thinks better of it and shrugs. "There's an event nearby that one of my friends told me about. I've been meaning to check it out, and my weekend plans fell through, so I figured I could come see my baby bro and check out the event."

Mona and Max exchange an inscrutable look. "What kind of event?" Mona asks, her voice slightly strained.

"A kinky one," Samantha says, seemingly unbothered by discussing the topic around her brother. "They have a monster night once a month, since this area seems to be loaded up with kinky paranormals. Honestly, it sucks that you guys get a cool event like that out here in the suburbs, while I'm living in the city quickly running out of monsters to match with on Bewitch'd."

"Oh, uh, cool." Mona frowns at Max, and he squeezes her shoulder.

"You can't go," he says firmly.

"Uh, yes I can. Since when do you get to decide what I do with my life?" Samantha scoffs.

"No, you can't," Max says.

Samantha rolls her eyes. "I never took you to be a prude, Maxie. I know you've never been a fan of your succubus side, but some of us like to fuck and get freaky."

I snort, unable to hold back my amusement knowing how wrong his sister is.

"What's funny?" Samantha asks with a frown.

"Oh, nothing!" I say, not wanting to expose Max and Mona's very kinky sex life to his sister.

Mona sighs. "Sam, Max and I had plans to go to that event.

We'd been, uh, looking forward to it. You being there would be way too weird."

"Oh!" Samantha gives Mona an assessing look, a salacious grin spreads across her face. "Nice." She turns to look at a beet red Max and grimaces. "Ugh. Gross."

"Yes. Like I said, you can't go."

"It happens once a month! You can go next time," Samantha protests. "I really need this. Work has been awful and I haven't been out on a date in weeks. *Weeks*. I'm going crazy with all my pent up succubus needs."

I expect Max to argue with her, but he just frowns and exchanges a look with Mona, who nods. "Alright, you can go. We'll stay home."

His sister claps her hands together in triumph. "Thanks, Maxie! This is why you're my favorite brother."

"I'm your only brother," Max scoffs. "You can go to the event tomorrow, but you have to promise not to go to The Vault unless you check in with me first ahead of time. No showing up randomly. It's an important part of my relationship with Mona, and I won't let you fuck that up by being there at an inopportune time because you're horny or bored."

Samantha nods solemnly. "I promise. Believe me, I've had enough of Mom and Dad's stories. I don't want to know what anyone else in the family gets up to." She shudders at the thought.

Max has the same reaction to the mention of his parents, and I can't help wondering what traumatized them so much. "Good."

"I'm disappointed that I never got to see it," I say, and all eyes at the table turn to me. It's a stray, slightly bitter thought I hadn't meant to voice out loud. "The monster night," I clarify. "Not Max and Mona. Or your parents," I add with a nervous snort, now that everyone's attention is on me.

"Come with me!" Samantha exclaims, the wave of excitement pouring off of her at the prospect making my pulse quicken. She sees me flush and winces. "Shit, sorry." Taking a deep breath, she makes her face as neutral as possible and the surge of energy dissipates. "No pressure, but it'd be more fun to go with someone."

"I, uh... I'm not sure that's a good idea. Sorry!" My appeasing smile probably looks more like a wince. "I'm not ready to, uh, do anything like that again."

Even thinking about attempting a scene with someone new makes the dinner I ate sit like lead in my stomach. I hate that I can't go out and fuck around and get Blair out of my system, but it didn't work after my divorce, so it sure as shit won't help after being with the woman who claimed my heart and introduced me to kink.

"Totally get it," Samantha says with a nod. "I'm happy to go as friends, though. I'd hate for whatever happened with your ex to keep you from doing something you're interested in."

I can't stop the rueful laugh that escapes from me. "It's a little late for that, sadly." I can't imagine submitting to anyone but Blair. Shit, I can't imagine wanting anyone else, period, which makes me seethe with anger. Makes me want to force myself to do something reckless to prove that wrong.

Samantha seems to pick up on that desire, her eyes twinkling with mischief. "Seems to me like you could use a night out, and seeing all those monsters in one place is a rare opportunity for a human. And who knows, maybe you'll find something to your taste?"

Max frowns at his sister, crossing his arm over his chest. "You don't have to go if it makes you uncomfortable, Grace. Sam is annoyingly persuasive, but she won't be upset if you say no."

"It's fine," I say, giving him an appreciative smile. I know he can sense the anger and pain burning inside me, but I don't think he gets that I want to lean into it. "You know what? Fuck it. I'll go. If I hate it, I can always go home." And if that happens, I'll just have ended up back where I would've been to start.

I refuse to let what happened with Blair keep me from living my life. I may be broken and bleeding on the inside, but I'm not giving in. I'm done being the sad and pathetic girl who spends her nights soaking her pillows with tears over people that don't want her.

39

BLAIR

For the second time in less than a week, someone is knocking on my door. It's almost 10 pm, which means it's not a solicitor. Did Nic decide I needed another in person pep talk? While I begrudgingly appreciate his support, his voice memos checking in twice a day are more than enough. Just because he got me to stop sleeping constantly, take a shower, and answer my texts again, doesn't mean I have it in me to spend time with him in person.

I groan and set down the paint roller in my hand, then head downstairs to answer it. I've been redoing the main bedroom to keep myself occupied. Or rather, to keep myself from acting feral again. It hasn't stopped the constant hollow feeling in my chest, but at least I'm doing something other than lying in bed and tormenting myself with nightmares and bad memories.

There's more pounding as I approach the door, filled with an urgency that sends a spike of panic through my gut. I fling the door open and find Mona on the other side, her expression stormy.

"Is she okay?" I ask immediately, the blood from my meal earlier thrumming in my ears as my body prepares to go into action.

"Why aren't you answering my texts and calls? I thought you stopped doing that shit!" Mona shouts, not acknowledging my question.

"*Is Grace okay?*" I ask again, my voice a growl as the monster inside me starts to take over.

"Whoa, calm down. Don't rip my throat out! She's not hurt or anything. It's not that kind of emergency," Mona says, taking a step back towards the edge of the porch with her hands up.

Her fear snaps me out of my agitation, and I realize I'm snarling, fangs distended. "Fuck. Sorry." My eyes drop in shame as I breathe past the unexpected adrenaline surge. "I'm not doing well."

"No shit, really?" Mona says, her humor laced with obvious concern. "I couldn't tell from the weeks you ignored me, or the massive bags under your eyes. I didn't even know vampires could get those." She steps back toward me hesitantly. "If I give you a hug, will you promise not to maul me?"

"I would never hurt you, Mona," I say, ashamed that I gave her even a second to doubt that.

A moment later, she's wrapping me up in a firm hug. I sink into the comfort like getting into bed after a long night of hard work. "This doesn't mean that I'm not still pissed at you."

"I know," I murmur. "I don't blame you."

AFTERGLOW

When I try to pull back, she clutches me tighter. "And me being pissed doesn't mean you're not still my friend."

"Okay." I don't know if I deserve it, but being held feels too good to argue.

There's an awkward moment of silence when she finally lets go of me, and when we break it, we both speak at the same time.

"Why are you—"

"Why didn't you—"

I nod for her to go first, even though I'm still worried about what would cause Mona to show up uninvited.

"Why didn't you answer your phone?" she asks, placing a hand on her hip.

"I was working on something upstairs and must've left it back in the kitchen or in my bedroom."

Her eyes narrow. "Are you sure you weren't ignoring me again? Because, as you can see now, showing up on your doorstep wasn't an idle threat."

When Nic left a few nights ago, I messaged Mona back, unable to bear the idea of two visitors in one evening. I needed time to think about what he said. I still need time.

I shake my head. "I promise. I was painting. See?" I hold my hands up to show her the flecks of dried pastel pink paint.

"Not your usual color. What are you painting?" Mona asks, brow crinkling.

I consider not telling her the truth. Making up something that won't make me seem insane. But she's here and hiding myself hasn't helped me feel more stable, so why bother?

"Come in, I can show you if you'd like. After you tell me what was so urgent that you needed to come over and bust down my door."

"It figures that it takes me doing that to see your house," Mona says dryly as she steps inside. Her eyes widen as I guide her through to the living room. "Damn, this place is amazing. I shouldn't be surprised because everything about you is cool, but—"

"Mona," I interrupt. "Admire my house later. Tell me what's going on."

She sobers and gives me a grim nod. "You fucked up."

"What?" I blink back at her.

"You fucked up and you're taking too goddamn long to come to your senses. If you don't do something soon, you won't be able to come back from this."

"Mona, I don't—"

"No," she snaps, holding her hands up to stop me from continuing. "Don't lie to me. You've hermited yourself up for two weeks. You look like shit. There's no way you broke up with Grace because you don't love her. You did it because you're a coward."

Her words slam into me, the unusual bluntness painful and comforting at the same time. "Mona—"

"Let me finish!" she says, raising her voice. "I love you and I love Grace, and I want you both to be happy. You're perfect for each other. Goddamn soulmates. I've had so many dreams about you two, together and so fucking happy I could still feel it when I woke up. I didn't tell you about them because I didn't want to freak you out. Prophecies aren't set in stone, though. You have to be brave enough to make those things happen."

"I know," I murmur.

"What?" Mona's puffed up posture from her impassioned speech deflates at my reply.

"I know." I say again, scrubbing my face with my hand. "I'm scared, and I've been trying to figure out how to get past that. Even if I can, I don't know how to undo the damage."

"You can start by not leaving boxes of blood on her doorstep with no other communication," Mona mutters.

I frown, disturbed by the implication of her remark. Did that upset Grace even more? *Fuck.* "I didn't think she'd want to hear from me, but I couldn't stop worrying about her being in pain. I made a promise to help her, no matter what. She said she didn't want to be my friend, so I thought she'd prefer it that way."

"Well, that backfired because she's pissed as hell now. Mad Grace makes reckless decisions. Normally, that means getting bangs or buying expensive equipment for a hobby she'll forget about in a month. But this time, she's more angry than I've ever seen her." Mona grimaces and levels me with a stern gaze. "She's going to monster night at The Vault tomorrow with Max's sister. His super flirtatious *succubus* sister, who will leap at the chance to encourage Grace to do something to get over you. Which is why I'm here, yelling at you to get your shit together and do something."

The thought makes my blood run cold. My instinct is to find Max's sister and tear her throat out. Instead, I clench my hands into tight fists and exhale sharply. "Grace has every right to be upset with me, and we're not together. She can do what she wants."

"She doesn't want to!" Mona huffs, exasperated. "She wants *you.* So you better figure out how to fix things. I'd suggest saving her life from a murderous demon, but that'd be a little derivative of my methods."

"Okay," I say, the word coming out of my mouth before I consciously decide. It's been building inside me since Nic told me about his wife. While I worked on the bedroom upstairs. And now with my best friend urging me to stop being scared, like I did for her back when she was struggling with her own relationship. I'm more terrified of letting myself love Grace than anything else in my life.

But after allowing myself a taste of what it's like to be with her, the agony of denying that love is far worse.

"Good," Mona nods, cracking a small, hopeful smile at me. "Now that that's settled, give me a house tour. I want to know what a vampire lair looks like, and you said you'd show me what you were painting."

40

GRACE

"What the fuck am I doing here?" I mutter under my breath as I cut the engine after pulling into the parking lot outside The Vault. Judging by how many cars are here already, it's going to be more packed than the last time I came.

Memories of that night swirl in my mind. The nerves, the excitement, the overwhelming pleasure, and the hopeful blossoming of my heart. My chest squeezes painfully and I fight back tears.

I check my makeup in the visor mirror, dabbing at my watery eyes with a tissue so I don't ruin my eyeliner.

I could turn around and go home. I don't have to do this.

And then what? Sob into my pillow again until I fall asleep and dream of Blair?

The woman who stares back at me in my reflection looks unhinged—sad, pissed, scared, and so, so tired of being upset.

No. I'm here and I'm doing this, dammit.

I reapply my hot pink lipstick, tug down the neckline of my dress, and give myself a determined look before flipping up the visor. I throw the car door open and haul myself out, flashing my panties to anyone nearby with my graceless exit.

Who cares? I'm here to be messy and reckless tonight.

Samantha waits by the entrance, her toned legs looking impossibly long in the white dress that barely covers her ass. If it weren't for how much skin she had exposed, I'd swear she looked like an angel under the glow of parking lot lights, her long white-blonde hair draped over one shoulder, soft, subtle makeup highlighting her striking features, and a sweet smile spreading her lips as I approach.

But the grin it morphs into as she checks me out is nothing but sinful, and I fight not to blush. I'm attracted to Samantha. It'd be impossible not to be unless you aren't into women even in the slightest. She's gorgeous and magnetic and probably everything I should be looking for in a rebound fling.

Yet, when I look back at her and wave, I don't feel anything other than a confidence boost from her obvious appreciation of my appearance. She's the most alluring person I'm likely to encounter, literally bestowed with powers of seduction, but I don't want her.

I wish I did.

Maybe that makes me a terrible person, wanting to move on to something else so fast, but desiring Samantha would be proof that I was being foolish with Blair. That my feelings resulted from the rush of trying something new and our kink dynamic, not a bone-deep connection that I'll never get over.

"Grace!" Samantha exclaims, tugging me into a quick hug, before pulling back and giving me another once-over. "You look so fucking hot, wow. Like I knew you were pretty, but *damn*."

I laugh at her compliments. "Thanks! You look incredible, too."

She does a twirl, showing off the back of her dress where there are long slits on the shoulder blades and a smaller one right above her tailbone. "Let's go inside and scope things out. Claim a spot to watch the bacchanal."

Samantha loops her arm through mine and leads me inside. Her presence at my side bolsters me enough that I don't immediately freak out being back in this space under very different circumstances. We check in with the bouncer, who unabashedly eyes up Samantha as he goes over the rules of the club.

"Most important one for tonight, other than consent, is no photos or videos. Humans leave their phones up here." The burly man holds his hand out expectantly to me.

"Huh? Why?" I ask, clutching at my purse defensively. Mona wanted me to text updates on how I was doing throughout the night. She's worried I'll freak out or do something I'll regret, and I could tell Max was concerned that Samantha would be a bad influence.

"Someone's guest broke the rule and now it's club policy. You don't want to give me your phone, you don't go inside."

I reluctantly hand it over, and Samantha nudges me reassuringly. "You can use mine to let Mona know I haven't used you in a kinky dark magic ritual or whatever she and Max are worried about."

"Damn, you're not going to do that?" I ask teasingly.

She laughs and shakes her head. "No, I save that for the third date." I must look surprised because she holds up her hands defensively. "Not that this is a date! Just two new friends casually watching a bunch of monsters get their freak on."

She winks at the bouncer, who perked up at her comment about us not being on a date. I have a feeling most unattached people here tonight will have the same relief when they find out we're not a couple.

As we head into the hallway connecting to the main room of the club, I grab her forearm to stop her before we go further. "You sure I won't get in your way? I won't be upset if you want to, uh, partake. I can stay to see all the monsters and then head out."

Samantha chews on her lip, considering my offer. "Honestly? I'm just here to watch, too. Absorb some of the energy. I've been feeling worn down lately, and I could really use a boost, but I'm not in the mood to fuck."

"A boost?" I ask.

"Oh! Yeah. So my mom is a succubus. She feeds off sexual energy and needs it to sustain her and she passed some of that need on to me. Not to the same extent, but I can definitely feel it when I haven't fed in a while."

"Whoa, okay. I bet this will be like a buffet for you then," I say. Knowing that won't be getting in her way, and she's going to spend the night just hanging out with me, I'm able to relax a little.

She smiles, her pearly teeth so bright they're almost the same color as her dress. "Exactly! Or actually, more like a B12 shot. Something to perk me back up."

"I'm jealous," I say with a soft chuckle. "I feel like shit all the time lately. It'd be nice to know a surefire way to improve that. Sorry, that's probably an overshare."

"No such thing tonight," Samantha says, placing a hand on my shoulder. "We're going to go in there, bask in the monster sex, and bitch about our love lives."

"Sounds good to me. The only thing missing are drinks to make this a proper lonely girls' night."

I'm joking, but Samantha looks around the hallway to make sure no one is coming, then digs into her cleavage and pulls out a flask.

"We're not supposed to have alcohol in here!" I squeak, motioning for her to put that away while simultaneously impressed at how well hidden it was.

"Relax." She chuckles and tucks it back between her breasts. "These places have that rule for consent purposes, and neither of us are taking part tonight. It's fine. Besides, it's fun to break the rules sometimes." She gives me a devilish grin, then adds, "When it isn't hurting anyone. Or is, but the pain is consensual. You know what I mean."

She loops her arm in mine again and we head into the main room of the club. It takes a minute to find an open couch for us to sit on, and once we settle in, someone is already coming around to let us know monsters are free to shift or let their human glamors down.

"Excited to see a succubus for the first time?" Samantha asks, waggling her eyebrows at me. "Even if you've seen Max in his demon form, I'm way hotter in mine."

I laugh, rolling my eyes at her comment. "What's up with that, by the way? You messing with Max."

She shrugs. "He's easy to tease, and it's fun to argue with him. He's always been the broody one of the family, too, so my sisters and I try to pester him to get him to come out of his shell more."

"And flirting with Mona?" I ask.

"Your best friend is a total babe. It's my nature to flirt. Trust me, if I actually wanted to steal Mona from Max, it would've already happened. No one can resist my charms." She gives me a decidedly filthy look and a wave of her seductive energy hits me, but it doesn't change my lack of actual interest. "Now hold my purse while I shift to my other form," she says, passing her bag over and sticking her hand up her skirt with no preamble.

"Whoa! You have to do *that* to shift?" I quickly avert my eyes.

"Huh? Oh!" she says with a boisterous laugh. "I have a spell-mark on my inner thigh that I have to touch to change forms. Don't worry, I'm not fingering myself."

I turn back around, my eyebrows shooting up when I see her new appearance. Her skin has changed to a pale pink that matches the bows on my dress, and small bat-like wings extend behind her, the edges tipped in silvery-white that matches the slightly altered color of her hair. Her violet eyes have an unnatural glow to them, and she has short, slightly twisted pink horns also tipped in white.

"If I weren't currently heartbroken and wishing I were with someone else, you'd be the magical monster girl of my dreams," I say, looking at her in awe. "I'm so jealous." I reach out to touch her skin, fascinated by the sparkling flecks that almost look like glitter, then freeze, face heating as I realize how rude that is.

Samantha leans forward and takes my hand, pressing it to her chest. "You can touch," she says, her tone more amused than seductive.

Her skin is unnaturally warm, and where my palm connects with her body, there's a tingling sensation that sends a small pulse of arousal through me. I gasp and pull back like I've been burned.

She chuckles. "Whoops! I'm burning hotter than usual. Usually it takes more than a casual touch to have that effect."

I narrow my eyes at her. "You're sure you weren't trying to seduce me after all?"

Her mischievous smile confirms my suspicion. "Alright, maybe just a little. Mostly, I wanted to get rid of that sad look in your eyes for a second. And it worked!"

"Next time, warn me," I say, shaking my head at her unapologetic grin.

"Ooo, so there will be a next time?" Samantha asks, licking her lips as she leans closer. "Because now that I'm in my succubus form, you're looking like even more of a treat."

Now that I'm getting used to her, I can tell there's no actual intent behind Samantha's words. She just enjoys getting under people's skin. I roll my eyes. "I'll pass."

"Damn," she says, laughing and sitting back, looking out to survey the room. "Wow, there's certainly a variety tonight."

I pull my eyes from her pretty pink demonic form to scan the room too, and can't help the gasp that the sight elicits.

There are monsters *everywhere*.

People are still chatting and getting settled in, but I see elfin creatures with glittering wings, a pair of werewolves, a woman with a long snakelike lower half of her body, and a hulking minotaur. Not to mention the person who looks like they're part-dragon. Or the tusked, green skinned... *orc*?

"Holy shit, orcs are real?" I ask, trying to keep my voice down as best I can so I don't come off as a gawking human.

"Out of all the monsters here, that's what's surprising?" Samantha asks, bemused.

"I'm a fantasy nerd," I say absently, eyes darting around the room in wonder. For the first time in weeks, the weight of my heartache eases and there's a glimmer of genuine happiness as I see the literal manifestation of creatures I've read about since I was a kid.

And then I see *her*.

Our eyes lock and the devastation comes crashing back in. My breath punches out of my lungs.

The crowd parts like the sea around Blair's preternaturally beautiful form as she stalks over to where I'm seated. I'm frozen, my traitorous body choosing neither fight nor flight when faced with seeing her again.

Then she's standing above me, staring down with an intensity that sets my body alight with a potent mixture of anger and yearning.

"Uh, can I help you?" Samantha asks, moving to position herself in front of me more.

Blair flashes her fangs and glares at the succubus like she's one second away from ripping her throat out. "No. You can't."

I finally find my voice, though it comes out far too shaky for my liking. "W-why are you here?"

Her red eyes lock back on me, softening into something that's far too similar to affection. To yearning.

No. She doesn't love me. She doesn't want me. She doesn't—

"I'm here for you."

41

BLAIR

Fuck, I've missed her so much.

My heart hammers in my undead chest at her proximity, her scent wrapping around me like a welcoming hug, reminding me how utterly idiotic I've been. That Grace is my home and trying to give that up was as futile as trying to stop the sun from rising each day.

It takes all of my willpower to not reach out to her and fold her into my arms. To steal her away from the succubus, who is so obvious in her desire for Grace that it makes me want to paint the walls with her blood.

"What do you mean, you're here for me?" Grace snaps, wrapping her arms around herself like she's trying to protect herself from more damage I might inflict.

All the thoughts I had about how to approach my apology fly out of my head now that I'm actually standing before Grace. Every beseeching word, every explanation for my behavior, is gone and I'm left scrambling to say *something* before I ruin any chance I have.

"I'll turn you," I blurt.

Grace's delicate golden brows shoot up to her hairline. "What?"

"I'll turn you. If that's what you want, I'll do it. I don't want to make you a vampire because it makes me sick to condemn you—the most brilliant, amazing person I've ever met—to an eternity of darkness. But if it means I can call you mine again, I'll do it with a fucking smile on my face. Even if you decide afterwards that you want something besides me."

A frown twists Grace's lips, the pain and anger I've caused carved into her expression. I want to smooth out the wrinkles on her furrowed brow and use my mouth on hers to apologize in a way I'm clearly not capable of doing with words.

"You've got to be fucking kidding me. I don't want to be a vampire! I only said I'd do it so we could be together. I don't care about anything but being with you. Not what your blood can provide, not the power you could give me, not even the kink or the pleasure. I just wanted *you*." Grace wipes at the water forming in her eyes and sniffs angrily. "You crushed me, Blair. You ruined me for anyone else. I'm sitting here with a goddamn succubus and all I can think about is how she's not you. How I never should've let myself fall in love with you."

I open my mouth to reply, but she keeps barreling forward, her anger gaining momentum. "And you couldn't even be bothered to leave a fucking note with the blood you dropped off. Like I'm an obligation, not the woman you said you'd give everything to. Hell, even if I was just your submissive and not your lover, I deserved better." She swipes at her tears, a streak of dark eyeliner smudging the back of her hand. "I deserved better," she says again, more softly.

My heart aches for her. I want to lay myself at her feet and beg for forgiveness.

So I do.

Kneeling at Grace's feet, I look up into her shocked eyes and hold them, begging her to see the sincerity of what I'm about to say. Someone nearby gasps, no doubt drawn by our raised voices and the sight of Mistress Bella on her knees. I don't give a shit about what they think. Grace is the only person who matters.

"You deserve everything, Grace. I thought you wouldn't want to hear from me, which is why I didn't leave a note. What was I supposed to say? 'I'm sorry I'm a coward and a monster, here's some blood?'"

Grace huffs out a humorless laugh. "That would've been better than nothing!"

"I know that now. I'm sorry."

Her lips flatten out into a line, and I continue before she tells me to stop. I have to tell her what she means to me, even if spilling it all out at her feet ends in her saying it's not enough.

"I'm flawed, Grace. I've spent all of my life and most of my undeath fighting for a semblance of control. I thought I'd finally found it, and then I met you and none of it mattered because you made me feel things I'd locked away so I wouldn't get hurt again." I clasp my hands tightly behind my back so I won't reach out and touch her. "And just when I let myself give into those feelings, someone visited me. Someone much older with more experience being immortal. I shouldn't have listened to them, but they terrified me with the reminder of how painful the difference in our life spans will be. I let that fear control me, let myself be selfish enough to think that I could cut my losses before my love for you became inescapable."

"Well, congratulations, you got what you wanted," Grace says, shrinking back away from me.

"No," I say, a choked sound erupting from me at how wrong she is. "There is no escaping my feelings for you, Grace. I started loving you the moment we met. Knowing you, being trusted with the real you, not the curated facade you let the rest of the world see, was more than I could've ever dreamed of experiencing. I feel the love for you in the core of my being and trying to reject that was more ruinous than being turned."

Tears slide down my cheeks, but I don't bother wiping them away. I'm shaking as I cast my eyes down, bowing my head before her. "I'm yours, Grace. Entirely yours to command. Give me whatever order you see fit and I'll follow."

"Wow." I turn my head and glare at the succubus gawking at me and Grace. She flinches under my attention, then slaps her hands on her thighs and stands. "I'm gonna go, uh...find somewhere else to be. Unless you need me to stay," she says to Grace, who silently shakes her head. "Right. Who wants to show off for a succubus?" she calls out to the small group of onlookers, expertly drawing them away from me and Grace.

There's a long stretch of silence between us as I wait for a response. When I can't stand it any longer, I risk looking up into Grace's eyes. Her expression is a storm of emotions—anger, fear, pain, and hope all flashing across her face like lightning.

"What if I order you to leave me alone? What if I can't accept what you've done?" she asks, scanning my face in search of something.

I can only hope that I show her what she wants as I reply. Please let it be enough. Let me be enough. "If that's what you want, I'll go." Grace's brow's raise and I swallow down the lump in my throat. "I don't know if I can promise I'll be able to stay away, but if you ask for that, I'll do my best to listen."

"What if I order you to stay on your knees and grovel the rest of the night? What if I make you my submissive, who only gets to move or act when I allow it?" Grace asks. Her expression is closed off now, and I can't tell if she's serious or not, but I don't care. I would walk out into the rising sun for her.

"Done."

"Really?" Grace scoffs, eyes scanning the room before narrowing back at me. "That seems bad for your professional reputation."

"Fuck my reputation. Submitting to the woman I love would be an honor."

Grace's eyes fill again at my mention of love, and this time I can't stop from reaching out to take her hand between mine as I look up into her breathtaking, beautiful face. "I love you. I won't hide from it again. However you need me to prove that to you, I will. Nothing else matters."

Her lip wobbles and tears spill down her cheeks, but she doesn't pull away. "What if I just want you to hold me?"

My heart leaps in my chest and I surge up to wrap my arms around her, gathering her against my chest. Grace sinks against me, burrowing her face into my shoulder as her breath shudders out, tears wetting my skin.

"I'm s-so mad at you," she says between shaking breaths.

I hold her tighter. "I know. I'm sorry."

There's nothing else to say. My heart is in her hands. I haven't believed in God or higher power since the night I was turned, but at this moment, I pray harder than I ever did when I was begging God to make me the daughter my parents wanted.

"You can't do this to me e-ever again," Grace whispers, the hurt in her voice like a knife in my stomach.

"I won't." It's a promise I don't have the right to expect her to trust, but I say it all the same.

She shudders, tension bleeding out of her warm, soft, perfect form as she lets me hold her. I want to resist when she finally pulls back, wiping at her face and gazing at me with longing and worry in her eyes.

"I get why you're scared," she says softly, then sighs, her breath catching slightly. "Fuck, when I wasn't bawling my eyes out because you broke my heart, I was sobbing because the thought of you being alone and in pain was devastating. You've been hurt so many times. I don't want to be the one that hurts you again. If being with me will..." Grace's eyes grow watery again, and she swallows heavily. "If I'm only making things worse for you in the long run—"

"No." I shake my head adamantly, reaching out to cup her cheek. A heavy teardrop falls from her wet lashes and I wipe it away with my thumb, locking eyes with her. "*No*, Grace."

"Are you sure?" The concern in her shining eyes makes my chest ache. She's looking at me like she'd do anything to keep me from being in pain again, despite how upset I made her.

My love for this compassionate, incredible woman threatens to overwhelm me. I nod, fighting back tears. "Avoiding grief isn't worth missing a life with you. I'm still terrified, but I refuse to let fear control me again."

Before I can stop myself, instinct kicks in and I'm kissing Grace with everything I have. She inhales sharply and I go to pull back, thinking I've gone too far, but then she's grabbing my head and kissing me back, hard and desperate. My hands rove her body, needing to remap every swell and dip of her form. Her arms, back, breasts, stomach, and hips. Everything I can reach in our tangled position as her tongue slides against mine and she lets out little breathy sounds of need.

When she pulls back to catch her breath, her cheeks and chest are flushed the same pink as her dress. Even with the tear tracks and smeared lipstick from our kiss, she's stunning. "Take me home," Grace whispers.

"Are you sure?" I ask. "I don't expect you to go back to the way things were right away. I'll wait as long as you need."

She shakes her head. "No, I'm not sure. I'm scared and hurt. But I'm so tired of being sad, Blair. I know you are, too. Please. Take me home."

GRACE

When we get to the intersection where we'd turn one way to go to my condo and the other to go to Blair's place, Blair hesitates at the stop sign.

"I'm taking you to my house," she says, and while it's not a question, I can tell it's her way of letting me correct her.

"Yes," I confirm.

Maybe it'd be better for Blair to bring me back to my place. I shouldn't let her back into my life right away. It's reckless. But I'm scared that if I let her drop me off at home, I'll wake up and this will all have been a cruel dream.

She nods, reaching out to grip my thigh as she looks back at the road. Her hand is shaking and I place mine atop hers to help steady her.

"I don't want you to go home," she says, still looking forward.

"We're going to your place," I say, confused.

"I mean when the sun rises. Please stay." Her voice trembles. "I know I have no right to ask you that, but—"

"Okay." I swallow the surge of emotion that threatens to choke me when I hear the fear and vulnerability in her request. "I'll stay."

Blair squeezes my thigh, then flips her palm up to thread her fingers through mine. "Thank you."

Neither one of us says anything for the rest of the drive, and though my thoughts race, the most important thing I keep coming back to is the anchor of her hand in mine. In the past, I would've worried that my palm was too sweaty and unpleasant, or if she was having a hard time driving with one hand, but now all that matters is that I'm touching her. That she's real, and she's squeezing me back as tightly as I am, like she can't bear the thought of letting go.

When Blair pulls into her driveway and cuts the engine, I give her hand a reluctant squeeze before releasing it. She gets out of the car, using her supernatural speed to round to the passenger side by the time I've opened my door, and proffer a hand.

I take it, letting her steady me as I step out, but I still stumble forward on my shaky legs. She wraps her arm around my waist, bracing me against her smaller frame. We stare at each other for a heartbeat, neither one of us willing to move.

Blair clears her throat and steps back. "I'm sorry. I'm having a hard time not touching you," she admits softly.

"Who said you have to stop?" I ask, closing the gap she made and pushing a strand of hair out of her face to tuck it behind her ear.

Her eyes close and she releases a shuddering breath before opening them to look up at me, her sad eyes glowing red in the moonlight. "I know you're mad, and it will take time to forgive me. The monster in me doesn't understand that. It only knows you're nearby and keeps screaming at me to hold you."

Something about her phrasing makes me smile. For all that she hates her vampiric nature, and calls it her monster, it doesn't sound that bad. "Such a mean, scary vampire, having a hard time controlling your need for hugs. Or is there more that it wants?"

Blair licks her lips, her eyes darting to my neck for a split second, where my pulse hammers in anticipation of what she might say. "Yes. There's more," she rasps.

"I shouldn't forgive you so easily. I should make you wait," I say, lowering my mouth so my lips ghost against hers.

"I'll wait as long as you need," she murmurs against mouth.

"What if I need you now?" I ask, lowering my mouth to her neck. She tilts her head to the side, offering me better access, and I scrape my teeth against her silky skin.

"Fuck," she hisses. "Anything you need, it's yours. I'm yours."

"Then take me inside," I say, kissing her neck.

"Yes," she breathes.

"Bring me to your bedroom and undress me." I press another kiss to her jaw.

"Yes."

"Take control so we can both forget the pain," I whisper, then mold my lips to hers.

Blair grips my hip to hold herself steady through the kiss, fingers sinking into my flesh hard enough to leave a bruise. "Yes," she growls, before claiming my mouth again.

We stumble inside, Blair cursing each time she has to pull away to keep us from crashing into a wall or lamp. When we reach the stairs down to her basement, she hesitates.

"Give me five minutes?" she asks.

"Need to hide the bodies?"

Blair laughs, low and throaty. "No. But I wanted the first time you slept over to be special, so let me go make my bed and light some candles, okay?"

My heart flutters, then squeezes painfully as I remember the hopes I had for our first full night together as well. I swallow down the lump rising in my throat. "Okay."

"I love you," she says softly, like she knows exactly what I'm thinking. "I'm sorry I ruined it that night."

I shake my head, even as a tear slides down my cheek. It hurts that things didn't go as planned, but I don't want to dwell on it. "We're here now. Let's focus on that."

42

BLAIR

I reach up to wipe the tear from Grace's cheek, my chest tightening with the need to make her pain go away. Her wanting to focus on the present rather than deal with what I did scares me. Will she regret using me to push away the sadness? Now that I've realized I need Grace in my life far more than I fear what will happen when she's gone, I can't handle the thought of her deciding I hurt her too much to forgive me once the passion of the moment fades.

But she's told me multiple times this is what she wants tonight, so I have to trust her decision. Outside of the brief time I had with my grandma before she passed, I've never truly loved someone—infatuation with Dominic doesn't count—let alone been loved back, so maybe it really is this simple. It feels impossible, but then again so did allowing someone into my cold, dead heart in the first place.

"Let me get you something to drink while you wait," I say, taking Grace's hand in mine and leading her into the kitchen.

She follows, her palm warm and comforting against my cool flesh, and I'm reluctant to let go.

"I've got a few different options," I say, opening my fridge to remind myself of what all is inside other than blood bags. "It's late, so you probably don't want any cold brew... I have some chocolate syrup that might taste good with the oatmilk, or there are some cans of vaguely grapefruit-flavored seltzer. Or I could make you a cup of tea."

Grace comes up behind me, and my breath hitches as she presses her chest to my back, placing a hand on my hip as she looks over my shoulder. I shut my eyes, fighting back tears at the overwhelming wave of emotions that hit me at her simple touch.

God, I love her so much. I missed her.

"Why do you have all this food?" she asks, seeing the groceries I panic ordered before I went to bed this morning. I figured I'd end up throwing them out, because there was no way Grace would agree to come stay. Now I'm glad I didn't resist the urge to get them.

Her hand on my hip slides to rest on my stomach as she leans in to look behind a bag of apples to where there's a whole cherry pie. "You have my favorite things," she murmurs, voice threaded with confusion. "Are these from... before?"

I shake my head. "No, I got them delivered earlier today. Not because I thought you'd come over tonight!" I clarify quickly. "I just... I wanted to be ready. I hated the thought that you wouldn't feel welcome if you ever stayed."

Grace moves to my side, eyes scanning my face, then flicking back to the stocked refrigerator. "Blair, this is enough food to last for weeks. How long did you hope I'd be here?"

"As long as you wanted," I say, the words tumbling out before I can think better of them.

Grace's mouth falls open in surprise.

"Shit. I'm sorry, I shouldn't have said that. I haven't earned your forgiveness. It's way too fucking soon to want you to live with me."

Her jaw drops even more. "You were thinking about me moving in?"

My stomach lurches at her obvious disbelief and shock, and yet instead of reassuring her or doing something remotely sane, I blurt out the truth. "Yes. I want to be with you. Not just for occasional date nights or when we can find the time. I want a life with you. I want it all."

"Blair..." Grace's brow furrows and my mind races, trying to find something to say that won't end in her running away.

"I know I can't expect you to want that soon, and I don't. Truly, I don't. But I need you to know that I'm done being scared and I'm done pretending not to want those things. I want someone to share a bed with. I want someone to sit and chat about nothing while we eat. Someone to force me to watch awful reality TV and nerdy movies. I want someone to help fill this lonely, empty house. Or, if you hate it here, find somewhere else to make ours. Where we are doesn't matter. I've spent my entire existence desperately wanting a place to call home, and when I met you, I finally found it."

I struggle to continue as emotion clogs my throat, tears sliding down my cheeks. "You're it, Grace. You're my home."

Grace moves so quickly, I let out a startled sound as her hand digs into my hair and an arm wraps around my waist, pulling me to her and claiming my lips. Her scent and the sweet taste of her mouth mingle with my coppery tears and the salt of her own.

🌹 363

Our tongues tangle as we melt together in the kiss. It's not rushed or frantic, like before. No, it's slow and painfully tender, a physical manifestation of us coming to an accord. We consume each other's sadness and yearning, until all that's left is overwhelming love and hot, aching need.

Grace pulls back, a slow smile stretching across her lips. "You know I'm going to want to add some color in here, right?"

It takes me a second to understand what she's saying. Another second to process the surge of shocked excitement. "We can paint the whole damn house pink if you want. I always wanted a Barbie Dreamhouse as a kid."

She snorts. "I was joking."

"I wasn't. Come on, I'll show you." I close the refrigerator doors and grab her hand.

"I don't need you to start redecorating right now! Your house is great the way it is, really it was a joke," she says, but lets herself be tugged behind me as I lead us up the stairs and to the main bedroom. "I thought you slept in the basement," she says as I open the door.

Grace gasps softly when I flick on the lights. I watch her face as she scans the freshly painted pink walls and the pink and gold rose-patterned wallpaper along one wall.

I grimace at her pinched brow. "I know it's certifiable for me to do this without even knowing if we'd get back together, but once I came up with the idea, it's all I could think about. Even if you couldn't forgive me, or if you never wanted to live together, I'd at least have somewhere that I could go when I thought of you."

Grace turns to me with watery eyes and buries her face in my shoulder, tears dripping onto my skin as she cries.

"If you hate it, we'll change it. It's just paint," I say, trying not to let her hear how crestfallen I am.

She pulls off my shoulder, sniffing. "I don't hate it! I'm overwhelmed. This is the most romantic thing anyone has ever done for me," she says, beaming at me even as tears spill down her cheeks. "I love it. I love you."

Grace kisses me, and I smile back at her. "Good. It was a pain in the ass to put the wallpaper up on my own, so I'm glad it's okay."

She laughs. "It's beautiful. Though I'm not sure why I need my own bedroom, so maybe I can use it as an office or something."

My chest squeezes at how casually she's discussing living here with me. "I thought it might be nice for you to have a second bedroom in case you got sick of sleeping in a dank basement with me."

"Hmm... I can't know if I'll want that without seeing it first," she says, eyelashes fluttering at me in an unsubtle hint of what she'd like to do once we get down there.

"Good point." I lick my lips, and she tracks the movement eagerly.

We head downstairs and back to the kitchen, where Grace grabs some coffee so she can stay up with me until sunrise. I reluctantly leave her to drink it in the kitchen while I race down to the basement to make things nicer for her.

I barely have time to make the bed and light some candles before I hear her footsteps coming down the stairs. She gives me a seductive smile when she steps into the bedroom, making desire pool in my stomach and my fangs emerge.

"Sorry, I couldn't wait any longer," she says, holding my gaze for a moment before letting her eyes drift to take in the space. "It's beautiful down here. Somehow exactly what I imagined, and yet even nicer."

"I'm glad you like it." I draw closer to her as my fangs ache at the thought of her being here, where I've dreamed of spending countless hours with her, fucking and feeding, or just holding her in my arms and feeling her heart beat against my chest.

She senses the shift in my energy, her pupils dilating as I approach. "Now what?" she asks, biting her lower lip.

Now, I keep you in my lair and never let you go.

The monster in me thinks it's crystal clear, but it's not that simple. Even if Grace moves in, living together won't change that I can't be in the sun, and she deserves to bask in its light. And there's the looming knowledge that she won't be able to stay forever, unless I turn her.

I shove down the welling panic and sadness. Those are worries for another night. No matter what happens, I'm going to cling to her for as long as I can, greedy for any scrap of Grace's light.

I give her an assessing look, hoping she can't tell how dark my thoughts were a moment ago. "Do you still want what you asked for earlier? For me to take control?"

"Yes," she breathes. Grace gives me a small smile, stunning me with how fucking lovely she is when she's vulnerable. "Maybe I shouldn't give it to you so easily, but I need that. If I let my mind lead, I'm worried I'll fall apart. I need you to show me I'm yours."

I nod, the weight of her words and the trust she's putting in me after I hurt her not something I take lightly. I'll do everything in my power to deserve her faith in me.

"Are you in any pain tonight? Anything I should avoid?" I ask, moving in behind her to brush her hair to the side and press a kiss to her nape.

"It's okay right now."

"Tell me your safeword, Grace." I thread my arm beneath hers and cup her breast, eliciting a small breathy inhale from her.

"Calico."

I kiss her shoulder as a reward for her response, and she arches her chest into my hand.

It would be so easy to command her to strip and feast on her blood and her pleasure, but the experienced dominant in me can sense she needs something different. She needs me to anchor her to this moment, keep her in her body so dark thoughts and anxieties won't pull her away.

She whimpers softly when I step away, watching me as I head into the closet to get what I need. I open the drawer where I keep my ropes, finding the pink cotton ones I bought with Grace in mind before we even started experimenting together.

Grace's eyes darken when I return with the ropes and safety scissors in hand, and her tongue darts out to wet her lips. "Are you going to tie me up?"

"Yes," I say, swallowing hard as I watch her pulse tick in her throat.

"Where do you want me?" Grace's gaze darts to the bed, and while that's tempting, I need to be fully present and in control for rigging. Grace in my bed, her legs tied open while I feast between them, will have to wait until a time when I'm not already half-feral for her.

"Stand by the chaise," I command, pointing to the other side of the room where I have an antique, blood red fainting couch.

"Yes..." Grace hesitates in her response. "Should I call you Mistress or...?"

"Just Blair for tonight, love," I say, moving in front of her and setting the shears and rope down on the edge of the chaise.

"Yes, Blair," she murmurs.

I hold her hand to keep her steady while she steps out of her heels, then circle behind her to unzip her dress and unhook her bra.

She shivers as I slip my hands under both the dress and her bra straps to push them off her shoulders.

Both garments fall to the ground at her feet, and I rake my gaze down her back, smiling when I see her heart-shaped birthmark peeking out from the edge of her high-waisted beige underwear.

"Sorry for the granny panties. I wasn't expecting anyone to see them," she says with a self-conscious chuckle.

I hook two of my fingers under the elastic of the waistband and pull it back before letting it snap against her skin. "I like them." I stroke my hand across the plain cotton fabric and down between her thighs, where there's already a small damp patch.

Grace inhales sharply as I tease that spot for a moment before moving away and pulling her underwear down. She steps out of it and I take a minute to soak her in now that she's bare to me.

"God, I'll never get over how beautiful you are," I murmur, eyes feasting on every dip and curve of her plush, perfect form.

"Enjoy it while it lasts," she says. My brow furrows, and she continues with a weak smile. "This is probably as hot as I'll be. It's all downhill from here."

"Didn't I just say I liked the granny panties?" I tease, even though I feel a lump rising in my throat at the reminder of her mortality.

Grace snorts. "You're supposed to tell me that you'll still love every inch of me when I'm saggy and wrinkly and you're still... perfect!"

"I will," I say solemnly. "I can't imagine not loving you. You're gorgeous, Grace, and I'd be lying if I said I didn't enjoy how sexy you are. But that's all surface stuff. I love you for you. The rest doesn't matter."

She sighs. "Yeah. Okay. Sorry, where were we? Oh right, you were going to tie me up."

I cup her cheek. "I was serious when I said I'd turn you. I've thought about it a lot... I don't want to, but it's your choice and I promise no matter what you decide, I'll support you." I hate that there's a small surge of hope at the thought of turning Grace that mingles with the more powerful dread at the idea of making her a monster.

"I... Ask me again in a few years?" Grace places her hand over mine as we exchange an understanding that both of us may reconsider our stance on the subject with the passage of time.

I nod and kiss her softly, bringing us both back into the moment. No matter what happens, I want to make every second I have with Grace count.

43

GRACE

My nervous chatter dies down when Blair trails her hand from my cheek down the side of my neck to caress across my collarbone, leaving goosebumps in her wake. She strokes down my arm and back up, grazing the side of my breast. I lean into her touch, savoring how right it feels to have her hands on me. She repeats the motion one more time, before circling around behind me and placing her lips against my shoulder.

"Sit for me, love," she commands gently, gesturing down to the floor.

I lower myself onto the soft carpet, sitting with my legs to one side. Blair lowers to her knees beside me, reaching over to grab one of the long strands of deep pink rope. My breath hitches as she runs it between her hands, wondering how she's going to use it.

Images from the night months ago where I saw her demonstrating her shibari skills float into my mind. Her submissive was still and obedient, letting her weave the rope around his body to create a beautiful harness. Blair was methodical with her use of the rope, all poise and control. So it surprises me when she moves behind me, setting down the rope so she can place her hands on my shoulders.

"It's crucial that you tell me immediately if any of this bothers your neck or you feel numbness or tingling anywhere," she says as her hands run down the length of my arms, then move to skim across my hips and stroke up my spine, in slow, soothing motions.

"I will." My eyes flutter closed as she draws hypnotic patterns along my skin with her fingertips.

Once I'm relaxed and leaning into her touch, Blair guides my arms above my head, and I instinctively turn to look at her. Our eyes catch over my shoulder, and I tilt my chin up, silently asking for her kiss. She grants my wish, her lips pressing to mine, stealing my breath with how tender the kiss is.

Blair only lets me linger in it for a moment before pulling back with a soft smile. She picks up the rope again, looping it around my waist. Her fingers trace along where she's placed the rope, slipping across my ribcage with enough pressure to not tickle. All of my focus is on her touch and the soft rope against my skin as she winds it around me again, and my breath hitches as she weaves the rope to frame my breasts, my nipples stiffening in response.

Each sensual, teasing touch and weaving of the rope builds until I'm almost panting, desperately wanting more. Blair pauses after completing a knot, closing the gap between us to press her chest to my back and wraps her arms around me to stroke across her handiwork. When she palms my breasts and kneads them gently, I let out a needy moan.

"Mmm, that's it, baby. You're doing so well," Blair murmurs in my ear, playing with my breasts for a moment longer, before pulling back to get more rope.

I whimper at the loss of her touch, but she doesn't chastise me. No, she leans back in and presses a kiss to the column of my throat, letting out a pleased hum.

She continues, making art of my body with intricate weaving and knots trailing down my stomach, then guiding me up to my knees to bind my hips and thighs.

I lose any sense of time or anything outside of her touch and the ropes. They should feel constraining but instead there's a potent relief, like each winding loop and knot is anchoring me in the moment. My mind can't focus on my worries or fears because it's too busy being held by the ropes, and in turn, held by Blair.

When she's done with the harness on my body, Blair moves on to my hands, binding them together until I'm truly helpless. She presses kisses to my palms as she finishes tying the ropes, and for a moment, rests her cheek against my hand. The raw, vulnerable look that crosses her face as she closes her eyes and leans into my touch knocks the breath out of me.

She needs this as much as I do. I crave the surrender and the knowledge that she'll take care of me, and Blair needs to know that I'm not going anywhere. At least not for a long time.

Blair checks the knots across my body, testing to make sure they're not chafing or too tight, then sits on the chaise, her eyes gleaming with desire and adoration as she takes in her handiwork.

In response, my eyes well with tears. I don't bother trying to hold them at bay, letting them slide down my cheeks.

"Tell me what you're feeling," she says, tilting my chin up gently so I meet her gaze.

There's no room for pretense that I'm not hurt from what she did. No hiding that I'm desperately in love with her, and that each messy, imperfect part of me is utterly hers. It feels right, laying my heart and body bare to her.

"Like I'm where I belong," I say. "Like I can finally let go because you have me."

"You can," Blair rasps, her voice thick with emotion.

We linger in the moment, neither one of us saying anything. Before I know it, she's kneeling beside me to undo my binds with care, pressing soft, reverent kisses to my skin where the rope touched. It's just as erotic having her remove them, and by the time I'm completely unbound, I'm desperate for more.

Blair helps me up from the floor, and once I'm next to her, my hands immediately go to the hem of her shirt to take it off. There's a hot gleam of hunger in her eyes as I remove it, then bend down to take her nipple between my lips through the thin lace of her bra, my hands digging into her ass to press her body close to mine.

"Fuck, Grace," she gasps, her fingers threading into my hair as I move to her other breast while she fumbles with her free hand to take her bra off.

I pull back and smile at her as I move to the bed, lying back and spreading my legs. A flash of something above me pulls my focus, and I look up to see a giant mirror hanging over the bed. Showing me sprawled out on Blair's bed, naked and wantonly awaiting her.

"Like what you see?" Blair asks, and my eyes snap back to her.

I flush. "Yeah, but I'll like it a hell of a lot better when you're here with me."

She chuckles and shucks her pants and underwear with a curse, then climbs over me. I loop my arms around her neck and pull her down into a kiss as she grinds her wet pussy against my thigh.

"Bite me," I beg between fevered kisses.

Blair drops her mouth to my throat with a groan, sucking at my neck but not giving me what I asked for. For a second, all I can see in the mirror above us is me, but then she appears in the reflection. The sight of her poised over me, and the stunning picture we create together makes me burn with the need for more.

"Please. I want you to bite me. Mark me. Make me yours again," I whimper as she slides a hand between my thighs to rub my clit.

An animalistic growl rumbles out of Blair, followed by sharp pain as her fangs sink into my throat. A moment later, hot, honeyed bliss pulses through my body as she laps at the blood flowing from me. Each pull of her sucking lips connects directly to my clit, and I come in long, languorous, unending waves.

"You're mine," Blair growls, crimson coating her lips and chin as she pulls back, only to move down to bite my breast as she slides her fingers inside my pussy, stroking them insistently in time with her swallows.

She's greedy for me tonight, consuming more than she ever dared before, until I'm lightheaded and euphoric. When she's finally sated, bites cover my body, throbbing reminders of her taking what she needed and claiming every inch of my body. It's the best feeling in the world.

Blair caresses my hair as she lies beside me, her eyes glassy from her own overload of pleasure.

"How are you feeling?" I ask, wondering what's going on inside her head.

She smiles, her expression warm and open. "Like this is where I belong," she replies, repeating my response from earlier. "Like I can finally let go because you have me."

I grab hold of her hand and bring it to rest on my chest. "You can."

THE REST of the night passes in a haze of pleasure, touch, and whispered confessions of love, fears, and hopes for our future together. We sleep through most of the day, and when I wake up in the late afternoon, Blair is still dead to the world. She doesn't stir when I sneak out of bed to get something to eat, my stomach clenching impatiently as I pour myself a bowl of cereal.

I still can't believe she got all this food for me. How did she even know what to buy?

I bet Mona told her. I pull out my phone, which I miraculously had the presence of mind to grab from the bouncer at The Vault last night, and open my texts to send Mona my thanks, only to find three missed calls from her.

Crap! I assumed Samantha would've told her what happened with Blair, but maybe she didn't go back to their place last night. Better call Mona back before she comes to bust down Blair's door for information about what's going on.

The phone rings twice before Mona answers.

"Grace? Where have you been? Are you okay?" Her voice is threaded with clear agitation.

"Whoa, relax. I'm good. I'm with Blair," I say, my heart fluttering at the dual meaning of my words.

"You are?" Mona sounds incredulous. "She's with Blair," she repeats in a hissed whisper.

"Told you!" replies an amused sounding Samantha, who must be hovering nearby.

"I can hear Samantha there. Didn't she tell you what happened?" I ask.

"She did but, I don't know... I didn't think you'd take her back right away."

"You didn't see what I did. It was romantic as fuck. And the emotions coming off that vampire...whew. I don't even know Blair, but I would've taken her back if she'd come to me like that," Samantha says loudly enough that I can hear her.

"Sam, go away and let Mona talk with her friend!" Max chastises, and the sound of them arguing in the background fades.

"Sorry about that," Mona says with an exasperated sigh. "I'm alone now. Well, Nugget is in here with me, but he's more interested in napping than your love life."

I laugh. "I respect his priorities."

"So...you accepted Blair's apology?" Mona prompts.

"Yeah." There's a flicker of worry that Mona is going to judge me for letting the woman who crushed my heart back into my life so easily, but I push that aside. I've made my choice and something in me keeps telling me it's the right one. "I know you probably think I'm being reckless, but I love her, Mona. And I believe her when she says she's sorry and wants to be with me."

"You do?" Mona asks, her voice growing softer.

Certainty swells inside me. "Yeah."

"Oh, thank god," Mona says with a gusty exhale. "I thought I was going to have to worry about the two of you being miserable for a lot longer. Not that I minded being there for you, but it's hard to see the people you love in pain. Especially when you keep dreaming about them getting married."

"Wait, what?" My heart leaps up into my throat. "Do you mean like, 'oh it'd be so cute if my best friends got married' or actual magic dreams of our wedding?"

"Shit, I... forget I said anything!" Mona lets out a falsely light laugh, trying to play off what she said.

"Mona! You can't do that to me!"

"What's she doing?" I almost drop the phone when I hear Blair's voice behind me.

I turn to look at her and my chest squeezes with affection at the sight. She's still half-asleep, with mussed hair and a worn, oversized t-shirt. The effect is equally adorable and enticing.

I'm so wrapped up in fluttery warm feelings seeing Blair that it takes me a second to realize that she shouldn't be awake. My eyes dart toward the sliver of late afternoon sunlight shining right beside her, and the phone clatters onto the floor as I drop it in my panic.

"What are you doing up? The sun!" I cry, standing up and pulling Blair into the kitchen and away from the light.

Blair's brows lift in surprise as she collides against my chest with a thud. I run my hands over her arms, then cup her face, looking for any sign of damage.

"I'm okay," she says, her voice a little hoarse from sleep.

"How?! I thought you couldn't be in the sun at all, but you had to walk through the living room to get here." My heart is slamming against my ribcage, and I ignore the faint sound of Mona coming from the phone, asking what's going on.

"I can't. Usually I can't physically bring myself to get anywhere near sunlight. But when I woke up, you weren't there, and the aversion to light wasn't as strong, so I figured I'd see what happened."

"What?! Why would you risk that? I would've come down soon." I hold Blair's shoulders and frown at her. "Did you think I left? I promised I wouldn't."

"No, I knew you were still here," she says, a hint of a smile curving her lips. "It wasn't a risk. There was a sense inside me like my monster knew it would be okay. And it was. I don't know why it didn't hurt." She wraps her arms around my waist, going up on her toes to press her lips to mine in a soft kiss. "Maybe you're magic."

I snort. "Doubtful."

"You taste pretty fucking magical," Blair says, kissing me again, deeper this time.

My breath hitches as she palms my ass. "Oh, yeah?" I ask. "Are you already hungry for more?"

Blair's eyes flare. "Yes."

"Hold that thought for one second," I say, pulling back despite a displeased groan from my vampire. I pick my phone back up, worried about Mona freaking out at my abrupt disappearance. She's hung up, so I send her a quick text to let her know no one is hurt before she drives over here in a panic.

"There." I set the phone back down and press close to Blair. "You were saying about needing more of me?"

She grins, flashing her fangs. "I'll never get enough of you, Grace."

44

BLAIR

6 months later

"Babe, do you know where I put the ice?" Grace yells, peeking her head into the kitchen from the door out to the garage. Her hair is still shoved up on the top of her head in a messy bun, and her eyes are wide with panic.

"It's in the cooler, out on the patio," I reply evenly, going back to arranging cookies on a tray.

Her face twists into a frown. "Wait, what? Did you put it out there?"

"Should I not have?" I ask, confused by her strong reaction. "You were busy finishing up with the decorations and people are going arrive soon, so I figured I'd lend a hand."

"Blair!" Grace exclaims, stepping into the kitchen and shutting the door behind her with a bit too much force. "It's still light out! What the hell were you thinking?"

I fight against the smile forming on my lips as I set down the last frosted, dick-shaped cookie and brush my hands off on the towel on my shoulder. Grace hates it when I find her frustration cute, but she gets this little line between her brows and her lips downturn into the most adorable pout. Plus, after living together these past months, it's clear what's exasperation and what's genuine anger.

"I was thinking you still need to get dressed, and I had the time," I deadpan. The furrow on her brow deepens, and I press a fang into my lip to keep from grinning.

"You know that's not what I meant!" Grace crosses her arms under her chest with a huff, and I'm momentarily distracted by how enticing it makes her tits look. Thankfully, she doesn't notice. "You could've been hurt, and I wouldn't have even known it."

We've had this conversation a lot lately. Since I started feeding on Grace regularly, my sunlight tolerance has grown. First, it was being able to be awake and in dim, indirect light for brief periods of time without the usual aversion and pain. Now I'm able to stand outside for a few minutes before sunset without issue. The light still feels unnatural, but short exposure doesn't harm me.

We still don't know why. Mona likes to say that it's because we're "fated". I'd dismiss her ridiculous theory more readily if the romantic hidden inside me didn't adore the idea. Whether it's magic or fate or a quirk of being a vampire I was never taught, all that matters is the end result—it lets me spend more time with the woman I love.

Now, I haven't told Grace about my increasing sun tolerance yet, because I've kept my experimentation to times when she wasn't home. If I'd done it while she was around, she'd have tried to block my exit from the house with her body. I appreciate Grace's concern, but it's unnecessary.

I sigh softly and close the distance between us, then place a hand on her arm. "Sweetheart, I'm fine. I was only out there for a minute." I stroke my hand down her arm and clasp her hand in mine. "I know it scares you, but it's clear that your blood has changed me enough that I can tolerate some sunlight."

Grace's angry expression softens slightly, like her body can't stay mad at me when I'm touching her, and she huffs out an exasperated sigh. "Fine. But next time, don't do it without me. I can't bear the thought of you out there frying to a crisp while I'm fucking around somewhere else."

"Deal." I kiss her, and she sighs again, this time sweet and breathy and far too delicious, given that guests are going to arrive soon. I step back reluctantly, and the flush on Grace's cheeks makes me think she's wishing we had more time, too.

"I'll finish up. Go get changed."

Grace nods. "Yes, Mistress." She gives me a flirty grin, snagging one of the pink pussy cookies from the tray I was working on before scurrying off to the basement.

She's such a tease and I love it.

I shift the cookies to fill in the gap she made, then bring the tray to the living room, where it looks like a demented sex fairy was set loose. Glittery cock, pussy, and boob decorations in a rainbow of colors fill the space, along with a spread of sex and kink-themed snacks and enough booze to get a giant drunk. It's garish and ridiculous, but Grace insisted we go over the top, and I'm sure Mona will think it's hilarious.

The patio is a little less obscene, but that's only because the phallic string lights that Grace ordered never arrived. I use some of the power in my blood to create a reflection in the glass doors, and snort at the hot pink "I love pussy" shirt with a sparkly eyed cat on it that Grace insisted I wear.

A year ago, I would never have been caught wearing this. I would've thought someone had lost their mind if they told me I'd be voluntarily inviting people I barely know over to my house. Granted, I'm still not a fan of having Mona's party guests coming into my private space, but the need to create that boundary from the rest of the world isn't nearly as strong anymore.

It's all because of Grace. She's utterly reshaped my life and continues to do so each day that we're together. In many ways, things were a hell of a lot simpler when I was alone and had my defenses firmly in place, but I never want to go back to that version of me. Simpler doesn't mean better, and any discomfort or friction from adjusting to having a partner is absolutely worth it.

A familiar pang of grief flickers inside me at the thought. Who knew grieving a loss before it happens was a thing? I keep thinking of how hard it will be to lose Grace. I'm still not sure that I'll survive after living like this. I've accepted that reality, but it doesn't make it any easier to cope with when the thought arises. All I can do is remind myself that she's here now, and that's what's important.

Easier said than done.

I finish up the last few party prep tasks, letting the work distract me from the flare up of sadness. By the time Grace returns, looking the very picture of innocence in her white dress and blonde hair falling in waves over one shoulder, I'm feeling a little better.

"You look gorgeous," I say, and she does a twirl, the hem of her dress flaring up. "But now I feel ridiculous in this shirt while you're looking so...demure."

Grace laughs and shakes her head. "Come closer." There's an amused gleam in her eyes.

I do as she asks, and her grin widens as she points to her dress, and now that I'm closer, I can see there's a subtle pattern of women sixty-nineing in the fabric of her dress.

"Nice," I say with a smirk.

"Anything else left to do?" Grace snakes her arms around my waist. "Or do we have a few free minutes before people show up?" She bends down a little to press a kiss to my neck, and I groan as my fangs emerge, my monster wanting a taste of her.

"Everything's done. Why? What did you have in mind?" I ask, heat coiling in my core.

"Me on my knees, eating you out," Grace replies with a wicked smile.

"Mmm, do you think you deserve that privilege?" I lick my lips at the prospect of feeling her mouth on me.

"I do, Mistress," Grace murmurs, her hand sliding down between our bodies to cup my pussy through my pants.

I know she's doing it to provoke me, and I don't resist taking the bait. I grab her hand and pull it away, spinning her around and pinning her arm behind her back as I grapple her against the wall. I raise up onto my toes and bring my mouth to her ear. "Such a naughty pet. I didn't give you permission to touch."

"S-sorry, Mistress. I'll be good," Grace says breathily, though there's still a hint of mischief in her tone.

"I'm not sure if I believe you," I murmur, scraping my fangs against the column of her throat.

Her breath hitches and I slide my free hand under her skirt. I'm seconds away from sliding my fingers into her panties and sinking my fangs into her neck when the doorbell rings.

"Ugh, dammit! Who the hell comes fifteen minutes early to a party?" Grace groans.

I chuckle, pressing a soft kiss to her neck. "It's alright. There wasn't enough time to do what I wanted, anyway."

She grins and smoothes the hem of her dress, then heads off to answer the door. I take a deep breath to compose myself, heart clenching, as I watch Grace walk away. I don't think there's enough time in the world to do everything I want with her.

"No way. You didn't!" Mona squeals, clasping a hand over her mouth as a muscular woman dressed as a barbarian, complete with a fake battle axe and faux leather bikini enters the room to a song that sounds like a sexy version of medieval tavern music.

When Grace said we needed to get strippers for the party, it was easy to find them, given my connections at The Vault and past burlesque experience. What was harder was finding ones who'd do a D&D-inspired routine, but I was determined to cater the experience to Mona's interests.

"Oh yes, we did," I say, grinning as the barbarian flexes and winks at Mona.

Grace whoops and their friends Devi and Rachel, who I've spent a few game nights with, gawk at the buff woman with a mixture of attraction and amusement. Caleb, a newer friend of Mona's, flushes bright red beneath his beard as the barbarian makes suggestive motions with the hilt of her battleaxe, while Ariana next to him laughs and claps. The delight in the room is infectious, and by the time she's done with her routine, I'm cheering as loud as everyone else.

"Holy shit, that was amazing," Mona exclaims, beaming at me.

"Just wait, there's another one," Grace says with glee, and that's my cue to start the music for the man dressed in wizard robes with slits up the thighs that bare his muscular legs.

He carries a tome in with him and flips through it, then sets it down in Mona's lap, sticking his ass out as he bends at the waist and winking over his shoulder at Grace.

My monster bristles at his attention toward her, even though I know it's all part of his act. He proceeds to perform very suggestive acts with a thick wand, and while he focuses mostly on the bachelorette, he keeps turning back in Grace's direction and making eyes at her.

I move to her side as subtly as I can, placing a hand on her shoulder. When he looks her way again, I flash my fangs in warning. It's quick enough to appear as a trick of the light when he does a double-take and sees a placid, fangless smile on my face. He doesn't look her way again, and finishes up his routine with a magic "explosion" that covers half the room in confetti and glitter.

Great, not only was he making eyes at my girlfriend, but I'm going to find glitter on things for months.

"You okay?" Grace looks up at me, and I realize I was gripping her shoulder a little too hard.

"I will be once he leaves," I mutter, politely applauding as the wizard picks up his robe and heads back to the guest room I set up for the performers to get ready in.

Grace grins at me. "Mmm, I like it when you get all possessive. But you've got nothing to worry about."

"I should hope not. I've got much better wands downstairs," I say with a wry smile.

She bites her lip, and I brush her hair away from her neck, letting my fingers run across her collarbone in a casual caress. Grace shivers and it takes all my willpower to pull my hand away and not haul her off to the basement to have my way with her while the party continues upstairs.

"Wow...that was *perfect*," Mona says, a huge grin on her face after the performances. "Max is going to be so jealous," she adds with a giggle, her golden brown cheeks burnishing. No doubt she's thinking about what he'll do to re-stake his claim on her when he hears about her wild evening.

The rest of the party goes by in a blur of raunchy, silly games and heartfelt wishes for Mona's marriage to Max. By the time everyone leaves, it's after midnight, and Grace crumples to the couch with an exhausted sigh.

I sit next to her and guide her to lay her head in my lap. She does so with a pleased hum and closes her eyes as I stroke her hair.

"Just give me a minute, and then I'll get up to start cleaning up," she murmurs.

"Leave it. I made plans for someone to take care of it tomorrow," I say.

"You hired a cleaner?" Grace asks, looking up at me.

"Not quite. Nic offered. He's doing it in exchange for a session next week." I brace myself for any sign of discomfort or jealousy the way I always do when I mention my clients, but Grace only smiles.

"He's such a sweetheart," she says, sounding entirely sincere. "It'll be nice to chat with him. It's been a while since he's been over to see you."

"I think he might be seeing someone. Or at least interested in them." After the bear shifter had his heart-to-heart with me about his wife while Grace and I had broken up, something shifted in him. When we have sessions, he doesn't want anything overtly sexual. Most of the time he comes over and helps me with housework with the thin guise of me dominating him.

"He deserves someone special in his life," Grace says wistfully, then lets out a soft chuckle. "Though, you'll have to find another sub you trust to do the heavy lifting around here if he ends up stopping his sessions."

"Eh, I'm apparently part of his pack in his eyes, so there's no getting rid of him, even if he's not a client."

"Aww, if I were twenty years older and not desperately in love with you, I'd be swooning for him." Grace grins when I pretend to glare at her.

"Tonight went pretty well, I think," she says, changing the subject.

"You saw the look on Mona's face the whole time. She loved it." I slide my fingers through Grace's hair, a question building inside me that I've been thinking about for a while. Since that night we got back together. Or maybe even earlier, but I was too afraid to acknowledge it.

"What's that look for?" Grace asks, far too perceptive of my subtle mood shifts now that we've spent so much time together.

"I... Would you like something like this?"

Her brow furrows. "Like what?"

"Like if you were to have a bachelorette party, would you want all the glitter dicks and strippers?" I say the words casually, but inside my stomach clenches in anticipation.

Grace sits up so quickly it startles me, spinning around to look at me eye-to-eye. "No way."

"'No' to the strippers? Or 'no' to the concept of a bachelorette party?" I ask.

"'No' to you bringing up getting married in such a roundabout way!" Grace huffs, crossing her arms over her chest petulantly. "If you want to get married, then just ask!"

"Okay." I swallow against the surge of emotion, attempting to make my voice steady. "Will you marry me?"

Grace blinks at me, her mouth falling open in surprise. After a second, she nods. "Yeah." Another second passes. "Fuck yeah, I'll marry you."

45

GRACE

"We should wait until after Mona and Max's wedding to say anything," I blurt a moment after agreeing to marry Blair. "If you're serious."

"I'm serious," Blair says, voice thick with emotion.

A grin spreads across my face as I take in how intently she's watching me. Blair is always reading me. Always looking for signs that I'm happy and comfortable, whether we're in or out of the bedroom. "Really?" I ask, even though I already know the answer.

Since the night Blair apologized, she's proven again and again that she's in this for the long haul. Her asking me to marry her was a given—I just didn't expect it so soon.

"Yes," she replies softly, taking my hand in hers. She frowns down at it. "Please pretend that I didn't already ask when I do this right in a few months. I refuse to have our engagement story be you sassing me into proposing. I don't even have a ring for you right now."

I laugh at the dismayed look on her face. "Such a romantic. Alright, babe. It never happened," I say, winking at her.

Blair squeezes my hand in thanks, a small smile forming on her lips. "What never happened?"

That makes me laugh harder and tug her into my arms. "I can't wait to spend the rest of my life with you," I murmur.

She holds me tight, like never wants to let me go. "Same."

Two years later

I LAUGH as Blair attempts to haul me into her arms, and fails with a dramatic grunt of exertion. She may have more strength as a vampire than someone as petite as her normally would, but that doesn't negate our size difference.

"I appreciate the attempt, but there's no need to throw your back out trying to carry me over the threshold," I say, tugging the fluffy tulle of my wedding dress back into place.

"It's good luck, though," Blair protests. She's been surprisingly adamant about adhering to a lot of conventional wedding traditions, and it took me a while to realize it was because she thought I wanted those things. All because one night when we were planning, I mentioned offhand that Zack didn't want to do any of the normal wedding stuff. So I've been humoring her need to make things perfect the second time around for me, even though I don't care at all.

"Here, let me try bending down and..." Blair moves to try to grab me again.

I swat her hands away. "Come here," I say, tugging her against me. "You know I don't give a shit about this, right? I just want to go inside, take off this dress, and get fucked by my wife." I grab her ass for emphasis.

"I can do it. Let me try again," Blair says, stubbornly ignoring my come on.

"That's it," I mutter, using my grip on her to hoist her up onto my shoulder unceremoniously and carry her inside the house. All my strength training for muscle stability to help my neck has really paid off.

"Grace!" she squeals, delighting me with how shocked she sounds.

I set her back down on her feet and kiss her cheek. "There. Happy now?"

Blair attempts to glare at me, but she can't keep from cracking a smile. "Yeah. So fucking happy." Her eyes rake down my body purposefully, then land back on my face, heat simmering in her gaze. "I'll be even happier when I have my wife naked and begging for me."

By all accounts, I should be exhausted after the wedding ceremony and small reception we had afterwards, but I'm practically buzzing with need for Blair. You'd think after years together, that desire would've dimmed, but it's only grown richer and more nuanced.

"That can be arranged," I murmur. "I'll need your help to get out of this thing, though." I gesture to my gown, which took both Mona and Samantha working together to lace up properly. "Preferably intact and without blood stains," I add, seeing the hungry, impatient gleam in Blair's eyes.

"Hmm." She assesses me, licking her lips. "But what if I want to ruin my pretty bride? Make a mess of what's mine."

"Fuck, Blair," I gasp, as she steps behind me and wraps an arm around my waist, pulling me flush with her body and scraping her fangs against my shoulder.

"Would you deny me that, pet?" she rasps, her hand skimming up my bodice to knead my breast.

We both know she's not going to destroy my wedding dress after it took me months to find, but the game still thrills me. I sink into my role easily after lots of practice submitting to Blair. Molten pleasure pools in my core as my body relaxes against her. "No, Mistress. I'm yours to do with as you please."

"That's right. You are." Blair steps back and I almost stagger at the loss of her support. "Come. I have a present for you."

I follow as Blair leads me down to our bedroom, pulse quickening as I wonder what kind of present she means. She's already given me everything I could ever want.

I try not to squirm with impatience as she slowly unlaces my bodice, taking more care than is necessary, brushing against the slivers of my bare skin as they're revealed in a maddening tease. When I'm finally able to step out of the gown, she takes her time hanging it up for me, then returns from the closet with a small rectangular box.

She sets the box on the bed, and I stare at it, wondering what's inside. A new vibrator? A special flogger?

"Kneel," Blair commands, coming to stand in front of me.

I obey, falling to my knees on the cushioned rug at the foot of the bed put here for this exact purpose. I keep my head bowed, waiting for her next order.

There's a rustle of fabric, most likely Blair taking off her wedding suit, but I resist the urge to look up. Time ticks by far too slowly and I clasp my hands together behind my back to keep from fidgeting.

"Such a good girl," Blair purrs, petting my hair. I lean into her touch, eyes closing in bliss at her praise.

"Thank you, Mistress," I whisper.

"Look up at me," Blair says, putting a fingertip under my chin.

My breath catches at the sight of her form as she looms over me, wearing only a black strap-on harness. She's been into trying out all kinds of unusual dildos on me lately, the most recent one with a knot at the base that took ages for her to stretch me enough to fit it inside my pussy.

I shiver at the memory. Maybe that's the present—a new addition to our collection.

She reaches over and grabs the box from the bed, and lifts off the lid. Inside, there's a pale pink strip of leather. My brow furrows in confusion, but when she removes it from the box, I realize what it is.

"I want you to wear my collar, Grace," Blair says, holding it out for me to inspect.

I take it in my hands, feeling breathless as I run my fingers over the buttery leather, finding on closer inspection that there are tiny roses embossed into it. "It's beautiful," I murmur reverently. "Will you put it on me?" I ask, holding it back out to her.

Blair gives me a wicked grin. "If I do, it means you're mine just as permanently as the ring on your finger."

"Yes." The thought makes excitement sizzle across my skin. "I'm yours. Forever."

Her smile flickers. "Before I put it on, I wanted to ask you something else." Her tone conveys that this is Blair asking me as herself, not as my domme.

"What's that? Is everything okay?"

"Yes. I just..." She swallows heavily. "You told me to ask you in a few years if you'd..." Blair looks at the floor, uncharacteristically avoidant of my gaze.

"If I'd what?" I ask, reaching out to touch her leg.

"If you want me to turn you." She meets my eyes again, her expression grave. "I'll do it. If you want me to, I will. I figured with all the talk of forever, it could be the perfect time."

"No."

I don't need time to consider. She's not the only one who's been contemplating our vows and wondering what it means for the future. I'd be lying if the thought hadn't crossed my mind, but I'm not ready. I'm happy how we are. Besides, we've been discussing what we want our lives to look like in the future, and there are some things we couldn't do if I became a vampire. Things I'm growing more certain every day that I want with her.

"I won't ask you to do something I know you're diametrically opposed to on our wedding night, Blair," I continue. "Even if I wanted you to make me a vampire. Which I don't."

"You don't?" she asks, a tinge of sadness mixed in with the relief in her tone.

"No. That might change, but right now, no. I'm so happy the way things are and I don't want to risk compromising that."

"It wouldn't. I promise I wouldn't hold it against you," Blair protests.

I shake my head. "I'm good. Your blood helps keep me from being in too much pain, and Max said that there are lots of records of regular doses of vampire blood extending human life spans."

"Okay," Blair says with a heavy exhale. "But you'll tell me if you change your mind?"

"I will. How about this? Ask me again in five years. Or no, in a decade. Who knows how I'll feel when I'm over forty?" I say with a laugh.

"Deal."

"Now, are you going to put that collar on me or what?" I ask, batting my eyelashes at her to try to pull her away from her worries.

"Not if you sass me like that," Blair says sternly.

"Sorry." I bite my tongue so I don't smile. "Please, Mistress?"

Blair shakes her head at me, unfooled by my false repentance, a springy coil of her hair that took her almost a year to learn how to grow out falling out of her updo. I smile up at her, stunned momentarily by how fucking beautiful my wife is. When she gives me an amused look, I break from my reverie and hold my hair up out of the way for her as she places the soft leather around my throat, the small o ring dangling in the center feeling heavy as I swallow. She checks to make sure it's not too tight, then closes the clasp.

A weighted sense of rightness and calm rushes over me.

Blair steps back to take in the effect. "Gorgeous," she murmurs. "Take off your underwear and get on the bed."

I quickly obey, standing and moving to sit on the edge of the bed.

"Lie back and spread your legs. Show me how wet you are for me, wife."

Fuck, I love her calling me that. It feels somehow reverent and filthy at the same time coming from her lips.

"I'm so wet," I murmur, lying down and spreading my legs shamelessly for her to see.

"Mmm, good girl." Blair moves to the nightstand and pulls out a dark gray drawstring bag that holds my favorite dildo, the one with the vibrating nubs at the base that can make us both come while she's using it on me. She situates it in the harness, then spreads lube along the length. "Does your needy pussy want me to fill it up?"

"Yes, Mistress," I whimper.

"Show me. Fuck yourself with your fingers," she commands, moving between my legs.

A spike of arousal hits me at the order. I bring two fingers to my entrance and sink them inside, knowing better than to touch my clit even though I desperately want to. If I don't follow her instructions to the letter, she might decide to not let me come at all.

Blair's eyes focus between my legs hungrily as I thrust my fingers inside my pussy, moaning with the need for more.

When my fingers make obscene slick noises and I'm soaking the bed with my arousal, Blair grabs my wrist and pulls my hand away from my pussy, pining it above my head as she uses her other hand to position the dildo at my entrance.

I gasp as she eases it inside me, thrusting shallowly to open me up for the considerable girth, before switching on the vibrations and sinking in to the hilt.

"You're taking it so well. Such a good girl. Tell me who this pussy belongs to," Blair rasps.

"You," I moan. "It belongs to you."

She works the dildo inside me with practiced precision, knowing exactly how to angle it to make me see stars.

When I'm writhing beneath her as she pins me down and fucks me, Blair lets out a dark chuckle. "Do you want to come, wife?"

"Please, yes, god, please," I gasp, praying she'll be merciful and give me what I need.

"You sound so pretty when you beg me," she purrs, her fangs

gleaming in the low light. She's as desperate as I am right now, which makes my need burn even brighter. "Do it again."

"Please. Please make me come."

Blair groans and brings the hand pinned above my head up to her lips. She teases me for a moment, then sinks her fangs in at the same time she thrusts inside me, and I shatter.

Pulses of pleasure suffuse my body as I come with each drag of blood she takes from me. Blair's movements falter as she comes with a deep moan, and when she releases my wrist, I loop my arm around her neck to tug her down into a kiss.

We melt together in a familiar dance of blood and ecstasy, each bite sending us both over the edge once more until we're too exhausted to continue.

Blair removes my collar, checking the skin for any chafing or marks, then guides me into the shower, where the fatigue of everything we've done today finally hits us. When we get back in bed, I tuck my body around hers, holding her tight to my chest as I let out a contented sigh.

"Thank you," Blair whispers, right as I'm about to drift off.

"For what?" I murmur, confused.

She rolls over to face me. "After I was turned, I thought that the best I could ask for was to survive and not get screwed over again. And I thought I was content with that. But you...fuck, Grace, you didn't let me hide any more. You shined your light into the darkest recesses of my heart and showed me how miserable I was. I'll never be able to express how grateful I am for you. How much I love you."

I squeeze her tighter, tears welling in my eyes at her confession. "You're everything to me, Blair. I never thought I could have love like this. Someone who is my friend and my partner, who respects me and makes me feel so cherished and desired."

"Loving you is the easiest thing I've ever done," she says, turning over to look at me, eyes glinting in the darkness.

"Psh, say that to me again when I'm hormonal and pissy next time I get my period." I nudge her playfully even as my chest fills with warmth.

Blair smirks. "I like when you have your period."

"Of course you do, bloodsucker."

"I don't see you complaining about me going down on you multiple times a day for a week," Blair teases back. "You get extra horny and want more orgasms, and I get a special treat. It's a win-win."

I laugh and roll my eyes. "Truly a match made in heaven."

"I like to think so," she says with surprising sincerity.

My brow scrunches. "I thought you didn't believe in God."

"I didn't. I still don't, at least not in the way I tried to as a kid. But it's hard not to believe that there's some kind of higher power or force when faced with a miracle like you."

"I'm not a miracle. You're the one with healing blood! I'm just... me," I say, dazed by how much I love this woman and how she loves me in return.

Blair kisses me tenderly, her adoration clear in the way she holds me close. She pulls back and holds my gaze with a breathtaking smile. "Yes, you are, Grace. You brought me back to life."

EPILOGUE

BLAIR

"What comes next?"

I look up from where I'm rolling out the pie crust. "Did you preheat the oven?"

"No. Fuck!" Allison's face twists into a grimace when I raise a brow at her language. "Sorry, Bear."

I shake my head at my great-granddaughter's sheepish expression and her using the nickname she came up with for me when she couldn't say my name properly as a toddler. I don't bother hiding my grin. "I know your mom doesn't like you cursing, but I've been around for more than a century, so frankly, I don't give a shit."

Her eyes go comically wide and her small iridescent wings

flutter behind her in excitement, almost knocking the colander of washed berries onto the kitchen floor. "Really? You're the coolest!"

I snort, grabbing the colander and moving it out of the way as she scurries over to turn the oven on. She's as much of a ball of teenage energy as her mother was at her age, though her dad's fae blood makes her even more excitable.

She's staying the week here while her parents go on a much needed vacation, and I can already tell I'm going to be exhausted by the time they come back to pick her up. I thought I'd gotten taking care of children down to a science after raising a son, and watching his kids, but this is the first time doing most of the work alone.

"Alright, while you're over there, go ahead and turn on the burner with the saucepan to medium," I say, grabbing the berries, sugar, cinnamon I had her measure out. "Dump these all in there. We need to cook the fruit and then thicken it up so the pie will set."

"How do you know how to do all this? I thought you didn't eat food," Allison says, staring intently down at the mixture as if watching it will make it cook faster.

It's no secret that I'm a vampire. Moonvale's protective ward has been in place for decades, allowing monsters living here to exist out in the open alongside humans. Thankfully, Allison doesn't seem bothered in the slightest when I'm having blood for a meal.

She gets that unflappable mentality from her fae dad. Her mother, my granddaughter, can't stand the sight of blood. You'd think a woman that's one-eighth vampire wouldn't be so squeamish, but monster genetics work in mysterious ways. That I was able to contribute to the creation of my son still boggles my mind, even knowing magic exists. Something dead shouldn't be able to create life, and yet you can see me in Benedict's face shape, coloring, and nose.

"I don't eat," I say with a shrug. "But back when I was a kid, a lot younger than you, my grandmother taught me. When I met GiGi, I got back into baking."

She doesn't need to know that I made my grandmother's pie for Grace after she asked me what her scent and taste reminded me of. I fed it to her, then tasted it on her tongue and in her blood as we made love afterward. It's one of my favorite memories.

We finish getting the pie ready for the oven, with only one mishap where Allison knocks the cornstarch onto the floor while excitedly gesticulating as she tells me about all the drama going on with her fellow freshmen at her high school. Apparently, a mothgirl named Sally is the hottest person in her class and everyone wants to date her, but she's not-so-secretly hooking up with a junior on the swim team who says he's full human but everyone thinks his dad is a merman.

Riveting stuff.

"It's going to be a while before this is done, and then it'll need to cool, so you're free to go FaceChat or whatever kids are doing these days."

Allison makes a disgusted face. "Eww, no one but creepy old dudes use FaceChat."

"Noted." I laugh, thinking about how Nic keeps trying to get me to download it so we can talk more often now that he's retired in the mountains. He's the opposite of creepy, but the man has got to be pushing 150 at this point. Shifters live two and a half to three centuries, so the bear still has some life left in him.

God, how did we get so old? It feels like it was just last year that he was bringing his twins over for a playdate with Ben.

My chest tightens at the reminder of how much time has slipped by. How much things have changed.

Allison scurries off upstairs to do god knows what, and once I've cleaned the kitchen up, I head to the den that's been converted into a bedroom for the time being. I pause at the door, listening for a moment, then open it as quietly as possible.

The ache in my chest from earlier deepens at the sight of my wife, asleep on the pullout couch, her long hair that's almost completely gray now splayed across the pillow. Despite my best efforts to come in quietly, she groans groggily.

"Shit, how long have I been asleep?" Grace asks, rubbing her eyes.

"About an hour. Don't worry, I kept the gremlin entertained."

Grace sits up, wincing as she moves her legs off the bed.

"You should've let me help you!" I protest, moving to her side in concern.

"Babe, it's been almost three weeks since the surgery," she says, rolling her eyes. "Besides, I'm supposed to move around and do things on my own."

"I remember the physical therapist saying that you weren't supposed to overdo it, yet you were standing for an hour earlier with Allison," I grumble. "At least take some of my blood for the pain."

"Yes, nurse." Grace smiles playfully, the lines around her eyes crinkling as she does.

I bite my wrist and hold it out for her, and her first suck against my skin sends a zing of arousal through me like it does every time.

Grace sighs as the effects of my blood take hold, then gives my wrist a kiss before removing her mouth. "Thank you." She rubs at her knee, testing it for any residual pain. Her smile falls and for a second I think it's still bothering her, but then she speaks. "I'm sorry."

"Why the hell are you sorry? I love it when you take my blood," I say in reassurance, but Grace shakes her head.

"I know, but it's got to be decidedly less sexy now that I'm relying on it so heavily. And..." Grace swallows heavily, her eyes growing watery. "I've had more time with you than I ever imagined I would. I'm over one hundred years old, with the body of a sixty-year-old, for fuck's sake. But after having the knee replacement, it really hit me how it's only going to get worse from here. I'm going to grow more and more decrepit, and you're..." A tear slides down her cheek. "I've been really selfish. I'm sorry that you're stuck taking care of me."

Her worry and guilt make my chest ache for her. "I'm not."

I haven't forgotten for a moment about Grace's mortality, though the accompanying fear and grief that comes along with it ebbs and flows. It's gotten easier to handle since she asked me to stop checking in about turning her after the birth of our first great-grandchild. Before that, I'd ask every ten years, and every time she'd tell me to ask again in the future.

At first, we decided to put off the decision in order to have Benedict. The impracticality of raising a child while being unable to go out in the sun meant we needed to at least wait until he'd moved out to broach the subject. Even with Grace's blood allowing me to be in the sun more than should be possible, raising a kid with one vampire parent was hard enough.

Then, it became a dance that was torturing us, but we were both too scared to admit that in our hearts, the decision had already been made.

Grace would've joined me in the darkness if I'd asked her to, but I couldn't extinguish her light. And I would've turned her, if Grace decided death was too frightening a specter, but she didn't, because the bravest person I know.

Knowing that it's not on the table has allowed me to accept things for what they are. And seeing my beautiful wife sitting next to me, the lines of a life filled with joy together written across her features, knowing about the faded stretch marks on her breasts and belly from when she was pregnant with Benedict that I love to map with my tongue, I wouldn't want it any other way.

"People already think you're my daughter or my live-in nurse, not my wife," Grace says with a soft sigh. "Does that not bother you?"

I narrow my eyes at her. "Since when have I ever given a shit about what anyone thinks? I only care about you and our family. The rest of them can go fuck themselves." I give her an assessing look, reaching up to brush the hair from her neck to stroke the delicate skin there. "They'd be lucky to have such a beautiful, perfect wife."

"I think your eyesight might be worse than mine," Grace scoffs.

"Do you need me to prove how much I desire you?" I murmur, leaning in to kiss her neck, her sugared berry scent making my mouth water.

Grace's heartbeat speeds up as I let my fangs press against her skin, and her breath hitches. "Later. The pie smells like it might be done and you know Allison will be down here banging on the door to share some silly random holo projection her friend sent her the second you sink your fangs into me."

I chuckle, reluctantly pulling away. "True."

I stand and offer her a hand, but she shakes her head with a stubborn gleam in her eyes. "I can do it on my own."

I keep it held out, glaring her down. "How many damn times am I going to have to say this? Just because you can, doesn't mean you have to. Don't forget, you're mine to take care of as I see fit." I let a hint of my dominance creep into my tone.

"Fine," she says sharply, but there's a hint of a flush to her cheeks as she does as I command.

I use my grip on her hand to move in closer and kiss her, pressing all my love to her lips.

She sighs and kisses me back, and I feel the same potent love in return.

"Eww, gross." I break the kiss and turn to see Allison standing in the doorway.

Grace laughs at her reaction. "Love isn't gross, Allie."

"Debatable," the feisty teen sasses back. "Is the pie ready? I'm starving."

The oven timer goes off a moment later and Allison's eyes light up. "Yes!" She races off toward the kitchen.

"It still needs to cool!" I shout behind her. "What are the odds that the pie is going to be intact when we get in there?" I mutter.

Grace laughs, the bubbly sound making affection swell inside me. She squeezes my shoulder. "About as good as my odds of getting carded."

Sure enough, when we enter the kitchen, Allison is putting a slice of the pie on a plate, hissing as some of the burning hot filling touches her finger.

I pretend to give her a stern look, but inside my heart fills with a surge of happiness that only deepens when Grace goes over to cut a slice for herself and starts chatting with our great-granddaughter.

How is this my life?

The little girl who snuck bites of her grandma's pie would never have dared to dream of this. The confused, fearful teen would've been desperately jealous of Allison's happiness and ease. And the broken woman who thought it was better to feel nothing than to let herself get hurt again? She wouldn't believe it was possible.

She was wrong.

Yes, there's been plenty of pain alongside the happiness, and I dread the loss looming on the horizon. But imagining what my life would look like if I hadn't let Grace in, it's clear that would've been an infinitely worse fate.

So I'll cherish Grace for as long as I can, soaking up every ray of happiness and pleasure until our time together ends. Even then, I know her light will still linger around me. In our family. In our friendships. In every facet of this incredible life we've built together.

I'm not scared of falling into darkness again, because I'll spend the rest of my existence basking in the afterglow of her love.

AUTHOR NOTES

Thank you so much for reading Afterglow! Writing this book was an emotional whirlwind. I laughed, sobbed, and fell completely head over heels for these women and the depth of their love and devotion. I hope you were able to experience some of that heartfelt journey as well, though I hope I didn't make you cry *too* hard.

When I was writing Behold Her, I hadn't planned on making Grace and Blair a *thing*, but their spark developed naturally as their characters interacted. So when it came time to figure out who would feature in the next book in the series, the answer was obvious. I didn't know at the time that these women would become my favorite couple I've written, or that writing their love story would be such a personal and cathartic experience. But I guess I should've expected it, because the more I write, the more I realize that it's impossible for me to not let aspects of myself bleed into my characters and the challenges they face.

Grace's struggles with chronic pain are based on my own expe-

AUTHOR NOTES

rience with degenerative disc disease and the things I've had to grapple with as I come to terms with being disabled. Her later-in-life queer awakening definitely bears a lot of resemblance to mine. So if you read the book and thought it was unrealistic that Grace would be so oblivious about her own sexuality, I'm living proof that people really can be that dense.

Blair's reflex to be detached to protect herself, as well as her need to be in control, are things I'm far too familiar with. I wish I could say that her general badass vibes were also based on me, but there's no way I'm that cool. Though I will threaten to cut a bitch if they mess with the people I care about.

While their story has a bittersweet ending, it's my favorite one yet. As I grew closer to the end of the book, I knew that there wouldn't be a magical solution to their mismatched lifespans, and that neither character would want Grace to become a vampire. This might be a divisive choice, but with how I write, discovering the story as I go and letting the characters dictate what happens, it didn't even feel like a choice at all. So if you're mad, blame Blair and Grace, not me 😂.

One minor note, because I have a feeling it might be contentious—the Twilight references aren't me, Emily, shitting on Twilight. They're written from Blair's perspective and lived experiences. I fully understand that this book might not even exist if it wasn't for how many readers got into paranormal romance via Twilight.

Huge thanks to my amazing alpha readers, Melissa and Kass, who both reassured me that the slow burn was worth it when I was freaking out that I'd reached 50k words and they hadn't even kissed yet. Thank you to my lovely beta readers, Amber, Ashley, Alexa, Laine, May, and Sofia, as well as my sensitivity reader, Havoc Archives—your feedback was invaluable! Much love to my ARC and

AUTHOR NOTES

Street teams, and to you, wonderful reader, for taking the time to read my book!

Want more Monsters of Moonvale?
Sign up for my newsletter to read my monster romance novella, Love Lights!

ABOUT THE AUTHOR

Emily loves cozy, emotional, and spicy romances with a monstrous twist. When she isn't musing on the merits of doting, dominant monsters, she reads an obscene amount of romance novels, and cultivates her eccentric recluse persona.